THE RELUCTANT COPILOT

Kelly Durham

THE RELUCTANT COPILOT

Published by Kelly Durham

THE WAR WIDOW, BERLIN CALLING and WADE'S WAR, also by Kelly Durham, are available at Amazon.com.

Cover design by Nat Shane

For

Bob Harmon, Joe Berly, Don Johns, John Rogers and

all who braved the skies over Nazi-occupied Europe.

Prologue

13 May 1943

Walt Biggs smiled, reached inside his sheepskin-lined flight jacket and plucked two cigars from his shirt pocket. Biggs popped one of the cigars into his mouth and, holding the other in his left hand, reached over and offered it to his pilot, Ervin Rhodes. Rhodes smiled and nodded his head, biting off the end of the stogie and clenching it between his teeth. Next, Biggs dug into his pocket and extracted his Zippo. Rhodes waved it away. "Bad luck!" he shouted over the din of the B-17's four huge engines, all running smoothly, thank God. The formation was descending, heading home from its latest mission over Nazi-occupied France, the English coast looming ahead through the scratched windscreen of the big bomber. Biggs nodded, pocketed the lighter and leaned back in his copilot's seat.

Rhodes, Biggs and the crew of *Rough Rider* had flown their final mission over occupied Europe, only the third 8th Air Force crew to complete twenty-five missions and earn a ticket home. With the ever-deeper penetrations the 8th's bombers were attempting over enemy territory, aircraft and crew losses had been increasing. The odds of successfully completing twenty-five missions seemed to be getting worse, not better. But today's mission had been a milk run. Light and inaccurate flak had been the only hazard as *Rough Rider* had joined eighty other bombers in an attack on aircraft factories at Meault, France. Due to the relatively short distances involved, friendly fighters from both 8th Fighter Command and the Royal Air Force had been able to escort the bombers all the way to the target and back. Now, as the group neared the English coast, Rhodes, Biggs and the eight other members of the crew began to relax as the realization that they had survived their tour began to sink in.

"Radio to pilot," the interphone crackled.

"Go ahead, Mike," Rhodes replied.

"Looks like the weather guys missed again, sir," radio operator Mike Rowell reported. "The field is reporting a twelve hundred-foot overcast with two-mile visibility and dropping." Low ceilings, poor visibility and lots of aircraft squeezing through limited airspace were part of the bomber crews' daily routine.

"Well, thanks for that cheery forecast, Mike. I wonder if the weather boys would be more accurate if they had to fly these missions themselves!" The truth was that the weather staff was composed mostly of permanent party officers and NCOs. Unlike aircraft crew, all of whom were volunteers, ground personnel were assigned for the duration of the war, with little chance to rotate back to the States. Well, thought Rhodes, too bad for them. Peering out the B-17's windscreen, he could see the coast growing closer and beyond it the layer of clouds he and the rest of the 91st Bomb Group would shortly have to penetrate to return to their field at Bassingbourn.

Rhodes' thoughts were interrupted by a voice on the group command frequency. "Blackfoot, this is Blackfoot Able. We're going to let *Rough Rider* lead the group home. Congratulations boys!" The group commanding officer, Colonel Reid, was flying copilot in the lead ship on this mission, with *Rough Rider* tucked in tight just behind his lead aircraft's left wing. Rhodes' smile widened and he winked at his copilot.

Rhodes flipped a toggle switch on the overhead panel and called to his crew, "Pilot to crew. The Old Man has given us the privilege of leading the group home in recognition of completing twenty-five missions. Hang on tight 'cause we're gonna have a little fun on the way down! Walt, run through the pre-landing checks."

Biggs directed each crew member to confirm his position was prepared for landing.

"Bomb bay doors closed; guns stowed," the bombardier responded from the aircraft's nose section.

"Antennae retracted; top window closed," came the call from Rowell, the radio operator.

"Ball turret stowed, locked and ready for landing, Skipper," Pete Johnson, the smallest member of the crew sang out.

Once the waist gunners and tail gunner had confirmed their guns were cleared and stowed, Biggs gave a thumbs up to his pilot. "Aircraft and crew prepared for landing," he reported for the last time.

The senior NCO on board, Staff Sergeant Larry Segars, took his pre-landing position behind the two pilots. As flight engineer, his duties included manning the top turret, monitoring the engine gauges and providing any other assistance needed. "Show 'em how to fly, Skipper!" Segars shouted, slapping Rhodes on his right shoulder.

As the formation descended toward the gray undercast, Rhodes slowly, carefully pulled his big bomber out of the formation. Within a few minutes, the rest of the formation disappeared as *Rough Rider* sank into the clouds.

Daylight all but disappeared as the overcast blocked out the sun. "Navigator, give me a position check," Rhodes ordered.

"We're about fifteen miles out. About six to eight minutes. The field should be at our two o'clock once we pop out of these clouds."

Rhodes was flying solely on instruments now; Biggs following every movement and Segars watching the engine gauges. It wasn't uniformly dark inside the clouds; there were lighter pockets, but still no visibility in any direction. Concentrating on his instrument panel, Rhodes didn't see the shadow as much as he felt it. In that tiny fraction of a second before comprehension, his mind recognized something was wrong, but didn't have time to figure out exactly what. Before he or Biggs could react, a pair of eleven-foot propellers were ripping their way through *Rough Rider's* aluminum skin; a spark, a flash and two aircraft disappeared in a catastrophic explosion of high-octane gasoline, leaving a hole in the clouds and showering the countryside below with a rain of debris and body parts.

Part 1

13 May 1943

The mission had been a milk run; light, inaccurate flak and very little trouble from enemy fighters. Because we only flew a little ways into France, we had friendly fighter escort the entire mission. That makes a huge difference. When our fighters are around, the bandits can't get to us to do any real damage. Our gunners came back with lots of ammunition still onboard.

So, you'd think with a mission like that, we would all have been in pretty high spirits, right? Not so. Although our squadron hadn't lost any aircraft to enemy action, two of them collided as we were descending through some thick clouds toward the field. You never know what happens in a situation like that, but our best guess was that Siefert, one of the newer pilots, somehow got out of position and smacked right into Rhodes. Like I said, we'll never really know.

That Rhodes' crew was one of the two that got erased was a real blow to everybody in the group. It was their twenty-fifth and final mission! They'd made it through a full tour of duty, something only two other 8th Air Force crews had done so far. They were sure to get sent home to the States, maybe do some war bond publicity, meet some pretty girls, see their families and then get reassigned to relatively safe training jobs. That would have been a boost to the morale of every American bomber crew in England. We were all pulling for them—and in a way for ourselves. And then in one blinding flash, they were gone.

We got the bad news during our debriefing. Captain Houser, from the intel section, was taking us through the mission, asking questions about enemy reactions; you know, number and types of planes, locations of flak batteries, accuracy and concentration of fire, all the usual stuff. Since we hadn't really been bothered by enemy fighters, none of the boys claimed any enemy fighters shot down or even damaged. About that time, Major Tucker, the group adjutant, came in and broke the news. Everybody got real quiet, real fast. It was sort of like when the visiting team wins on the last play of the game.

It was 1930 hours by the time we finished debriefing. Christy, Joe, Don and I, as was our post-mission custom, agreed to meet at the Officers' Club for sandwiches and beer after we'd had a chance to shower and change. By 2015, we were gathered around a small table in the corner of the club, close enough to the radio to hear the jazz music Radio Berlin was playing. We were a pretty somber bunch. Although he'd been at Bassingbourn a few months longer than we had, we'd known Rhodes and the rest of his crew pretty well. We went to the same briefings, flew the same missions, drank at the same O Club bar, danced with the same local girls at the occasional dances. Rhodes had been a good pilot and a good egg.

"To Rhodes, Biggs and their crew," Don said, raising his glass in a salute. We all clinked our glasses together and drank. Don was our bombardier and armaments officer. He, our navigator Joe, Christy and I had been together for six months. We'd been assigned as a crew, along with our non-commissioned officers, when we finished our advanced training. We'd met the previous November at our combat crew training base in Omaha, Nebraska, but you'd have thought we'd known each other for years. Same with our NCOs. A bomber crew is different than, say, an infantry platoon. Every man's life depends on every other man's actions more so than in any other military outfit. And everybody's at the mercy of the pilot. I felt that responsibility and I wasn't going to do anything to let my crew down.

"Who's that?" Don asked, tipping his head toward three Lieutenants who'd taken a table across the room from us. We all glanced over at them, but I didn't recognize them.

"Must be replacements," Joe observed. "Haven't seen them around here before."

The music on the radio had stopped, replaced by Lord Haw Haw, an obnoxious English turncoat who broadcast propaganda for the Nazis. He was always rambling on about some nonsense. We only listened for the music, but then Don said, "Shhhh. . .!"

"Too bad about those boys in the 91st Group at Bassingbourn. You know the ones; they'd just finished their twenty-fifth and last mission and then 'poof,' up in smoke, so to speak. It's a real shame, but you boys must realize that even if the gallant knights of the *Luftwaffe* don't get you, the poor training, equipment and leadership of the 8th Air Force will. Do the math. The odds against completing twenty-five missions are simply staggering. How lucky do you feel tonight?"

"Bastard!" Christy muttered.

"Amen," Joe agreed. Joe tended to say "amen" a lot. He'd been raised a Southern Baptist in Virginia's Shenandoah Valley.

Across the room, the three new Lieutenants burst into laughter, diverting our attention from the radio and Lord Haw Haw, who'd gone on to other news. The four of us stared at the new arrivals who were having way too much fun for this particular night.

"I'm going to say something," I said, wiping my lips on my napkin and standing up.

"I'll go with you," Christy said, standing. Now, that's one of the things I liked about Christy. He was loyal to a fault—and smart too. A little older than the rest of us, Christy had left law school to join the Air Corps right after Pearl Harbor.

"Good evening, gentlemen," I said, approaching their table. "I guess you fellows are new here and I guess you didn't know we lost a crew today."

One of the new guys, a sturdily-built, blond-headed fellow, pushed his chair back and stood. "We didn't mean any disrespect. We just flew in this afternoon. We haven't heard about your lost crew. I'm Harmon Roberts III; that's Bud Daly and that's Martin Wells," he pointed to one of the Lieutenants and then the other.

"Well, Lieutenant Roberts, we lost the Rhodes crew today. They'd finished their twenty-fifth mission. They were descending to land when another aircraft collided with them. They were done, on their way home and now they're dead and this doesn't seem like a very good night for a celebration."

"Was he a friend of yours?" Roberts asked.

"What difference does it make?" I snapped back. "He was a good pilot with a good crew and they all deserve a little more respect than you and your friends are showing!" Christy touched me on the sleeve but I didn't care. I was mad at the whole damn mess and Roberts just happened to be a convenient target for my anger.

"Well, like I said," Roberts stammered, "we didn't—
"

The door to the club swung open and Major Tucker strode in. He came to the edge of the bar, stopped and looked around the room. Conversation slowly ebbed as the twenty or so other officers in the place stopped whatever they were doing and focused their attention on the adjutant. There was no more dour, officious officer in the 91st than Tucker. His demeanor had earned him the nickname "Jolly."

"Gentlemen," Tucker began, his face pinched, his voice all nasally, "the bar is closed. The 91st is alerted for tomorrow morning."

The 91st Bomb Group (Heavy) was based at Bassingbourn, about fifty miles north of London and about eleven miles southwest of Cambridge. Of all the 8th Air Force's English bases, Bassingbourn was the best. Constructed in peace time for the Royal Air Force, the field avoided the sacrifices in planning and construction caused by the urgent wartime needs and short timelines which afflicted so many other stations. For instance, most of our peers in other groups lived in Quonset-style huts with coal stoves for heat—and we needed a lot of heat, especially during the colder months. At Bassingbourn, we lived in brick barracks kept comfortable by steam heat. Ah, luxury!

But you forget just how luxurious you have it when you're rousted out of the sack at 0300. Baker, one of the headquarters orderlies, had the task of waking officer air crews—and he seemed to relish the job. "Good morning, sirs!" he would sing out, swinging open our door and flipping on the overhead light. "Breakfast in thirty minutes; briefing in one hour!" Then, he'd be off to the next room.

Christy, Don, Joe and I shared a room featuring two sets of bunk beds and four stand-up lockers. The NCOs on our crew were likewise billeted together. We'd meet up for breakfast, then go as a group to the mission briefing.

"Oh, how I hate to get up in the morning!" Joe sang, rubbing his eyes and swinging his feet over the side of his upper bunk. As the pilot and copilot, Christy and I had commandeered the lower beds. Joe and Don slept above us.

"Cheer up," Don called, climbing down, "it could be worse."

"How?"

"Well they could be waking us up to tell us we have to go fly a dangerous mission over enemy territory or. . . never mind."

We walked down to the showers at the end of the hall and shaved quickly. We'd all learned fast that an oxygen mask is uncomfortable, but an oxygen mask over whiskers can be agonizing. After a quick shave, we dressed and headed toward the mess hall. There was really no point in showering before a mission. We'd be bundled in heavy clothes and surrounded by the smells of aviation fuel and oil, exhaust and smoke and who knows what else for most of our work day. Showers would come after the mission.

The mess hall was big, filled with rows of picnic-style tables and attached benches. The kitchen crew served from two lines. They had to get all the air crews, at least one hundred-eighty guys, fed and on their way to the mission briefing in about thirty minutes. Breakfast fare didn't vary much: powdered eggs, bacon, SOS, potatoes, toast and lots of coffee. There was plenty of racket in the mess hall as forks scraped against plates, mugs thumped against tables and servers dished out food, but there wasn't much talking. We were all still sleepy—and also nervous. In a few minutes, we'd find out how and where we were going to risk our lives for democracy on this May morning.

Christy made sure all our crew was present. That was never a problem with these guys. They were disciplined and worked really well together--a strong team that I was proud, and lucky, to be a part of. I knew that each man would do his job and, if necessary, do his crew mate's job, too.

A line extended from inside the briefing building out into the cool, dark morning. A small vestibule had been added onto the front of the building. Inside it sat two burly MPs checking the names of the crews as they entered the building. If you weren't scheduled to fly, you didn't get in--which always struck me as kind of funny because who in his right mind would want to get in who didn't *have* to get in? We presented our ID cards to the MPs and then stepped through a set of blackout curtains. In front of us was a center aisle flanked on both sides by rows of wooden benches. Our crew filed in from the back; Christy, Don, Joe and I made our way up front. Stan Martin, Phil Fox and all the other pilots sat close to the front, too. As pilots, navigator and bombardier, it was essential that we got all the information about the mission we were about to fly. The other guys mostly were there to defend our aircraft. We had to make sure it got where it was supposed to, when it was supposed to and that it delivered its cargo.

Once we got seated, Joe pulled out a pack of Luckys and passed it around. Half the room lit up as matches or lighters flared in the dim light. Several of the group staff officers were already on stage. Behind them, covered with black drapes, were large maps, ordnance charts and assignment boards that would shortly be revealed to paint a picture of the day's mission.

"Atten-hut!" came a cry from the back of the room. We all sprang to our feet like marionettes as Colonel Reid strode down the aisle, trailed by his adjutant Major Tucker.

"At ease, gentlemen," Reid called, hopping up the one step onto the stage. "Be seated and smoke 'em if you got 'em. We've got a tough mission today, so listen up and take good notes." Reid gestured to the operations officer to begin the briefing and took a seat on the stage.

Captain Ballard had a red-and-white-striped pointer that looked like a rehabilitated pool cue. He pulled back the drapes from the map board and declared, "Today's mission is the U-boat yards at Kiel!"

"Damn!" muttered Christy as a collective groan went up from the assembled crews.

"Amen," agreed Joe. The German Navy's U-boats were threatening to choke the shipping flowing into Great Britain, shipping that carried food, fuel and clothing for not only the civilian population, but also for those of us in uniform.

"This will be the 91st's deepest penetration yet into Nazi Germany," Ballard said, using his pointer to highlight the red lines of yarn on the map, lines that represented the group's flight path into occupied Europe, to the target and then back out over the North Sea to return to England. Areas of known flak batteries were circled on the map in red. The idea was to avoid those areas on the way in and on the way out. That was usually feasible, but the red circles around the target itself always proved more of a problem.

After Ballard finished, the weather officer briefed us on the meteorological conditions we could expect at takeoff, assembly, enroute, over the target and on the way home. Today's forecast looked to be pretty favorable once the inevitable morning fog dispersed.

Ballard returned to center stage, reviewing bomb loads, fuel loads and expected enemy opposition. He shifted to formation assignments next, telling which aircraft were to fly lead and which squadrons would fly high, middle and low in the group. A group formation is sort of like a carefully choreographed ballet. Every aircraft has to be in its proper position in order for the formation's combined defensive firepower to ward off attacking enemy fighters. The least desirable spot is the bottom corner of the low squadron. Fortunately, we were assigned to the high squadron for today's mission. There are no guarantees on a mission like this, but high is almost always better than low! Formation is also important for bombing accuracy; the tighter the formation, the more bombs will hit the target. "Takeoff time is 0630," Ballard concluded.

Reid stood up and faced us as Ballard moved off the stage. "Let's fly tight today, men. Let's give the Huns a good pounding and knock out these facilities. If we can weaken the Nazis' U-boat effort we can keep England's lifeline open. Let's get it right today so we don't have to go back!" Reid's left arm came up and he pulled his sleeve back. "Hack your watches, gentlemen," he said and we all followed his lead. "0455 on my mark. . .three, two, one, mark!" We all set our watches to his. "Good luck and God bless you!" With that, Reid dismissed us to our position briefings—pilots and copilots; navigators; bombardiers; gunners; radio operators—everybody had a specific job and everybody needed to know how his fit into the overall picture.

It was still dark as we exited the briefing theater and made our way to the equipment shack. We turned in our personal papers, money and valuables and drew our flight gear. Insulated, heated suits were a must at the altitudes at which we flew. Flak jackets and helmets provided some protection from the Germans' anti-aircraft fire. Parachutes, escape kits, side arms and maps were all part of our basic equipment for missions over enemy territory. The gunners picked up their heavy machine guns from the armorer's shack, along with a full load of belted ammunition.

Joe always took a few minutes to duck into the chapel and pray before we boarded the vehicles that carried us out to our aircraft. Most of the other guys would use the few spare minutes to smoke or talk quietly. Once we were all ready, the officers jumped into a jeep and the NCOs mounted up into the back of a deuce-and-a-half truck for the short trip to the hardstand and our waiting B-17.

I hopped out of the jeep as it pulled to a stop in front of the nose of *Hitler Hunter*, an olive drab B-17F. A picture of Elmer Fudd holding his shotgun graced the painted aluminum skin of the aircraft below the pilot's window. The F model, with its heavier armament and larger bomb load capacity, was an improvement over previous models of the B-17. Two things that hadn't changed, though, were the airplane's forgiving flight characteristics and its ability to withstand severe damage and keep flying. I walked around to the rear of the aircraft where I found Master Sergeant Tee Spence drinking coffee from a dirty mug and staring through sleep-deprived eyes at his "baby."

Tee and his team of mechanics worked all through the night to make sure our plane was ready to fly its next mission.

"Good morning, Tee."

"Morning, sir. She's just about all set. Full fuel and five thousand-pounders on board. What time's takeoff?"

"It's supposed to be 0630," I answered, peering through the darkness at the dim silhouettes of other airplanes stretched out along the taxi way to the right, "but this fog's gonna have to lift off before we can."

"Yes sir. Well, the old girl is ready when you are. We patched a few holes and ran engine checks and everything is running fine. Where to this morning?"

"We're off to Kiel. A U-boat base up there is going to have a very bad morning," I grinned with more confidence than I felt.

"Where's that?"

"Just south of Denmark, on the Baltic Sea."

Tee thought for a moment and then said, "Seems like a long way to go to find trouble when there's plenty of it a lot closer by."

"If I didn't know better, Tee, I'd think you were worried more about the airplane than me."

"Now sir, you know you're my favorite pilot," Tee grinned. "I'll see you when you get back this afternoon. Take good care of my baby."

Before we boarded the aircraft, our ritual was a final crew briefing. We'd gather under the left wing, near the nose hatch, in a huddle not unlike a football team's. "Okay, fellows," I began, as the first hints of dawn crept through the fog. "We can expect enemy fighters today because our friendly fighters don't have the range to go all the way to the target with us. So keep a sharp look out and if you see something, sing out right away. If you don't see anything, then stay off the interphone. We don't need a lot of jabbering up there. Let's save it for when we need it." I stopped, realizing that someone was missing. "Where's Willie?" Willie Trapp was our right waist gunner, a quiet kid from Kentucky, but a very good shot.

"He'll be right here, sir," answered our senior NCO Sandy Sanderson, the flight engineer and top turret gunner. Sandy was standing astride a canvas bag full of tools and small repair parts. He always carried it on our missions in case we experienced an in-flight emergency.

"I asked where he was, Sandy, not when he'd be back." My tone was a little sharper than I intended, but this was no time to play games, not when we were getting ready for our deepest penetration yet over Hitler's Germany.

"He's right over there, sir," Sandy answered, jerking his thumb toward the small stand of trees that separated ours from the next hardstand to the left.

"What's he doing over there?" I demanded.

"Maybe the Lieutenant would like to see for himself," Sandy answered. His formal tone sent a clear message that I'd embarrassed him in front of the crew. I got the message and resolved to make amends, but having gone this far, I decided I'd better go all the way. I broke free from the circle and stomped over to the trees in my heavy flying boots. Willie was bent over, his hands on his knees, breathing heavily. He turned when he heard me and straightened up.

"We're having our crew briefing, Willie," I snapped. "Maybe you'd care to join us?"

Willie wiped his mouth with the back of his sleeve. "Yes sir. I'm sorry," he coughed.

"Then let's go!" In my annoyance, I had initially missed that something was wrong with Willie. "Hey, what's the matter?"

"Nothing, sir, it's nothing."

"Well now, Willie, it looks like it might be more than nothing. You can't go off on a combat mission like it's a Sunday drive through town. You've got to be at the top of your game--not just for your sake but for the sake of the whole crew."

"I'm okay sir, really," Willie stammered, "It's just that I get a little sick before we fly. It's just nerves. I'm fine once we get up in the air."

"You mean this happens *every* flight?"

"Pretty much," he answered sheepishly.

"Why don't you go to the flight surgeon? He could take you off flight status until this goes away."

"Oh, no sir! I'm fine now. I couldn't let you and the boys go without me, sir!"

That was the way most of these guys were. They'd endure just about anything before they'd let down their crew mates. I wanted to put my arms around Willie and give him a big hug, but that would have been two members of the crew I'd embarrassed. Instead I said, "All right then. Come on back over to the *Hunter* and let's get this show on the road."

Willie grinned in the gray dawn.

Our takeoff time kept getting pushed back by the fog. Finally, we got off the ground about 0910, formed up in sunny, blue skies and set out over the Channel on an easterly heading flying toward Holland. Crossing the enemy coast, German flak was moderate, but not very accurate and none of the high squadron aircraft received appreciable damage.

We flew on through clear, blue skies for twenty minutes before Sandy shouted over the interphones, "Bandits! Three o'clock high!" It was now 1140 hours; we were about twenty minutes from our target. Christy stared out the window to his right; I concentrated on the wing of the aircraft in front of us and kept the *Hunter* in as tight as possible.

"Willie, Artie, Rick, look alive! Looks like twenty or thirty bad guys headed our way!" Christy was a cool customer. He'd decided early on that calling our crew members by name got their attention more effectively and reinforced their responsibilities to the rest of the crew. With the enemy fighters approaching from our right, Christy had alerted our right waist gunner, ball turret gunner and tail gunner. Sandy, in the top turret, already had them in sight. The fighters were still too far away to determine their type, but they were closing fast—and diving.

"FWs," Sandy reported after a few seconds. "They're going after the low squadron!" FWs were Focke-Wulf fighters, not quite as maneuverable as the Messerschmitts, but better armed. The fighters dived toward the airplanes below and on the left of our formation, wheeling and turning, winks of light flashing from their wings as they fired at our comrades.

I looked out my window to the left and glanced down toward the low squadron. A furious battle was raging as the massed firepower of six Flying Fortresses attempted to swat the German fighters away.

"Ball turret to pilot," Artie Holmes called. "One aircraft has a smoking engine."

"Which one?"

"Tail end Charlie, sir."

I glanced over at Christy; he shrugged. At the moment, neither of us could recall from the morning briefing which crew had drawn the short straw of having to fly on the lower left position of the lower left squadron. Inevitably, it was against this aircraft, the most susceptible of the formation, that the Germans focused their attacks.

"Right, Artie. Keep an eye on them and let me know what develops. All of you keep watch on those fighters. Just because they're hitting low doesn't mean they'll stay down there!"

Up ahead, small red balls of flame were turning into harmless-looking puffs of black smoke. Flak was anything but harmless; we were losing almost as many Forts to flak as to the enemy's fighters. Fortunately, the gunners on the ground hadn't found our range; they were aiming left of our flight path and so far, at least, well below our altitude.

"Bombardier to pilot." It was Don this time, reporting from the bombardier's position in the Plexiglas nose of the Fortress. "IP coming up."

The IP, or initial point, marked the beginning of the bomb run. At the IP, the bombardier took control of the airplane through the automatic flight control equipment and the top secret Norden bombsight. The Norden was one of America's secret weapons in the air war; it gave us the ability, under ideal conditions, to put our bombs on the target with pinpoint accuracy. Of course, when you're flying at twenty-six thousand feet, enemy fighters are darting through the formation and anti-aircraft shells are exploding all around you, conditions are never "ideal"!

"All right, Don," I replied, keying my throat-mic, "you've got the airplane." On the bomb run, Don would control heading and drift, I would maintain the correct altitude and airspeed. We were still in formation, of course, so we also had to hold our position relative to the lead aircraft. Now, once we were on the bomb run, we were sitting ducks. We couldn't take any evasive action; we had to continue straight and true to the target. That meant the job of the anti-aircraft gunners got a lot simpler. Our altitude, speed and heading were now constant. All the gunners had to do was lead us like a hunter leads a duck. Fortunately, Kiel's protectors weren't having a very good day!

Even before Don shouted "Bombs away!" we all knew. When he toggled the switch releasing our lethal load, the aircraft jumped up like a fisherman's float when the fish lets go. All of a sudden we were five thousand pounds lighter. We immediately climbed along with the rest of the formation. After the seemingly endless bomb run, a change of altitude would provide another margin of protection from the flak batteries below.

"Artie, Rick!" I called out to the ball turret and tail gunners, "let me know what you see back there!" The ball turret gunner rode beneath the belly of the Fortress in a hydraulically-controlled turret. He had the best view of what was happening below us. Likewise, Rick Gonzalez, our tail gunner, had the best view of what was behind us. "Everybody keep a watch on those fighters." The enemy fighters were still swooping in and among the low squadron, but so far all the Fortresses were still in formation.

After another fifteen minutes or so, the fighters began to fall away. Like our fighters, the Germans' aircraft had limited fuel capacity. At some point, they had to break off, return to their fields, refuel and rearm.

"Ball turret to pilot."

"Go, Artie."

"That same Fort with the smoking engine is starting to fall behind. Looks like he can't keep up."

"All right, keep an eye on them as long as you can. . . and say a little prayer for those guys. We still have a long way to go."

By the time we got back out over the North Sea, heading west toward England, the wounded B-17 had fallen way behind. Fortunately, no additional German fighters had come after us. That gave the crippled aircraft at least a chance--however long--to make it home.

"They're getting really low, Lieutenant," Rick reported from his tail gunner's seat. "Looks like they're gonna ditch."

Ditching was a sort of controlled crash into the sea. The pilot aligned his airplane parallel to the waves and landed it in the troughs between them. It was a lot simpler in theory than it was in practice. Hit the waves wrong and the airplane would bust apart like an egg dropped on a sidewalk. If that happened, it would be devilishly hard to get the crew out and into the life rafts, which in the frigid waters of the North Sea was your only chance of survival.

"Splash!" Rick called out.

"How far back to you estimate they are, Rick?"

"Maybe three miles or so, Lieutenant."

"Any sign of rafts?"

"No sir."

I instructed Rick to keep watching, but by the time he lost sight of the plane, no rafts had appeared.

We flew for another couple of hours out over the sea, our eyes straining into the sunlight, searching for the dark smudge of England on the horizon. Most of the crew had relaxed by now, the threat of enemy fighter attack diminishing with each mile.

"Top turret to pilot."

"Go ahead, Sandy."

"Shall we prepare all positions for landing?"

Christy glanced my way and I nodded. It wouldn't be more than a few minutes until we were back over the English countryside. Christy gave the order and the crew began to stow their gear and break down their machine guns. Work done now, as we neared the base, was work that would be finished by the time we landed.

Flying a big, heavy bomber is a challenge. The pilot has to keep his left hand on the yoke to control pitch--that's the up and down movement dictated by the elevators--and roll, the side-to-side movement determined by the ailerons. He has to keep his feet on the rudder pedals, which control yaw, the lateral movement of the ship. With his right hand, the pilot manipulates engine controls for the four big twelve hundred-horsepower Wright Cyclone engines that pull the Fortress through the air. That's a lot of work! Even though I shared flight time with Christy, by the time we landed back at Bassingbourn, I was physically and mentally exhausted. We had completed our tenth mission as a crew. I was proud of our team, grateful to Almighty God to be back on terra firma and eager to relax for a while. But first, we had to complete the tasks that go along with a successful mission.

We taxied back to our hardstand and I turned the *Hunter* back over to Sergeant Spence.

"Nice trip today, Lieutenant?" Spence asked, his eyes scanning the airplane for any signs of damage.

"Under the circumstances--world war, flak, enemy fighters and all that jazz," I answered, "yes. No damage that I'm aware of but Al was complaining that his suit wasn't keeping him warm once we got back over the sea. You might want to look at his outlet." Al Norris was our left waist gunner. He and Willie had the unenviable privilege of flying to work each day at twenty thousand feet with the windows open. Standing hunched over in the waist of the B-17 and pointing their .50 caliber machine guns out into the slip stream, theirs were the coldest of the crew's positions.

"Will do, sir. Tell Al to get the suit checked out, too. All it takes is a broken wire and he'll stay cold regardless of what he's plugged into."

The gunners removed their guns and ammo and we climbed into the vehicles that would take us back to the armory. Next, each crew went to debriefing where each got his regulation shot of whiskey before the intelligence staff questioned us about the mission.

"We saw one aircraft ditch in the sea," I reported to Captain Schiff, our debriefer. "Couldn't tell who it was, but it was the Tail End Charlie from low squadron." Our whole crew was seated around a small table in the briefing shack, one of a dozen or so similar meetings going on as the aircraft crews trickled in from the flight line.

Schiff checked his notes. "That'd be Broley in *Hell's Angels*," he said looking back up. "Any rafts, anybody get out?"

I glanced over at Rick. He shook his head and replied, "No sir."

We went through the usual stuff, pointing out the locations of flak batteries and grading the gunners on accuracy and volume of fire. We reported how many, where and when we'd seen enemy fighters and evaluated their tactics.

"Okay, fellas," Schiff said after we'd covered the routine topics. "Thanks. Good job. It sounds like you hit the target pretty hard. Lieutenant Foster," he turned to me, "Major Tucker asked to see you when we finished debriefing."

Terrific, I thought. Here I wake up at three o'clock in the morning, spend six hours flying through enemy airspace, I'm physically and mentally beat and now I have to go talk to Jolly. "Yes sir," I said and pushed my chair back from the table. That was the signal for the rest of the crew that our duty day was done. Well, theirs was anyway.

As ordered, I had dragged my weary body to the headquarters building where Major Tucker eagerly awaited my company. I reported in and Tucker hemmed and hawed for a minute before he cleared his throat and asked me to take the seat opposite his desk.

"We've got a bit of a situation here in the 91st," his voice escaped through his nose. "We have a new pilot who needs some special handling." My eyebrows shot up as my tired mind went to full alert. "You're going to help us," Tucker continued. He used an old letter opener to flip open a personnel records file on his desk. I couldn't see whose it was, so I assumed it was mine. You know what they say about assuming.

"Harmon Roberts III," Tucker said, looking up to meet my gaze. "Does that name sound familiar?"

"It does," I nodded, "but I don't remember why."

"Well, my sources tell me that you and First Lieutenant Roberts had a bit of a run-in at the club last night."

"Oh, sure," the memory light flickered on in my brain. "He and his buddies were a little too happy after what happened to Rhodes. I had a little talk with him about how things are around here."

"Did he make a good impression on you?" I wasn't sure why Tucker cared and I couldn't tell where this conversation was going.

"Not particularly." Sometimes short answers are the best.

"That's odd, because he's been at or near the top of his class in each phase of his training so far. He did so well at Omaha that he was held back as an instructor. He seems to be a pretty hot pilot." Tucker was watching me through squinty eyes and it dawned on me that he was tired, too.

"What's this got to do with me. . .sir?" I added the "sir" a little late, hoping to convey my disinterest without being overtly rude. Or insubordinate.

"Well, as I said, we need your help. The name Harmon Roberts doesn't ring a bell with you?"

"No, not really."

"Harmon Roberts, Jr., is a United States Senator from Ohio. His namesake Harmon Roberts III reported for duty here with the 91st two days ago. As a new pilot, he would normally be assigned to an experienced crew as copilot for his first five missions in order to gain experience before being entrusted with a crew of his own in combat. You know how it works."

"And you want me to take him on as my copilot?" I'm afraid a little aggravation crept into my voice, but Tucker continued on.

"I said, 'normally'." Tucker paused now and took a deep breath. I had the impression he was about to deliver bad news. I've got to learn to trust my gut. "The PR boys have been all over the Old Man on this one. They need an all-American hero, someone who flies and who fights." I was thinking that the group was full of guys like that, including Yours Truly. "We need authentic heroes and young Roberts is going to be one. You're going to help him."

"I've got a great copilot already! I'm reluctant to break up a good crew just to help the PR boys with their problem. McKnight is good enough to get his own crew," I protested.

"Oh, the Old Man and I agree completely." Jolly smiled as though I had walked right into a well-laid trap. "McKnight is getting his own crew and you're getting Roberts."

"Why me?"

"I picked you," Major Tucker said, looking me directly in the eyes even as my mouth hung open. "The CO asked me to select a good pilot with a good crew. You were one of three names I recommended. He approved the three and then directed me to choose."

"Okay, fine!" I said, too weary to continue the fight. I hated losing Christy, but he did deserve his own crew. "I'll take Roberts on as copilot." I capitulated and hoped I wouldn't live to regret it. Regret travels faster than you expect sometimes.

"You don't understand, Lieutenant Foster." Jolly was smiling again. "You'll be the copilot. Roberts is taking over your crew."

Losing my crew was a pretty hard blow to take. Losing it to Roberts made it even harder. After a quick shower, I met Christy, Joe and Don at the club for our customary post-mission beer. "I've got some good news and some bad news," I said when we sat down. Their faces turned my way. "The good news is that Lieutenant McKnight there," I tipped my head in his direction as I lifted my bottle, "is being promoted to pilot!" Joe and Don smiled and reached over to clap our crewmate on the shoulder. We all raised our bottles, clinking their necks together, and then we took a swig. "The bad news, of course," I continued, "is that we'll be losing Christy to another crew."

It didn't take long for that to sink in before Don asked, "Who's our new copilot?"

"Lieutenant Roberts will be joining our crew," I said, resting my bottle back on the table and avoiding eye contact with my friends.

"Ain't he the fella that you. . ." Joe's voice trailed off.

"When's all this happening, Bob?" Don asked, his thumb picking at the label of his bottle.

"Right away," I replied. "That's why Jolly wanted to see me. Christy will be assigned a new crew within a few days, but Roberts flies with us on our next mission." As if on cue, Tucker pushed open the door to the club and strode to the edge of the bar.

"Gentlemen, the bar is closed. The 91st is alerted for tomorrow."

It felt strange when Baker woke us up the next morning and Christy didn't get out of his rack. He rolled over, wished us luck and went back to sleep. Joe, Don and I repeated our pre-mission ritual. This would be our eleventh mission.

We'd eaten breakfast and reached the briefing hut when I felt a tug on my arm. "Good morning, Lieutenant Foster," a voice said from behind me. I turned to find Roberts extending his hand. "I know we got off to a bum start the other day. I'm pleased to be flying with you and the crew."

I wasn't sure what to say, so I shook his hand and mumbled, "Follow me."

We checked in with the MPs and took our seats along with the rest of the air crews alerted for the mission. Like the previous day's target, this one was a port facility servicing the Germans' U-boat fleet, only this time our target, Wilhelmshaven, was slightly closer, on the North Sea rather than the Baltic. We listened to the operations briefing, taking careful notes; to the weather briefing; the flak briefing; the communications plan; the formation assignments. *Hitler Hunter* would be flying in the number three spot of the high squadron. I suspected Roberts and his inexperience might have been the reason for that, but whatever the reason, it was a good spot to be in.

We drew our equipment, boarded the jeep with Joe and Don and drove out to our hardstand. I noticed Willie wander over to the elm trees that separated our hardstand from the Royston highway.

"Morning, Lieutenant," Tee Spence greeted me. "Lovely day for flying. Where to this morning?"

Roberts walked up beside me. "Sergeant Spence, I'd like you to meet Lieutenant Harmon Roberts III," I said as Roberts shook hands with Tee. "The CO has seen fit to give Lieutenant McKnight his own crew, so Lieutenant Roberts is joining ours."

"Pleased to know you, sir," Tee smiled in the dim light of the dawning day. "Now, you make sure to take good care of this airplane and it will take good care of you."

Roberts chuckled. "It's a deal, Sergeant Spence. Nice to meet you, too."

"Let's get started," I said curtly to Roberts and we walked back to where the crew was waiting under the left wing. Willie, I noticed, had rejoined the others. There was one extra figure standing in the shadows, but I couldn't tell who it was in the darkness.

"All right, fellows," I called out as Roberts and I reached the ragged circle. "This is Lieutenant Roberts."

"Good morning, men," he began. "I want first of all to tell you that I feel privileged to lead this experienced crew." A couple of the boys glanced at each other. "I know it's unconventional to make a pilot switch like this, but we're all fortunate that Lieutenant Foster will continue as our copilot. I know you and he have built up a lot of trust in each other and I want you to know how much I respect him and the track record you've achieved. The Old Man and Major Tucker both had the highest praise for your teamwork and skill. We'll need that today. We'll need every man alert and on guard. We're going back to

Germany. . ." I lost interest in what my new pilot was saying. I was humiliated as the truth sank in. My crew, guys I'd flown with into enemy airspace ten times, were all shifting their stares from Roberts to me and back to Roberts as if to ask "What the hell is going on?"

"All right, that's it," Roberts concluded. "Let's load up."

Joe and Don were the last to head toward the hatch. Joe reached over and squeezed my shoulder, but he didn't say anything. Don looked at me and shrugged.

"Lieutenant Foster," came the familiar nasally voice from out of the darkness, "a word with you, please." Tucker had been standing just on the edge of the circle, listening to Roberts and watching. He took me by the elbow and led me away toward Willie's pre-flight spot. "I know you'll do your duty, Lieutenant."

"Of course I will," I seethed. I was working very hard to control my temper and just barely succeeding. "It's my ass on the line up there too, you know. Mine and eight other guys I feel responsible for."

"Nine other guys," Jolly smiled. "Make sure you take very good care of Roberts. He's very important to the morale of the 8th Air Force. And his father is very important to the war effort. Don't forget that."

"Yes sir. I've really got to go now, Major," I said taking a step toward the *Hunter*. Tucker's arm blocked my way.

"One more thing, Lieutenant. As big a PR weapon as Roberts can be for us, he can also be one for the Germans. Make sure he doesn't fall into their hands."

"What does that mean?"

"Don't get shot down."

"I should have thought of that myself. Come to think of it, Major, maybe you should just order everybody not to get shot down. We'd have the war won by Independence Day and we could all go home!"

"Let me put it another way then," Jolly leaned in so his face would be near my ear. "Make sure Roberts isn't taken prisoner."

I stood still, searching Tucker's face in the dawn light, trying to understand what he was saying. To the right, a B-17's engine coughed and sputtered to life. I had to get into the cockpit and assist my new pilot, my new boss, with pre-flight. "I'm still not sure what you're telling me, Major."

"I think you are. You've got a sidearm, haven't you?"

For once, the mission got off the ground on schedule. No fog. The sky was clear and visibility was excellent so forming up in our squadron, group and wing formations was a lot easier than on a cloudy day. I was a little uncomfortable flying from the right seat; everything seemed to be on the wrong side. My left arm, the one with which I usually handled the yoke, was now relegated to the less physically demanding tasks of throttle and engine control. My right arm wasn't used to the exertion of heavy control forces necessary to keep the aircraft in its assigned position. The other thing that was different from the copilot's seat, at least when flying in the number three position, was that our lead aircraft was to our left. Roberts, sitting in the left seat, the pilot's seat, had a much better perspective on the lead aircraft and was doing an admirable job of keeping formation.

We'd had beautiful weather in England, for a change, but crossing the enemy coast, we caught up with a thickening undercast of clouds. As we flew deeper into enemy territory, the clouds became thicker.

"Radio to pilot."

I reached for my throat mic, but before I could answer Roberts did.

"Go ahead, radio."

"BOXCAR reports the target is 10/10, sir. He's aborting and will look for a target of opportunity." BOXCAR was the radio code name for Captain Moore, who was leading the 91st Group. 10/10 meant that the cloud cover over the target was complete; no breaks would allow us to salvo our bombs onto the target with any hope of accuracy.

The formation began a slow turn to the north, which carried us back out over the cold waters of the North Sea. As we cleared the enemy coast, the clouds fell behind also. The blue water stretched out before us, the golden sun hanging in the sky to the southwest. Within a few minutes, Red Sutton, our radio operator, was back on the interphone.

"Radio to pilot. BOXCAR signals target ahead. Enemy airfield."

"Roger. Bombardier, get ready to toggle when the lead drops his bombs."

Don, alert and ready as always, was quick to respond. "Bombardier standing by."

I leaned forward and stared out the front windscreen of the *Hunter*. With the sun slightly behind us, visibility was as good as I had seen it. Two small islands were maybe ten miles away off our airplane's nose. Intersecting runways marked the smaller of the islands with an X clearly visible from this distance. Talk about a target of opportunity: X marks the spot!

We closed the distance quickly. Don toggled our bomb load and cried "Bombs away!" The *Hunter* lurched upward and Roberts hugged the lead aircraft as we made another turn, this time toward the southwest and England.

"Pilot to tail gunner and ball turret gunner. What do you see down there?"

Artie in the ball turret responded first. "Plastered the bastards, sir! There's so much smoke down there I can't even see the field."

Rick spoke next. "Formation looks good, sir, nobody damaged that I can see. No bad guys either."

Our operations plan for this mission called for us to rendezvous with friendly fighters on the way home. Sometimes the fighters failed to show up when and where we expected them, but with such good visibility aloft, I didn't think that would be a problem today.

Sandy from the top turret was the first to see them. "Little friends, ten o'clock high." We used the face of the clock as an indicator of where to look when calling out enemy or friendly aircraft. Our aircraft's nose represented twelve o'clock, off the right wing was three o'clock, the tail six o'clock and so on. The friendly fighters Sandy sighted were to our front left, still some distance away.

"Copilot to crew," I announced. "Prepare your positions." It was customary for the copilot to issue general instructions to the crew. That freed the pilot to concentrate on flying the plane. Each crew member had certain tasks to accomplish at his station before we could safely land the plane. Guns had to be cleared of live ammunition to prevent tragic accidental firing as the airplanes of the group converged on the field. Turrets had to be positioned and locked for landing, radio antennae retracted, stuff like that.

The hospitable shores of England were looming large before us when Sandy's frantic voice screamed into the interphone, "Bandits! Four o'clock low!" We'd been caught with our pants down!

"Tell me what you see!" Roberts commanded.

Guns from our neighboring aircraft were flashing, but our crew had already begun stowing our guns and none were firing at the deadly threat racing up behind us!

"Four FWs, closing fast at four o'clock!" Willie shouted.

The *Hunter* shuddered as a twenty mm canon round flashed through Red's radio room. A shaft of sunlight illuminated the compartment and a high velocity stream of cold air ventilated it. Machine gun fire from a second Focke-Wulf stitched a line of holes into our right wing.

Fortunately, our fighter escort, a flight of P-47 Thunderbolts, had closed fast on our formation. The German fighters couldn't attack us and protect themselves from the P-47s at the same time, so they wisely chose the latter, much to our good fortune.

"Everybody OK?" I asked. The crew checked in one-by-one. We'd had a close call and had suffered minor damage to the aircraft, but fortunately no wounds.

Roberts taxied the *Hunter* to our hardstand and shut down the engines. He pulled off his headphones and tugged a handkerchief out of the pocket of his flight suit. He wiped the perspiration off his face and turned to me.

"Get the crew together. I want to have a little talk before we go to debriefing."

"They're bound to be worn out and we really should get to debriefing as quick as we can. It's first come, first served. If a bunch of other crews get ahead of us, we could sit there for an hour waiting our turn."

"Since when are you a stickler for routines?" Roberts forced a smile. "Get the crew together." With that, he unplugged his suit, took off his throat mic and pushed himself up and out of his pilot's seat.

I hustled to catch up and gathered the men together under the left wing. They were all glad to be back on the ground and were eager to be on the way to debriefing. Don and Joe gave me inquiring looks as I told the crew that Lieutenant Roberts wanted to talk with them. Roberts, who had walked back toward the midsection of the *Hunter* to assess the damage to the radio room, now appeared from the direction of the right wing.

He looked at the youthful but tired faces of his crew and chuckled. "That got pretty exciting, didn't it?" A couple of the guys smiled and nodded their heads. "I don't know how you are used to doing things," Roberts resumed, "but breaking down our guns before we're back over friendly territory seems pretty foolish if we want to survive our tours." He hadn't raised his voice, but it was clear that Roberts was angry from the intensity of the gaze that he focused on each man in turn. "If our fighter escort hadn't shown up like the cavalry, we'd be swimming in the Channel right now. Let's not ever make that mistake again! Everybody understand?"

I had to take up for my crew. "It was an innocent mistake, Lieutenant," I began, but Sandy cut me off before I could continue.

"You're right, sir," he responded to Roberts, looking his pilot in the eye. "It won't happen again. Will it, fellows?" He looked around the circle. A chorus of mumbled "no's" and "no sirs" tumbled from the chastened crew.

"All right," Roberts nodded toward a deuce-and-a-half that pulled up in front of the *Hunter*. "Mount up and let's get to debriefing before the rest of these guys try to take all the credit for knocking out that airfield."

"Yes sir!" the crew responded and picking up their gear ambled over to the truck.

Roberts hung back a moment, watching as the crew climbed up into the back of the truck. "Bob," he said, turning toward me. It was the first time he'd called me Bob. "It's important that you don't ever appear to question my decisions or my authority. If you disagree with me, fine, tell me in private; never in front of the men. Understand?"

"Understood!" I replied, the tips of my ears burning in the cool afternoon shade. I was fuming now. I'd screwed up in the air in a way that could have gotten us all killed. My mistake to prepare prematurely for landing had been waved in front of the crew like a red cape before a bull and Sandy--Sandy of all people-- had backed the new guy over his former pilot. Well, I got the message and how--he thought Roberts was right!

All of the sudden, I could see the benefits of getting shot down. I'm kidding. Maybe.

A B-17 is a big, four-engine airplane; I may have mentioned this before. The four engines provide power for lift and speed. They also provide a measure of safety. A B-17 can fly on three engines, even on two, but not as high and not as fast.

I'm sharing this technical detail because it came into play on our May 19th mission. We were again alerted for Wilhelmshaven and the U-boat facilities there. This was the target a few days earlier when we had to abort because of the cloud cover. It had been an important target then, it was still one now.

We were flying in the low element of the low squadron of the group, the most hazardous and exposed position in the formation. Crews rotated among these positions and our number had come up. We were all wound a little tighter than normal; there was less banter as we loaded into the *Hunter*, more attention to our duties.

We lifted off shortly after 1000 hours. Roberts was cool and focused, flying tight formation. By the time we crossed the enemy coast, there was no chatter on the interphones and the boys were busy scanning the skies ahead and above us. Ahead of us, we could see another group and there were at least two more behind us. That gave us confidence as the old adage of strength in numbers certainly holds true in a bomber formation.

"Look at that," I shouted to Roberts, peering out the windscreen at the dozens of small, black clouds filling the sky ahead of us. What looked like a field of black cotton was really German anti-aircraft fire, both accurate and intense. Some clouds and haze in the area probably kept the flak from being worse than it already was. The closer we got to the flak bursts, the rougher our ride became as the *Hunter* lurched and bucked through the turbulence created by the exploding shells. Shrapnel rattled against the thin skin of the aircraft and small holes began to appear, made conspicuous by the shafts of light they allowed into the aircraft. A bright flash to my right compelled me to glance over in time to see the scattered pieces of a Fortress raining down through the rest of the formation, the victim of a direct hit.

A bright flash and a concussion wave rolled through us. The *Hunter* skidded to the left, but Roberts leveled the wings and regained control. "Number one engine is losing oil pressure!" I shouted. "RPMs dropping!" Number one was the outboard engine on the left wing. Roberts had a better view of it than I did.

"It's smoking!" he shouted. A smoking engine on a car is a problem. A smoking engine on an airplane can lead to catastrophe. "Shut down number one!" Roberts ordered. I quickly feathered the prop while I still had the oil pressure to do so, and then cut the fuel to the engine. That would reduce the risk of fire and worse, explosion.

We were already losing speed, the distance between us and our lead plane increasing with each second. A B-17 that couldn't keep up with the formation was like a wounded deer; it wouldn't be long before the wolves arrived to tear it apart.

Roberts put the *Hunter* into a gentle, descending turn, eager to get us pointed back toward England so far distant. "Pilot to crew. We've got a little engine trouble up here, boys. Keep your peepers outside. Look for fighters in all directions and sing out if you see anything." Then he added words that sent a chill all the way down my spine: "Looks like we're on our own."

It seemed like only seconds before Sandy and Joe shouted at the same moment. "Fighters twelve o'clock level!" I sat up a little straighter and peered over the instrument panel. Three German fighters were heading straight for the *Hunter's* nose, closing on us at an incomprehensible rate. Blinking lights along the edges of their wings meant they were firing at us. Above and behind me, Sandy's twin .50 caliber top turret guns pounded back. Machine gun rounds hammered through the cockpit, sending sparks and bits of metal ricocheting. The enemy fighters flashed past us, wheeling away to begin another run.

"Keep your eyes on 'em, boys!" I shouted over the interphone. "Don't waste ammo! We're going to need all we got!"

Artie called from beneath the airplane, "They're peeling off to the left!"

"Watch 'em!" I repeated. I looked back at Roberts. He was focused on flying the airplane, exactly what he should have been doing. He was pushing the yoke forward, putting the *Hunter* into a shallow dive. That would give us more speed, but he had a more important objective in mind: punching a hole into one of the white, fluffy clouds loitering below us.

"They're coming around again!" Sandy shouted.

Down in the nose of the plan, Don or Joe--I couldn't tell which-- cut loose with the smaller .30 caliber machine gun as the German fighters closed for a second attack. Up above, Sandy's guns spit lethal darts as I'm sure Artie's ball turret guns did as well. I forced myself to look away from the onrushing fighters and to concentrate on the engine gauges. Once again, bullets thundered through the flight deck, puncturing a tank and sending a stream of compressed oxygen hissing into the cabin. Sandy shouted and I looked back half expecting to see blood. Instead, he clambered down from his turret, scratches on his face.

"They knocked it out sir!" he shouted over the drone of the remaining engines and the rush of the slipstream. "My turret's stuck!" Sandy's top turret was our best defense against a head-on attack. If he couldn't bring his weapons to bear on the enemy fighters, we'd gone from the proverbial frying pan into the fire.

"Holes in the right wing, sir! Fuel leaking!" It was Willie's voice, I think. I looked out my side window and everything went white. That's it, I thought. We've blown up; we've all been sent to Kingdom Come. Then I realized that Roberts had reached a cloud. I looked over at him and he was actually grinning.

"Pilot to crew," he said, sounding a lot calmer than I felt. "We're going to stay in these clouds just as long as we can, but keep a sharp look out. Let us know if you see anything: shadows, good guys, bad guys, geese. . . Joe give us the most direct heading to the coast. Copilot," Roberts turned to look at me, "let's get an injury and damage report."

I nodded and proceeded to poll the crew. A spent round had nailed Al Norris, the left waist gunner, in his ribs. Since Al had been wearing his heavy flak jacket, he'd escaped with a painful bruise. Otherwise, the crew was unharmed. The *Hunter* was not so lucky. In addition to losing number one engine, we'd lost one of our oxygen systems and the fuel tank in the right wing was still leaking.

"Navigator to pilot. Best course is two hundred eighty degrees."

Roberts pushed down on his right rudder pedal and rolled the aircraft gently to the right before leveling out on the new heading. "We're about eight thousand feet and descending. You can take off your oxygen masks." We needed oxygen above ten thousand feet, but here at this lower altitude and in the relative safety of the clouds, we wouldn't feel the loss of our damaged oxygen system.

Roberts reached over and slapped me on the arm. "Take over!" he shouted. I took control of the airplane, maintaining the heading and altitude. Roberts stretched his arms over his head and looked around the cockpit. Despite the aggressive attacks by the German fighters and the damage they'd caused, the *Hunter* was still flying. With a little luck and an assist from the clouds, we might just make it home.

At 1420 hours, we broke out of the cloud layer. Just ahead was the coastline. "Where are we, Joe?" Roberts called down to our navigator.

"That should be Amsterdam off to the left about thirty miles," Joe reported. "We're about one hundred sixty miles from Bassingbourn." We were approaching the northern limits of the English Channel, beyond which lay safety. Out of my side window I looked down on the Netherlands and saw what appeared to be a couple of merchant ships hugging the coast and steaming north. I reached over and tapped Roberts on his arm and motioned for him to remove his headphones.

"Hey, Lieutenant!" I shouted over the thunder of the engines. "There are two ships down there. We still have a full load of bombs on board and since we don't want to take 'em home, why not share them with someone who can actually use them?" Roberts smiled and nodded, then slipped his headphones back in place and keyed his throat mic.

"Pilot to bombardier. There are a couple of enemy ships down below just to the north. See them?" Before I knew what was happening Roberts had again put the *Hunter* into a shallow dive and was banking to the right. "See if you can hit 'em. We'll make one pass and then head for home!"

Roberts leveled the aircraft and turned the controls over to Don, who was using the bomb sight to make the attack. We were just off the coast, far enough away from the flak batteries around Amsterdam and low enough that we probably hadn't been identified as a threat. As we droned toward the two ships below, Roberts was back on the interphone. "Pilot to navigator. Note the position of these two ships so if Don doesn't sink 'em we can alert the Royal Navy when we get back."

"Roger!"

"Bombs away!"

Roberts took control of the plane and banked it to the southwest, out over the water. "Look out below! Ball turret, tail gunner, let us know what you see!"

Artie was on the interphone a few moments later. "It looks like we hit pretty close, sir. Big water spouts and I can't see one of the ships at all right now. The other one is heading up the coast still." By the time the smoke and mist from our bombs dispersed we were too far away to assess the damage.

"They were right about here, sir." Joe Johnson placed his index finger on the map, "North of Amsterdam and right between these two inlets."

"You pretty sure about their location, Lieutenant?" Captain Schiff from the intelligence section asked. We were in the midst of debriefing our mission. Because we'd had to abort before we reached the target, we'd been one of the first crews to return. Roberts was still out on the hardstand going over the damage with Sergeant Spence.

"Real sure, sir. Lieutenant Roberts made sure I noted the precise location so we could report it to the Royal Navy in case we didn't sink them."

"If you ask me, sir," Don spoke up, "Lieutenant Roberts did a mighty fine job of putting us into a position where we didn't have to waste our bombs. If he hadn't gotten us into the clouds when he did, we wouldn't be sitting here." A couple of the other boys nodded.

Schiff smiled. "That was good thinking. We'll send this location report over to the Navy right away." Schiff jotted some notes on a message form and then dispatched it via an orderly to the communications center. Schiff continued to query the crew, asking questions about the fighter attacks. He wanted to know about aircraft markings, numbers, tactics and so on. The Germans were formidable and the fighter pilots in particular were always trying new ways to blow us out of the sky. Anything we could share that would help defend our bombers would be passed on to all the crews in the 8th Air Force.

Roberts finally appeared in the briefing hut, a scowl on his normally relaxed face. He joined us around the table, downing his regulation shot of whiskey and answering the Captain's questions. Because Schiff had already gone over the mission in detail with the crew, he got little new information from Roberts.

"OK, fellows," Schiff said finally, "nice work on making it back and good work on those enemy freighters. Take the rest of the day off." That brought a chuckle from the boys, but not from Roberts.

As we all stood up to leave, Roberts pulled me aside. "We've got one unhappy crew chief!" he frowned, referring to Tee Spence. "He was bitching and moaning, stomping from one wing to the other and back."

"He'll get over it." I shook my head. "He's like a teenager with his first car."

"Well, he may get over it, but it's going to take a few days before we can fly our aircraft again. Number one's got to be replaced, there are a lot of holes to patch and he's got to replace one of the wing tanks. Then there's the minor stuff, top turret, oxygen tank. . ." Roberts's voice trailed off. I could see that he was exhausted. His eyes were red-rimmed and underscored with dark pouches.

"Maybe we'll catch a break," I said, "get a few days off to rest up."

"I hope so." He attempted a smile. "I don't want to get stuck with one of those hangar queens." Nobody wanted to get stuck with one of the replacement planes. You never knew what was going to work on them--and more importantly, what didn't!

Two days later, the 91st took to the air again, but the Roberts crew did not. Nope. Headquarters had something else in mind for us.

It was nice to have a Friday when we knew we wouldn't be alerted for a mission. It was also nice to sleep late and enjoy a leisurely breakfast. I'd thought about corralling Christy, Joe and Don and heading down to London for a couple of nights of merriment, but Christy was flying with his new crew and somehow it didn't seem right to go without him. I still hadn't adjusted to Harmon Roberts as pilot of my crew.

I was sitting in a nice comfortable arm chair in the O Club reading *Northwest Passage*, a novel about the French and Indian War. It was one of many books the YMCA had donated to our base library. I was just starting to get into it when the door opened and Baker, the headquarters orderly, walked in. He glanced around and once he saw me headed straight over.

"Major Tucker's compliments, sir," he began as I set the open book across the arm of the chair. "You and the rest of the Roberts crew are to report to the headquarters building at 1100 hours."

"What time is it now?"

Baker cocked his arm and eyed his wrist watch. I could have looked at mine, but I wanted to see if he could tell time. "1038 hours, sir."

"Major Tucker wants the whole crew? What, are we in trouble or something?"

"Oh no, sir." Baker brightened. "It's for an awards ceremony!"

I didn't know anything about any awards, but it's not like I would have been in the loop on something like that. Since Roberts was now the pilot and leader of our crew, I now felt some kinship with "Cactus Jack" Garner who while serving as vice president during Roosevelt's first two terms had famously noted that his office "wasn't worth a bucket of spit." Of course "spit" was the published quote, but I'm pretty sure Garner used a more colorful term.

I straightened my tie and opened the door to the headquarters shed just a couple of minutes before 1100. The rest of the crew was already there, neatly turned out in their uniforms, standing around Baker's desk and sipping mugs of coffee. A photographer was sitting in a straight-backed chair fiddling with his camera.

"Good of you to join us, Lieutenant Foster," Tucker greeted me, rising from behind his desk in the corner. "I'll tell the Old Man you're all finally here." Tucker headed toward the closed door to the CO's office. "When I signal you," he said over his shoulder, "file in and form two ranks; NCOs in back and officers in front. Understood?"

"Yes sir," Roberts and I echoed each other. Tucker knocked once and then disappeared into Colonel Reid's office.

"What's this all about?" I asked Roberts as Joe and Don crowded around.

"All I know is what Baker told me," Roberts answered. "He said be here at 1100. So here I am."

"Amen," Joe said.

"Me, too," said Don.

The CO's door opened and Tucker waved us in. As instructed, we formed two ranks and then left-faced so that we were facing the front of the Colonel's desk. Reid, standing behind the desk, returned our salutes.

"At ease, men," Reid smiled. Colonel Reid was well-respected by all of the flight crews. He led many missions himself, having already completed eighteen. And he didn't put up with a lot of chicken shit. "This is one of the more pleasant duties a commander is privileged to perform," he said, stepping around his desk and holding out his left hand toward Tucker. The Major handed him a small blue box. "Your quick thinking the other day resulted in a productive mission even though you had to turn back. If all the crews of the 91st were as resourceful as you fellows, we'd have the Huns on the ropes in no time flat. Major," he said glancing over at Tucker.

"Attention to orders!" Tucker commanded and all of us snapped to attention except for the photographer who was busy snapping pictures. "The President of the United States takes pleasure in presenting the Distinguished Flying Cross to First Lieutenant Harmon Walker Roberts III, United States Army Air Corps for service as set forth in the following: For heroism and extraordinary achievement in aerial flight as pilot-in-command of a B-17 Flying Fortress assigned to the 91st Bomb Group, 8th Air Force in action against German forces in occupied Europe on 19 May 1943. Despite heavy damage to his aircraft from enemy fighters and anti-aircraft fire, Lieutenant Roberts skillfully evaded additional enemy attacks and located highly valuable targets of opportunity. Lieutenant Roberts successfully attacked two enemy freighters, damaging both, one so severely that it was immobilized. Further, Lieutenant Roberts wisely noted the location of the ships and was able to report this to Allied Naval forces which subsequently attacked and sank one of the ships. His commitment to the mission, initiative, courage and devotion to duty were in keeping with the highest traditions of the United States Army Air Corps. For the President, Henry L. Stimson, Secretary of War."

Reid snapped open the blue box and extracted the Distinguished Flying Cross. He stepped forward and pinned the medal to the front of Roberts's tunic. "Congratulations, Lieutenant Roberts." Reid stuck out his right hand. Roberts shook it and then saluted. "Well done!" Reid looked to Roberts' left and right, making eye contact with each of us. "Well done all of you!"

Once we were back outside, the fellows all gathered around Roberts admiring his medal and shaking his hand. All except me. He'd stolen my crew, my airplane, and now, my medal. Mine were the eyes which had seen those ships. My initiative had suggested we drop our bombs on them. I was getting the short end of the stick on this deal and I was sore about it.

"Bob, let's ride into town and celebrate at the pub." Joe was pulling at my sleeve, urging me to catch up with Don and Roberts.

"You guys go ahead. Maybe I'll catch up with you later."

Joe hesitated, but then he turned and walked back over to Don and Roberts. I watched as they stood talking. After a few moments, Don and Joe shook hands with Roberts and walked away toward our quarters. Roberts looked over at me and started walking toward me.

"I guess you don't like me so much," he said as he approached.

"I guess not."

"You hold me responsible for losing your crew, don't you?"

"Yep."

"I'd like you to understand that I had nothing to do with that. I didn't hint for it, didn't ask for it and I turned it down when it was offered."

I looked him directly in his baby blues and asked, "Then how come you're the pilot and I'm the copilot?"

"Because after I turned it down, the Old Man ordered me to take your crew. You see, I'm not just another hot shot pilot to them," he jerked his thumb back toward headquarters. "To them, I'm just a propaganda tool." Roberts held my gaze. "I'm just like you, Bob; I'm doing what I can to help win this war so I can go home and get on with my life. So, if that means I have to take over your crew and your airplane, that's what I'm going to do. You can blame me for that or you can accept it, but that's how it is." He continued to stare at me.

I thought for a minute. Maybe Roberts's head wasn't "up and locked." Maybe he really was an OK guy, just following orders, doing his best to survive. Well, I had my orders, too; orders he knew nothing about; orders that might make him question all the "do-my-duty" crap he'd just shoveled my way. Maybe I'd have done the same thing in his shoes. Maybe not. Guess we'll never know, because I'm not in his shoes. "Have a good afternoon, Lieutenant," I said and walked away.

The *Hunter* wasn't ready to fly the next day, but it didn't matter. Weather kept the whole group on the ground. Despite no mission, my day didn't start out so hot. I was just rolling out of the sack about 0900 when a knock sounded on the door to our quarters. "Lieutenant Foster?" came the voice of Baker the headquarters orderly. I cracked open the door and stared at his whisker-less cheeks. "Major Tucker's compliments, sir, and he requests you drop by and see him at your earliest convenience."

"What if it's never convenient?"

"Huh?"

"Never mind. Run along and tell the Major I'll be there shortly." I took my time getting ready. We got up so early, so often, that on a day like this I just wanted to float along in no hurry for nobody. I showered, shaved, dressed and spent a good few minutes brushing my hair. It didn't really make any difference to how I looked, but it felt really good--and it wasted time.

Finally, about 1130 I sauntered over to the headquarters building. I took the scenic route, past the theater, the O Club, the small guest house. Baker was banging away on the keys of an unfortunate typewriter when I walked in. Stacks of papers and Army folders were piled on his desk. He looked up, nodded and pointed toward Tucker's desk, which was stuck in the front corner of the building between two windows.

As I headed over, Tucker looked up from whatever essential mission he was working on and waved me to a seat in front of his desk. I sat. Tucker cleared his throat. "You look well rested today, Lieutenant Foster."

"Thank you, sir," I replied. What was I supposed to say?

"How's our boy doing?"

I wondered if he'd heard about the snafu with the enemy fighters. I decided not to bring it up unless he did. "He's a very competent pilot, sir," I answered, adding "just as you said."

This elicited a rare smile from Jolly. "Very good. And the crew? Has the crew accepted him as their new pilot?"

I flashed back to Sandy. "Yes sir, I'd say that they have." I still wasn't sure why I was there.

"That's excellent, really excellent," Jolly smiled again. He was clearly having a happy day. "The 91st is scheduled to host a big war bond rally next week. There will be a dance, a band and some celebrities. The Old Man suggested I ask you if you'd be willing to escort one of them to the dance."

"It's not Walter Brennan, is it?"

Jolly actually laughed. I'm so witty. "No, no it's not. Someone I think you'll find much more appealing. Her name is Candy Cain. Ever heard of her?"

"The actress? Sure!" Candy Cain was one of the young, up-and-coming starlets of Hollywood. She'd gotten good critical reviews as the oldest daughter in *The Brookridge Girls*, a western set during the California gold rush. She was knockout good-looking, too. "Why me?" I asked, not really caring to hear the answer.

"Theirs not to reason why. . ." Tucker quoted.

"Hey," I protested, "I know the rest of that line and it doesn't end well!"

"Well, the Old Man feels you're a real team player with the way you've handled the Roberts thing. He appreciates your good judgment. Look at this as a consolation prize."

I thought for a moment, nodded and accepted the Major's kind offer. A beautiful girl on my arm, a night of dancing and who knows what else; things could be worse, right? Unwilling to leave well enough alone, Tucker added: "Remember your orders about Roberts; he is not to fall into enemy hands."

The enemy was the farthest thing from my mind as I stepped out of the staff car that had been assigned to me for the evening. We'd just pulled up in front of the base guest house precisely at 1759 hours, giving me one minute to reach my objective. The guest house was a ten-room facility that had been completely overrun by the Hollywood contingent. The big bond rally included a dance on Friday night and opportunities for every man on base to assign part of his paycheck back to Uncle Sam. The 91st Group was standing down so all the fellows, including the ground crews, could enjoy the festivities--and do their patriotic duty to help finance the war effort.

One of the big hangars on the flight line had been specially decorated for the dance and my mission was to pick up Miss Cain and escort her there. On the way, we were to make some carefully choreographed stops, all of which would be duly recorded by a newsreel crew and the 8th Air Force public affairs staff. We were scheduled to visit a ground crew that just happened to be finishing up repairs on a battle-damaged B-17, some wounded airmen at the base hospital, NCO quarters, and the mess hall. Then, we'd be whisked away to the dance, where Miss Cain and I would entertain the rest of the jealous men of the 91st with our ballroom dancing skills. Just kidding--but not about the jealous part.

Two photographers were waiting beside the front door of the guest house. They nodded and followed me through the main entrance, past the small front desk and down the corridor to room Number 5. I straightened my uniform jacket and tie and then knocked boldly on the door. As if my visit had been planned to the minute, which it had, the door opened. The beautiful face of Miss Candy Cain, movie star, smiled at me from beneath curls of honey-colored hair.

"Miss Cain," I nodded, smiling, "I'm Bob Foster, your escort for this evening." My hands were a little sweaty, but I had practiced my opening line for several hours that afternoon and it seemed to come out all right.

"Why, good evening, Lieutenant Foster," she smiled. Lovely, just lovely. "Edna," she called out over her shoulder, "Lieutenant Foster's here. We're going now."

From behind her, a matronly-looking woman of about 128—years, not pounds—called back, "Have a good time, dear!"

I held out my arm and Miss Cain slipped her hand through. I started to step off, but she held me back for just a moment. "Let the photographers get in front of us," she whispered from the corner of her mouth.

Now, Candy Cain was at that moment and remains to this day the most beautiful specimen of the gentler sex that I have ever laid eyes on. She had bright blue eyes, two rows of perfect white teeth, rosy cheeks and a figure that would make a bull dog break his chain. Her evening gown was made of some kind of stiff, frilly material, and it left little to the imagination with its low neck line and tightly cut fit.

"Where to?" she smiled up at me as we exited the guest house.

"First stop is the flight line," I replied as I held open the door of the car. Once she was inside, I hustled around to my side and hopped in. I quickly introduced Sergeant Marks, the driver, and off we went.

As the escort, my job was to get her where she was supposed to be, more or less on schedule. Her job, at which she was quite competent, was to pose, flirt, compliment, pose, inspire, thank and pose. She posed with the ground crew working to repair a combat-weary B-17, holding a big engine wrench in one hand while she wrapped her other arm around a grease-stained crew chief. At the hospital, she held hands with several of the boys while sitting on the side of their beds. She willingly signed every scrap of paper thrust under her nose and had the official photographers take her picture with practically everybody she met. I'd hate to have to pay the film and developing bill she must have racked up!

Next, we drove to the NCOs' quarters, where the crewmen of the *Hitler Hunter* were waiting out front, turned out in their best uniforms. I introduced her to Sandy at the head of the line and he in turn escorted her down the row so she could shake hands with each man. Rick Gonzalez, our tail gunner, was the last guy in the line, but next to him, as if he was part of the formation, sat a small brown dog. "What a charming little fellow," Miss Cain gushed, leaning down, patting the mutt on his head and eliciting a tail wag. "Is he your mascot?"

"That's Joe," Rick answered. "He's a Boykin."

"How did you find such a handsome dog in the middle of such a bustling air base?"

"Well," Rick scratched the back of his head and smiled, "he wandered over one day when we weren't flying and we were sitting under that tree over there drinking a few beers. Next thing you know, we'd found an old cup and poured some out for Joe. He seemed to like it and he ain't left since."

Candy Cain didn't know what to say, so she threw back her head and laughed.

"What wonderful boys," she said to me as we settled back into the staff car for the short ride to the mess hall.

"Yes, they're great fellows," I agreed. "Tell me, do you ever get tired of being on public display like this?"

She looked at me sideways, her automatic smile still in place. "Well, I'll tell you what: this seems like a pretty swell gig compared to what you boys are doing. I think I can tough it out a little longer." She winked and scooted a little closer. It was my turn to laugh.

Joe, Don, Harmon and Christy were waiting, along with a couple of hundred other guys, when we arrived for our evening meal at the chow hall. Tucker had allowed me to pick our dinner companions and I added Roberts at the last minute as a goodwill gesture. I made quick introductions, Candy waved to all the unlucky guys standing outside and in we went.

Once again, she turned on her hundred-watt charm, chatting with and smiling at every one of the cooks and attendants, posing for pictures when practical and generally being your average, run-of-the-mill, drop-dead-gorgeous, down-to-earth-friendly movie star. We got our trays and sat down with Christy to Candy's left, me on her right and Joe, Don and Harmon seated across from us.

"So what do you call this?" she laughed, poking at the meat on her plate.

"It's probably some variety of Spam," Christy offered.

"Yes," Don agreed, "since we promised to stop bombing Vienna, the Germans have stopped sending us Vienna Sausages." Candy leaned back and laughed, her hand on my thigh to steady herself. She asked the boys where they were from and about their families and how long they'd been in England. She was an enthusiastic conversationalist, which was good, because we probably stared more than we talked, so unaccustomed were we to being in the company of a beautiful woman--or any woman for that matter. Except for Roberts. While he'd been somewhat taciturn in my presence, perhaps from guilt at having stolen my crew and airplane, he seemed quite capable of carrying on a conversation with Miss Cain. Roberts was better-traveled than all the rest of us put together. I'd made more trips to Germany, but that didn't really count. Anyway, he'd been to California a couple of times with his father the senator and he seemed quite comfortable discussing with Candy some of her favorite Los Angeles restaurants. Next, the conversation turned to her work.

"What's your next picture going to be?" Roberts inquired.

"Funny you should ask: I'm scheduled to start shooting a picture for MGM when we get back from this tour. It's about a bomber pilot flying out of England like you boys."

"Need a co-star?" Don asked, drawing chuckles from the rest of the table.

"I suspect you could teach Spencer Tracy a thing or two about flying!"

"Spencer Tracy! No kidding!" Joe was star-struck.

Candy nodded her head, "Oh, he's swell, just like you boys," she leaned forward conspiratorially, "except when he's drinking and then, oh my!" she rolled her eyes and leaned in toward my shoulder. She smelled wonderful, despite the Spam, and the pressure of first her hand and then her shoulder was most pleasant.

AT 2000 hours, Candy Cain, Hollywood starlet, escorted by Yours Truly, made her grand entrance into the war bond dance. Hundreds of airmen, ground crew men and permanent party personnel along with a large contingent of girls from the surrounding towns and villages applauded as I escorted Candy into the hangar. Colonel Reid, with the group staff arrayed behind him, greeted her with a smile and a bouquet of roses. I should have thought of roses. A stage had been constructed on the right side of the hangar facing one of the group's newest, undefiled B-17s. Bright red, white and blue streamers stretched from each corner of the cavernous structure, meeting at a center point of the ceiling. Bunting adorned the stage and the largest American flag I've ever seen was the back drop to a twenty-five piece band. Refreshment tables lined the rear wall of the makeshift dance hall. Finger sandwiches, punch and even Cokes, formed in neat rows, filled the tables. Clearly this shindig was being produced by some entity greater than the 91st. It had all the marks of a big Hollywood production—and now it had one of Tinsel Town's stars, too.

"Good evening, boys!" Candy sang out from the big floor microphone on the stage as two spotlights converged on her shapely figure. She was greeted with a loud cheer and many a whistle. Reid stood behind her, smiling broadly. "All of us in the good old USA want to say thanks! Thanks for fighting for our country and our freedom! Why, if *Herr* Hitler could see what I've seen here at the 91st today, he'd just go ahead and throw in the towel!" This brought more cheers. "I bring you special greetings from Hollywood and hope you all enjoy the dance this evening; and look at all these pretty girls! Looks like we'll have lots of fun."

"Before we get to the fun, I want to get serious for a minute," she continued. "You know, beating the Germans takes more than skill, more than bravery, more than guts--it takes money. To make sure that 'We the People' provide you our soldiers with the best weapons and other material you need to beat the Germans and win this war, we're asking every American patriot to buy bonds. For as little as $18.75, you can buy a bond that will pay you back a full $25 upon its maturity. What do you say fellows, any bonds today?" At that, the band struck up the tune of the same name and Candy turned to Colonel Reid. "Colonel, would you do me the very great honor of leading the first dance?" He was happy to oblige.

A lottery had been held, don't ask me how, to award dances with Candy. After tripping the floor with Reid and five of his senior staff officers, including Jolly Tucker, Candy paused for a brief rest. She was still smiling, flirting and conversing with everyone who approached her. I went over to the refreshment table and grabbed a Coke, then elbowed my way through the crowd of officers surrounding her. I caught her eye and held up the bottle. She nodded and winked and held her hand out. "Thanks, Bob!" she said over the hubbub. Then she grabbed my arm, pulled me closer and leaned in to my ear. "Next time," she teased, "bring me something stronger!" That smell again, and another wink.

Candy downed the Coke quickly and was ready to dance again by the time the emcee began calling the names of the ten lucky NCOs who'd won the coveted dances with the star. "Looks like my dance card is pretty full," she said to me as her dance partners lined up behind me. "But I'm saving something special for you." I wasn't sure what that meant, but thinking about it was awfully pleasant.

She was a great sport, continuing with the same friendly, open demeanor she'd displayed hours earlier on the flight line, at the hospital and in the mess hall. I decided this was one movie star who was more than just a pretty face.

When the band played the last dance at 2300 hours, I could tell she was bushed. Still she smiled, signed autographs, posed for pictures, kissed cheeks. It was almost like she was running for office. Finally, Colonel Reid guided Candy back to me. "Miss Cain," he said, shaking her hand and standing between us, "I can't tell you how much your presence means to these men. After everything they've gone through to see you standing up on that stage and dancing with their comrades, well it's a big lift for their morale, I can tell you that. Thank you so much for spending time with us here at the 91st."

"Colonel, it's been not only a great pleasure but a truly great honor as well."

"And now, Miss Cain, I'm entrusting you to one of our finest pilots, Lieutenant Foster, who will see you safely home. Good night and thank you."

I again took Candy's arm in mine and walked her out of the hangar to the staff car. For the first time since I'd met her, there were no photographers around. A misty rain was falling, but it hadn't dampened the evening's festivities. The men were slowly fading into the darkness, heading back to their quarters. The English girls were climbing into the trucks that would carry them back to town. I opened the rear door and Candy fairly collapsed into the back seat. I crossed behind the car and slid in beside her.

"OK, Sergeant Marks. Back to the guest house, please."

Candy had kicked off her shoes and now she swung her feet up into my lap. "Sergeant," she began sweetly, "could we just ride around for a little while?"

"Sure thing, Miss Cain," Marks grinned into the rear view mirror and put the car in gear. He slowly pulled away from the hangar and headed toward the airfield.

"Rub my feet, Bob, will you? They're killing me." Even in the darkness of the back seat, even after what seemed like a hundred dances with a bunch of clumsy GIs stepping all over her, she still flashed that seductive smile. I slowly kneaded her feet, starting with my thumb on the arch and working my way up to her toes. "Oh God, that feels great!" she sighed. It felt pretty good to me too.

Sergeant Marks worked his way to the top of my list by driving us around the entire base, including the airfield, three times. During her impromptu foot massage, Candy talked about her life, her family in Colorado, and making it big in Hollywood. She asked me about our missions, what they were like and about the guys who weren't coming back. Then she asked about me. It was nearly midnight when Marks finally stopped the car in front of the guest house and I reluctantly climbed out.

I escorted her inside, past the desk, down the corridor and stopped at Room Five. "I guess this is goodbye," I smiled into her lovely eyes.

"That sounds like a line from a movie," she said wistfully. Then she reached up with her left hand and pulled my head down until my lips met hers. She was pressing up against me and within seconds I knew she could feel my growing excitement. My hands crept down to her waist, then lower, pulling her tighter. I don't know how long we kissed, but suddenly the door to Room Five swung open and light flooded the hallway.

"There you are! I've been worried sick!" shrieked the old broad I'd seen earlier.

Candy broke away from our embrace. "Relax, Edna," she growled. "I'm on an Army base. The bad guys can't get me here."

"My dear, the 'bad guys' are all over the place!" Edna snapped, scowling at me. "Stop pawing her, young man!" she snarled. "You, young lady, march right into this room right this second!"

Candy sighed, took her hand off my shoulder, smiled and said, "Thank you, Bob, for a lovely evening. It was so kind of you to escort me."

"It was my pleasure. I hope to see you again someday," I said without conviction. Candy winked at me again, brushed past Edna and disappeared into the room.

"Now, young man," Edna wagged her finger at me, "you remove yourself right now before I call the Military Police!"

"Yes ma'am," I said, tossing off a casual salute and heading for the door. Even that old crow couldn't ruin my evening after Candy's good night kiss.

I continued to give Harmon Roberts a wide berth, except when we were flying, which wasn't very often as May turned to June. We took the *Hunter* up for a check ride after Sergeant Spence and the ground crew completed the replacement of engine number one and the patching of the holes incurred during our last mission. Even after Roberts certified that the aircraft was once again battle-worthy, we still weren't flying. We'd be alerted for missions, awakened at three or four o'clock in the morning, briefed, pre-flight the aircraft and then the mission would be scrubbed; bad weather over the continent or lousy weather over the field. It was almost as if the gods of war had decided to give the 91st a break. Maybe they were just letting us rest up for the trials to come.

"Gentlemen, this will be 8th Air Force's first large scale raid into the Ruhr Valley. This is the industrial heart of the German war machine," Colonel Reid stated from the stage of the briefing hut. "Knocking out the synthetic rubber factory at Huls will put a severe strain on the Nazis. But don't think this is going to be easy--"

"Seriously?" Christy whispered to me. "Since when has any mission been easy?" We were sitting next to each other, in between Roberts on my left and Christy's copilot Tom Hamilton on his right.

"--if we know it's an important target, you can bet the Huns know it, too," Reid continued. Christy and I sat side-by-side through the entire mission briefing, listening with increasing concern as the group staff reported on the target (deep into Germany), expected weather (mediocre to poor), anti-aircraft (heavy around the target) and expected enemy fighter opposition (fierce). I was starting to wonder if I would ever see the good old briefing hut again, or any part of Bassingbourn for that matter. As usual, the Colonel ended the meeting by having us all synchronize our watches to his. Next, we hustled to our position briefings and then to draw our flight gear.

It was the first day of summer and we could tell. It was already daylight even at this early hour as I climbed into the jeep with Roberts, Don and Joe. I jumped in the back and Roberts dropped the jeep into gear. It was a short trip from the operations area to our hardstand and the cool morning air was very pleasant. We pulled up next to the *Hunter* and I could tell something was different, but wasn't sure exactly what, at least for a moment.

"Look at this, fellows," Roberts said to the three of us as we climbed out of the jeep. "I found a guy at group headquarters who used to be a cartoonist for *The New Yorker*. I commissioned a little upgrade to our noble bird there," he jerked his head toward the *Hunter*. Only it wasn't the *Hunter* anymore. In place of Elmer Fudd, a new design stood out against the olive-colored skin of the aircraft. In bright yellow letters trimmed in sky blue, the words "HARM'S WAY" had been painted on the aircraft's nose just below the pilot's window. "How do you like it?" he asked no one in particular, staring at the painting as though it were a Rembrandt.

"Looks good," Don laughed.

"Amen," said Joe.

"Are you kidding?" I protested. "Who do you think you are changing the name of the *Hunter* without even talking it over?" I was getting a little hot. Fortunately, the rest of the crew hadn't arrived yet; it was just us four officers. "Besides being just a little bit self-serving, it's bad luck to change the name of a plane! Are you crazy?"

Don and Joe were staring at me open-mouthed. Roberts was looking at me with a bemused grin on his face.

"Now don't tell me you're superstitious, Bob." It was almost as if he was admonishing me in front of my crewmates.

"I'm not superstitious, damn it! I just don't want to tempt fate!"

"You know," Don interrupted, "this is our thirteenth mission."

Roberts threw back his head and laughed. "Not you too, Don! All right, listen: here comes the crew. I promise to bring us all back safe and sound, bad luck or not. No more of this scaredy-pants crap in front of the men. Put on your big-boy britches and let's go to work." He was still smiling like it was some big joke, but I was getting more and more uncomfortable with this mission. With good reason as it turned out.

The trip into Germany had been remarkably unremarkable. We were flying in the high element of the high squadron, off the right wing of the squadron leader. This was a really good spot as the lead squadron and low squadrons, both below us in formation, would make more appealing targets for the Germans. We'd encountered sporadic, inaccurate flak on the way in, a testament to the good planning of the group staff. They had clearly routed us to our target without sending us through known areas of heavy anti-aircraft. By the time Roberts turned the airplane over to Don at the initial point, the group formation was still intact, except for the aircraft that had aborted due to mechanical troubles. There must have been two hundred B-17s plowing through the morning skies as Don homed in on our target.

"Holy smoke!" I cried as the sky in front of us suddenly filled with black smoke. Here at the target, the Germans were letting loose with everything they had, throwing up a barrage of anti-aircraft fire as thick as a storm cloud--a very lethal storm cloud. I guess the Old Man was right: the Germans did know this was an important target, one they were hell-bent on protecting. As we got closer to the target, our good fortune held. The deadly flak continued to fly forth from below, but was still concentrated on the lower squadrons. Our ride was getting a little bumpy from all the turbulence of the exploding 88 mm shells the Germans were lobbing at the formation, but so far, we'd sustained no damage.

Harm's Way, nee the *Hitler Hunter*, leapt upward as Don toggled the bomb release. Red left his radio compartment with the big Kodak camera we used to record our bombing accuracy. He steadied himself against the two hundred mile-per-hour slip stream in the still open bomb bay, snapping pictures of the target area as bombs began to explode below. As bad as it was flying through flak and enemy fighters, I've always believed being on the receiving end of one of our cargoes had to be a lot worse. Huls was about half covered by clouds, but Red reported a few moments later that it looked like the group had really plastered the target.

As the formation began to tighten back up after the turn toward home, Sandy in the top turret called out, "Fighters ten o'clock low. Fighters four o'clock low." From around the ship, calls came from the other gunners. It seemed as though every fighter in Germany was closing on the formation and from all directions at once.

"Pilot to crew. Call 'em out but stay calm. Don't waste ammo, we're going to need all we have."

"Ball turret to pilot. Low squadron's drawing them off. There are about thirty FWs buzzing in and out down there."

"Six o'clock low, five fighters, FWs," Gonzalez reported from his tail gunner's seat. So far, none of the fighters had bothered to climb up to molest the high squadron. There was easier fruit to pick.

The formation was now on course for the coast and beyond it, the safety of England. But we still had a long way to go and more German fighters were appearing by the minute. "A dozen more, eight o'clock low," Artie reported from the ball turret.

"Pilot to ball turret. Give me an estimate of the number of fighters attacking."

"It's easy fifty to sixty, sir. They're swarming like bees around a hive."

We could see the guns on the B-17s below us spitting tracers into the cold air and the answering flashes from the wings of the enemy fighters. *Harm's Way* hadn't fired a shot. So far.

"Low squadron, two planes smoking!" Al Norris called from the left waist. The low squadron was taking a pounding, the enemy fighters concentrating their malevolent attentions on our comrades below.

"Eight, no ten, fighters, one o'clock high!" Sandy shouted over the interphone. This unwelcome news jarred us. Fighters coming in from above us meant that we were now the target! I looked out of my side window and saw the black lines of the fighters' wings rapidly thickening as they closed the gap between us with sickening speed. Their wings lit with lethal flashes as they fired machine guns at us and then disappeared beneath us. All the guns on the ship were hammering back as another flight of three FWs converged from head on, twelve o'clock level. Sandy's twin .50 caliber machine guns thundered away just a few feet above and behind me. The ship vibrated and gun smoke filled the cockpit as every man except Roberts and I defended our aircraft.

"Three o'clock, three o'clock!" I turned to look out my side window and saw three more fighters blazing away. The ship thundered and rattled, jerking through the air like a bronco trying to unseat his rider. Five neat holes appeared in the bulwark behind my head; five tiny streams of light seeped into the cabin.

"I'm hit!"

"Who's hit? Who's hit?" I shouted into the interphone.

"It's Willie!" Al shouted from the other waist gun. "He's down!"

"Red! Take over Willie's gun!" Although we needed Red to monitor the radios, his weapon was of little use in a fight like this because visibility from the radio compartment was limited to only the airspace directly overhead. This fight looked more like one of those westerns where the wagon train forms in a defensive circle and the Indians attack from all directions.

"Copilot to pilot. I'll go check on Willie!" Roberts glanced over at me and nodded, his forehead glistening with sweat despite the sub-zero temperatures at twenty-two thousand feet. I pushed myself up out of my seat and stepped into a pile of brass casings from Sandy's twin-mount machine guns. As I did, they thundered again and more casings rained down onto the floor. I snatched a portable oxygen bottle and plugged my supply hose to it.

Now a B-17 is a large airplane, built to carry ten men and tons of bombs, but the crew compartments are nonetheless tight. I had to pick my way carefully, through the growing pile of brass, along the narrow bomb bay catwalk and through the now vacant radio room. Dozens of pinholes of light each represented a German bullet that had punched through our aircraft's thin skin.

I had a portable oxygen bottle, but now out of my seat, my flight suit was unplugged and I was cooling off fast. I pushed on, stepping around Artie's ball turret and into the waist section. Al and Red were blasting away at the legions of German fighters that continued to swoop past us. Here again, brass shells tumbled from their guns onto a growing pile. Willie was lying motionless, his left pants leg bright red with blood. I pulled off my leather flying glove and the silk liner beneath it. I had to work fast to avoid frostbite. I ripped open the first aid kit that Red had dragged with him from the radio room and found a bandage. I'm no doctor and couldn't tell how badly wounded Willie was, but the blood from his leg was seeping, not spraying. I sprinkled a packet of sulfa powder on the hole in his leg and then tightly wound the bandage over it. One of the few advantages of fighting a war at high altitude is that blood tended to clot faster in the extreme cold. I checked Willie's suit to make sure it was still heating. We didn't want to stop the bleeding only to let him freeze to death.

During a lull in his firing, I shouted for Red to keep an eye on Willie and headed back toward the cockpit. Even over the steady vibrations of our engines, all of which were mercifully running smoothly, I could feel the jerking recoil of our guns as they continued to spit bullets toward our attackers. I waded through the shells on the floor, stowed my walk-around oxygen bottle and climbed back into the copilot's seat.

"Need a break?" I shouted over at Roberts. He nodded and removed his tired left hand from the control wheel as I took hold of mine with my right. I locked my eyes on our lead aircraft and noted that Roberts had been flying tight off its wing. Even though we didn't gee and haw very well, Roberts was a good pilot. He skillfully flew the aircraft through coordination of engine power and control inputs. But I'm a pretty good pilot, too, and now was my chance to prove it. As I've mentioned before, on missions deep into Germany, where we don't have friendly fighter escort, tight formations offer our best defense against the kind of relentless fighter attacks we were now suffering. I was determined to keep *Harm's Way* as tight on the lead as possible to take full advantage of the overlapping fields of fire from the other ships in our squadron.

"Bandits, ten o'clock high!"

"B-17 below is smoking!"

"Which one?" I shouted over the calamitous noise of the engines and our busy machine guns.

"*Witch's Brew*!" Artie grunted. "Number four engine!" You could tell he had more important things on his mind than the lives of ten of our friends--he was busy trying to keep the same fate from befalling us! *Witch's Brew* was piloted by Stan Martin. He frequently entertained us at the club with a spot-on imitation of James Cagney. We'd gone through primary and advanced flight training together. I hoped he could catch a little luck and get his plane back to England, but there wasn't much I could do to help him.

"Twelve o'clock level--five abreast!" Don's anxiety carried over the interphone throughout the ship. Up ahead and closing fast came the flashes from their wings as tracers raced the fighters into our formation. No rounds from the head-on attack hit us, but a new threat was about to test us.

"Three fighters, three o'clock level, coming in fast and hot!" It was Red, calling in from the right waist. I chanced a quick glance over my right shoulder and saw flashes, and then jerked my eyes back to our lead aircraft. We were too close to look away for more than a moment. *Harm's Way* shuddered and the control wheel came all the way back into my stomach as the plane nosed over into a steep dive. Before I could shout to Roberts, he reached over and engaged the autopilot. The aircraft immediately began to level off. We'd fallen out of position, but not so far that we'd be easy pickings for the German fighters.

I nodded a quick thanks to Roberts and then lifted the headphone off my left ear. There were times when I didn't want to use the interphone because I didn't want the whole crew to listen to the conversation between the pilots. This was one of those times. They had more important things to do. Roberts and I had to keep *Harm's Way* flying.

"You fly!" I shouted. "I'll see if I can fix anything!" Roberts nodded and put his headphones back in place.

"Pilot to crew. Keep after those Jerries, boys. We've got a little problem with flight controls, but we've switched on the autopilot and that will give us time to make repairs. Keep those fighters at a distance.

Once again, I grabbed an air bottle and climbed out of my seat. Normally Sandy would have been our first choice to make repairs, but as I mentioned, we needed him more on the guns at the moment. I grabbed his canvas repair bag from behind my seat and worked my way back to toward the bomb bay. I had a pretty good idea what had happened.

My guess was that one of the FWs had hit us with his twenty mm canon and had severed our control cables. Now, this is why we loved to fly the B-17: the engineers who designed her ran two sets of control cables. One set of manual cables was tied into the pilot's and copilot's control wheel. A second set of electrical cables linked the control surfaces via servo motors to the autopilot. When Roberts saw the control wheel come all the way back into my stomach, he guessed immediately that our manual cables were severed. His quick thinking in flipping on the autopilot probably saved ten lives. The only problem with our current situation is that we were no longer in quite as tight a formation as we would have liked. Oh yeah, one other thing: We couldn't land on autopilot. That wasn't a major problem at the moment, but it would become more important to us with each passing mile.

I looked along the top of the fuselage, aft of the top turret and found the problem in the bomb bay. Ragged ends hung down on both sides where unbroken cables had run before. I set the repair kit down and began looking through it. Something fast and angry whizzed past my head and another shaft of light penetrated the interior of our bomber. Sandy, God bless his soul, always carried extra parts in the repair bag. He'd obviously paid attention to the experiences of others and had included in the bag extra lengths of cable and some cable clamps. I was using a portable oxygen bottle, but I was cut off from the rest of the crew because there was no way I could plug into the interphone.

I set to work. I'd pull off my gloves, work for a couple of minutes, then stop and put my gloves back on to warm up my fingers. This went on for several days. Okay, it seemed like days, but it was really probably less than a quarter of an hour. I was making slow progress when Sandy appeared by my side. Apparently, the enemy fighter attacks had let up. He slapped me on the shoulder and pointed to a portable oxygen bottle in his hand. He was telling me it was time to change bottles, that mine was about out. He swapped with me and disappeared back through the door to the flight deck. A couple of minutes later, he was back with the portable bottle he had refilled from our oxygen system.

Working together, taking breaks to warm up and to refill our oxygen bottles, Sandy and I spliced in new cables, restoring the manual control of the rudders, ailerons and elevators to the control wheels of the pilot and copilot. The cables were looser than normal and the handling of the airplane would be mushy, but we ought to be able to land. By the time we finished and got back to the flight deck, we were back over water and still more or less in formation.

Because of our wounded man on board and the damage we'd sustained, we were among the first to land. Roberts had to be exhausted, but he made a good approach to the field. Once we were lined up to land, I fired a red flare out my side window. That was the signal for the ambulance crews that we had a wounded man aboard. *Harm's Way* came in a little wobbly, like a drunk after a night at the pub, but Roberts sat her down and our rollout was uneventful. All the boys pitched in to help get Willie on a stretcher. He was ashen-faced but still breathing as the medics loaded him into the ambulance.

I stood staring after him as the ambulance sped away. I felt a hand on my shoulder. "That was really good work up there, Bob." Harmon Roberts said. "I think you and Sandy saved our bacon. Thanks."

"Yeah, well just remember who promised to bring us all back safe and sound!" I snapped, jerking my shoulder from beneath his hand. "I think you've got some explaining to do to Willie." I walked away. I can be a real jerk sometimes.

By the time we got to the O Club that night, I was ready for more than a beer. For the second straight mission, we'd gotten personal attention from the *Luftwaffe* and sustained serious damage. For the first time, we'd also suffered a serious wound. Willie had been hauled off to the hospital; we'd go check on him in the morning--if we weren't flying. I grabbed a seat at the table near the radio. Jazz music was playing so I figured we weren't listening to the BBC. Jazz usually meant Radio Berlin.

I looked around the club. Officers were slowly trickling in; the clack of billiard balls punctuating the mostly quiet conversations taking place around the room.

"Who are you looking for, Bob?" Don asked after a minute.

"Christy."

Joe and Don looked at each other for a second, and then Don cleared his throat. "Christy's ship didn't make it back. They went down somewhere near the Dutch-Belgian border."

I was stunned. "Why didn't somebody tell me?"

"We watched him go down. I even counted eight chutes. I counted them off." Joe nodded his head in agreement.

"I don't remember hearing any of that."

"It all happened while you and Sandy were fixing those cables. I'm sorry," Don apologized. "I didn't realize you didn't know."

Damn. First I lose my aircraft and my crew, then my replacement wins a medal for following through on my idea and now my best friend goes missing. I was having a bad run--but I guess not as bad as Christy.

We didn't fly for the next couple of days. On Friday, I was once again summoned to group headquarters. On a day off, I had better things to do than hang around headquarters and mingle with the pencil pushers, but Major Tucker had sent for me so I figured I'd better show up.

I'm respectful of rank and I understand that everybody has a job to do to help win this war, but Jolly Tucker rubbed me the wrong way. He was a "kiwi," a non-flyer and one of those self-important, by-the-book officers who thought adherence to regulations was the way to beat the Germans. Of course he was also one of those guys who would never see enemy territory, never inflict harm on the enemy and never have the satisfying experience of having the enemy shoot at him without effect.

I entered the headquarters building and strode past Baker's desk. He was banging away on a typewriter, no doubt mangling some form or something.

"You wanted to see me, sir?" I said, stopping in front of Tucker's desk.

"Well, Casanova, isn't it?" Tucker asked sarcastically, a sneer on his face.

"Sir?"

He held up a letter. "This, for your information, Lieutenant, is a letter of complaint from a Mrs. Marsh. Do you recognize that name, Lieutenant?"

"No sir. Any reason why I should?" I wasn't being a wise guy; I didn't know anyone named Marsh, not here and not back home.

Tucker looked from my innocent face back to the letter. He continued, "Mrs. Edna Marsh just happens to be the chaperone for Miss Candy Cain." He looked back up at me, his eyes trying to burn holes through my skull. "Ring a bell?"

"Sure, I remember her. What's her beef?"

"She reports that you were pawing Miss Cain in the guest house hallway! Damn it, Foster! You were supposed to be her escort, not some kind of wolf!"

This was almost comical. Almost. "Hey, look, Major, she initiated the good night kiss."

"There's nothing wrong with a kiss on the cheek, but that's hardly what Mrs. Marsh is describing here!" he waved the letter in the air. "She's threatening to report this to General Eaker and then pack up Miss Cain and take her home!" Eaker was the commander of the 8th Air Force; a man whose attention I didn't want to attract.

"I'm sorry, Major, but I don't see that I did anything out of line. Candy's on the road all the time and she just needed somebody to talk to. You assigned me the job and I did it. Nothing happened."

"Candy? Well that's not the way Mrs. Marsh saw it and based on her report, I'm going to have to address this with the Old Man. I swear, Foster, I would never have given you this assignment if I thought you'd turn into some sort of masher!"

"Yeah, well, if you wanted a eunuch to be Miss Cain's escort, you should have taken the job yourself!" Baker's typing ceased and his mouth fell open. Sometimes I go too far.

Tucker's neck, face and ears turned a bright crimson, like a character in one of those cartoons. I half expected smoke to start pouring out of his ears. I held my breath, waiting for the eruption. Instead, in a very low growl, Tucker said, "Get your ass out of my headquarters."

Now, I was tempted to point out that it wasn't actually his headquarters, that it was the Colonel's, but occasionally, my better judgment actually does kick in. I saluted, stepped back and pivoted toward the door. I winked at the dumbstruck Baker on my way out.

I almost ran into Colonel Reid as I exited the building. I quickly saluted and said "Good morning, sir!"

"Good morning, Bob," he smiled in return. "What're you doing over here on a day off?"

"I, uh, just had an appointment with Major Tucker, sir."

"What about?" I didn't know if he was testing me or if he really didn't know, so I decided to play it straight.

"Well, sir, he, Major Tucker, that is, he's a little concerned about the way I handled my escort assignment with Miss Cain. He, uh, thinks I got a little too friendly with her."

"And why does he think that?" the Colonel asked, trying to suppress a smile.

"It seems Miss Cain's chaperone sent a letter of complaint."

"Hmmm," the Colonel rubbed his chin. "Bob, I saw Miss Cain and the rest of her entourage off the morning after the big dance. She had only the highest praise for you. She called you thoughtful and gentlemanly. In fact, for a moment I thought she had gotten you and me confused." He laughed. I thought that was a good sign. "Well, you didn't do anything any normal red-blooded American fighting man wouldn't do, did you?"

"No sir!"

"Any letter addressed to this headquarters will eventually hit my desk. I'll take a look at it and let you know if I have any questions. Fair enough?"

"Absolutely, sir!"

"Take off and go do something fun!"

"Yes sir!" I saluted and followed his order, thinking that I wouldn't hear anything more about the incident. I was surprised when I was ordered back to headquarters the very next day.

In a theater of war, Saturdays and Sundays are indistinguishable from Mondays, Tuesdays or any other days. We liked to joke that we'd only fly on days that ended in "Y." But, the weather had remained crummy, with low ceilings and plenty of rain and the weather over the continent apparently wasn't much better, so on this particular Saturday, we weren't flying.

I was thinking about borrowing a bicycle and riding into the village, maybe visit The Red Lion pub or something, you know, just to get off the base for a while. Don came into our room and deflected that plan with one line.

"Old Man wants to see you," he said, a look of concern on his face.

I was just knotting my tie. "What for?"

"Well, he didn't confide in me, Bob. Would you like me to run back over and ask him his intentions?" Don can be pretty sarcastic sometimes, but I like him anyway.

"Was Tucker with him?"

"Yes."

Damn. I was surprised and disappointed. I had thought the Old Man would brush off the letter from that old wind bag. I guess I had a lot to learn about human nature and the responsibilities of command.

I pulled on my uniform blouse and followed Don back out. We got to headquarters and Don held the door open and let me go in first. I was startled to see Roberts, Joe, Sandy and the rest of the crew, less Willie of course, waiting for us. I glanced at Don and he smiled and shrugged.

"Good morning, sir!" I said to Colonel Reid, ignoring Major Tucker who was standing off to his right.

The Colonel gave me a tight smile and shook my hand. "Lieutenant Foster. Sergeant Sanderson, please come and stand beside Lieutenant Foster." I was really confused at this point. The Colonel glanced at Tucker and nodded. "Major, if you please."

Tucker straightened and began, "Attention to orders!" The rest of the boys, along with Baker, popped to attention. Tucker proceeded to read from the papers in his hands. When my addled brain caught up with what was happening, I realized that Sandy was being awarded the Bronze Star for helping patch *Harm's Way* back together on our previous mission. I thought this was well-deserved, but still didn't understand why I was standing next to him. Once Tucker finished reading the order, Colonel Reid stepped forward and pinned the medal to the left pocket flap of Sandy's uniform. He shook Sandy's hand and stepped back. Sandy saluted and the Colonel returned the salute. Without missing a beat, Reid nodded once more to Tucker.

"Attention to orders!" Tucker repeated. This time, he called my name as he read the citation for the Silver Star medal. It seems that I had been given the bulk of the credit for repairing the ship and saving all of our lives. I was okay with this. Reid pinned the Silver Star on my swelling chest, shook my hand and we exchanged salutes. He looked tired. Then all the boys were applauding and slapping Sandy and me on the back. I have to admit, it felt pretty good. Then Roberts was in front of me, his hand extended.

"Well done, Bob!" he said. "I'd like to buy you a drink. Sort of a congratulations. What'd'ya say?"

Before I could answer, the Colonel stepped over to us and said, "Bob, I'd like to see you in my office for a moment before you go. Give us just a minute, Harmon?"

"Of course, sir," Roberts answered, stepping back.

I followed the Colonel into his office and he shut the door behind us. "Have a seat," he directed, pointing to one of the straight-backed chairs in front of his desk.

"This hasn't got anything to do with Miss Cain, does it, sir?" I asked, my anxiety getting the best of me.

"I'm afraid it does, Bob," he said, moving an ash tray aside so he could sit on the front of the desk.

"Sir, I give you my word that I didn't do anything out of line. I didn't make any unwelcome advances--"

Reid held up both his hands. "Hold it, Bob," he said, a new tone in his voice. He stared into my eyes for a moment, then down at his hands. "I'm sorry to have to tell you--" Oh great, I thought, here it comes, "--Miss Cain and the rest of her entourage were killed yesterday afternoon. Their C-47 crashed into a mountain up in Scotland somewhere. They were going up there to entertain at some training post and the weather deteriorated and they couldn't find their way in. The news hasn't been released yet. The War Department is working on notifying next of kin. I thought you should know."

I was stunned. I looked away and shook my head. I hadn't really expected to ever see Candy Cain again, but still I felt an intense loss. Reid leaned forward and patted me on the shoulder. "I'm sorry to have to share sad news. There's plenty of that around here without something like this." I realized that after just about every mission, this man had to write letters of condolence to loved ones telling them their sons, fathers or husbands were dead, wounded or missing. No wonder his eyes looked so tired.

I shook my head. "It doesn't make any sense, does it, sir?"

"None at all."

"Thanks for telling me. Thanks for telling me in here," I said, looking up and meeting his eyes again.

"Congratulations on that Silver Star. You can't order those from the Sears catalogue," he smiled, standing and tugging on the bottom of his tunic.

"Thank you, sir."

"Don't thank me. Lieutenant Roberts was behind the recommendations for both you and Sergeant Sanderson."

I shook his hand again and left his office, passing by Tucker's desk and then Baker's and exiting the building. Don was waiting on me. "Congratulations, hero!" he smiled. "Hey, what's the matter? You don't look very happy for a medal winner." I told him about Candy. He looked down at his shoes and shook his head.

"I guess Spencer Tracy'll have to find a new co-star."

Don figured I needed some cheering up and talked me in to riding into town for drinks. He also invited Joe and Roberts. I was starting to get the message, finally, that the rest of the boys had accepted Roberts as part of our crew. I seemed to be the only holdout.

We pedaled into the village of Bassingbourn, which was only about a mile or so from the base, and turned right onto High Street. From there, it was a short ride to the heart of the village and The Red Lion pub. We parked our bikes, put on our caps and stepped into the dark interior of the pub where we took our caps off again. It was just before noon and we took a table by the window facing the street. We each ordered a pint of dark ale.

"Four bob please, gents," said the proprietor, a beefy man wearing a white apron over a white long sleeved shirt. We dug in our pockets and handed over the coins, which he dropped into a pocket of his apron.

Once the drinks were served, Roberts raised his glass and said, "Good fortune and good comrades."

"Amen," Joe agreed.

"Congratulations on your medal, Bob," Roberts added. "You saved the airplane."

"Thanks. Thanks for recommending the award. I thought I was in trouble when Don came and told me I had to report back to headquarters."

"Why'd you think that?" Roberts asked as a couple of patrons entered the pub.

I spent the next few minutes relating the story of my unpleasant visit with Tucker the day before; how he'd chewed me out and threatened to go to the Old Man with Mrs. Marsh's letter. Don kept looking away, glancing out the window. Joe was smiling. Roberts was following the story with a mixture of bemusement and disbelief.

"She really threatened to go to General Eaker?" Roberts asked.

"Hell yes."

Don fell over laughing, banging his head on the table. Joe erupted with a spasm of his own. Roberts smiled, more amused at our crew mates than at the story.

"Anyway," I resumed, "when Don told me to report to headquarters, I was sure the Old Man was going to end up busting me back to flying cadet."

Joe couldn't contain himself any longer and began slapping the table. Tears were streaming down Don's cheeks. Now, I thought it was pretty funny in hindsight, but not *that* funny.

Joe started to speak, and then succumbed to another wave of giggles. Finally, Don caught his breath. "I wish I'd seen the look on your face. . .and on Jolly's too! He wasn't very observant."

I was confused now. "What do you mean, he wasn't very observant?"

"Well," Joe cleared his throat and spoke up, "did he show you the envelope or just the letter?"

"He just waved the letter in front of my face. He didn't actually let me read it and I didn't see the envelope."

Joe started to laugh again so Don picked up the conversation. "The dumb jerk should have paid a little more attention to the post mark. If he had, he would have noticed that it was mailed from Bassingbourn two days after Mrs. Marsh and the rest of the troupe left town."

"How could she do that?" Roberts asked.

"She didn't do it," Joe snickered. "We did!"

The look on my face must have been quite comical, because Joe and Don again collapsed in fits of laughter. "You two. . .?"

They were laughing so hard now all either could do was nod his head. I looked at Roberts and asked, "Did you. . .?"

He quickly threw up both hands in protest. "Not even a little!" That's when the trouble started.

In our merriment, Joe's and Don's in particular, we had been oblivious to the fact that The Red Lion was filling up with its regular lunch time patrons. Our laughter, apparently, was a little more than they were accustomed to hearing. This didn't really register with me until I felt the presence of someone standing over me.

"You Yanks are having quite a time of it, hey?" I looked up to see a mountainous fellow looking back at me. "Having a merry time, are we?" We might have been, but he clearly was not.

I kept staring up at the man who must have been six feet tall and two hundred thirty pounds. "We're just minding our own business, friend," I replied with a smile. Joe and Don had stopped laughing. Finally.

"Well, I'm just minding mine, Yank and you're interfering with my enjoyment of my dinner." The man, like I said, was big, with muscular arms and hands the size of baseball mitts. They didn't look as soft, though. "I advise you to finish your pints and leave."

"I advise you to go back over and finish your lunch," I replied sweetly. "I've flown thirteen missions over Europe, I'm due a little bit of fun and I'm going to have some of it here."

"Oh, a hero, eh?" the big man snarled and started rolling up his sleeves. "Well, hero, let's the two of us settle this outside."

"Why?" I asked, acting far more stupid than usual. "You afraid to get your ass whipped in here?" For some reason, the big man took that as an invitation to knock my head off. He would have, too, if Harmon Roberts III hadn't kicked his legs out from under him quick as a cat. Next thing I knew, Roberts had me by the back of my collar and was hustling me out the door while Joe and Don acted as rear guard. Roberts practically threw me onto the bike, giving me a shove to start me back down High Street.

It didn't take long before Joe, Don, Roberts and I were called on the carpet, standing at attention in front of Jolly Tucker's desk. The Old Man had gone down to High Wycombe for some commanders meeting, leaving Tucker in charge of headquarters. Tucker, apparently, had received a call from the town mayor. Baker had driven the good Major into the village and the mayor had crawled him up one side and down the other. A fuming Tucker had returned to base ready to make examples of four lieutenants.

"I'm not surprised to see you in here again, Foster," Tucker ranted, "but in the rest of you--you in particular, Lieutenant Roberts--I am both surprised and disappointed. What could possibly have gone on in your mind to become involved in a disturbance like this?" Already, Tucker's color was rising.

Before I could speak, Roberts intervened. "It was completely my fault, sir. I was frightened and I struck the first blow; the only blow as it turned out."

"Frightened? That stretches credibility, Lieutenant Roberts!" Jolly's voice was rising in volume and in pitch. "There were four of you young, brave American fighting men against one middle-aged Englishman!"

"He was a big guy, sir," Don added.

"At ease!" Tucker snapped. "I ought to have all four of you thrown in the Hoosegow!" He paused for a moment and I got the impression that the guardhouse really wasn't a very likely landing strip for Harmon Roberts III, war hero. Since Roberts had already confessed to being the only one of us to actually strike a blow, the guardhouse didn't seem likely for any of us. "Lucky for you the gentleman wasn't badly injured and chose not to prefer charges or you'd all be up before a general court-martial. I needn't tell you how important it is for us to maintain good relations with our hosts."

"Maybe you need to remind our hosts. . .sir." For some reason, I like to see how far I can push Jolly and still come out unscathed.

"I've had quite enough trouble out of you, mister! First the Marsh incident and now this." From the corner of my eye, I could see Joe was struggling to maintain a straight face. I guessed Don was, too, because Tucker shifted his stare away from me. He was shaking his head, his lips pursed, hands on his hips. "You men had better come out of your spin and be quick about it. If I see any of you in here again on similar business, I'll recommend the Old Man throw the book at you! Now take off!"

We were safely outside and breathing a little easier when Roberts said, "Joe, I thought for sure you or Don was going to confess in there." And the laughter started again.

We visited Willie in the hospital. He was going to be okay, but it was going to take a while for him to regain his strength. He'd be reassigned with another crew to finish his tour of duty once he fully recovered. That meant a new waist gunner for the Roberts crew, an eighteen-year-old kid from Princeton, New Jersey named Samuel Gold. By the time he was assigned to our crew, Gold had already flown five missions filling in for guys on sick call or what have you.

"Pleased to meet you, sirs," Gold saluted Roberts and me. Baker from headquarters had brought him over to meet us since we expected to be flying together any day now. We saluted back and then shook hands.

"So, you've already been on a couple of missions, Sam?" Roberts asked.

"Sammy, sir. I was up on the Wilhelmshaven and Bremen missions and also on a couple of milk runs over France. I don't remember the names of them places; I couldn't pronounce 'em anyways."

"Well, Sammy," Roberts continued, "our right waist gunner caught a fragment in his leg and we need a straight shooter to take over his spot. Think you can handle it?"

Sammy smiled. "You bet I can, Lieutenant. I've got 20/15 eyesight and I scored 'expert' in aerial gunnery school. The chief instructor said I was the best gunnery student he'd ever seen. On our ground-to-air final exercise, I severed the target from its tow plane," Sammy chuckled. "I can't wait to get back up in the air and smoke one of those Nazi bastards!"

It was rare to see such enthusiasm from someone who'd actually flown a combat mission. I attributed it to a lack of imagination.

"I suspect we'll be back in the air any day now, so you won't have long to wait!" Roberts stuck out his hand, smiling. "Welcome to the team, Sammy!"

Independence Day fell on a Sunday, another of those days ending in "Y" and another of those days on which the 91st was alerted for a mission. We took off into mostly clear skies shortly before 1000 hours, formed up over southeastern England and headed south over the Channel. Our target was an aero-engine factory complex at Le Mans, France, about a hundred miles south of the Normandy coast. Five groups participated in the raid, led by the 91st with Colonel Reid, the mission commander, flying in the copilot seat of Ed Morgan's B-17, *Red Robin*.

We had an escort of RAF Spitfires over the Channel, but they soon had to turn back due to their limited fuel capacity. "What we need," Don suggested from the nose of the aircraft, "is a fighter with long range."

"That's a brilliant idea, Don. When we get back, let's compose a memo to General Arnold. I'm sure he'd be enlightened by your keen observation," I said. Roberts grinned, but slashed his hand across his throat, telling us to knock it off. We were now approaching enemy territory and our attention rightly needed to be focused on our mission, not on playful banter.

Flak was sporadic and inaccurate as we crossed the coast. Once a few miles inland, we were flying over mostly farm country. Below I could see a checkerboard of neat fields bordered by roads and trees. It was a pleasant day to fly--at least so far.

In the clear weather and with a target easily identifiable due to its proximity to the Sarthe River, Don laid our five thousand pounds of bombs right down the factory's smokestacks. It was one of the most accurate bombing runs I'd ever seen.

Twenty to thirty enemy fighters came our way, but made only one pass. One of the other groups got a lot more of their attention and lost a few airplanes, but the 91st emerged unscathed. We were back on the ground at Bassingbourn before 1500, a relatively easy mission. I thought the boys would be pretty happy to chalk up one more mission, but one of them seemed a little steamed.

"Those bastards must've heard Sammy Gold was riding shot gun!" Sammy ranted as we unloaded *Harm's Way*. "Did you see those cowards, El-Tee? They didn't even come in range! I woulda knocked 'em right out of the sky. 'Knights of the Sky' my ass! More like 'Cowards of the Clouds' if you ask me!"

"Don't fret, Sammy, my eager, young friend," I consoled, slapping him on the shoulder. "There are still plenty of *Luftwaffe* pilots left for you to shoot at."

It must have been show season at Bassingbourn. First, we'd enjoyed the big war bond rally with the late Candy Cain. Now, another star was scheduled to entertain the 91st Bomb Group. The show was scheduled for Saturday and was to be transcribed for later broadcast over the National Broadcasting Company network back in the States. Roberts insisted that Joe, Don and I accompany him. I'd been pretty rough on Roberts, but something was telling me that it was time to cut him a little slack. I mean, he was doing what he was ordered to do, just like me. The rest of the boys had all embraced him as their leader. I could remain a jerk and probably no one would blame me. Okay, I wouldn't blame me. But, he had recommended me for the Silver Star and he had kept me from getting a broken face at The Red Lion and he had taken the blame with Tucker. I agreed to go.

We were alerted for what sounded like a tough mission on Saturday. Our target was the rail yard at Hannover, Germany, deep into the Reich. We took off about 0830 and immediately had trouble. The visibility was poor, even at high altitude and a couple of squadrons were late forming up with the rest of the wing. Several aircraft aborted rather than try to catch up. We were flying extremely high, twenty-seven thousand feet, due to the weather and winds aloft. It didn't help. Enemy flak and fighter opposition were weak, but it didn't matter; we couldn't find the target because of the cloud cover. We couldn't even find targets of opportunity, so Don toggled our bomb load over the Rhine River. Who knows if we hit anything—other than fish. We were back to the base by 1300 hours, giving us plenty of time for debriefing and cleaning up before the big show. Just another day at the office.

A large stage had been constructed across the mouth of the main hangar. A twenty-piece band sat on its left tuning instruments and arranging music stands. A black curtain hung down separating what we could see out front from whatever was going on backstage. In front of the stage, ten rows of folding wooden chairs had been set up for the brass and VIPs. I could see Colonel Reid talking to a general officer I didn't recognize. I didn't know if he was from wing headquarters, VIII Bomber Command or 8th Air Force.

Tucker was also up front, brown-nosing with a couple of Colonels. I couldn't tell what he was up to, I just knew to give him a wide berth. Tucker hadn't tapped me for escort duty for this show, a fact that hadn't escaped my keen powers of observation. I hoped my relationship with Tucker wouldn't be permanently scarred by Joe and Don's little prank. Actually, I didn't care.

There were probably a couple of thousand guys gathering on the macadam waiting for the show to start. The day's mission had gone pretty well for the 91st, so spirits were high and everyone was looking forward to a break from the monotony of life at Bassingbourn--monotony interrupted by occasional moments of stark terror.

Most of the men were smart enough to bring blankets to sit on. Joe and Don spread one out, careful to pick a spot with a good line of sight to the stage. As they settled down, Roberts caught me by the elbow.

"Come on," he said quietly. Then, turning to Don and Joe, he said more loudly, "Hey, fellas, we'll be back in a few. Save us a spot."

Still holding my elbow, Roberts led me to the edge of the gathering crowd and around to the side of the stage. "Where're we going?" I asked.

"You'll see."

As we rounded the corner, we could see a lot of activity and a lot of clutter. There were cases for costumes, musical instruments, sound gear and lights scattered among cables snaking across the concrete floor. People were milling about wearing headsets and holding clipboards and, of course, there was an MP; a rather large MP.

"Sorry sir," he said holding up his hand, "this is a restricted area." This guy looked like he'd just stepped off the pages of *The Sporting News*. He was about six foot, two inches tall, broad shouldered and had Hollywood good looks.

Roberts pulled a folded letter from his shirt pocket as he looked the big man in the eye. "I'm Harmon Roberts III. I was asked to come back stage." He handed over the letter and the big MP looked it over. "Sir, if you don't mind waiting just a second." The MP carried the letter over to a middle-aged, balding man holding a clipboard. We couldn't hear what was going on, but could see the MP pointing back toward us and the other guy staring at us--well, at Roberts. The two men came over together.

"Hi, Lieutenant Roberts, I'm Marty Malone, the field producer," he said extending his hand.

Roberts smiled, shook hands and introduced me to Mr. Malone. "This is my copilot, Bob Foster." Then it was my turn to smile and shake hands.

"Come this way, fellows." Malone nodded to the MP and led us around the crates, cases and small knots of people. He led us through another curtain and clearly here we were in with the entertainers. Malone wove through folding chairs haphazardly scattered around lighted make-up tables and traveling clothes lockers. He headed toward a man who was standing with his back to us, one foot propped up on a chair, and concentrating on the sheets of paper he was holding in his hand.

He cleared his throat, causing the man to turn. "Bob," Malone said, "Here's Harmon Roberts."

"Harm! Hey, great to see you, kid," said Bob Hope, throwing an arm around Harmon's neck. Harmon reciprocated with an arm across Hope's back and turned him toward me.

"Good to see you, Bob! I'd like you to meet the best copilot in the ETO, First Lieutenant Bob Foster," Harmon said nodding toward me.

Bob Hope stuck out his hand and smiled his famous smile. "Great first name!" he winked. "I'm very proud to meet you!" Hope was wearing a white shirt with a navy blue tie and light gray, wool slacks. "How have you been?" he asked Harmon. "Your dad asked me to look you up when I got over here."

"So far, so good, thanks to Bob here. He single-handedly saved us two missions ago." Harmon related the *Reader's Digest* condensed version of our mission to Huls, giving me more credit than I was due, but hey, he's the pilot, right?

"Well, I want to shake your hand again, Bob!" Hope said. "Wow, two authentic heroes!" he was smiling broadly, almost as though he was more excited to meet us than we were to meet him!

Malone cleared his throat and tapped his watch. "Five minutes, Bob."

"We'll let you go!" Harmon said. "Thanks for coming all the way over here to do this. It means a lot to the boys. Tell Father that everything's good here. And tell him you met Bob. He's keeping me out of trouble."

"Will do, kid. You boys enjoy the show." Handshakes all around and Malone ushered us back out.

As we made our way back toward Joe and Don, I had to ask, "How do you know Bob Hope?"

"He's a family friend. He's been a supporter of Father's. We've had dinner together a couple of times."

"I'm impressed. Bob Hope as a family friend? I guess your father's pretty influential, huh?"

"He was. Before Pearl Harbor. Father was an isolationist. He didn't want to see us get mixed up in another European war. He came over here in 1918 and never forgot the misery he experienced. He always said the Great War was an avoidable tragedy and he wanted to make sure it didn't happen again. Unfortunately, his method of avoidance was to pretend the troubles over here didn't affect us."

"How's he feel about you being over here?"

"He wasn't too happy when I wrangled this assignment." A shadow passed over Roberts's face. "We had some bitter words over it. We got into an argument and I ended up pushing him out of my way and leaving the house. I felt bad about it afterward, but Father was trying to make decisions for my own safety, not for my own good."

"Why?" I asked.

"Why does any father try to protect his son?" A slight smile curled up the corner of Roberts's lip. "I shamelessly dropped his name to get sent over here. Sometimes having a famous name can work to your advantage." I remembered Tucker's instructions to me about Roberts and thought, Not always. "After I got to England I went down to one of those photo studios in London and had my picture taken in my uniform, wings, 8th Air Force patch and all. I sent it to him along with a letter explaining why I had to be here, not stateside. "

"Could you have just waited this mess out in some training post somewhere in Podunk, USA?"

"Probably. But some day, it's going to be very important how men of our age answer the question, 'What did you do in the war?' My answer is going to be that I did my duty just like everybody else." He glanced over at me. "And that I served with some awfully swell guys."

I laughed. "You sound like you're running for something."

"Maybe," he replied with a smile that belied his seriousness. "Maybe someday."

"How did your father respond to the letter?" We'd made it back to Joe and Don by then.

"He didn't."

"Where'd you go?" Don asked as we settled down on the blanket.

"I was just saying hello to an old family friend," Harmon replied.

A man walked out on stage and a bright spotlight bathed him in white. He stopped behind the big NBC microphone and said, "Good evening to the officers and men of the 91st Bomb Group and special guests. I'm Bill Goodwin and it's my distinct pleasure to welcome you to tonight's entertainment extravaganza!" This was met with cheers and applause. "Tonight we're here under special arrangement by General Hap Arnold, commander of the

Army Air Corps, and General Ira Eaker, commanding officer of the 8th Air Force. Our great group of entertainers includes Jerry Colonna--" applause, "and Frances Langford--" enthusiastic applause, " but first, here's the star of our show, the multi-talented star of stage, screen and radio, our comedian-in-chief, Mr. Bob Hope!"

The band struck up a tune and Hope, now wearing a double-breasted jacket, strode out on stage. He was smiling and nodding and holding the same pages we'd seen him with backstage. The applause finally died down and Hope took his mark behind the mic. "Hey it's Bob-great-to-be-with-the-91st-Bomb-Group-Hope! Boy, it's great to be here at Bassingbourn—the country club of the 8th Air Force!"

"That'll never get past the censors," Harmon muttered to me from the corner of his mouth.

Hope unloaded the punch line: "What a great place to hide from your draft board!" This brought cheers, whistles and applause. "And what a friendly bunch of guys! Colonel Reid took me up for a courtesy flight in one of your big B-17s. What an airplane! I wasn't frightened, but at two thousand feet one of my goose pimples bailed out!"

I'd seen Hope in a couple of movies and I'd heard his show on the radio, but seeing him live was a whole lot more interesting. He was much funnier now that I'd actually met him.

"And how'd you like this English weather?" We all groaned. "I tell you, all this fog makes it really hard to conduct war games; you can hardly see the numbers on the dice!" The boys liked that one.

"Say I know you fellows had a big bond rally here at the base a month or so back. Yeah, you probably didn't know it but I've been helping sell bonds too. I've been offering to kiss every movie star who bought a five-hundred-dollar war bond. So far, I've only sold one and Boris Karloff wants his money back."

Hope went on for fifteen minutes by which time we were all tired from laughing. He was a nice break from the routine, which consisted of boredom, orders, briefings, missions, terror, fatigue and back to boredom. Taking time to just laugh, for somebody to entertain us, just us, that added a little dose of humanity back into our world, if only for an evening. The next act was even better; singer Frances Langford was the best-looking woman to hit Bassingbourn since Candy Cain.

The blond-haired Langford was short, beautiful and built like a dream! She was stunning in a blue, low cut gown that sparkled under the attention of the spotlight. "I'd like to sing a little song for you fellows," she started out in a sexy voice. "It's called 'I'm In the Mood for Love.'"

From behind us someone bellowed out, "You've come to the right place, baby!" I thought I recognized the voice of Sammy Gold.

It was five minutes before the cheers and laughter died down and Langford could sing.

We flew again a week later. Our target was an aluminum factory in Norway, making this the first raid ever carried out by American bombers on that country. It was also, at more than three thousand miles, our longest round trip of the war so far. It was a butt-numbing mission for the pilots, I can tell you that. Hour after hour we hugged in tight with the rest of the aircraft in our formation. Flying in tight formation, even for a few minutes, is tiring. It takes intense concentration, good coordination and a mastery of the flight controls and characteristics of the aircraft. Harmon was really good at formation flying, but even he needed frequent relief from wrestling with the controls of our big bomber.

Don put our bombs right in the pickle barrel and our strike photos showed that the group's bombing was very effective. I don't think our German friends will be getting aluminum from Norway any time soon.

This flight was also unusual in that we spent little time over enemy territory; our flight path to and from the target was almost entirely over water, most of it the North Sea. The North Sea isn't exactly hospitable, but it's a far sight better than flying over enemy-occupied Europe! Flak at the target was light and inaccurate. Face it: the Norwegians just aren't used to getting bombed. No enemy aircraft came up to challenge us. This all seemed pretty swell to most of us, but not to Sammy.

"I tell you, sir," he began once we were back on terra firma, "those Kraut bastards are afraid to tangle with Sammy Gold! They must have heard I was on the guns and decided to stay in bed!"

"I don't think they expected us so far north," Harmon replied with a smile. "Don't worry. You'll get a shot at 'em soon enough." This mission was the beginning of "Blitz Week," a week that would see the 8th Air Force fly six missions in seven days.

The next mission for the Roberts crew was scheduled for July 28. We were awakened, fed, briefed and equipped. We took off on time for another deep penetration into Germany, this time to bomb an aircraft engine factory near Kassel. It seemed that every two weeks or so the pencil-pushers at 8th Air Force Headquarters cooked up another "deepest ever" mission somewhere. "Deepest penetration yet into Germany" became a running joke among the aircrews. "Where you headed?" we'd ask each other. "I'm making the deepest penetration yet into the mess hall," would come the sarcastic reply. Things started getting a little out of hand when some of the boys began to apply the phrase to their female acquaintances.

Anyway, our newest, "deepest penetration yet" to Kassel turned into a real bust. Our entire formation was recalled due to multiple layers of cloud cover stretching across the continent. No flak, no fighters, no bombing, but we did get credit for the mission since we'd crossed the enemy coastline. That was the last easy mission we'd fly, and the last one Sammy could gripe about.

That last week of July, the group flew on six out of seven days. We were all physically and mentally exhausted. The strain of flying was one thing; the strain of flying while being shot at was even more severe. On the 30th, we were alerted for yet another mission, another raid to finish our uncompleted business at Kassel. The factory there made Messerschmitt 109s, one of the two main fighter aircraft of the *Luftwaffe*. We were briefed that we could effectively destroy five hundred Messerschmitts by destroying the target. Killing them on the ground was a whole lot easier than knocking them out of the sky!

We took off very early, even by our standards, at 0640. Flak on the way to the target ranged from light to moderate, wild to fairly accurate. Once over the target that all changed. Heavy, accurate flak peppered our formation. *Harm's Way* was riddled by shell fragments, but so far nobody'd been wounded. We dropped our bombs and clobbered the factory, which was easy to find due to the good visibility and the adjacent four thousand-foot runway. Then things got interesting.

All around us, bombers were taking hits from the flak. *Red Robin's* number three engine was smoking, but Morgan kept her in formation. Miraculously, despite all the holes in our aircraft, no vital systems and none of the engines had been damaged.

We were pointed back in the right direction, toward England, when Sandy called out, "Top turret to crew. Little friends twelve o'clock high!" I strained my eyes to find the friendly fighter escort we'd been briefed to expect. Sure enough, some twenty miles away and closing fast, I could see the tiny black specks in the sky. I smiled and glanced over at Harmon. Little friends meant that our ride home would be relatively uneventful; enemy fighters had a hard time attacking our bombers when they had to defend themselves against our P-47s!

As they got closer, we could make out the big black-painted noses of the P-47 escort. They were a little early for our rendezvous, but a welcome sight nonetheless. "Pilot to crew," Harmon was on the interphone, "those guys are way too early. Keep a close eye on them." I smiled. I liked it when the pilot was on his toes, but Harmon was being overly cautious. I held to that thought until Sammy Gold jumped on the interphone.

"Those are Krauts, El-Tee!" he shouted. "Those are FWs, not 'Jugs'." Jugs was our nickname for the heavy-nosed P-47s.

"All right, Sammy and all the rest of you guys!" Harmon replied. "Friend or foe, I want every gun tracking those airplanes until we know for sure. Sandy, you've got the best view. Keep 'em in sight and provide position reports."

"Yes sir! They're circling around the formation just like our escort normally would."

"I'm telling you, those guys are German!" Sammy repeated.

Sammy was right. As soon as they had taken positions above and behind the formation, the "little friends" began diving through our bomber stream in flights of two and three, guns blazing. Chatter filled our headphones as our gunners reported from where the next threat was coming.

Sammy was the most vociferous. "Come on in here, you little bastard!" Our guns were hammering away, vibrating the entire aircraft and filling it with spent shell casings. Tracers decorated the air as a thousand guns from a hundred B-17s chased the enemy fighters. "I got something for you to eat!"

"Two coming in four o'clock level!" Sandy shouted. I looked back over my shoulder to see flashes from the wings of two fighters closing incredibly fast, then felt *Harm's Way* shudder as their rounds hit their target. I watched helplessly, mesmerized by the yellow flashes and the streaking tracers. There was no way for me to fight back; I just had to take it. Before I turned back to the instrument panel, I saw debris flying off one of the attackers, and then a much larger, brighter flash as his engine burst into flame.

"Scratch one Hun!" Sammy shouted gleefully.

"Good shooting, Sammy!" Sandy echoed.

I don't know if the other German fighters felt challenged by Sammy's victory or if they simply hadn't noticed in all the chaos, but they continued to press their attacks against the formation and against us. By now, *Red Robin* was gone and two other aircraft were smoking. I'll say this for the *Luftwaffe* fighter pilots: they may have been fighting for the wrong side, but they were skillful and daring. They squeezed their fighters through the tiniest gaps in our formation, twisting, turning and guns blazing all the while. Their tactics made it hard for our gunners to get a good shot at them. Except for Sammy. After thirty minutes or so, when the enemy fighters finally broke off the attack, Sammy had shot down one more FW and damaged a third! He'd lived up to his self-promotion and at the best possible time, in the best possible way.

Blitz Week may have looked like a success to the generals and staff at High Wycombe, but to the aircrews it felt like something else entirely. By the end of July, we were exhausted both physically and mentally. My arms were sore from hauling on the heavy controls of our bomber. My brain was frazzled by the seemingly constant flash of flak explosions and the deceptively alluring flashes of the wing guns on German fighters. My ears were numb from the drone of our engines and the staccato hammering of our machine guns. I was weary, always tense from anticipation of the next mission alert, the next spin of the wheel of fortune. The rest of the boys were tired, too. We all dealt with it differently. Some sought escape in the villages surrounding Bassingbourn where, despite our experience at The Red Lion, most of the natives were friendly and appreciative. Others gambled; there was always a dice game or a hand of poker going on somewhere on base. Some drank. Some read books; our little library had been stocked by generous donations from folks back home, the tiny library in nearby Royston and shipments from the YMCA.

The 91st Bomb Group had lost five aircraft during Blitz Week. We didn't know it at the time, but that week's six missions had whittled the 8th Air Force's bomber strength from three-hundred-thirty aircraft all the way down to two hundred. That was a lot of lost airplanes—and even more lost men.

Following Blitz Week, we got a break. I don't know if it was because the weather turned lousy again or if the brass figured out that we couldn't maintain the pace without punching ourselves out. Maybe it was a little of both. For almost two weeks, we flew only training missions over England, helping incorporate newly-arriving crews and aircraft into the ways of combat flying. For nearly two weeks we didn't cross the Channel. We did, however, plan a raid on London.

On Friday afternoon, Harmon, Joe, Don and I hitched a ride on a jeep for the short trip to Royston's train station. From there, we boarded the four o'clock train into London. A little over an hour later, we pulled into King's Cross, the biggest train station I'd ever seen, in the biggest city I'd ever visited. We hefted our overnight bags and asked directions to the Regent Palace Hotel. We hopped on the Underground and rode for twenty minutes or so, exiting at Piccadilly Circus.

Coming up from underground, we were greeted by bright sunshine and the roar and honk of motor vehicles.

Most of the traffic was military trucks, but the occasional fire truck, black taxi and red double-decker bus also rolled past on its way to some important destination.

"Come on," Harmon said, stepping off to our right. "This way." We hiked a couple of blocks and entered the ornate entrance hall of the hotel. The lobby was teeming with people of all sorts. In a glance, I took in a dozen different colored military uniforms from God-only-knows how many different countries. Harmon led us up to the registration desk and spoke to a clerk wearing a formal morning coat. When he turned around, he was holding two large keys in his hands.

"If I didn't know better," I said, "I'd think you'd done this before."

"A time or two," Harmon laughed and handed one of the keys to Joe. "All right, faithful navigator, see if you can find these rooms." We took the lift up to the fourth floor and found our rooms, which were on opposite ends of a long hallway. Harmon and I took one room and Joe and Don the other. "We'll meet downstairs at 1800. That's six o'clock, Don," he teased.

He closed the door behind us and we each threw our bag on one of the twin beds in the center of the small room. "Have you really been here before?" I asked.

"London? Sure, a couple of times with Father. We stayed over at Claridge's though, not here."

"Sounds pretty swanky."

"It is. Was, anyway. I hear the brass have just about taken over every nice place in the city."

"What brought you to London?"

"Father was on a fact-finding trip. He was trying to gauge how serious the Brits were about standing up to *Herr*

Hitler. This was back in the spring of '39. I think even then he realized how dangerous this whole mess was becoming. I think that's why he wanted to keep us out of it. Any way, we were here for about three weeks. I actually got to meet Chamberlain and Halifax."

"What about Churchill?"

"No. We saw him in Commons one day, but I didn't meet him. I don't think Father did either."

"So, who are we dining with this evening? George and Mary?"

Harmon laughed again. Off the base and out of the airplane, he was as relaxed as I'd ever seen him. "I don't know, but I'm sure we can find something fun going on."

We met up with Joe and Don in the lobby at six pm. We were standing in a loose huddle, my back to the entrance, discussing which London hot spot would be favored with our presence when I noticed Don's eyes go wide. I felt a hand clamp down on my right shoulder.

"Well, well, well, if it isn't the notorious Bob Foster," said a familiar voice, turning me around. My mouth must have fallen open because Christy McKnight threw his head back and laughed. "Not surprised to see me, are you?!"

I laughed and shook his hand, slapping him on the shoulder. I couldn't stop grinning. Neither could Joe and Don. Harmon stood just to the side, all of a sudden seeming a little out of place in this unexpected reunion of old crew mates. Finally, Don noticed the awkwardness.

"Christy, you remember Harmon Roberts."

"How could I forget! The man who got me my own crew! Nice to see you again, Lieutenant Roberts," he smiled.

"Good to see you," Harmon replied politely.

"Wait, wait, wait," I interrupted. "You can't just waltz in here and pretend nothing happened! Where have you been and how'd you get here?"

"If you'll buy me a drink and some dinner, I'll tell you the whole story."

The five of us stepped out into the evening sunshine and walked west, toward Brook Street and the famous bar at Claridge's. Harmon assured us it was worth a visit. Central London had been hit hard by the Germans, not as hard as we were now hitting Hamburg and other German cities, but hard nonetheless. I could still see a lot of damaged buildings and even some empty lots where buildings had once stood. Even though the Blitz had ended two years earlier, there were still sandbags surrounding many doorways and still a few windows covered with wood. There weren't many vehicles on the streets, but there were plenty of people walking along the sidewalks enjoying the summer evening.

We wedged our way into a round booth in the corner of Claridge's Bar and ordered drinks from a waiter who looked old enough to be Churchill's father. Drinks were more expensive here than at The Red Lion, but the accommodations were somewhat nicer and there weren't any big farmers lurking about to dampen our enthusiasm at being out on the town.

"So, how'd you end up here?" I asked after the waiter had delivered our drinks.

Christy took a sip of his drink and stared down at the glass. "Luck. A lot of it. We lost two engines and that was pretty much that. We couldn't maintain formation and we couldn't maintain speed. Once we fell out of formation, the fighters were on us like flies on garbage. Our interphones were shot all to hell so I hit the bail-out bell and held the plane steady until everybody got out. I trimmed it for straight and level, climbed out of the seat and hooked on my chute." He looked back up. "You know those damn Germans kept shooting at me. Here they see all these guys jumping out and their chutes popping open and they're still shooting at me!" He shook his head. "The right wing's on fire by now so I go out the bomb bay. Anyway, my chute opens and I'm hanging there watching this lovely countryside floating up toward me. Then I hear an airplane, a fighter diving on me. Except he's off to my right and he's not diving on me, he's diving on Steve or Tom or one of the other boys in my crew. They were too far away for me to tell who it was. And this German bastard opens up on him. Bang. He circles away and goes to the next chute. I saw him do that three times. Killed three of my men who had escaped a burning airplane and were hanging harmless and helpless under their parachutes. He must have run out of gas, because he flew away to the south after that. So, I was just lucky, that's all."

"Jesus!" Don muttered. We all stared down at our drinks, afraid to make eye contact. All except Harmon.

"There was nothing you could have done, Christy. No way you could have changed the outcome. You did everything right. You held the plane steady, you were the last one out. You couldn't have done anything more." Christy didn't answer; he just shook his head.

"You going back to Bassingbourn?" Joe asked after a moment.

"I doubt it. Regulations won't allow me to fly over occupied territory. Having successfully evaded capture with the help of some brave Belgians, the brass won't take a chance on me getting shot down a second time and captured. They're afraid that if I was shot down again and captured, I might give away the escape route or the people who helped me." He took a swig. "That's a very wise policy which I fully support."

I lifted my glass. "To brave Belgians."

"To my brave crew," Christy added. We all drank.

To change the mood, Joe asked, "So, tour guide, what's our dinner plan?"

"There's an officers' mess set up a couple of blocks from here on Grosvenor Square," Harmon replied.

"We can do better than that," Christy interjected. "I got ferried over on a little fishing boat, two days on the Channel, stuffed down in a smelly, slimy hold, seasick half the time. But when I reached the dock, the first guy in uniform I ran into happened to be a classmate of mine from law school. He was at the dock supervising shipments. He works for the Services of Supply headquarters. Believe me, those guys aren't eating at an officers' mess. They've got their own deal going."

"Can you get us in?" I asked.

"Like you had an engraved invitation," he smiled.

The party, for it had no resemblance to any officers' mess I'd ever seen, was raging by the time we got there. Christy had talked our way into the noisy, crowded, smoke-filled apartment with little effort and no trouble. Once inside, I was amazed at the spread of foods on the long buffet and the scores of bottles on the shelves above the portable bar. There were American officers, British officers, Canadian officers, Polish, Dutch and even a couple of French officers. And there was a woman on every arm.

After we heaped cuts of roast beef, turkey and ham on our plates and added cheeses and bread, we maneuvered to the bar. All I wanted was a beer, but Christy and Harmon ordered Scotch. I saw Christy wave and catch the eye of a young Captain, who threaded his way through the crowd.

"Boys," Christy grinned broadly, "meet Richie Spencer!" We all shook hands. "Richie's one of the worst students to ever gain admission to law school, but a pretty damn good procurement officer!" Christy laughed, hoisting his Scotch.

"Pleased to meet you fellas," Spencer replied. "It's nice to rub shoulders with the boys who are doing the real fighting. I wish I could get into some real action!"

"Don't be so sure," Christy replied, his smile tightening.

"After all," Harmon interjected, "we couldn't do what we do without you doing what you do."

"So, what is it exactly that you do?" Spencer asked our group. We explained we were a bomber crew from the 91st Group, that we'd been together since coming over from the States and that when Christy had been promoted, Harmon had joined us. I glossed over the part about Roberts usurping my status as pilot, my airplane and my crew, but I figured that was a little more than Spencer needed to know.

"Listen, eat and drink as much as you want. Just look at this as a 'thank you' from General Lee and the fine folks at Services of Supply. But," he paused, "do watch out for the Colonels. They tend to get a little uptight when they see unfamiliar faces in here. If anybody challenges you, just tell them you're my guest. And be careful of the women. Some of them are 'Piccadilly Commandoes.'"

"What's that?" Joe asked.

"Those are the ones they warned us about in the contagious diseases briefing," Don answered knowingly.

After we'd all gone back for seconds, or maybe it was thirds, Christy and I ended up sitting by ourselves at a two-seat table in the corner of the flat. He was on his second, or maybe it was his third, Scotch. "I'm sorry about what happened to your crew," I mumbled.

"Thanks. I still see it every night when I close my eyes. I appreciated what Harmon said. He really seems like an okay sort."

"I guess he is; just not as good as the guy he replaced." I laughed. I didn't want to get all sentimental, but over the months we'd been together, Christy, Joe and Don had become like brothers to me.

"Yeah, well, I'm glad I wasn't with you guys when I got shot down. You wouldn't be here tonight."

I needed to turn the conversation in a more positive direction, so I asked, "How did you escape? You said you came over on a boat."

"That's right. When I hit the ground, it knocked the wind out of me. By the time I recovered, I looked up and there was this farmer standing there jabbering at me and trying to lift me to my feet. I couldn't understand what he was saying, but it was probably something like 'get the hell out of here.' He hustled me to the edge of the field and pointed toward some woods. I took off running and once I got into the trees a little ways I burrowed under some thick bushes. I smeared some dirt on my face and hands and tried to conceal myself as best I could. About ten minutes later, I heard people coming. It's either a rescue party or the Germans, I figured. Well, it turned out to be the Germans, looking for me and the rest of my crew--the ones they didn't slaughter anyway. I tried to make myself small and invisible. This one guy came so close I could smell him." Christy took a sip of his drink and then continued. "Then he unbuttoned his fly and peed right on me! But he didn't see me. I stayed there until it got dark. I'm wiggled out from under these bushes, filthy dirty and smelling like a garbage dump, and I heard voices and people moving in the woods again. This time it's the farmer and a couple of other guys. I went 'psst' and they froze, like I scared the hell out of them. Then I did it again and they came over to where I was. Of course they all started talking at once and I couldn't understand any of it. I took Spanish in college. Nobody in Belgium seems to speak that for some silly reason. So one of them handed me some old clothes and motioned for me to put them on, which I did. They took my flight gear and off we went. We walked for maybe half an hour and by then it was really dark. We came to this farm and there was a little shed out back and in I went. Turned out to be a smokehouse, which was good because nobody could smell me in there. They gave me a jug of water and a loaf of bread and I stayed there for a whole day. The next night, I moved again, this time with different guides. About all I can tell is that they moved me toward the west, which is good, because that was away from Germany! I moved every day or two, to a barn, a house, a village, a city, and finally to the coast. I hid in a tiny attic overlooking a little harbor for four very long days. I could see German soldiers walking the streets in the day time. Finally, on the fifth night, this guy came and got me. He smelled like fish and diesel. I shook hands with my hosts and sneaked out the back door. The guy walked me straight to the pier and right onto this little fishing boat. It was maybe thirty feet long. He opened a hatch on the deck, pointed at me and then pointed down the hatch. I leaned over and the smell almost knocked me down, but I figured the longer I stayed on deck, the more dangerous for everybody, so down I went. I stayed down there puking my guts out for two nights and two days until we reached Ramsgate. That's where I ran into Richie. He vouched for me and turned me over to the Home Guard and the next day I'm on a train to London."

"What happened to the fisherman?"

"I don't know, but I hope he got paid a king's ransom and that he shares it with all those people who helped me. After seeing the conditions in Belgium, I have no doubt God's on our side."

"Did you before?"

"Not really," he smiled. "I need a refill," he held up his glass. I watched him as he walked to the bar. I always admired Christy for his intelligence and the way he was always able to size up a situation. He never flew off the handle, never acted rashly like his old pilot sometimes did. He had deserved his shot as pilot of his crew. Well, now that shot was over. He'd done the best he could, the best anybody could, and he'd live with the outcome for the rest of his life.

"Is this seat taken?"

I looked up to see a lovely young lady with big brown eyes smiling at me. "No, please join me," I said standing and completely forgetting about Christy McKnight. I held the chair for her and then took my seat across from her.

"I don't think I've seen you around here before," she said. "My name's Bea."

"Like the queen bee?" I asked, smiling.

"No," she laughed, "like Beatrice." She had a lovely, lilting laugh and a pleasant smile. Of course most any woman's smile would seem pleasant after living for two years with only men. "Tell me, what is it that you do to help win the war?"

"I brave enemy anti-aircraft fire and the *Luftwaffe* to fly my big bomber over Germany and drop bombs. How about you?"

"Oh, I'm in charge of morale. So you fly a bomber? What type?"

"A Flying Fortress, the B-17. The best bomber in the skies."

"Is it really better than the B-24? They say the Liberator can fly faster, farther and carry more load."

"Are you kidding?" I laughed. "The Banana Boat is the best escort we have. Why when we fly missions with B-24s, the Germans always go for them. They're not as maneuverable and they can't take punishment like a B-17." Here I was, talking to a pretty girl and we were discussing the relative merits of heavy bombers! "What do you like to do for fun, Bea?"

"Oh, I like parties and meeting handsome pilots and talking about how we're finally winning the war for a change." I was about to suggest we continue our conversation someplace more private when Harmon walked over.

"Sorry to interrupt, but we need to leave!" Bea and I looked up, puzzled. "Really!" Harmon reached down and tugged on my arm.

I resisted. I was pretty happy right where I was. I thought things with Bea and me were heading in a promising direction. "Bea, this is Harmon. Harmon, this is Bea. Why don't you go get us drinks from the bar, Harmon?" I tipped my head toward the bar, hoping Harmon would interpret my gesture as "Get the hell out of here and leave me alone with this brown-eyed beauty." Alas, he did not.

He leaned in close to me and just loud enough to ensure Bea could hear said, "MPs are on the way. They're shutting everything down and getting everybody out before this party gets crashed!"

"Oh my!" Bea exclaimed, standing up and extending her hand. "Well, it's been quite nice to meet you both!" And she was gone. I watched her as she gracefully crossed the room, hips swaying beneath her tight skirt, and exited the flat.

"Still want that drink?" Harmon smiled, sliding into the seat just vacated by Bea.

"What are you doing? Don't we have to scram?"

"You see anybody else leaving?" I looked around the room. I could detect no change in the buzz of the crowd, could detect no urgent or excited response to the threat of a raid by the Provost Marshall.

"What the hell was that all about?" I asked, anger seeping into my voice. "I was having a really nice visit with Bea. I think that might have gotten me somewhere!"

"It would have gotten you 'somewhere', I guarantee it. Probably on sick call." I didn't quite get what Harmon was telling me and he read that in my expression. "Come on, Bob; she's a prostitute!"

"She is not. She just knows a handsome, virile man when she sees one," I protested. "Any way, how would you know?"

"Because when I was in the men's room earlier, she was in there servicing a client." I couldn't tell if he was being smug or was simply amused. Either way, the tips of my ears were burning. "I probably saved you from a nasty case of clap. You should thank me." He was smiling now.

"Thanks," I grunted and just shook my head. I wondered how Christy would have handled it.

Saturday morning was slow and leisurely. We ordered breakfast in bed and were treated to good, hot coffee, toast and orange marmalade. Along with the food was a copy of the morning paper.

The *Times* ran a series of aerial photos taken over Hamburg and credited the RAF for the devastation depicted in the pictures. No mention of the gallant boys of the 8th Air Force which, unlike the RAF, flew in broad daylight and bombed point, not area, targets. I'll bet a lot of the damage in those pictures had been wrought by American flyers, not by the British alone. The Russians were celebrating some big victory over the Germans at a place called Orel. I was never much for geography and didn't know where that was, but hey, any win for the Russians was a win for us, right?

The *Times* was an interesting paper. Classified ads and announcements ran on page one; news was found inside, on pages two, three and four. There were few advertisements, but one that caught my eye was from a tobacconist's shop in Scotland. For eight pounds, you could send a tin of cigarettes to any member of the British forces, anywhere in the world, including, the ad claimed, to POWs, provided they weren't being held by the Japanese. Eight pounds was a lot of money, equal to about 32. As that was ten percent of my monthly pay, I was glad I didn't know anybody serving in the British forces!

We spent the afternoon at an honest-to-goodness baseball game. Wembley Stadium hosted a game between members of the Canadian forces and American forces. Baseball may have seemed out of place in London, but we felt right at home, sitting in the warm sunshine, drinking beer and watching the Americans prevail 6-3.

After that, we elected to take in a picture. There were several to choose from: *Five Graves to Cairo, Crash Dive* and *Road to Zanzibar* were the ones that caught our attention. Two were war pictures. War pictures are made by civilians, for civilians. They really don't know any better I guess. Well, maybe Londoners do. Any way, we decided we were on break from the war and that included our entertainment so Bob Hope, Bing Crosby and Dorothy Lamour got our vote. Now that Bob Hope was a friend of mine, I felt an obligation to support his work.

After the show, we found a dance hall, paid our two shillings and danced until late, then stumbled happily back to the Regent Palace and our freshly-made beds. Breakfast the next morning was a repeat of Saturday, with the exception of the paper, which wasn't available on Sunday.

We wandered around Westminster, Buckingham Palace and Parliament, seeing the sights, and then caught a late lunch at the Grosvenor Square mess.

"What's next for you, Christy?" Harmon asked the question that had lingered on my mind all weekend.

"I've got another couple of days here going over things with the G2 staff, and then I'm up to High Wycombe. They're going to make a pencil-pusher out of me. I'll probably lend my keen analytical ability to calculating the precise bomb loads, aiming points and altitudes for your next fifty missions!"

"Count me out!" Don laughed. "I'm not sticking around that long!"

Christy saw us off at King's Cross and we were back in Bassingbourn before dark. We'd had a good break in London. It was the last prolonged period of rest we got.

Our London adventure had been a nice break, but we all knew it would be short-lived. Favorable flying weather had returned to the continent and we were alerted for and flew missions on August 15th and 16th. Both times we were attacking *Luftwaffe* airfields in France and both times we enjoyed relatively easy missions. We had friendly fighter protection to and from the targets, so our main worry was flak. Our twentieth mission was to Le Bourget, the famous Paris airfield where Lindbergh had finished his cross-Atlantic flight in 1927. It seemed a shame to bomb a historic place like that, but a greater shame to let the *Luftwaffe* use it as a base from which to attack us! We lost one aircraft on these missions, so the butcher's bill wasn't too bad. That was about to change.

We were alerted again on the 17th, our third mission in as many days. Nobody had cleared it with the bomber crews, but clearly we were well into a whole new Blitz Week. We were awakened early and fed. Lots of coffee and cigarettes were consumed as the boys tried to clear their sleepy brains. We crammed into the briefing theater, Harmon, Don, Joe and I sitting together on the second row. The closer we sat, the better we could see and hear; the better we could see and hear, the better our chances of getting back in one piece.

From the back of the room came the command, "Atten-hut!" and we all sprang to our feet. Colonel Reid, followed by his staff, strode down the center aisle and hopped up onto the low stage. "At ease, take your seats. Today, we're going to be part of an anniversary celebration--"

"Oh yippee," Don muttered quietly.

"Today marks the anniversary of the 8th Air Force's first bombing mission over occupied Europe. One year ago, we sent eighteen B-17s to bomb a railroad yard in France." The Old Man paused for a moment, scanning the faces of the aircrews before him. "Today, gentlemen, we're going to launch a few more than eighteen ships against the enemy. Today, the 91st will lead more than two hundred bombers against a key strategic target deep inside Germany. In fact, we're celebrating this anniversary with --"

"--our deepest penetration to date," Don whispered.

"--our deepest penetration yet into Germany," the Colonel echoed. He nodded to the operations officer, Captain Ballard, and then stepped to the side of the stage and took a seat.

Ballard, pointer in hand, pulled back the black curtain that had been shielding the map board and said, "Today's target is Schweinfurt!" Schweinfurt was indeed a long way away; a long way through enemy territory, a long way past our fighter escorts' range. A low groan swept the room. A couple of the fellows whistled. "Our target is the KugelFischer ball-bearing works. This complex manufactures the bulk of Germany's ball-bearings, without which they cannot successfully prosecute this war." I glanced at Harmon. He was focused on the briefing; already scratching notes on his pad. "While the 91st is leading our wing to Schweinfurt, another wing will be bombing a different target in southern Germany. This two-pronged attack will confuse the enemy air defenses and split their fighters so that neither wing will face the full force of enemy fighters."

"Haven't we heard that story before?" Don whispered without taking his eyes off the map.

Ballard continued. "This complex of buildings here," he tapped his pointer on an aerial reconnaissance photograph that was being projected on a screen next to the map, "is our target. We expect good visibility over Germany today and the target should be easy to pinpoint due to its proximity to the river, here," he tapped the photo again, "and the railroad bridge here. Each aircraft will carry five thousand pounds of high explosive bombs."

The weather guesser was next, and then squadron and formation assignments were covered. Ballard issued instructions on radio communications and call signs and then the Colonel was back on his feet. "Knocking out the Germans' ball-bearing capacity will render a mortal blow. Remember, it's easier to prevent them from producing new fighters than it is to shoot them out of the sky, like Sergeant Gold over there." The Old Man pointed toward Sammy who swelled up so I thought he was going to bust. The Old Man was good at stuff like that. The Colonel pulled back his sleeve and I could hear rustling throughout the room as we all followed suit. "On my mark, the time is 0625. . . mark!" We set our watches to his. "Take off is 0715. Good luck to you all and God bless you. Let's get to our airplanes and make this a day the Huns never forget!" It would indeed be a day to remember, but not for the reasons Colonel Reid intended.

Our scheduled takeoff time came and went, a heavy mist settled over the airfield, preventing departure. We were all a little on edge, facing an historic mission on an historic day and watching the clock tick. Part of the strategy for committing such a large force against such a deep target had been the idea that the two large formations would confuse and split the enemy defenders. If we were still sitting at Bassingbourn waiting for the weather to clear, what was happening to the other wing? Had they departed on time?

"Hey, El-Tee!" Sammy called out. Most of the Roberts crew was sitting under the broad wings of *Harm's Way* enjoying some shelter from the dampness. I'd been leaning against one of the large main tires of the landing gear hangar flying with Harmon. I walked over to where Sammy was sprawled over his flight gear.

"What's up, Sammy?"

"El-Tee, I hear we got fighter escort all the way on this mission."

"How's that?" I asked, knowing that our P-47s would only be able to cover us part-ways into France.

"We got P-47s to Paris and Messerschmitts the rest of the way!" The boys laughed and I joined them. Nothing like a little gallows humor to lighten the mood. Now all we needed was something to lighten the weather.

We didn't get off the ground until well after 0900; only then did the sun finally exert itself sufficiently to chase away the mist. We were already hours behind schedule. Over the Channel, the group in its combat formation, Harmon gave the boys the go ahead to check their guns. Vibrations rattled *Harm's Way* as ten machine guns spit out test bursts. Visibility, which had so delayed us in England, was excellent as we approached the enemy coast. The sky was a deep, clear blue with only a thin band of haze at the horizon.

P-47 fighters were flying above us, providing top cover and scouting ahead for the enemy fighters we knew were lying in wait. The Germans' radar would have seen our massive formation of bombers assembling over England. They would know we were coming.

"Copilot to crew," I called, as the P-47s began a slow bank to the left. "Our little friends are leaving us. Look sharp. Let us know if you see anything." I should have said "when." It didn't take long.

"Bandits eleven o'clock; still pretty far away," Sandy reported from the top turret. We were heading east, into the sun, and I couldn't make out the bad guys yet.

"Keep an eye on 'em, Sandy. Let's see where they're headed," I said.

"Two o'clock low, looks like they're taking off from their base and forming up to the south," Artie shouted from his perch in the ball turret. This group of fighters I could see. They were climbing like a swarm of angry hornets. We now had two formations of enemy fighters in front of us--and they were heading our way.

The 91st was leading the bomber stream on this mission. We were out front, the point of the spear. *Harm's Way* was the lead aircraft of the low squadron, not the worst place to be, but close. Usually, the Germans liked to pick off the Fortresses in the low squadron and work their way up. The rationale for this tactic was that the low squadron had no supporting friendly fire from below or behind.

The fighters continued to grow larger through the windscreen. We were closing at around four hundred miles per hour, that's nearly seven miles per minute, so we were only a few minutes away from battle!

"They're staying high," Sandy reported. "That bunch to the south is still climbing."

"Messerschmitt 109s in that group on the right," Sammy chimed in. They were getting to the point now where his eagle eyes could make out the aircraft type. Tactics were pretty much the same, whether our attackers were Messerschmitts or Focke-Wulfs, but the FWs had heavier armaments with their twenty mm nose cannon. That's what had severed our control cables on the mission to Huls back in June. We watched with growing anxiety as the distance between our formations and the fighters dwindled away, forgetting about everything else but the on-rushing threat to our lives.

"Here they come, here they come! They're peeling off in bunches!"

Both groups of fighters had now merged into one enormous swarm of malice. In an instant, two-, three-, four- and five-plane groups were knifing through our formation, guns spewing lethal pellets of lead at our engines and cockpits. Our gunners began to hammer back as the fighters twisted and rolled through our formation. In a flash, the attack was over--for the moment.

"They're curling away at seven o'clock!" Rick called from his tail gunner's seat. "Looks like they're going to hit the next group behind us." That was welcome news for us. We didn't wish ill fortune on any of our guys, but we also didn't mind if the Germans picked on someone else.

"Any damage? Anybody hurt?" I called out. One by one, starting with the bombardier in the nose of the airplane, the crew reported in; everybody was okay. Except for a few new ventilation holes, *Harm's Way* was all right too; no vital systems had been hit.

I glanced over at Harmon and gave him a thumbs up. He responded with a tight grin, his forehead shiny with sweat. We were halfway to the target.

Anti-aircraft fire had been spotty and inaccurate, but as we neared the City of Schweinfurt nestled along the banks of the Main River, the flak increased in intensity. From his bombardier's panel down in the nose, Don took control of *Harm's Way* at the initial point and began our bomb run. Anti-aircraft explosions rocked us violently and sent vicious chunks of hot shrapnel slicing through the thin skin of our craft. Bright red flak bursts erupted on all sides, rattling us like a jalopy riding over a corrugated road. The bursts faded to yellow and left behind menacing black clouds. It was a very rough ride. Harmon struggled to keep the airplane in tight formation as we were pitched and jostled by the seemingly endless flak bursts.

"Target straight ahead! Thirty seconds!" Don shouted. Our formation plowed through the angry clouds, through the concussion waves, absorbing shrapnel, pitching and bucking on a ride through the gates of Hell itself.

Then we heard the sweet words, "Bombs away!" and felt *Harm's Way* leap into the air as five thousand pounds of high explosives began a relentless plunge toward the sinister ball bearing works below. Within seconds, the group began its climbing turn to the northeast and, suddenly, we left the flak behind.

Harmon shouted over to me. "Check the crew!"

I repeated my earlier check of each position. Miraculously, everyone was all right. We'd picked up dozens of new holes and the boys had been rattled around, but again, no vital systems had been damaged.

"All right, gang!" Harmon shouted, "watch for enemy fighters! All eyes on the skies!" We leveled off at twenty-two thousand feet, the afternoon sun again in our faces. The cold air made for much smoother flying than the turbulent, flak-filled skies over the target. We were headed back toward England. It was 1500 hours. Our ordeal was about to begin.

So far, the 91st had gotten off easy as enemy fighters had made one aggressive, but relatively harmless pass. Now, our crew began calling out fighters approaching from all directions.

"Fighters two o'clock!" We were deep inside Germany, flying through the *Luftwaffe*'s home skies.

"Four o'clock and closing, looks like ten to twelve!"

"Fifteen fighters at ten o'clock!"

The reports were so numerous that the interphones were a constant jumble of excited words, shouts and expletives. "Four abreast, nine o'clock level," grunted Al on the left waist gun. I was flying the airplane, giving Harmon a badly-needed break. I couldn't see the attackers, but I felt the rounds from their guns smack into our ship. Our gunners were firing back, shifting from one target to the next as each subsequent wave swept toward us.

"One o'clock, one o'clock!" shouted Sandy and I felt the familiar shudder and heard the ear-splitting reports as his twin .50 caliber machine guns erupted just above my head. I could hear the firing from Don and Joe below the flight deck, each swinging his single gun in its limited arc as they chased after our attackers. I heard a loud "pop" and felt rushing wind over my shoulder. I glanced back to see Sandy slumped on the floor, his left arm a tangled, bloody mess.

"Take over!" I shouted to Harmon. I climbed out of my seat and stumbled back to Sandy.

"Six in a line coming right at our nose!" Don shouted. I froze for a moment and stared through the windscreen at the onrushing carriers of destruction. Their wings were winking at me. Rounds punctured the windscreen and slammed their way into our instrument panel. Wind from the slipstream now raced through the cockpit, lowering the temperature even further and adding to the cacophony of battle noises. I grabbed the first aid kit from behind my seat and dug out a bandage. I unrolled it and turned to lash it around Sandy's wound. I couldn't. His left arm was shattered, the upper bone exposed. It remained attached to his body only by muscle tissue. Even in the frigid air, he was bleeding like a slaughtered animal. A tourniquet seemed the best hope for saving Sandy, but there was so little arm left above his wound that I couldn't tie it off. I used two bandages and lashed his arm to his torso as best I could. I found a morphine syrette, peeled away Sandy's ripped flight overalls, eased the needle into his shoulder and squeezed the medicine into him.

"*Bathing Beauty* is falling away, number one and two engines smoking!" Joe called out as the Fortress on our left slid out of the formation.

"Watch for chutes!" Harmon directed. Meanwhile, the fighter attacks continued. Gray messengers of death darted and dove through our formation. Chunks were flying off of our bombers and their attackers as each fired relentlessly at the others. "Get on that top turret, Bob!" Harmon shouted as a group of enemy fighters lined up for another head-on pass at us. Our best protection to the front was the top turret. Without it, we'd quickly be overwhelmed. I pulled Sandy's feet out of the way and climbed up into the blood-spattered turret. I reached up and grabbed the gun handles and attempted to turn the turret toward the attacking fighters. Nothing happened! From my perch above the flight deck, I could see tracers smacking into our wings and sparks flying from our two left engines. The fighters zipped past me in a blur. I ducked down and twisted my head to look at the electrical cables that controlled the turret's rotation. The round that knocked Sandy out of action had done the same to his turret; the electrical cables were tattered and shredded.

I climbed over Sandy's supine form and leaned over the back of Harmon's seat. "Top turret's out of action!" I shouted. "And Sandy's going to bleed to death unless he gets treatment fast!"

"Cover his wounds as best you can, then hook his chute on him. His only hope is to get out of this airplane. Maybe somebody on the ground will help him!" Harmon shouted back.

I reached behind Sandy's turret and hauled out his parachute, clipping it onto his harness. As a rule, the boys all kept their harnesses on in flight, even in combat, but usually they set their parachutes out of the way; they were too bulky and hindered movement in the tight spaces of the airplane's interior. Next, I stuck my head down in the nose and shouted for Joe to lend a hand. As gingerly as I could, I maneuvered Sandy's inert form so that his feet hung down where Joe could pull them. Gently I lowered him down into the nose. Don helped lay Sandy down. *Harm's Way* shuddered again as we took more enemy fire. I shouted instructions to Joe and Don. They exchanged quick glances and then nodded back at me. I watched as they opened the nose hatch. Air and noise whipped through the compartment as anything not secured scattered in the hurricane-like wind. They eased Sandy into a sitting position and dangled his feet out of the hatch. Don steadied him by holding him around his waist. Joe grabbed the D-ring on his chute and nodded. Don scooted Sandy out the hatch. Joe pulled his hand back; the D-ring in it no longer attached to Sandy's chute.

I climbed back into my seat feeling extremely tired and gasping for air. My brain was falling behind the action. I realized that I'd neglected to hook up to an oxygen bottle when I left my seat. I quickly plugged back in and began to gulp in the precious oxygen.

While I'd been off the interphones, Don must have told the crew about Sandy, because as soon as I put my headphones back on Artie reported, "His chute opened! I can see him!" We'd done all we could. Now Sandy was in God's hands.

"Three more coming in from the left; four more!"

Harm's Way rocked violently as a new attack raked the ship. "Down, down, down! Al's down!" Sammy shouted.

"Smoke on engine one!" Joe called out. "Here they come, here they come!" Rounds punched through the bulkhead windows above my seat and burrowed into the throttle quadrant between the two pilots' seats. "Number one's on fire!"

Harmon and I reached for the fire extinguisher button. He hit it first. Nothing happened. "Cut the fuel to one!" he ordered. I reached to my left and turned the lever to cut the fuel supply to our outboard engine on the left. "Feather it quick, before we lose oil pressure!" Feathering the propeller turned its blades into the headwind, reducing drag and helping us maintain as much speed as possible on just three engines.

"Three from eleven o'clock level, four from two o'clock level!"

Most of the time, flying in a B-17 is so noisy that sounds from outside our aircraft can't penetrate the racket. Most of the time. A tremendous explosion rocked *Harm's Way*, shoving us sideways. I looked to our right and the Fortress that had been there a moment ago was gone, replaced by a sinister cloud of the blackest smoke. Our comrades had simply disintegrated in a thunderous flash. *Harm's Way* was now the last aircraft left from the low squadron. We were in an ominous position and it was worsening by the moment.

Harmon was fighting a losing battle to maintain speed and close up with the group's lead squadron. With each foot we fell behind, our survival became more precarious. Sandy was gone; Al was down, though we didn't know how badly he was hurt. Our top turret was out of action. We were down to three engines. But the enemy wasn't finished with us. The attack, which seemed to have lasted for hours, continued unabated. *Harm's Way*, now in obvious distress, attracted the German fighters like sharks to blood.

"Cylinder temps are climbing on two!" I reported to Harmon. If we lost a second engine, we were doomed.

Another head-on attack materialized with three FWs wing-tip-to-wing-tip charging straight at us. Flashes from their wing-mounted machine guns and their nose-mounted cannons sent shudders through me. Twenty mm cannon rounds exploded on our Plexiglas nose. I called Joe and Don on the interphone, but got no response. If we lost their guns, we'd have no defensive fire to the front. Chunks of our right wing and aileron flew off under the new assault. "Check on the nose!" Harmon directed.

Again I clambered out of my seat, this time grabbing an oxygen bottle. I climbed down into the nose. Maps, logs and other papers were swirling around in the 150 mile-per-hour hurricane ripping through the holes in the Plexiglas. Joe was sitting dazed against the fuselage, a blue lump on his forehead, his flight suit ripped and torn. Don was in worse condition, a fist-sized hole in his lower left torso, seeping blood. He was unconscious. I dug through the swirling debris and found the first aid kit. I plugged Don's wound and gave him an injection of morphine. I checked his oxygen mask to make sure it was functioning. I turned my attention to Joe, slapping him on his cheeks until his eyes came back into focus. I double checked his oxygen too. "You keep an eye on Don!" I shouted over the roar of the wind. "And keep shooting at those fighters!"

Before I could climb back up to the flight deck, another pair of fighters rolled in on us, guns blazing. Rounds marched across our wings, punching holes in our fuel tanks. The slipstream functioned as a syphon, sucking gas out. "Look!" Harmon pointed out his window, before I could sit back down. Flames were licking the cowling of engine two. "Cut the fuel!" I reached for the fuel lever and twisted it, but the flames were already spreading, fanned by the headwind. Starved of fuel, engine two spun to a halt. We hadn't had time to feather the prop. Now, all our thrust was being provided by the two so- far-undamaged engines on the right wing.

Harm's Way was now doomed. I knew it and I suspect Harmon knew it, although he was fighting valiantly to milk every ounce of power from the remaining engines. He was practically standing on the right rudder pedal in an effort to keep the aircraft flying straight ahead. He reached up his right hand and grabbed me by the shoulder. "Get the crew ready to bail out! Check their chutes and harnesses!" He looked me in the eyes for a fraction of a second. In that moment, I could see that he knew it was over, that we only had a few minutes remaining.

I worked my way past the frozen pool of Sandy's blood and pushed across the narrow catwalk that traversed the bomb bay. By the time I got to the radio compartment, Red was already clipping his chute on. "Lieutenant Roberts said to prepare to bail out!" he shouted at me.

I nodded. I leaned close to his ear. "Get Artie out of the ball, help him with his chute and get ready to jump!" Then I headed toward the waist.

Sammy's was one of the few guns still firing. He was standing ankle-deep in spent brass. I knelt beside Al, but he was already dead, his head torn open like a can of Spam. I glanced out of the left waist window and nearly panicked; flames were streaming from engine two all the way back to the trailing edge of the wing. Sammy's firing diverted my attention. He fired his gun and I looked past him to see another fighter winking back. Those bastards didn't know when to quit. I slapped him on his shoulder. "Put on your chute and get ready to go!" He gave me a thumbs-up and squeezed off a few more rounds at a target I couldn't see. That left Rick, all alone in the tail. I started to wiggle my way back through the narrow tunnel to the tail gunner's position. Then I stopped. The escape hatch was open and Rick was already gone. I pushed myself back out. That's when I heard the bell. B-17s were equipped with an audible alarm in the form of a bell. Its ringing was used to let the crew know to bail out.

Sammy was clipping on his chute and followed me out of the waist and into the radio compartment. Rounds streaked right in front of my face, in on the right side and out the left, not bothering to linger. Artie had his chute on, as did Red. "Get out! God bless you!" I yelled over the racket, slapping them on their shoulders. Smoke was seeping into the plane.

The others followed me into the bomb bay where they jumped through the open doors. I moved back onto the flight deck. It was filling with choking, blinding smoke. Harmon looked like a contortionist, standing on the right rudder pedal and holding the yoke as steady as he could. I leaned over and adjusted the rudder trim fully to the right to relieve some of the pressure. We were now losing altitude rapidly. It was going to be a challenge to get him out of his seat and get out of the airplane before it went out of control. If it went into a spin, the centrifugal force might pin us against the fuselage, preventing our escape. A small fire had broken out on the top of the instrument panel on the copilot's side. I was glad I wasn't in my seat.

"Let's kill the other engines and put her in a controlled glide!" I suggested, leaning in next to Harmon. He nodded. Even though it was probably twenty degrees below zero, he was bathed in sweat, so strenuous were his attempts to maintain control. I pulled the throttles back on engines three and four and all of a sudden, things got eerily quiet. Well, not really quiet, but certainly as quiet as I'd ever heard in a B-17 at altitude. I looked over at Harmon. I nodded. With the plane in a shallow dive, he was no longer fighting unbalanced thrust. Keeping us level had actually gotten easier for the moment.

"Get everybody out! I'll hold her steady!" he shouted. Past him, out the window, I could see the left wing beginning to glow. We were running out of time. Fast!

I clambered down into the nose section again. Joe had clipped on both his and Don's chutes. Don was still unconscious. "Okay," I screamed, with my face just inches from Joe's, "we've got to do the same thing we did with Sandy! I'll move him into the hatch and you hold his D-ring!" Joe nodded. I wasn't sure he was clear-headed, but we didn't have time to linger. Joe grabbed the ring in his hand and I pushed and hauled Don to the hatch. "Ready?" Joe nodded. I pushed. Joe pulled and the D-ring came off in his hand. I pressed against the window to see if Don's chute had opened. To my horror, it had. The chute billowed as soon as it hit the slipstream, even before it cleared the wing. There was a bright flash as the flames from the wing ignited the parachute silk, a wisp of smoke and the chute vanished. Don plunged from sight.

Joe hadn't seen what happened. I turned back to him and faked a smile. I pointed at his chest and said, "Your turn! Make sure you're clear of the plane before you pull your chute!" Joe nodded again and I silently prayed that he understood my instructions. Joe went out feet first. I wanted to stay and watch for his chute to open, but I knew that Harmon and I were already tempting fate.

I scrambled back up to the flight deck and slapped Harmon on the shoulder. "I'll hold the wheel! Put on your chute!" He crawled out of the pilot's seat, so weak from fighting for control of the big bomber that his hands and arms were shaking from fatigue. I was a little concerned that he wouldn't be able to get his chute on, but I guess adrenaline kicked in. *Harm's Way* was sliding into a gentle turn, the precursor of a spin. I didn't know which would kill us first: our exploding wing tank or getting pinned inside an out-of-control aircraft!

"Let's go!" Harmon shouted. A last glance at the wing; it was now red hot. We were down to seconds. *Harm's Way* continued to turn--and to burn.

"Don't pull your chute until you're clear of the plane!" I repeated my instructions as I pushed him toward the open bomb bay. He sat on the edge of the cat walk, pushed with his arms and disappeared. I dropped to my knees and swung my feet out over the void. A bright yellow flash blinded me. Then there was nothing.

I don't know how long I was unconscious, but when I came to, I was falling through the sky, wind whipping at my flight suit. I was cold and confused and it took me a moment to realize what had happened. I began to look around and realized that I was falling at a rather rapid pace and that I should release my parachute. I did, and my hurtle through space was brought to a sudden stop! Now the wind noise fell away to nothing and I searched the skies around me. Smoking debris was falling nearby and I gathered that was all that was left of *Harm's Way*. I scanned the sky around me and saw two more white chutes. One was below me, that was most likely Joe; the other above me. That was probably Harmon. He would have released his chute shortly after leaving the airplane. I had fallen much farther before coming to and releasing mine.

That's when I heard the high-pitched whine of a fighter. He screamed in from my right, his nose pointed right at me. He had me lined up for a quick kill. I started to pull on the risers of my parachute in an attempt to swing myself back and forth. A moving target is harder to hit, right? The Focke-Wulf flashed by and I could see the pilot grinning. He began a tight curve, banking his wings steeply and I knew he was coming around for a second pass. Now that he knew my swinging tactic, I had no idea how to make him miss. I decided I'd turn sideways to him and present the smallest possible target. Although the parachute was supposed to be saving my life, it was like a big arrow, pointing me out to the blood-thirsty fighter pilot while holding me relatively still so he could center me in his sights.

He began his second run; I twisted to offer him the narrowest profile possible. As he flashed by again, he was still laughing and now waving as well. I watched as he circled the other two chutes and then broke off and flew away.

Not until I landed in a pasture did I realize that I was barefoot. Apparently, my boots, socks and shoes had been blown off when the airplane blew up. This was a rude surprise because my feet were no longer calloused and rough as they had been when I ran barefoot through the summers of my childhood. The landing left me with a sprained left ankle and cuts on both feet. I hobbled in the direction where I'd seen Joe's chute come down, grimacing as my feet found rocks and twigs among the grass. Joe was sitting just as he'd landed. I figured the landing had knocked the wind out of him. I figured wrong. I limped over to him and saw that he was dead. I couldn't tell if it was from the wound he'd received in the attack, or from the way he'd landed. Poor Joe; first Don, now him. I didn't have time to bury him. All our briefings on escape and evasion had stressed the need to move out smartly and put as much distance as possible as quickly as possible between ourselves and our landing site.

I could see Harmon coming down another two hundred yards away, so I began the painful trot toward him. In the distance, I heard another engine racing. I looked over my shoulder and saw a gray truck speeding along a narrow dirt track about a mile away. Harmon landed right next to some trees. His chute collapsed onto one of them and hung there, as if to send a message to every German in France: here he is!

By the time I got to him, he was free of his chute and was doubled over puking at the base of the tree. As I leaned down, I saw why. When Harmon and I left the flight deck, the airplane had been in a steepening turn. It must have gone through one hundred eighty degrees, because directly to Harmon's left were the charred remains of a parachute harness and the battered, lifeless body it was supposed to have saved, would have saved if I'd thought of a better plan to get Don out of the airplane.

The truck was now only a quarter of a mile away and would reach us quickly. We were in a pasture. There was no place we could hide, no brush we could crawl beneath, no farmer to come to our aid. There would be no escape for us as there had been for Christy. In a rush of despair, I saw the face of Jolly Tucker and heard his voice echo in my head: *Make sure Roberts isn't taken prisoner*. What a shitty day, I thought, as I unsnapped my holster. Harmon was still leaning over, spitting bile out of his mouth. I slowly pulled my .45 out and stared at the back of Harmon's head.

The thunder of the gunshot surprised me.

Part 2

17 August 1943

"Hände hoch!" shouted the gray-clad soldier as he chambered another round. His first shot had whizzed past my head and gently prompted me to drop my pistol to the ground. He was still some fifty yards away, cautiously moving toward us.

"Harmon," I said, slowly raising my hands above my head, "do exactly what I say, do it now and without questions." He wiped the yellow spit from his mouth and nodded. "Take your ID tags and shove them in the knot of that tree to your right!" He obeyed immediately. "Now, crawl over to Don and slip his tags off and put them around your neck."

"But Bob--"

"Do it quick!"

Harmon inched his way over to Don's body and gently pulled the necklace holding his dog tags from around his neck. He lowered his head, almost as if he was praying, and slipped them around his own neck, sticking them down beneath his shirt. He sat back on his haunches and wiped his sleeve across his eyes.

"Steh auf!" barked the soldier, gesturing with the barrel of his rifle for Harmon to get to his feet. The soldier looked to be about twenty years old and he was now standing about fifteen feet from us. Two of his comrades were coming up behind him. I guess he was the fastest of the three.

"You're now Don Berly!" I said to Harmon without taking my eyes off our captor. "Got it, Don?"

"Nicht reden!" our guard shouted. He seemed to be stuck on two-word phrases. Harmon rose slowly to his feet

and raised his hands up. I noticed he still had both of his shoes.

"Understood," he replied quietly.

"Stille!" commanded our captor.

With a little luck, the Germans would overlook Harmon's hidden ID tags. With a little luck, they would conclude Don's tags had somehow become separated from his body in battle. With a little luck, Don would be reported as a prisoner-of-war and Harmon Roberts III would be listed as missing-in-action. It was a cruel course to take, more so for Don's family than Harmon's, but I had my orders and I had to keep Harmon Roberts from falling into the enemy's hands. It might work; it had to work. With a little luck.

"Wie heisst er?" The soldier barked at us, gesturing toward Don's body. He'd already searched the corpse unsuccessfully for some type of identification. Harmon and I were now standing side-by-side, our hands up. The soldier was sweating, and it occurred to me what a beautiful day this was. The sky was blue, with a few fluffy white clouds drifting lazily overhead. The sun was warm; the grass smelled sweet. Don lay dead just behind me; Joe two hundred yards away. *"Seinen Namen?"*

"I don't speak German," I ventured.

"Ruhig!"

Harmon looked at me from the corner of his eye and then back to the soldier. "He wants to know D-- the dead guy's name."

"We don't speak German," I repeated. Then, for Harmon's sake added, "Neither one of us. Do you speak English?" At that, our captor shrugged his shoulders and shouted something to his comrades. One of them handed his rifle to the other, who slung it across his shoulder. The unarmed soldier walked over and picked up my .45, ejecting the chambered round and stuck the pistol in his belt. He sauntered over to us and put the first two fingers of his right hand to his lips.

"Zigaretten?" The universal language.

I slowly lowered one hand and fished around in my pocket. I found a pack of Luckys and deliberately removed it, holding it so he could see that it was nothing worth getting shot over. I tossed it to him. "Share those with your pals," I instructed. He held the pack up to show his two buddies and quickly stuck a fag in his mouth. Then he turned back toward Harmon and me. He held up his fist, with his thumb on top and pantomimed the spinning of a lighter's flint. I glanced at Harmon. So now the little bastard expected me to light the cigarette for him? I looked back at our captors and just shrugged. I actually had a lighter, but enough is enough.

The soldiers started talking again. They seemed to be arguing but I wasn't sure. If Harmon understood them, he wasn't talking either. For all the time we'd spent together, I realized that I didn't know if he understood German or not. If he did, I was hoping he'd keep that to himself. That could give us a slight advantage and we needed every advantage we could come by.

The first soldier turned his attention from his pal to us, said something and pointed toward Don's body. Harmon and I stood still. He spoke again, a little more intensely. The unarmed soldier stepped toward me and grabbed me by the shoulder. He spun me toward the corpse, and then he bent down and lifted Don by his shoulders. After easing Don back to the ground, he stepped aside and motioned for me to pick up the body. The soldier pointed to Harmon and then to Don's feet. Then, he pointed toward the truck.

We loaded poor Don into the back of the truck, stopping once for Harmon to puke again. I felt sorry for the guy; I don't know how he had anything left to throw up. My ankle was killing me, swollen and pink, but moving Don's body away from its landing place was a good deal for Harmon and me; it got us away from Harmon's ID tags and virtually assured that the Germans wouldn't search for them.

The soldier who'd bummed my cigarettes seemed to be in charge. He drove the truck and left the other two in the back of the bed with us. We drove back to where Joe was slumped over and dismounted. The Germans stood around and smoked while we unclipped Joe's chute and loaded him in beside Don. Then we covered both with the silk from Joe's parachute.

The Germans clearly weren't concerned about us making an escape attempt. They stood near the tailgate smoking and holding on to the sideboards as the truck traversed one dirt track after another. A cloud of dust floated upward behind us. I scooted as close to Harmon as I could and spoke just loudly enough for him to hear me over the sound of the engine.

"We know Joe. He was our navigator. We don't know the other guy. He must be from another airplane, another unit. We don't know him." Harmon nodded his understanding.

"Hier! Verstummen Sie!" one of our guards ordered, motioning us to slide apart on the rough bench seat. The

truck turned right on to a hard-surfaced road. A yellow sign said, "Philippeville 8 km."

Harmon waited until the soldier looked away then asked, "What happened to your shoes?"

The truck rolled in to a small town. The signs on the buildings were in French, but I wasn't sure whether we were in France or Belgium. As we wound our way through the town, the roads became narrower, the buildings older. There weren't many people on the streets and no vehicles save our own. We'd been riding for thirty minutes or so when we pulled to a stop in front of an official-looking building. Out front was a flag pole flying the red, white and black Nazi flag. A heavy, iron-banded wooden door and barred windows marked the building as some type of jail. Our captors jumped down from the truck, crushed out their cigarettes--which were really *my* cigarettes--and motioned for us to hop down. Harmon complied effortlessly and then helped me down. By now, my ankle was swollen three times its normal size and was pounding like the bass drum in a polka band. Harmon helped me up the steps, one soldier leading the way, one holding the door and the other trailing behind us.

My eyes took a few moments to adjust from the bright sunshine outside to the artificially lit interior of the building. We were led to a large, raised wooden desk, behind which sat a portly man in a light blue uniform. I was pretty sure he wasn't German and guessed that he was the sheriff, police chief, constable or whatever they called the law in this part of the world.

The soldier in charge spoke German to the official and the man handed him a ring of over-sized keys and pointed toward another heavy, wooden door off to the side of his desk. Our escort looked at us and pointed toward the door, then stepped off in that direction. I leaned against Harmon to avoid putting any weight on my bad ankle and we followed. Sure enough, on the other side of the door was a long corridor with a barred window facing the street on one end. Along the corridor were several small rooms, each with its own heavy, wooden door and each of these sporting a small square opening guarded by vertical metal bars. Harmon and I were invited, at gunpoint, to make ourselves at home in one of these cells. The soldier swung the door closed behind us and we heard the lock tumble closed and the key removed. The soldier looked through the opening in the door, smiled and said, *"Aufwiedersehen,"* then disappeared back into the office area.

"Well," Harmon said, "here's another fine mess you've gotten me into." He sat down on the iron bunk. "Not quite the accommodations I'm used to. Better get off that ankle."

I sat down on the bunk across from him and gingerly raised my leg up. The throbbing was a little less pronounced, the colors more vivid. I turned my head toward him. "Listen," I spoke quietly, "the Germans can't know they've captured Harmon Roberts III. They'd parade you out as the biggest propaganda coup since Rudolph Hess flew to Scotland. That's why you have to become Don Berly. Memorize his service number. And that's all you give them: name, rank and number. Understand?"

"Got it," he nodded. "How long do you think we'll be here?"

"It depends on where 'here' is and how near we are to a *Luftwaffe* base."

"Why does that matter?"

"Geez, didn't you pay attention in all those escape and evasion briefings? The *Luftwaffe* is in charge of Air Corps prisoners. At some point in the next few hours, a *Luftwaffe* officer is going to open that door and take possession of us."

"Well," Harmon replied, "something to look forward to." It would happen a lot sooner than we expected.

I hadn't realized how tired I was, for despite the pain in my ankle and my anxiety at being imprisoned, I fell into a light sleep. I guess getting up at two o'clock in the morning, flying for hours at twenty thousand feet, fighting for your very life, being thrown from an exploding aircraft, parachuting to the ground, being shot at and taken prisoner tire a man out. Anyway, there I was dozing when a loud racket out in the street startled me awake. Harmon was standing, peering through the bars on our door, trying to get a glimpse out the window at the end of the hallway. We heard the unmistakable sound of a motor vehicle, its gears grinding against themselves in a tooth-rattling vibration. I sat up on my bunk.

"What do you see?"

"Nothing," Harmon answered without leaving his post. A few moments later, we heard the heavy door to the building open and footsteps out in the office area where we'd originally entered.

We could also hear voices, which reminded me, "Do you speak German?"

"A little," Harmon answered, his face still at the door.

"Well, pretend that you don't. At least for now." Harmon looked down at me and nodded. The voices were louder now, as though their owners were arguing. "Can you tell what they're saying?"

"No, but it's about us and they sound a little angry."

I didn't like the sound of that, but my options just at that moment were limited. After another minute or so, the voices lowered. Harmon could no longer hear what was being said and so had no opportunity to translate. The subject, which seemed to be us, and result of the conversation were left to our imaginations. But not for long.

The thick door separating the outer area from our corridor was pushed open by the fat guy in the blue uniform. Behind him strode a young man in a wrinkled, gray flight suit and tall black boots. He was smoking a cigarette, his blue eyes squinting as he inhaled, his blond hair short and matted. The fat guy stopped in front of our door, the keys in his hand, and looked back at the German flyer.

"Ja, ja!" the German pointed at our door. The fat man frowned, but stuck in the key and twisted the lock. He swung the door open and stepped aside.

"Guten Abend, meine Herren," the German smiled. He made for a rather handsome figure. There were tiny crow's feet around his eyes. I could see the marks on his face left by his flight goggles and noted the white scarf tucked inside his suit. Harmon and I didn't look quite so dashing. "My name is Louie Weber. I would be pleased to take you to supper."

Harmon and I looked at each other. Our escape and evasion training hadn't included invitations to dinner.

Harmon cleared his throat and spoke. "I'm afraid we didn't pack our dinner jackets."

The German threw his head back and laughed. "Well, *Herr* Leutnant, we are all then in the same boat, as you Americans say!" He looked us over, starting at my dirty, bare feet and working his way to the top of my head, then spoke swiftly in German to the fat guy. The fat guy started to argue, but Louie held up his hand and said, *"Jetzt!"* The fat man disappeared back through the door.

"*Monsieur* Lambert will find some shoes for you, my friend. Now, as I have already introduced myself, please tell me your names."

"Bob Foster," I said. I was a little surprised when the German stuck out his hand; and a little surprised when I shook it.

"How do you do, *Leutnant* Foster?"

He turned to Harmon. "Har--" Harmon caught himself just in time and covered his mistake by coughing. "Harumph! Excuse me," he continued. "I'm Don Berly."

After shaking Harmon's hand, the German swept his arm back to his left and said, "Please follow me." I was a little nervous about all of this, but Harmon followed him like a puppy. In the back of my mind, I had this image of a squad of soldiers standing in front of the jail, ready to shoot us as we attempted to escape. We passed by the raised desk and *Monsieur* Lambert stood and handed a pair of muddy, wooden clogs to the German. He passed them to me. "Here, try these on."

To my surprise, they fit; not snugly, but with the condition of my ankle, that was a good thing. He led us outside and opened the door to a small, gray military car. It had a canvas top that had been pulled down. Harmon crawled in the back to allow me and my ankle the relative luxury of the front seat. The German, Weber, closed the door and skipped around the back of the car to the driver's seat.

He started the vehicle and shifted into first, resulting in a fierce grinding sound that made the hair on the back of my neck crawl, then we were moving. "I know a good French café nearby," he smiled, turning his head to address both of us. "Is this pleasing to you?"

I shrugged, but Harmon was more social. "As you wish."

We drove to the edge of the town in silence, passing a few pedestrians who gawked at the strange sight of a German chauffeuring two American airmen. Weber parked the car in front of a small restaurant with two tables sitting on the sidewalk. "To avoid undue attention and so that we may enjoy our meal, let us dine inside," he said, leading us through the door. The proprietor greeted us and seated us near the front window. Weber sat where he would have an unobstructed view of both the entrance door and his vehicle in the street. I got the idea that maybe not all the Belgians were friendly and that he couldn't leave his toys unattended.

"And so, gentlemen, here we are," he smiled again. "May I recommend the chicken quiche with a bottle of Riesling?"

I had no idea what quiche was, but felt certain it was better than what *Monsieur* Lambert had planned to serve. Harmon nodded and so I said, "Sure."

Quiche turned out to be some kind of eggy, cheesy pie. It wasn't too bad once you got used to the idea. The older man waiting on us, probably the owner, brought us a bottle of white wine and three glasses. Weber poured the wine and offered a toast. "To peace," he said, raising his glass to eye level and looking past it into my eyes. We tapped glasses and drank.

"So, my friends," he continued after a sip, "where are your homes?"

"Thank you for your hospitality Lieutenant Weber--"

"*Hauptmann,*" he interrupted me. "I am a 'Captain,' *Hauptmann* in German." He said this in a friendly manner and was still smiling.

"*Herr Hauptmann,*" I resumed, "forgive us, but we can only share our names, ranks and service numbers with you, according to the Geneva Convention."

"Of course, of course," he waved my comment away with his hand as if shooing flies. "But that is for formal questioning, not for a friendly dinner. I am making no notes, you see," he gestured toward the table where in fact there were no notepads or pens set out. "I am simply a pilot privileged to be in the company of gallant fellow pilots. I would much rather talk about flying than about war. I have no desire or need to collect information from you. I only wish to be a pleasant host for the evening."

"In that case," Harmon responded, "I'm from Missouri." I was both concerned and relieved: concerned that he seemed willing to talk with Weber but relieved that he had adopted Don's home state as his own.

"Ah, the wild west, yes?" Weber smiled with delight and then turned to me. "And you, *Leutnant* Foster?"

Okay, I decided; a little friendly chit-chat was likely to do us a lot more good than ill. "North Carolina, in the south."

"Do you live on a plantation?"

"No, those are all gone. I lived on a tobacco farm."

"Yes, American cigarettes are the best. These are made from your tobacco?" he asked pulling a pack of Chesterfields from his pocket.

"Probably not," I answered. "Those are made in Virginia." I wondered if I'd just revealed a military secret. "How did you get those?"

"Yours is not the first bomber I've shot down. These were a gift from one of your comrades after a fine meal like this," he smiled, leaving the cigarette pack on the table.

"How many have you shot down?" Harmon asked.

"At least ten," Weber answered, stuffing a bite of quiche into his mouth. "There, you see. I'm telling you about my experiences; I would enjoy hearing about yours. I understand that we are on different sides in this war, but we can be friendly with each other this evening. After all," he smiled, "you are now out of the war."

"Were you the pilot who buzzed us in our parachutes?" I asked.

"Yes! I wanted to see that you were all right and to see where you were going to land. Then I knew where to start looking for you."

"Why?"

"Isn't the answer obvious?" he asked with a puzzled expression. "I wanted to dine with you!"

I wasn't sure what to make of Weber. I couldn't tell if this was really his idea of a good time or if he was trying to butter us up so he could interrogate us without our suspecting what he was up to. I decided to play along. "I was afraid you were coming back to kill us," I said, watching his face for his reaction.

He met my gaze and replied, "I would never do such a wicked thing! We are enemies, yes, but honorable enemies. A man under a parachute--as I myself have been--is no longer a combatant."

"Not all of your comrades feel the same way," I said.

"Be careful not to fall for your government's propaganda. It would characterize all Germans as brutal thugs. This is not the case."

"Do you deny that some of your fellow pilots have murdered parachuting airmen?"

"Do you deny that your bombs fall on homes and schools and hospitals? I have seen this with my own eyes. Have you yourself seen any of your comrades murdered in the way you describe?"

For a moment, I thought about sharing what Christy had described. Fortunately, Harmon rescued me from Weber's awkward question.

"You were shot down?"

"Yes. A Spitfire got the better of me one spring day over Dunkirk. He hit my propeller and knocked it out of balance. Before I could escape, the shaft bent and my engine quit. I jumped before he could come around and finish me off."

"Once you got out, did the English pilot shoot at you again?"

"Of course not! That, as the English say, 'wouldn't be cricket!'" Weber chuckled.

"Where's your base? It must be pretty close."

"Yes, Florennes, only about ten kilometers from here."

"How long have you been there?"

Weber laughed. "Now you are interrogating me! I must protest!" He emptied the wine bottle into our glasses. "I know you are from a B-17 Flying Fortress. I know at least one of your fellow officers, probably two, were killed in the battle today. You are part of the 91st Bombardment Group and you are based at Bassingbourn in Cambridgeshire. Today, you bombed a factory, several shops and a few homes in Schweinfurt. I am sorry for the loss of your crewmen. Can you say the same for those who were killed by your bombs? You tend only to see targets--a factory or a harbor--but you must remember that your bombs drop on innocent civilians who have no part fighting this war."

"The same 'innocent civilians' who support Hitler and his conquest of France, Belgium and Holland?" I was unnerved that he knew as much as he did, but I wasn't going to let him push us around--at least not until after he paid the check.

"Don't forget Luxembourg," Harmon added.

Weber chuckled again. "I apologize, gentlemen. I have allowed politics to intrude on our dinner. Let us talk about more pleasant matters. What do you do back home?" he asked Harmon.

I saw Harmon hesitate, so I intercepted the question. "I worked on my father's farm. A tobacco farm."

"Yes, this you mentioned before. And when did you begin to fly?"

"I started as a teenager. A fellow near Chapel Hill set up a crop-dusting business. I'd walk to his air strip and work for him in exchange for rides which eventually turned into lessons. When the war broke out, I already knew how to fly. I just had to learn how to fly complex airplanes. What about you?"

"I was in the Hitler Youth, in its flying program. We learned to fly gliders. Those of us with aptitude were selected for flight training. I fell in love with flying from the beginning. There's something about soaring in the blue sky and looking down on God's beautiful creation!"

"And shooting down your fellow man." I interjected.

Weber smiled again and wagged his finger at me. "No war talk. Not tonight. Let us enjoy the evening."

We soon figured out that, if we'd let him, Weber would do most of the talking and Harmon and I could enjoy the food and the wine. We listened, commented occasionally and enjoyed being out of the jail. As darkness began to fall on the long summer day, I ventured a question. "*Hauptmann* Weber, what happens to us now?"

"Louie, you must call me Louie since we are now friends."

"Okay, Louie. What happens to us now?"

Louie drained a second bottle into his glass. "I will deliver you back to *Monsieur* Lambert who will keep you safe for tonight. Sometime tomorrow, you will be collected and taken away."

"Where," Harmon asked, "where will we be taken?"

The anxiety in his voice sobered Weber. "To Frankfurt, I suppose. There is an interrogation center there. After that," he shrugged, "to a prisoner-of-war camp. But don't worry. Camps for downed airmen are run by the *Luftwaffe*, not the *SS*. You will be well-treated there."

We couldn't vouch for that, but Weber certainly treated us well. And he picked up the check.

It was dark by the time we pulled up in front of the jail. Fortunately, the moon was just a couple of days past full so Weber could see pretty well even with his headlights hooded. Of course it helped that there was no other traffic on the road.

We climbed out of the car and Weber led us back inside the jail. I had to lean on Harmon for support as I was now unable to put any weight on my left ankle. *"Guten Abend!"* he called out to a visibly relieved Lambert, who stood up behind his desk, a bowl of vegetable soup steaming on its corner. He handed the keys to Weber and watched as we limped along slowly in his wake.

"I regret putting you back in here," Weber said as we reached our open cell. "It would be far better to carry you back to our base and find suitable quarters for you there. Unfortunately, I cannot do this."

"Why not, Louie?" I asked smiling. "I thought we were friends."

He chuckled again. He seemed to be a happy guy for someone who would fight until he was shot down once too often or until the war ended, whichever came first. "Friends, yes! But still also enemies, no?" He shook hands with both of us and then pushed the door closed and locked it. He peered at us through the bars. "I take my leave. Adieu and good luck!"

"Louie!" Harmon called out. He reached in his pocket and pulled out a pack of Luckys. "Thanks for dinner," he said as he passed the cigarettes through the bars. "Good luck to you as well."

Weber pocketed the pack, smiled and disappeared back down the corridor.

A pail of water, a tin cup and two thin rags had been placed inside our cell during our absence. On each bunk, a wool blanket had been folded. The only light in the cell was what filtered in from outside, which at this time of night, even with a full moon, wasn't much.

I sat on my metal bunk and kicked off my clogs. "Let me look at your ankle," Harmon said, kneeling in front of me. He studied my ankle for a minute, then reached behind him and picked up on of the rags. "This is going to be yours," he said, holding the rag up for me to see. "Don't mess with mine." He was kidding. A little. Harmon grabbed the tin cup and dipped it in the water, then poured the cup's contents over the rag. He wrung it out on the floor. I didn't think the maid would notice. Very gently, he began to wipe my ankle, then my foot. "You've got a couple of nice scratches to go along with your sprain," he said without looking up. I twitched at the pressure on my ankle and he noticed. "Still pretty sensitive?"

"And how!"

"Well, if I was a doctor, I'd tell you to ice it down to reduce the swelling, take a couple of aspirin and keep it elevated."

"But you're not a doctor."

"Nope; but you should still elevate it." Harmon moved to my good foot and rinsed it off. "A couple of scrapes here too. My goodness, you must have had a busy day. Tomorrow, I'm going to ask for a doctor to look you over."

He wet the rag again and handed it to me so I could wipe the day's sweat and grime off my face. He did the same with his rag. It had been the longest, most traumatic day of my life. I was emotionally and physically spent. I stretched out on the bed and covered myself with the blanket. I thought about Don, about Joe and about Al. I wondered about Sandy, if he'd made it down alive and if someone had gotten him the medical care he needed in time to save his life. I pictured the rest of the boys and hoped they'd landed without injury and that they hadn't been caught. Maybe they'd gotten lucky and been found by friendly Belgians who would help them hitch a ride on a fishing boat like Christy had done.

It was cool in the cell and sleep finally granted me a reprieve from my worries.

I woke up to find Harmon standing again at the door, peering out into the corridor. It was light in our cell and I realized the sun was up. I checked my watch; it was eight o'clock.

"Good morning," I mumbled, clearing my throat and pushing myself up. My ankle was a wicked purple, still swollen and sore.

"Ah, Rip van Foster!" Harmon turned and smiled. "You sure can sleep through a lot!"

"What did I miss?"

"Not sure. Something's going on though. I heard a truck pull up a little while ago. At least it sounded like a truck." He pointed toward the door separating our wing of the building from the entrance area. "I can hear a discussion going on out there."

After a few minutes of ineffective eavesdropping, the corridor door swung open with a loud creak and three uniformed Germans marched through, *Monsieur* Lambert leading the way. He stopped in front of our cell, the only one that seemed to be occupied, and unlocked our door.

Lambert stepped aside and a German Captain filled the door way. *"Aus!"* he commanded, motioning for us to vacate the cell. *"Kommen Sie!"* He turned on his heel and marched back into the outer office area. Two German soldiers with their rifles at port arms shepherded us behind him. The Captain stepped up behind Lambert's big desk and stood looking down at Harmon and me. *"Leeren Sie Ihre Taschen!"*

I had no idea what he wanted, but Harmon began to turn out his pockets so I did the same. I'd already given up a pack of smokes, but I still had my fountain pen, a couple of pencils, a pocket knife, a small note pad and my lighter. The Captain glared down at me. *"Die Armbanduhr."* He tapped the surface of the desk. The blank look on my face annoyed this impatient man and he pointed to my wrist watch and again tapped the desk. I unfastened my watch and laid it beside my other belongings. Satisfied that our pockets were empty, the German officer barked a new command at the two soldiers. The next thing I knew, Harmon was being pushed forward. One of the guards pulled his arms up and placed Harmon's hands on the edge of the desk. Using his legs, he prodded Harmon's legs apart and pulled them backwards. Harmon was now off balance, holding himself up by hanging on to the edge of the desk. With his comrade still holding a rifle on our backs, the soldier frisked Harmon. Finding nothing, he turned his attention to me. As quickly as I could, I assumed the same position from which he'd searched Harmon. The last thing I needed was to get kicked on my bad ankle. Satisfied that we weren't hiding contraband, the officer barked new orders at his men. One opened the door to the street, the other took position behind us.

"Herr Hauptmann," Harmon addressed the officer, *"Mein Kamerad braucht medizinische Hilfe."*

The German hesitated. While he was distracted, I reached up and snatched my watch off the counter. He seemed surprised that Harmon spoke German. *"Vielleicht am Ziel,"* he replied, then cocked his head toward the door. I stuffed my watch into my pocket and hobbled along behind Harmon, down the steps and to the back of a waiting truck. Harmon climbed up into the canvas-covered bed, and then he and one of the guards helped me up. My ankle was certainly not healed, was still swollen, colorful and painful, but at least I could walk without leaning on someone. We sat side-by-side on a narrow wooden bench along the outboard side of the truck's bed. The two soldiers climbed in behind us and closed the canvas curtains blocking our view of the outside.

I waited until the engine started to lean over and ask Harmon, "What did you say?"

"I told him you needed medical attention, for your ankle."

"I wish you hadn't tipped them that you understood German."

"Yeah, me too, for all the good it did. He said maybe when we get where we're going."

I couldn't chance a look at my watch and with no ability to see outside, it was impossible to tell how long our trip lasted. I guessed it was about an hour before the truck stopped and the curtains were thrown back. When my eyes adjusted to the brightness of the summer morning, I could see we were in a railroad yard. The truck had stopped close to an open freight car. Our guards dismounted and then helped us down. I was careful to land on my good foot. They pointed toward a freight car with its door open. With Harmon's help, I limped across some side tracks and hoisted myself up into its wooden deck. It was dark inside, but I could sense movement and figured that other prisoners were already lurking in the shadows.

Our guards slid closed the heavy wooden door of our freight car. Before too long, we started moving, slowly at first, then gathering speed. Our eyes were now adjusted to the darkness of the car. The only light within was that seeping between the wooden slats making up the walls. Every now and then, a train would pass us going in the opposite direction and we'd feel the buffeting of the air being pushed along in front of it.

Inside the car were about a dozen prisoners, all airmen and all American. There were even two from Bassingbourn and even though I didn't know either of them well, it was still good to see a familiar face. We shared our battle stories and asked for news of common acquaintances. I had coached Harmon to keep up his identity charade even with friendlies; you never knew when someone might slip up and say the wrong thing.

Our train stopped several times during the day and often new passengers boarded our car. A couple of the newer guys were Brits, probably some of the night bomber crews, because by now I guessed we were too far away from the coast for fighters to have reached.

We were allowed out of the car during an early evening stop at a large rail yard on the outskirts of

Luxembourg City. Although we couldn't see beans while traveling inside the freight car, the European stations were always well-marked with signs letting us know about where we were. We were definitely moving east, toward Germany. The sun was already below the trees, but still reflecting off the top of the yard's switching house. I counted twenty-five prisoners in our group.

We reached Frankfurt well after dark. The city was blacked out, but the moon was still bright and we had no trouble moving from our original car to another, smaller train nearby. We were now guarded by about ten armed soldiers, but I didn't see their Captain. Our prisoner group had grown with some more pick-ups at stops along the way and we now numbered about forty. This time our transportation was a passenger coach with windows. We sat on comfortable benches, pleased to be off the bug-infested, straw-covered floor of our previous conveyance.

As best I could tell, we headed north, away from Frankfurt's massive marshalling yards. We rocked along at a slower speed here, maybe because we were moving through the city, maybe because of the narrower gauge of the tracks. We rode for about forty-five minutes or so, most of us dozing off. There was no light to be seen inside or outside the car except for the moonlight.

The train finally stopped and the German Captain who had picked up Harmon and me that morning strode into our car. *"Aussteigen!"* he barked. Harmon and a couple of other prisoners stood up.

"He wants us to get off," Harmon explained. We all stood and trundled down the aisle, to the end of the car and down its steps. Harmon helped me down the last step onto the platform at a small station with a sign reading

"Oberursel." The guards kept us tightly bunched, the Captain shouting directions and issuing orders. One of the guards counted us and reported to the Captain, who seemed satisfied.

"How many were there?" I whispered to Harmon.

"Zwei und Viersig," he answered. "Forty-two."

"Rechts! Rechts!" the guards now shouted at us. Harmon turned to his right, so I did the same. Most of the other guys followed suit. Those that didn't turn received help with their directions from the guards who were all really friendly and seemed to be enjoying their twenty-hour work day and fringe benefits. Not really.

"Vormarsch!" the Captain ordered and we all started walking. The Captain trotted to the front of our ragged formation so he could lead the way.

One of the good things about our train ride was that I hadn't had to walk all day. I'd spent most of the day sitting or lying down, which had provided some relief for my ankle. Now, however, I was putting the most stress on it since we'd been shot down. I was marching in a formation, trying to keep up and not knowing where we were going or how far away it was.

I wasn't the only guy beat up and pretty soon, about five of us were dragging along at the back of the formation. This attracted the attention of the guards, who prodded us along.

"Wie weit?" Harmon whispered to one of the guards as I leaned heavily on his shoulder.

"Zwei kilometer."

"Only two thousand yards or so, Bob. You can make that can't you?" Harmon said quietly.

"Piece of cake," I grunted. By now, my ankle was hurting again, hurting as badly as ever. I was working hard to keep up, sweating heavily and dreading the pain of every step. And Harmon was doing half my work for me.

"One step at a time, Bob. One after another."

Needles of pain stabbed into my ankle every time my foot landed on the road. Now my foot was aching as well. My wooden clogs were made for the soft ground of the field or garden, not for marching down the center of the street in the middle of the night.

Our silent parade finally, mercifully halted in front of the gate of a tall, barbed-wire fence. Over the top of the gate was a sign. "What's that say?" I asked Harmon, careful to keep my voice low.

"It's some kind of *Luftwaffe* camp. I'm not sure how it translates, but literally it's a 'through way camp.'"

We marched, or limped in my case, inside the gate, which swung closed behind us. We continued a ways into the camp and then were halted outside a one-story, wooden structure. A bare flag pole stood out front. Two steps led up to a wide porch. Our guards turned us to face the building and the Captain disappeared inside.

I was ready to get off my feet and grab a little shut eye. Not that it mattered to the Germans.

The best thing I can say about the next couple of hours is that it was August and therefore still fairly comfortable outside even in the wee hours of the morning. We'd have lots of cold mornings to compare this one to over the next two years. A couple of guys sat down, but were immediately prodded back to their feet by the guards.

We stood in our loose formation half-asleep until the dawn broke.

"Achtung!" shouted an officer emerging from the building. Just behind him was an older but trim-looking man in a light blue *Luftwaffe* uniform with gold patches on his lapels. He stopped at the top of the steps and looked over us as if we were cattle at an auction. The younger officer stood just behind and to his left.

By this time, we hadn't shaved or showered in more than two days. We were pretty fragrant and also pretty grungy looking, a fact the German *Kommandant* made clear when he finally spoke. "You are prisoners of the German Reich," he said in thickly-accented English. "You will wash, you will shave and you will look and behave as soldiers. You will obey orders and cooperate."

I was a little underwhelmed. I thought after standing in the dark for half the night we deserved something a bit more eloquent and uplifting. Still, I was not disappointed to finally be herded into a large wash room. The room had six circular sinks, each about six feet in diameter and each with four spigots spraying water out from a center pipe. We all crowded around and washed as best we could in the cold water.

"Shave!" one of the guards yelled.

"We haven't got any razors, you bloody arse!" one of our British comrades politely responded.

"Da!" the guard shouted, pointing at the top of the pipe. There, balanced on the pipe, was a solitary safety razor. *"Alles!"*

"Who's Alice?" I mumbled to Harmon.

"He means all of us," Harmon replied, reaching up and taking the razor in his hand. We were all nicked and bleeding by the time we exited the wash room, but I was grateful that Harmon had passed me the razor when he was done; the small bar of soap was exhausted long before the last of us was shaved.

"Remember, Weber said this was an interrogation center," I said quietly as Harmon and I waited outside for the others to emerge. "Don't tell them anything they don't already know. And make sure you stay in character."

"Got it. I'll be fine. How's your ankle holding up?"

"It feels like a tree stump, except that it hurts too much to be wooden."

We were re-formed and counted. The Germans really seemed to like to count things: forty-two prisoners, Third Reich. . . We were marched through another gated, barbed-wire fence to an inner compound where we halted in front of a long, low wooden building. Here we were separated and each man was placed into a tiny room. The rooms were just wide enough for a wooden bed and a small table holding a pitcher of water. A thick, wooden door defined one end of the narrow room with a barred window opposite.

The guard nudged me in and closed the door behind me. I heard the latch thrown into place on the outside. There was no light in the room save what shone through the window. No light, no chair, no food, nothing to read, nothing to do. I didn't like the idea of solitary confinement. Man is a social animal. We need contact with each other. This is especially true when our stories have to match up. I was concerned that I had no way to coach Harmon on what his story should be. I considered complaining to management, but since I'd been up for most of two days, I laid down on the bed, painful ankle and all, and fell asleep in a wink.

The "thunk" of the door lock woke me. I was disoriented for a moment, but my razor-sharp mind quickly recalled my predicament. I swung my legs over the side of the bed and sat up as a young soldier entered.

"Kommen Sie mit mir," he said, motioning for me to stand up. I stood as he pivoted back toward the door and motioned for me to follow. He led me back outside and through the inner compound to the gate. My dog tags were checked against a clipboard by the gate keeper and we were passed through. My escort guided me to a white, wooden building set in some fir trees behind the headquarters building. We walked up the steps and entered the building, then continued down a center corridor. The architecture here was all of a piece: low, wooden structures, center hallways and rooms off to each side.

We stopped in front of a door on the right marked with the number "four" and my escort knocked.

"Come!" a voice answered in English. The guard tipped his head toward the door and I opened it. "Come in, come in," said a *Luftwaffe* Lieutenant with a smile. *"Danke,* Hans," he said to the guard, crossing behind me and closing the door. He turned and grabbed a wooden chair and placed it squarely in front of the desk. "Sit, please, sit!" He seemed to be quite happy to see me. I hobbled over to the chair and settled into it. "You're hurt?" A look of concern erased his smile. "You've seen a doctor?"

"No. I've received no medical treatment since I've been in German custody," I replied. I thought it was important to establish our adversarial roles right away.

"This is unforgivable!" He retreated behind his desk and picked up his telephone, glancing down at the blotter on his desk. *"Ja, hier ist Sonntag. Senden Sie, bitte, den Arzt um Zimmer vier."* He hung up and looked back at me. "I have called for the doctor. He will have a look at your ankle. I hope your discomfort is not too great."

"I'm getting used to it."

"My name is Felix Sonntag," he said, once again coming from behind his desk and this time offering his hand. "And you are?"

I figured he already knew who I was but I also figured I'd play along. I shook his hand and replied, "First Lieutenant Robert Foster, United States Army, 0-376080."

"I am pleased to meet you, Lieutenant Foster. Other than your ankle, have you been injured anywhere else?"

"No."

"Good." Sonntag sat on the front edge of his desk and twisted around to pick up a buff colored file. "Now, let's see," he opened the file and ran his finger down the page. "You were shot down on Friday, is that right?"

I smiled. "First Lieutenant Robert Foster, United States Army, 0-376080."

Sonntag returned my smile. "Very good. I see you have been well-trained and that you are a highly-disciplined man. That makes for a formidable combination. Please understand that I am merely being friendly; 'small talk' is what you call it, yes, until the doctor arrives."

"Why haven't I been offered medical treatment before now?"

"An oversight, I am sure. Perhaps you were not near a German facility where medical care was available."

"Maybe not."

"Now, according to my notes—"

"Where do your notes come from?" I interrupted.

Sonntag smiled and looked up at me. "They come from many sources, including reports from our fighter groups. Would you like to see?" He unclipped a page from the file and handed it to me. I looked it over carefully. It was, of course, in German, which, as we've already covered, I don't speak or read. I think Sonntag had already guessed this and knew he was taking a minimal risk in sharing the report with me. I handed it back.

"So," he began again, "do you dispute that you were shot down on Friday?"

"No."

"Good." A rapping on the door intruded on our friendly discourse. The door opened and in walked the doctor, a chubby man in a tailored uniform. I could tell he was a doctor because he carried one of those little black bags doctors always carry. Behind him, just outside the door, Hans the orderly waited. "Ah, Dr. Franck! It seems Lieutenant Foster has sprained his ankle." Franck knelt beside me and slipped the wooden clog off my foot. He gently held my foot in his hand and slowly flexed my ankle, stopping when the pain made me flinch. He spoke rapidly to Hans who was still standing in the doorway. Hans disappeared, off on another errand of mercy no doubt. Franck opened his bag and took out a small pill box and a tiny paper envelope. He counted some pills into the envelope and stuffed the tab inside to keep them from spilling out. He handed them to Sonntag and spoke to him quickly but quietly. I gathered the doctor was giving instructions for the care of his new patient.

"Alles klar. Danke," Sonntag nodded as Dr. Franck turned and exited the room. The door was left open behind him. I guess they didn't think I was much of a risk to flee.

Sonntag resumed his perch on the front of his desk. He handed me the pill packet. "The doctor believes you have suffered a sprain, nothing more serious. He prescribes that you take one of these pills twice a day until they are gone. He also says you are to stay off the ankle and keep it elevated." At this point, Hans showed back up. He was carrying what looked like a pair of leather bedroom slippers. "Thank you, Hans," Sonntag said, taking the slippers. "You may leave us now." Hans backed out of the room and closed the door. "The doctor also recommends that you trade in your clogs for these shoes. They will be more comfortable." He handed the slippers to me and I transferred my feet into them. My feet have rarely felt so relieved!

"Now, where were we? Ah yes, shot down on the 17th, which you admit. A B-17 crewman, an officer, which means you served in one of four positions. Were you the pilot?"

"Look, Lieutenant," I said, "we've already been over all this. I can only give you my name, rank and service number; which by the way I've already done twice!" Sonntag held eye contact with me, but unfortunately wasn't put off by my protest.

"Lieutenant Foster, you may as well confirm what I already know. Cooperate with me and things will be very agreeable. I have provided medical treatment to include medication. I can even ensure that you are able to rest your ankle. Cooperate with me and I will help you, just as I helped Lieutenant Morgan. You remember him, don't you? He was also from the 91st Group. A very friendly chap."

I did remember Ed Morgan and he was a very friendly chap. I wondered what compromises Ed had made--and what I'd be forced to compromise. Now, I was happy to have gotten some medicine and a pair of comfortable shoes, but what I really wanted was food and rest. Maybe I should follow the advice I'd given to Harmon and tell them what I knew they already knew. As if by design, another knock on the door again stopped our conversation. Hans came in carrying a tray of white sausages, sauerkraut and a glass of beer.

"Thank you, Hans," Sonntag stood and pointed to the corner of his desk. "Just put it right there." Hans did as instructed and again left the room. Sonntag stepped around behind his desk and sat in his chair. He reached out and pulled the tray toward him. He unfolded a white cloth napkin and tucked it under his chin, then he stabbed one of the sausages with his fork and took a bite. My mouth was watering and my stomach was growling as loudly as a B-17 in flight. "Forgive me," Sonntag said, chewing his sausage. "We've been so busy here the last few days that we must eat when we can. On Saturday, for example, eighty-two new prisoners arrived--eighty-two! Can you imagine? One wonders how long you Americans can sustain such losses." He glanced up at me as he chewed. "We've been working around the clock." He took a sip from his beer and then paused with his glass in mid-air. "You must be hungry. Would you like some of this?"

"I would," I nodded.

He picked up the phone and after a moment spoke into the handset. *"Hans, noch ein bier, bitte. Und eine andere Gabel."* He set the phone back on its cradle and looked at me. "91st Bomb Group, yes?"

"Yes."

I've never liked cooked cabbage. I don't like Brussels sprouts either, but that's another story. I can eat cabbage raw, like in slaw or a salad, but cook it and it turns my stomach. But by the time I finished eating Sonntag's meal, sauerkraut was my new favorite vegetable. "What do you call those sausages?" I asked, licking my fingers as I chewed the last one.

"Weisswurst. There're very good, aren't they?"

I took advantage of my beer to swallow one of the pills. "What kind of pill is this, anyway?"

"Aspirin. Germans invented aspirin, did you know that? Bayer is a German company. I love Americans. That's the thing I like most about this job, but as a group, you are rather chauvinistic."

I wasn't sure what "chauvinistic" meant, so I just nodded and took another sip.

"Now, tell me: what was your role on your crew?" he subtly switched back to interrogator.

I belched and said, "Copilot." Sonntag knew that as an officer, which my ID tags confirmed, I was the pilot, co-pilot, bombardier or navigator. Of these, the position of least interest to him was probably copilot. And it happened to be the truth--easier to remember.

"And so Lieutenant Berly, who was captured with you, he was the pilot?"

"No. Berly was the bombardier. I don't know what happened to the pilot. I didn't see him after the plane blew up."

"It blew up?"

"Kaboom!" I spread my hands apart to mimic an explosion.

"Heavens! You must have been lucky to escape."

I hesitated. I didn't feel lucky. Here I was sitting in a German POW camp. I didn't feel lucky at all. Then I thought about Joe and Don. Luck is relative. "I suppose so."

"How did you get shot down?"

"What does your report say?"

Sonntag picked up the file again and flipped over a couple of pages. "It says you were attacked by a number of fighters making repeated passes; that one, then another of your engines was disabled; that several of your crewmembers parachuted out of the plane. This is accurate?"

"Pretty much."

"And you were shot down on your way home from the target? What was your target?"

"I thought you already knew that too."

"Well, we know some things and some things we deduce. You can confirm our deductions. Your group bombed Schweinfurt and your specific target was. . .?"

"What do you think it was?"

"I think it was a factory."

I nodded. I had already decided not to go much further than that in answering questions about the target.

"What kind of factory was it?" Sonntag persisted.

"I have no idea," I lied. "In our briefings, they'd tell us it was a factory. They'd never tell us what kind of factory because they didn't really want us to know, you know, in case we ended up here talking with you." I smiled.

Sonntag smiled back. He really was friendly and he'd treated me way better than I had expected to be treated. "Bob," he said, "I am a *Luftwaffe* officer, not *SS.* I am much easier to deal with, believe me. You've had no experience with the *SS* and take my word for it: you want to keep it that way; they can be much more difficult. Now, I believe you are being less than candid with me. You knew very well what your target was, didn't you."

"Of course."

"Tell me, please."

"No, Felix," I answered. "Thank you for the meal. It was the best food I've had since I arrived at your little Shangri La here. You know what we bombed and you know we hit what we aim at. So you already know what our target was. Stop playing games with me like I was some sort of mouse and you were the cat."

"The KugelFischer Werks. Why did you target this factory?"

"As clever as you are, I thought you had figured out by now that we're doing all this to kill Germans, destroy Germany and win the war. Hadn't you heard?"

Felix leaned back in his chair, placed his palms together and brought his hands up to his lips. He paused for a moment, his blue eyes staring directly into mine. "I found Lieutenant Morgan to be somewhat more cooperative."

"What did he share with you?" I asked.

"Well, he was willing to confirm certain circumstances about the mission he was on. For example, he was able to recall which organizations participated in the mission, some of their radio code names, bomb loads, commanding officers, formation leaders, just some of the little details that go together to form the bigger picture. Are you sure, in light of the kindnesses I've already shown you, that you wouldn't like to assist me as well?"

He had a good point. Food, beer, aspirin. I was already feeling better. "Okay, Felix," I said, "here's the big picture, the one you're trying to piece together like a jigsaw puzzle: the 91st Bomb Group and the rest of the 8th Air Force are getting bigger and stronger every day. Yes, we can sustain the losses. We're going to keep coming, we're going to keep bombing until you square heads come to your senses and get rid of the Nazis or until we bomb Germany back to the Stone Age, whichever comes first." I stood up. "I think I've had enough for today." I turned and walked to the door. It was time we both understood who was the boss.

Apparently, Felix had the same thought because he said, "Sit your ass back in that chair, Lieutenant. We're just getting started."

"So, you claim that Lieutenant Berly was your bombardier," Felix resumed our session seated behind his desk with the folder open in front of him. "Who was Lieutenant Johnson?"

"He was our navigator."

"What happened to him?"

"He died."

"Yes, I know he died. How did he die?"

"He was wounded in the battle. I didn't see any blood, but he had a big lump on his forehead. I don't know if that killed him or if something happened after he left the airplane."

"What about the rest of your crew?"

"Our top turret gunner had his arm nearly blown off. We bandaged him the best we could and then threw him out. His chute opened."

"Where was this?"

"I really don't know. It was maybe ten minutes before we all bailed out. It was before we lost our second engine."

"What is his name?"

"Sanderson. Eric Sanderson. We called him Sandy."

Felix made a note on a pad next to the folder. "And the others?"

"Al Norris, our waist gunner, got hit in the head. He was dead when I got to him. He stayed in the plane."

"Everyone else got out?"

"I think so."

"So we have Lieutenant Berly, Lieutenant Johnson and you accounted for. Your Sergeants are accounted for. We seem to be missing a pilot."

"Like I said, I don't know what happened to him."

Felix frowned, scanning his notes, then looked back up at me. "What was your pilot's name?"

I hesitated. If I told the truth, the Germans might begin to put the puzzle together. If I lied and Harmon didn't tell the same story, we could really cause ourselves a lot of trouble. I kicked myself for failing to anticipate this question, for failing to have a good answer ready. "I don't know what happened to him," I repeated.

"I understand," Felix replied in a sympathetic voice. "Tell me his name and perhaps we can locate him. A reunion would be pleasant, yes?"

"In England, yes; here, I'm not so sure."

Felix laughed. "His name?"

"Harold Robertson." It had to be a lie that would survive casual scrutiny, one that I could remember and one that I could relay to Harmon--if I got the chance. Felix wrote the name on his pad.

"Who was the dead man?"

"Lieutenant Johnson," I said, feigning boredom. "I already told you that. You're trying to trip me up aren't you; find holes in my story, right?"

"No, although I think there are some holes in your story, as you say. Who was the other dead man in the field where you and Lieutenant Berly were captured? According to the report, Lieutenant Berly was kneeling next to a corpse when you were apprehended. Why? What was he doing?"

"Puking his guts out."

"Surely he's seen dead men before?"

"Well, apparently this guy's chute didn't open or something. His body was smashed to pieces. It was rather gruesome."

"So you maintain that you did not know this man?"

"We did not."

"He was not from your aircraft?"

"No." Felix stared right through me for twenty minutes. Okay, it was more like twenty seconds, but you get my point. He dropped his gaze back to the file and flipped back a couple of pages. He looked back up at me. "What rank is Robertson?"

"First Lieutenant, like me."

"We don't have any record of Lieutenant Harold Robertson."

"Well, I guess your records aren't complete."

"I suppose this is true." Felix looked at his watch. "I suppose also that you have had enough for one day. As the good doctor said, you need to elevate your ankle and get some rest. Perhaps we can resume our conversation tomorrow."

"I can't wait," I smiled.

I learned later that every prisoner brought to the interrogation center was kept, like me, in solitary confinement for the first few days. Some guys, real hard cases, were kept for a month or more. My room was small. I had a bucket in which to relieve myself, a blanket, a pitcher of water, a small table, a wooden bed and a window. And time, I had lots of time.

I didn't see Felix the next day, or the day after that either. I kept going back over my story, trying to find a way to explain the fictional Lieutenant Robertson, but I was having a hard time coming up with a plausible story. I wasn't sure if it mattered anyway. Why would the Germans care about one guy, pilot or not?

My ankle was getting better. Staying off it and taking daily aspirin had greatly reduced the swelling and the pain. It no longer hurt to put weight on it though it was still sort of stiff. I would take my aspirin with my daily meals. I got a piece of black bread in the morning for breakfast. In the late afternoon, I was served supper: a piece of black bread. My water pitcher was refilled with each meal. My accommodations were not lavish, but no one was shooting at me.

By the time I was finally summoned for another interview, four days had passed since my arrival at the camp. I put on my slippers and followed my escort back to Sonntag's office. His door was open and as I walked in, he was putting on his uniform cap.

"Hello, Lieutenant Foster!" he said with a smile. "I thought perhaps you and your ankle might like some fresh air." He shook my hand and then led me out of the office, down the long corridor lined with numbered rooms and out into the sunlight of a summer morning. "You know, I much prefer being with Americans. The British officers always expect tea and biscuits. It's a wonder how they ever built an empire! How is your ankle?" he asked as we walked toward the main gate.

"Much better, thanks. The aspirin and the rest have helped a lot."

"Excellent. Is there anything else you need?"

"I'm still hungry," I said without thinking and immediately regretted my error. That's the thing with interrogators: anything you tell them, they intend to use against you.

"Yes, I imagine the rations you're served here are somewhat less filling than what you are used to. Perhaps I can find for you a can of Spam."

"You know about Spam?"

"Everyone knows about Spam!" Felix replied as he nodded to the gatekeeper. The wire on the gate gleamed in the sunlight as one side was swung open to accommodate our stroll. We passed through and Felix spoke again, "I thought some fresh air would do both of us some good. There's a trail here that meanders through the forest," he added, pointing up a shallow incline to our right. We were climbing a small hill that rose up behind the camp.

"Your English is really excellent, Felix. Not many Americans use words like 'meander.' How'd you learn English?"

"Oh," a smile spread across his narrow face, "I lived in California for two years, near Los Angeles."

"Thinking about going into show business?"

He laughed. "Me? No, I'd never make a good actor. I don't think I'd be good at pretending to be someone else. No, I was trying to break into the vegetable and fruit business. I was planning to make a fortune selling tomatoes and lettuce from California to overseas markets. I am a great admirer of your capitalistic system."

"So what happened?"

"Storm clouds began to gather and I thought it best to return here. What about you? What did you do before the war started?"

My ankle was feeling better from the walk. It felt great to be in the warm sunshine. The forest was quiet and fragrant. I was feeling pretty relaxed. "I was a crop duster."

"Of course," Felix nodded. He removed his cap. "We had those out in California. Some of the pilots were rather daring. How long did you dust crops before the war came along?"

"About two years, I guess."

"I'll bet you picked up military flying quickly."

"Well, you would think so, I mean I certainly understood the basics of flying, but you know, in the military there's only one right way to do something, so that took a little getting used to."

"What's the main difference between flying a small crop duster and a large bomber?"

"Just the complexity of the aircraft. Ailerons, rudders, elevators, all that stuff is the same. But with a big airplane there are just so many systems that you have to understand: radios, interphones, super chargers, fuel pumps. It's just a lot to keep up with."

We walked through a shaft of sunlight beaming down through the boughs of a tall fir tree and into the shadows of the woods. The temperature here was pleasingly cool, the forest floor neatly manicured. "No wonder it takes two pilots!" Felix offered. "Most of our bombers fly with just one."

"Did you fly, Felix?"

"Yes, for a while at least."

"But not anymore?"

"No. I crashed and two of my crew were killed. It was my fault. One of our engines faltered on takeoff and I pulled the throttle back immediately. The only problem was that I pulled power off the good engine. Do you know how quiet an airplane gets with no engines? I pushed the nose down and tried to restart the good engine, but of course it was too late. We crashed into some trees and that was that. I asked for a ground assignment and here I am."

"Bad luck," I said. Felix grunted. "What did you fly?"

"The Dornier, the 'flying pencil.' I liked it. Very maneuverable and faster than your B-17. Good bomb load, too."

"Faster than a B-17?" I wasn't buying that! "I'd be willing to race you. My B-17 against your Dornier!"

"I once reached a ground speed of two hundred fifty miles per hour in level flight!" Felix boasted. He stopped walking and turned to face me. "I bet you can't beat that."

"Two hundred eighty-five miles per hour!" I laughed. "Of course that was maximum speed. We only cruise at about one hundred eighty."

"Well, you win the bet. I suppose you could carry more bombs too. Our load was typically two thousand two hundred pounds."

I smiled, because I like to win. "Five thousand pounds!"

"And your planes are very rugged too. I've heard some of your men tell the most incredible stories about flying on three, two, even one engine." Felix began walking again.

We continued to walk and talk and I was both relieved and a little surprised that Felix didn't ask any more questions about Harold Robertson. He asked about North Carolina. I asked him about growing up in Bavaria. To Felix, it was the most beautiful part of Germany--and therefore of the world. We were both single, though at twenty-eight, Felix was a few years older than me. Even though I was strolling through woods deep inside of Germany and walking with an officer of the *Luftwaffe*, I felt relaxed and at ease.

Out of deference to my ankle, Felix kept our walk brief. After no more than forty-five minutes, we were back through the gate and in his office. "I enjoyed our walk, Bob. We must do this when our schedules allow. The exercise is good for both of us." I started to make a wise-ass remark about my schedule being pretty flexible, but before I could do so Felix reached into his desk drawer and pulled out a sheet of paper. He held it up for me to look at. "I don't suppose you can read this, but it is a report from a hospital in Bonn. Do you know Bonn?" I shook my head. "It doesn't matter," he continued. "What matters is that your Sergeant Sanderson is a patient there. I regret to inform you that they could not save his arm, but they did save his life. In fact, based on what little you've told me, your decision to shove him out of your bomber saved his life. I congratulate you."

"Thank you, Felix," I said quietly. I was at once sad and elated.

"Well," he said replacing the report in his desk, "I must now get back to work." He leaned over and opened one of the lower drawers of his desk and stood back up. When he did, he held out a blue can. A can of Spam. "Here. This will supplement your camp diet."

I reached out to accept the gift, but before he let go of it, Felix looked me in the eyes and asked, "Who is Harmon Roberts?"

"I don't know." I returned his stare and kept my face blank. We stood there for a moment longer before he released his grip on the Spam. "Thanks for the information on Sanderson. I really do appreciate it." I tried to sound sincere and nonchalant at the same time.

Felix continued to stare at me and I felt his disappointment in me. I liked Felix, but he was still the enemy. If he was disappointed, I thought, that was his problem. I was still pretty naïve at that point.

I spent a week alone. Twice a day the guard came to empty my slop bucket, bring me a piece of bread and refill my water. That was my only contact with another person. I had nothing to do, nothing to read, to write on, to listen to. Occasionally I would hear footsteps and voices, sometimes in the long corridor outside my door, sometimes from outside my window. The next time I met with Felix, if there was a next time, I decided I'd tell the truth. Up to a point. In the meantime, I rested; you can't do too much on two pieces of bread a day.

Felix was seated behind his desk when the guard brought me in. He didn't stand to greet me as he had in the past. "Hello, Bob," he said with a strained smile. "You look well-rested." I sat down in the chair across the desk from him.

"Very rested," I agreed. I didn't want to spend another week all by my lonesome. Agreeable seemed to be my best strategy.

Felix stared at me for a moment. Felix was an accomplished starer. "I wonder if you'd like to reconsider what you've told me so far."

"About what?" Agreeability still had to have limits.

"Harmon Roberts. Who is he?"

"Why are you so obsessed with this Roberts guy?" I laughed.

"I will level with you--that's the saying, isn't it?" Felix leaned forward, his forearms resting on his desk. "Roberts seems to be a mystery man. He turns up here and there but we can't put our fingers on him. That makes me very curious. What secret is being hidden along with

Harmon Roberts? Now, I've been candid with you, Bob; will you be candid with me?"

Here goes, I thought. "Harmon Roberts was the pilot of my aircraft."

Felix exhaled and leaned back in his chair. *"Ach so!* And why have you lied to me before? What in heaven's name is so important about Roberts that you have continually lied to me? I have not lied to you Bob, ever! We may be on opposite sides but I have treated you with nothing but respect and kindness." This was true and for a moment I felt a little guilt. For a moment. "Now, tell me please the truth about Harmon Roberts."

Truth-telling time was over. "Roberts was my pilot. I don't know what happened to him. I didn't see him after the plane blew up. If you want to know more, I'm sorry, that's it."

"You're still lying to me, Bob. You must remember that you are not the first enemy officer I have questioned. That's right, I used the term enemy! I like you. I have been kind to you. But you must understand that I intend to do my job. Why are you lying about Roberts? What's so special about him?"

"We didn't want Roberts to be captured."

"And why not?"

"Because he's Hitler's bastard son and we were afraid you'd use him for propaganda!"

Felix stared at me--again. Then he threw his head back and laughed. He laughed until tears came to his eyes. He wagged his finger at me as he wiped his eyes. "I really enjoy talking with you, Bob." He became serious again. "Why did you lie?"

"I don't know what happened to Roberts. If I report that I saw the plane blow up with him in it, his family will get a telegram saying he's dead. I don't know that's the case. Maybe he got out and the underground is hiding him."

"There is no underground," Felix smirked.

"Anyway, I'd hate to be the cause of that telegram and the cause of the anguish that goes along with it when I don't know if it's true."

"So, you make up a name? "

"So I make up a name; a name you can't check on; a name that won't generate a telegram."

"But you think Roberts is dead?"

"I really don't know, Felix." Now this was technically true because I had not seen Harmon in several days. I didn't think he was dead, but I didn't know.

Felix picked up his pen and made some notes across the bottom of my file. He opened his desk drawer and pulled out an ink pad and a rubber stamp of some sort and smacked it down on the page. He closed the file and looked up at me. He picked up his telephone and spoke a rapid phrase in German. Then he turned his attention back to me. "And so your time here comes to an end." He stood. I stood.

"Thank you for your kindness to me," I said, and I meant it.

"Good luck to you, Bob. Remember what I told you: you may be able to make me laugh, but should you ever attract the attention of the SS, a more cooperative approach will serve you better." We shook hands and the guard took me back to my cell.

Two days later, I was rousted from my bunk early in the morning. The guard led me outside into the cool air, the sun still below the horizon. I joined a formation of eighty or so other prisoners and we stood sleepily in our rows while a *Luftwaffe* officer checked our identification tags against a list on his clipboard. By the time he finished the sun was just beginning to warm our faces, a few of which I recognized. Besides Harmon, who I could see about fifteen yards away, there were at least three other 91st alumni in our ranks.

"Vier und achtzig," the officer concluded, handing the clipboard to a Sergeant and receiving his salute. With that, the Sergeant ordered us to march and we proceeded to the gate. Here, we were counted as we passed through in our ranks, four abreast. From there, we crossed the outer compound to the main gate we'd entered about two weeks earlier. Another count and we were on our way, marching back through the village of Oberursel to the train station.

The march this time was far easier. My ankle was much stronger and more limber. And my shoes, my slippers, were much more comfortable than the clogs I'd arrived in. It was a pleasant morning for a walk and I thought it must surely be good weather for bombing as well. I wondered where the 8th Air Force was heading today.

We stayed in our formation even after we reached the station, our *Luftwaffe* guards moving up and down our ranks and making it impossible to talk to anyone. I really wanted to talk to somebody, especially Harmon. I needed to find out what he'd been asked and what he'd said to determine if the danger was behind or ahead of us.

A short train pulled into the station at seven o'clock according to the large clock above the platform. The last two cars were empty and we were herded aboard. Our guards stood in the aisles as we made our way south, again preventing conversation. We passed through fields, then through increasingly built-up areas. It was clear we were headed back into Frankfurt. We arrived at a large rail yard and our train came to a halt. This time, I could climb down on my own. The guards formed a loose cordon around us, channeling us to a pair of waiting freight cars. It looked like we had another, longer ride ahead of us. Our formation loosened as we picked our way over the rails and cross ties between our last train and the waiting cars. I took advantage of this to move closer to Harmon and when we reached our conveyances, I was only a couple of bodies away from him. I wanted to make sure we ended up in the same car.

The same *Luftwaffe* officer reappeared, taking the clipboard from the Sergeant. Based on how we were standing in front of the two freight cars, he divided us fairly evenly. Then, he and the Sergeant did what they liked to do most: they counted us. As the officer counted one group, the Sergeant counted the other. Then they switched. Then they compared counts and only when satisfied that their counts matched each other's and that the total was indeed eighty-four, were we allowed to load into the cars.

"I'm glad to see you," I whispered as I climbed up beside Harmon.

"Likewise," he muttered with a smile. He had been in front of me in the formation and so had not seen me and hadn't known I was in the group. He pulled me along as he went to the far corner of the straw-covered floor of the car. "Don't talk until they close the doors," he whispered.

The longer we sat, the more whispers and low mumbling we heard from the forty or so other men stuffed into the car with us. Those with cigarettes--and there weren't many-- lit up and soon a low cloud hung just over our heads. After about an hour, we heard shouts outside and one of our guards slid the wooden door of the car closed, throwing us into darkness. In the several minutes it took our eyes to adjust to the now darkened interior of the car, we could feel it being pushed and coupled to other cars. We finally started moving, slowly at first, then settling in to a steady roll. There were several cracks in the boarded sides of the car and these let in some slivers of light as well as ventilation, which soon cleared away the cigarette smoke.

"Where do you think we're headed?" Harmon asked once he deemed it safe to speak. I craned my neck and tried to locate the sun, but I wasn't near enough to one of the cracks to make an educated guess.

"I don't know. How did it go back there? I wanted to get word to you about my visits with the interrogator but I couldn't figure out how."

Harmon leaned back into the corner. "Better than I thought it would. No bamboo shoots under the fingernails or anything like that. The only thing that caused me any concern was that after we'd been there a week or maybe a little more he began to ask if I knew Harmon Roberts. That threw me!"

"What'd you say?"

"I told him that Roberts was our pilot but that I didn't know what had happened to him."

I took a deep breath and patted him on the knee. "Good thinking. That's pretty much what I told him, too. What was your interrogator's name?"

"Major Neumann. Cool, professional, a little aloof. How about yours?"

"Sonntag, Felix Sonntag. Great guy. Spent time in the States back in the thirties. When I told him about Sanderson and us pushing him out of the plane with his arm nearly shot off, Felix did some investigating and guess what! He found Sandy alive in a German hospital!"

Harmon smiled, "That's a relief at least." We shared our interrogation experience and how we passed the long days in between sessions. We were having a good time catching up and we were both relieved that the Germans hadn't caught on to our lies about Harmon Roberts! The level of conversation in the car had now reached a low murmur which included much speculation about our eventual destination.

From our spot in the front- right corner of the car, we had a pretty good view of the rest of the car and watched in the semi-darkness as a figure made his way through the crowd of men. He reached us about forty-five minutes into our journey. "Ross Wilcox," he said extending his hand. "379th Group out of Kimbolton. We're establishing a chain of command to deal with whatever issues arise during our journey. There's a Captain over there. Either of you guys rank him?"

"Bob Foster," I replied, shaking hands with Wilcox. "I'm just a lowly first Lieutenant."

"Me, too," said Harmon, extending his hand. "Don Berly." If I'd been more perceptive, I would have noticed the fleeting look that crossed over Wilcox's face. I said "if."

"From the 91st, right?" Wilcox asked, cocking his head.

"How'd you know that?" I asked.

"Well, I know the 91st led the Schweinfurt raid and a lot of the boys I've already talked to got here courtesy of that little adventure. Lucky guess, really."

"So, who's the Captain?"

"Mike Huff, 303rd Group. He's the guy standing up over there looking out the window." The window was a larger than average gap between the boards on the opposite side of the car from where we sat. "I think he's trying to figure out where we're headed. Where you fellas from?"

"Missouri," Harmon answered.

"North Carolina," I said. "How about you?"

"Washington State. I used to watch Boeing make B-17s before I even knew what a B-17 was." He looked around in the dim light. "Well nice to meet ya. Don Berly, right? And Bob Foster?" We nodded and watched as he picked his way to a group of men nearby.

"From what I can tell," Captain Mike Huff shouted to our group over the noise of the clacking rails, "we're heading east. That probably means a permanent camp. While we're on this train and stuck in this car, we'll maintain military discipline. I appear to be the senior officer, so if anybody has a problem, come talk to me about it."

"What a jerk," I muttered to Harmon.

"Oh, I don't know, Bob. Somebody's got to be in charge; it might as well be him. You know, make decisions for the group, coordinate with the Germans."

"We'll share rations evenly," Huff continued, "until we get wherever we're going. Is anybody injured?" A couple of hands went up. "All right, you and you," Huff pointed to the faces beneath the raised hands. "Anybody with any kind of medical training higher than the first aid merit badge?" Three more hands went up. "Great! Make your way over to the south forty," he pointed to the left-front corner of the car, near the "window." He continued, "Let's talk for a minute. Depending on how long our little journey lasts, we will appoint a fire watch. Like I said, let me know if you have any issues."

Our train continued to roll eastward all morning. In the early afternoon, we began to slow and eventually stopped. We heard footsteps trooping by outside, our big side door was slid back and we were blinded by bright sunlight.

"Raus! Raus!" the German guards shouted, motioning for us to get out. We were on a sidetrack in a wooded area. We couldn't see anything past the trees lining the track on both sides. I saw Huff talking to the *Luftwaffe* officer, but wasn't close enough to hear what they were saying. After a moment, I saw Huff nod and the German moved to the car behind ours where the other group of POWs had spilled out on the tracks.

"Listen up, men!" Huff called to our group. "Hauptman Steiner says we can expect to be here for twenty minutes. Take a pee break in those trees but then come straight back. Steiner's going to feed us before we get back on the train. Nobody wanders off or we all pay for it. Understand? Be back on this side of the tracks in five minutes."

Harmon and I took advantage of the break to relieve ourselves. It was a nice day to be in the forest and reminded me of the day Felix had taken me for a walk. We were back where we were supposed to be on time. I'm such a rule-follower. Huff walked over to us. "You're Foster?" he asked.

"Right, Bob Foster," I replied, sticking out my hand. He looked at it and then back to my face.

"I hear you were very cooperative back there at Oberursel, Foster," he said accusingly. "You might want to remember you're still in the American Army and still subject to the Articles of War."

"Hold on a minute, pal! First of all, where are you getting your information? There were only two people in the room when I was being interrogated and you didn't get a report from me!"

"It's Captain, Lieutenant," the jerk actually pointed at the silver bars on his collar. He was leaning in now and I decided to lean back.

"Consider the source of your information, Captain, and try to apply a little professional judgment. Any information about my interrogation came from the enemy. You might want to keep that in mind, Captain!"

"You might want to remember that you're addressing a superior officer, Lieutenant! Do you deny that you gave the Krauts the flight characteristics of the B-17?"

My stomach turned over as I remembered my pleasant walk in the woods with Felix.

"Gentlemen, please," Harmon stepped between us. "This isn't the time or place. Captain Huff, during the course of my own interrogation I was told that several of our brother officers had been very cooperative. The

Germans were using the tactic to make me, and I suspect all of us, relax a little and let down our guard. I'm sure at some point or other they've portrayed each of us as cooperative. I have no hesitation vouching for Bob's patriotism."

Huff paused and seemed to cool off a little. Thank goodness for Harmon. "Well, I'm sure you don't, Lieutenant Berly. I'm sure you don't." Huff pointed his finger at my chest. "I'm going to keep my eyes on you two. Remember that."

"Wasser! Brot!" came a call from between the prisoners' two rail cars. The Germans had set up two folding tables and were handing out chunks of black bread and giving drinks of water from tin cups.

"Go get something to eat and drink," Huff ordered.

When we were a few paces away, I turned to Harmon and said, "Thanks. That was going to get ugly."

"It already was. That dumbass should have better sense than to pick a fight like that in front of everybody, especially the Germans."

"Yeah. Felix used that 'cooperative' line on me a bunch. He mentioned Ed Morgan. Remember him?"

"Sure."

"So who'd they tell you was 'cooperative'?" We'd reached the bread table. Harmon looked at me with a pained expression on his face.

"Nobody," he said.

I avoided Huff and his sycophant Wilcox for the rest of the trip and they gave me leeway as well. We stopped every couple of hours and when we were moving, it wasn't always at a rapid pace. I figured we were often shunted aside to make way for higher priority military traffic. I remembered the *Times* of London articles about the big Russian victories in the east and imagined that the Germans would be sending reinforcements along these same tracks.

We stopped in the early evening and were fed and watered again. This time our stopping point was beside a fallow field. The cool air reminded me that September had replaced August.

"Pretty countryside," Harmon said from over my shoulder. I had crossed the tracks and was standing on the edge of the field, enjoying the view as it sloped away from us and ended in a copse of hardwoods.

"It is," I agreed. "Any idea where we are?"

"A couple of the guys said we passed through Chemnitz."

"Yeah? Where's that?"

"It's almost due south of Berlin. Our deepest penetration yet into the Third Reich," he chuckled.

"And we're heading in the wrong direction," I added. I looked down at my slippered feet. "Listen, thanks for defending me back there with that jerk."

"Think nothing of it," Harmon smiled. "Anybody who feels like he has to pull rank in a situation like this has got his head up and locked." Then to steer the conversation to more solid ground, Harmon said, "I wonder how much further we have to go."

"Well," I ventured, looking up at the gathering dusk, "wherever it is, we aren't going to get there before dark." A whistle interrupted the pleasant moment and we re-crossed the tracks and climbed back into the freight car.

Our train moved fitfully through the night. We were only seven or eight cars long and apparently not carrying anything valuable--to the Germans at least!

Several times during the night we were shunted to a sidetrack while a faster, longer train blasted past us, pushing a concussive wave over us as it sped by. I could only guess at its destination and cargo.

At mid-morning of the second day, our train began to slow, the steady rocking of the cars fading away. From his post by the window, Huff attempted to determine where we were. We'd passed through a mountainous area in the early morning, before dawn, and the temperature had fallen noticeably. We'd reached flatter ground and warmer weather by the time we stopped.

"Sagan," Huff called out. "Anybody ever heard of it?" No one had. Most of us were just ready to get out of the box car, out of stale air fouled by the odors of forty unwashed men. When we heard boots tramping along the track outside, we began to stand in anticipation of another break.

The routine began again: the door slid back, the bright light flooding in, the cries of the guards to climb out. Once on the ground, we found ourselves in yet another railroad yard. Two sets of tracks led into the large yard from each direction. From our vantage point, I could see the yard widening out to a dozen sets of tracks. I'd never heard of Sagan, but apparently they got a fair amount of railroad traffic through here.

I looked around for the bread and water servers, but didn't see them. Maybe this was just a pee break, I thought, although those were usually out in the country. The *Luftwaffe* officer who had accompanied our group marched toward us from the locomotive at the front of the train. He was shouting at our guards, who responded by shouting at us. They gestured with their rifles and pointed and yelled until they had us back in a sloppy formation facing the train.

Either Huff was the senior officer from both cars of prisoners, or he was just a jerk, for he took position at the front of the formation. He shouted "Attention!" and saluted the *Luftwaffe* officer. I glanced at Harmon out of the corner of my eyes and he smothered a smile. I guessed this was Huff's first command. I could hear the German speaking, but not what he was saying. Huff was nodding his pea-head up and down. Huff saluted again and crisply about-faced.

"Listen up, men," Huff projected. "Our destination is through the woods behind me. *Hauptmann* Steiner says it's less than a mile. Let's move out smartly and show our hosts what good soldiers look like! Right face! Forward march!"

"You've got to be kidding me," I said to the back of Harmon's head. "'Let's show our hosts what good soldiers look like'? He's been watching too many training films."

We moved down the tracks flanked on all sides by rifle-toting guards and then Huff ordered a column right to exit the rail yard onto a straight dirt road that disappeared into an evergreen forest. As we approached the limit of the yard, a fence with a very small gate blocked our way. "Column halt!" shouted our fearless leader. He stepped around to the front of the formation and pushed the gate open himself. "File from the left, forward march!"

"How'd this guy escape the infantry when he's so good at drill and ceremony?" I muttered.

"No talking in the ranks!" Huff barked.

On the other side of the gate, we reformed and stepped off once again. It actually felt good to be outside and moving. It was cool in the shade of the trees and their fragrance was a welcome improvement over that of the box car. I couldn't see *Hauptmann* Steiner anywhere, which meant that he was behind me somewhere, probably riding in a staff car.

Steiner was good to his word and within fifteen minutes, we could see a clearing in the forest ahead and low wooden buildings springing up out of the ground. As we drew nearer, I realized the complex was far more than just a few buildings. It spread out in front of us for acres. The entire development was surrounded by a pair of ten-foot high fences, one about six feet or so inside the other and both topped with barbed wire. Tall watch towers stood about every two hundred feet, their occupants leaning on machine guns and smoking, their attention focused inside the camp. Outside of the fences, soldiers and mean-looking dogs patrolled on foot. They turned to stare at us as we marched by. On the other side of the wire, we could see men wearing a hodge-podge of uniforms standing in small groups watching us. This didn't appear to be a very friendly place.

Huff continued to bark his marching cadence as though he was auditioning for Sergeant-Major. We continued to walk along, enjoying the sunshine, but awed at the size of our new home. Off to our left front, several buildings were under construction, the fall of the carpenters' hammers disrupting the pleasant morning. Guards swung open the large double gates and Huff led us through. They closed again immediately behind us. Huff halted us in front of what must have been the headquarters building as it was the only one with a flag pole. The red, white and black Nazi flag was hanging lazily in the still air. On his command, we all turned and faced Huff. He ordered, "At ease," and then sharply turned about and stood at ease himself.

We stood quietly in the sunshine for a few minutes, taking in what we could see without breaking formation. This place was twenty times the size of the interrogation center and with its snarling dogs, armed patrols, fences, barbed wire and machine gun towers, twenty times as intimidating.

The door to the headquarters opened and a *Luftwaffe* officer stepped out, down the two steps and quickly approached Huff. Huff looked back at us from over his shoulder and commanded, "Attention!" The German appeared to be another Captain and he walked with a slight limp. Huff saluted like a marionette and the German returned the salute. He spoke quietly to Huff and Huff again ordered, "At ease!"

"Good morning, gentlemen, and welcome to *Stalag Luft* III," the German officer began in lightly-accented English. "My name is Handelmann and I am *Oberst* von Linden's adjutant. This camp is run by the *Luftwaffe* for Allied airmen who have become prisoners of the Third Reich. Within the camp, your own officers have established a chain of command. You will be counted"--I knew he was going to get to that at some point--"and assigned to a barracks. Your predecessors will help you learn camp routine. As you move from the *Vorlager* here," he gestured to the headquarters area in which we now stood, "into the compound behind you, you will be checked against our list of prisoners, searched and issued a Red Cross parcel."

Handelmann paused and his eyes swept over the formation. "Act honorably and so you shall be treated." He turned his attention back to Huff, who, like the puppet he was, popped back to attention and saluted. Handelmann saluted and returned to the steps of the building.

Handelmann turned and watched as we filed through another set of double gates, this separating the *Vorlager* from the prisoners' area. Standing between these two fences were parallel rows of German guards dressed in distinctive blue coveralls. As a group of us drew abreast, we would be stopped and the blue-clad men would quickly search us. I guess the guards had all the watches they needed because they let me keep mine. Occasionally, one of the guards would smile and hold up a pen or a pocket knife or something else that he felt would make a nice souvenir. Once through this gauntlet, we were prodded into the prisoners' compound where we were met by more blue-suits who handed us our Red Cross parcels. The only good thing about this experience was that my new pal, Huff, was shunted over to the West Compound which was still under construction. Unfortunately, we weren't so lucky with Wilcox.

We received our parcels and were released into the compound. We quickly found ourselves at the tender mercies of our British allies. They say "The sun never sets on the British Empire" and that was certainly true at *Stalag Luft* III. Inside the wire, the British had taken over. Two small tables cobbled together from the remains of packing crates stood in front of us. Behind each sat a British officer with a chart of some type on the surface in front of him.

"Next, please," the Brit called out, waving Harmon forward. "Name, please," he said without looking up.

"Berly, Donald, first Lieutenant, United States Army." The British flight Lieutenant ticked the name on a roster and then consulted his chart, a rough diagram of the barracks with some numbers written alongside each building.

"We'd prefer billets together, if possible," Harmon said, looking down. "We're crew mates."

The flight Lieutenant looked up, squinting in the sunlight. "Would you, now? Well, that should be easy enough to accomplish. Ocean view or mountains?"

Harmon laughed and replied, "Best available."

"Right! That would be ocean view," he consulted his chart again and penciled a number next to a box on the page. "And your name, please," he peered around Harmon to look at me.

"Foster, Robert, first Lieutenant, United States Army."

"Just so! All right, Yanks," he said scribbling a note on the chart, "off you go to Hut 112. Straight ahead and then turn left at Hut 109 and then just past the cook house. Welcome to Sagan and good luck!"

With parcels under our arms, we walked across the dirt grounds. "You've got that Don Berly thing down pat," I said to Harmon as we explored our new home. I didn't realize that Wilcox was right behind us.

Hut 112 looked just like all the rest of the barracks. It had a low, peaked roof broken only by chimneys serving bunk rooms on either side of a central corridor. The building sat on low brick pillars so that one could see underneath. The exception was the solid foundation in the center of the building where water pipes came up from below ground into the washrooms. Each room was fitted with a large window and each window with exterior shutters that had to be latched from the outside.

Harmon and I stepped up the two steps and into the corridor of Hut 112. It would be our home for many months, though we didn't know it at the time.

"Hello, chaps," a voice called out from the first room on the right. We stuck our heads inside and discovered three men sitting around a makeshift table.

"How do you do?" Harmon said, stepping through the doorway. "I'm Don Berly, 91st Bomb Group. This is my copilot Bob Foster."

"Hugh Jeffers, this is George Travis and Harold Mayhew. You're with the group just in this morning then?"

"We are," Harmon nodded, "and we've been assigned to this barracks."

"Well then, you've arrived at the right place," Jeffers said, standing and extending his hand. "I'm the barracks chief. We'll put you right down the corridor." We followed Jeffers about halfway down the length of the building and he showed us to two bunks in a compartment on the left. "You two get settled in and I'll come back for you in a few minutes. Then I'll take you to meet our C/O."

Jeffers headed back down the hallway. I didn't think it was going to take me long to "get settled in" as all my possessions were either on my body or in the box in my hands. "How do you like that, their own C/O inside a German prison camp? No wonder these guys ruled the world." I opened my Red Cross box to find welcome necessities. In addition to a razor, blades, tooth brush and powder, soap and a comb, it contained towels, socks, underwear, shirt and tie, but no shoes. There was a pipe and some tobacco, a sewing kit, toilet paper, a wool sweater and a first aid kit. I knew that it would soon get cold and the sweater would come in handy. I hoped I wouldn't need the first aid kit.

Harmon and I took our new towels, soap and razors and headed to the wash room. We were pretty foul, having gone more than two weeks without a shower, and welcomed the chance to clean up and put on mostly new clothes. By the time Jeffers returned, we were at least presentable, which is good, because that's exactly what he had in mind.

"Group Captain Walling, may I present First Lieutenants Berly and Foster," Jeffers began. We were standing in Hut 102, in the small office of the SBO, the Senior British Officer. He was the commander of the prisoner side of the camp. Walling was tall, with an erect bearing and narrow features. His brow was creased and he had tiny crows' feet bracketing his brown eyes.

"Good of you to join us, gentlemen," he smiled. "Welcome to Sagan. We like to maintain military discipline here. It provides us some very limited measure of freedom. The Germans allow us to administer on this side of the wire. As long as there's no trouble, we get along fairly well. I'm sure Jeffers has briefed you on our standing procedures. As questions arise, feel free to call on him for assistance. Won't you please sit down?" he motioned to two Red Cross crates standing in front of the table behind which he stood. As we sat, he settled on to a crate of his own, leaned his forearms on the table and peered across at us. Jeffers remained standing behind us while two other officers sat on crates to either side of Walling. I noticed that it was dim in the room, that the windows were shuttered.

"This is Flight Lieutenant Jones-Hatton," he nodded to his right, "and this is Squadron Leader Hastings," he waved a hand to his left. "They are members of my staff. Tell me," Walling resumed now that we all knew each other, "what outfit were you with?"

"The 91st Bomb Group out of Bassingbourn," I answered. Harmon and I had agreed that since I was the copilot and he was pretending to be the bombardier, it would be more natural for me to speak.

"The both of you?" Walling asked with a raised eyebrow.

"Yes sir. I was the copilot and Don here was the bombardier." Harmon nodded.

"Denys," Walling looked to Jones-Hatton on his right, "we've got some chaps from the 91st, haven't we?"

Denys was flipping through some loose pages clamped on clipboard. "Yes sir. I'll see who I can round up." With that, he left the room.

"You were shot down?"

"Yes sir."

"Fighters or flak?"

"Fighters, sir, a lot of fighters."

"When was this, Lieutenant?" He pronounced it *Leftenant* in that goofy way the English have.

"17 August, sir."

Walling nodded. "I see. Decent treatment so far?"

I was tempted to complain about Huff, but I was pretty sure he meant the Germans so I said, "Yes sir. I sprained my ankle pretty badly when I landed and a *Luftwaffe* doctor looked at it and gave me some aspirin."

"Hmmm." Walling turned his gaze to Harmon. "And you, Lieutenant Berly?"

"No complaints, sir."

"The Germans can be quite civil when they choose to be, quite beastly when they don't. They can also be quite devious, which is why this little chat is so important. Every new prisoner must be vetted until we are confident you are who you claim to be. The Huns have attempted on a couple of occasions to infiltrate informers disguised as Allied airmen." I heard a door open and close and footsteps out in the hallway. Within a moment, Denys was back and with him a familiar face.

"Sir, you remember Lieutenant Hamilton? Tom was a member of the 91st Bomb Group until he was shot down in June." Tom Hamilton had been Christy's copilot when their plane was shot down on the mission to Huls. He nodded at us and grinned.

"Of course," Walling smiled at the new arrival. "Good of you to spare us a moment."

Tom Hamilton smiled at Walling and replied, "I had nothing planned for today, sir." The others chuckled like that was funny. I hadn't adapted yet to British humor, but apparently Tom had.

"Well, Tom, these gentlemen claim to have arrived here following service with the 91st and we were wondering if you could identify them." The red flags in my mind shot to the top of the pole.

"Sir, if I might--"

"Not so fast, Lieutenant Foster," Walling held up his hand, "procedures to follow." He nodded at Hamilton.

"Sir, this is Lieutenant Bob Foster, copilot on one of our B-17s and this," he pointed at Harmon, "is Lieutenant Harmon Roberts, the pilot."

A puzzled look flitted across Walling's face. "Thank you, Tom. Would you mind hanging about for a few minutes? We might have one or two other questions."

"Of course, sir," Tom answered and left the room.

When he heard the hallway door close again, Walling looked from Harmon to me and back. "We seem to have a discrepancy in our stories, don't we?"

"Sir," I began, "I respectfully request that we be allowed to meet with you in private?"

"Your respectful request is denied, Lieutenant Foster. My staff are both trustworthy and discreet. Now, perhaps you will share with us the rationale behind your subterfuge."

It took me twenty minutes to explain why Harmon Roberts III was masquerading as our dead crewmate Don Berly. I'd even thrown in the part where Jolly ordered me not to let Harmon be taken alive. That raised a few eyebrows and the hair on the back of Harmon's neck.

After I explained the reason for the deception, Walling called Tom Hamilton in a second time and asked what he knew about Harmon and me. He confirmed that Harmon's father was a United States Senator from Ohio and that Harmon was indeed the pilot of our crew. Once Walling was finally satisfied that we were who Tom said we were, I made the case for denying the Germans a cheap propaganda victory and continuing the ruse.

"Does anyone have an argument to the contrary?" Walling asked. No one did. Walling gave orders that

Harmon would continue to be known as Don Berly. Tom and the others agreed and Tom was dismissed for a second time.

From there the conversation turned to other matters, including any skills Harmon or I could add to camp administration. I was assigned to camp sanitation owing to my crop dusting work with pesticides. Harmon was delegated to assist with billeting. It seemed ironic that in a camp full of highly trained aviators, we had no use for pilots. We were winding up our interview when the officer to Walling's left, Hastings, spoke for the first time. He was on the smallish side, with intense eyes and a high-pitched voice.

"Sir, I'm sorry to intrude," he spoke to Walling.

"Go ahead, David."

"Well, I've been sitting here for the longest time staring at Lieutenant Rob—Lieutenant Berly and it's just now struck me who it is he reminds me of. From this angle, sir, he's a dead ringer for Dalberg."

Denys stood up and walked behind Walling to view Harmon from David's angle.

"Dalberg?" Walling looked confused.

"Yes sir, the ferret who's always harassing us with unannounced searches."

Walling leaned over to his left and ogled Harmon. "My word, David, you're quite right! My word! I'm surprised I hadn't noticed it before! Let's wait a couple of days so 'Don' here can learn his way around and then match these two up with the X, will you? I'm confident they can make some use of your most keen observation."

"Yes sir!"

I had no idea what the Brits were talking about, but we'd find out soon enough.

"Would you really have shot me?" Harmon asked as we traipsed back to Hut 112. It was now late afternoon and already part of the camp lay in shadows.

"I would have after you painted over Elmer Fudd and got Al shot," I laughed, giving Harmon a playful shove with my hand.

"That's it? That's all I get?" Lieutenant Wilcox complained as the cook ladled a cup full of stew into his mess tin. It was our first full day in the camp and our first meal at the cook house. A long line of hungry Allied airman stood under a cool, gray September sky. Through some witheringly bad fortune, Harmon and I had ended up just behind Wilcox.

"Sorry, mate," the cook replied. "We've got to stretch the supply to meet the demand. Economics, you know."

Wilcox stomped off. Now, I could see why Wilcox was a little put out. The portion was not only small, but very thin, more like soup than stew. A thumb-sized piece of bread was served with it, but we got all the water we could drink.

Harmon and I leaned against the wall of Hut 112 to eat our meal. We could have gone inside to our tiny room, but even though it was overcast, we preferred to stay outside. We knew autumn was just around the corner and winter would follow. We needed to take advantage of our opportunities to be outside. Dining al fresco also gave us a chance to continue looking around our new home.

We'd been assigned to the North Compound of *Stalag Luft* III. The Germans and their Polish laborers were working daily on a new compound to the west. Clearly they were expecting more guests. To the immediate south of our area was a smaller compound. Russian prisoners were kept there. From what little we'd heard so far, the Russians were being starved and worked to death.

The North Compound consisted of fifteen barracks arranged in five rows of three building each. In addition, there were also the small hut where we'd met Group Captain Walling and his staff, the cook house, bath house and a theater where the prisoners held plays, concerts and other entertainments. A single ten-foot fence separated our area from another smaller area which contained a couple of storage buildings, sick quarters, and the cooler, where prisoners were relegated to solitary confinement. I wasn't yet sure what kind of behavior landed you in the cooler.

I spooned a mouthful of stew. It actually didn't taste too bad. I chalked that up to the well-known culinary skill of the British. I'd just nibbled a piece of bread when a voice from beside us said, "I know what you're up to." It was our friend Wilcox.

"Really," I said, not bothering to look at him. "And what would that be?"

"You're working for the Germans. You're trying to infiltrate this camp and keep an eye on things for the Krauts. Well, the game's up, buster. I know he's not Don Berly!" Wilcox pointed at Harmon with his spoon. "You're probably not who you say you are either, Foster!"

"Why do you think I'm not Don Berly?" Harmon asked calmly.

"Because I knew Don. We were at bombardier school together in New Mexico." I noticed that he'd cleaned his plate. "I'm going to turn you guys in!"

Harmon looked over at him and said, "You should do what you think best, Ross." With that, Wilcox stomped off again. It was all I could do not to laugh. What a wiener!

Harmon returned to his meal. "You don't think he's dumb enough to start trouble, do you?" he asked, looking at the dwindling amount of food still on his tin. "I'd hate to get my rations cut for causing trouble."

"Him?" I snorted. "He couldn't cause trouble in a bull ring with two red capes." Maybe I was a little too confident.

Once we walked the perimeter a couple of times getting the feel for the layout of the camp and looking for familiar faces, there really wasn't much to do. We visited with Tom Hamilton and shared with him Christy's miraculous tale of escape. Tom had been less fortunate and had been apprehended within hours of being shot down.

"As I see it," Tom told us, "the two main problems are that there isn't enough to eat and there isn't enough to do. When there isn't enough to eat, you begin to lose strength. When there isn't enough to do, you begin to lose your mind. Some of these birds have been here a long time. Walling was shot down in 1940 over France. When you start feeling sorry for yourself just remember that he's already got three years on us."

"Say, Tom," Harmon said as we walked along, "what's with the low strand of wire there?" He pointed toward a single strand of knee-high barbed wire running parallel to the perimeter fences.

"That's the warning wire. Get between it and the fence and the guards will shoot you. Don't cross the wire."

"I think I like it better on this side anyway," Harmon allowed.

It was my turn to ask a question. "What's the X?"

"Keep walking," Tom said. We followed him away from the fence and toward the center of the rows of huts. "Each of you face a different direction and if you see any of the ferrets lurking about, stop me." We'd learned by now that "ferret" was the prisoners' name for the guards in the blue uniforms. Their job was to maintain security in the camp. As such, they would enter the compound at any time, day or night, alone, in pairs or in groups and conduct searches. They would search for contraband, which was just about anything that the Germans or the Red Cross hadn't provided. They were also always looking for information about escape attempts. We casually took positions from which I could see the main gate, Tom could see the west compound and Harmon could look to the east fence. We didn't figure we'd have to guard against the Russians.

"X is the escape committee. It's all top secret. A British squadron leader's in charge of it. He keeps Walling informed, but he runs all escapes. The way the Brits play it, if you or I want to go over the wire, we have to clear it first with the X."

"That seems sort of bureaucratic doesn't it? I mean if I want to go, why can't I just go?" I said.

"Technically, I guess you can. But if you need support of any kind, the committee can help."

"What kind of support?" Harmon asked.

"Depends on what kind of escape. Maybe you speak pretty good German and you want to take a train. They can get you a ticket. Maybe you're going to hide in the day and walk to the English Channel by night. They can get you a map or a compass."

"How can they do that?" I could tell Harmon was impressed. I was, too.

"Beats me," Tom replied, "but I bet half the Brits in camp provide some type of support from time to time. Why are you asking this stuff?"

Harmon spoke up. "Well, apparently, I look a lot like one of the ferrets and David, one of Walling's staff, is supposed to introduce me to the X."

"Well, be very careful. I hear the guy's pretty intense and that he hates the Germans. Don't let him talk you into something stupid."

"You're new, aren't you?" asked the German guard escorting our work group. Jeffers, another British officer named Lewallen, and I had been delegated to come up with a solution to the fly problem. The flies were getting disgustingly thick around the bath house and latrine and as a result threatened to spread pestilence throughout the camp. Both Walling, the SBO, and von Linden, the *Kommandant*, recognized the potential hazard to health and morale. They had agreed that it be a top priority and so naturally had assigned their top new man to the job.

"Yes, I arrived a few days ago," I said. "My name's Bob, Bob Foster." I extended my hand to see if he would shake it. I had been told that some of the guards were very friendly and that others would keep us at arm's length. This guy seemed to be one of the former.

"Freddie Sommer," he smiled and shook my hand. Freddie was a ferret, one of the blue-uniformed guards who had free roam of the camp. His job was security. He wasn't with us to help solve the fly problem; his job was to see what he could learn about what was going on inside the wire. In particular, Freddie and his comrades were looking for the skinny on escape attempts. I had not seen or heard of any, but I'd been assured by Jeffers that a number of small jobs were always in the planning stages and that the best time to "have a go" was during the dark of the moon. That wouldn't come around until the end of the month.

"So, *Leutnant* Foster," Freddie leaned in close, "what can be done about these swarming flies?"

I thought a little charm was called for so I laid it on thick. "How'd you learn to speak English so well, Freddie?"

He smiled at the compliment and said, "I have a good ear for languages. I speak English as well as many Americans and better than most Canadians!" I laughed at the joke. Mr. Friendly.

"Well, you really do speak it well. I wish I spoke German as well as you speak English. Then I could escape and take the train to Berlin." It was my turn to joke, but the smile vanished quickly from Freddie's face.

"No joking about escapes! You'll go to the cooler! You won't like that!"

"Relax, Freddie! I'm only pulling your leg!" Freddie glanced down at his legs and then back up to my face, a puzzled expression on his own. "I'm sorry. It's just an expression; it means I'm joking with you, I'm pulling your leg."

"Ach so. Pulling your leg." Freddie nodded and smiled. Then, he was back to business. "No more jokes about escapes. Now, what about these dirty flies?"

The four of us were standing at the southeast corner of the bath house, closest to the theater. Big, hairy, black flies were swarming around the soggy ground at the corner of the building. "My guess," I explained looking from Jeffers to Lewallen to Freddie, "is that some of the drain tiles inside have collapsed, so the water isn't draining into the sewer. Instead, it's leeching out into the ground. The flies love it."

"Any recommendations?" Jeffers asked.

"A couple pop into my head. First, we should have the drain dug up and replaced. We'd need a work party of about five to ten men with picks and shovels and some tile. We could finish in a day or two. Second, some insecticide scattered around this area would help reduce the fly population." I turned to Freddie. "Do we have any DDT here?"

"DDT?" he repeated haltingly.

"Yeah, it's a chemical insecticide. It was just coming in to use in the States before the war, but some egghead here in Europe got credit for using it as a bug killer."

"I don't know. What's an egghead?"

"Oh, sorry. It's slang for a scientist or a professor. Because they have big brains so they have heads shaped like eggs. . . Get it?" Freddie responded with a blank look. "Never mind. Do we have any chemicals like that around here?"

Jeffers, Lewallen and Freddie all looked at me and shrugged. "Well, Hugh," I addressed Jeffers, "think we can find out?"

"Right on it," he nodded. "We'll go and check with Walling and he can address it with von Linden. Come along, James," he said to Lewallen.

Once they were out of earshot, Freddie spoke again, "*Leutnant* Foster, your shoes, they're not regulation, are they?"

"No," I replied somewhat ruefully, "and they're starting to fall apart, too." My slippers were soft, which is why they had felt so welcome on my feet at first. But clearly they weren't going to last a whole lot longer and cold weather was fast approaching. I shared a cigarette with Freddie while I explained how I'd been blown out of my airplane and landed barefoot; how Louie had commandeered a pair of wooden clogs for me; and Felix had obtained these more comfortable slippers. "It seems like all my shoes are courtesy of my captors," I grinned.

"Perhaps I can continue this tradition," he replied, blowing smoke at a couple of large flies buzzing around his face.

"You've got my attention," I said as I watched Jeffers and Lewallen walk past the cook house.

"Soon the weather will be wet, then cold, then cold and wet. You really must have some decent shoes. What size do you wear?"

"American size nine. Can you get me some?"

"As you Americans say: for a price."

"How much?" I asked without seeming desperate.

Freddie held up his right hand, his fingers spread apart. "Five packs."

I let out a low whistle. Five packs of cigarettes was the entire ration in a Red Cross parcel. Handing over the whole bundle to Freddie would mean I'd have no other bartering currency until the next parcel. I'd been told to expect a parcel every week or so, but as much as I loved the Red Cross, I knew ultimately that the parcels had to pass through at least three governments and lots of greedy hands before they reached us. Still, cold, wet feet held little appeal. I made up my mind. I'd be living on charity for a while.

"Deal," I said. "Three packs up front, two more on delivery."

"Deal," Freddie smiled.

"What's up, hot shot?" I asked, slapping Harmon on the back. I'd just returned to the barracks from my assignment. I figured Jeffers and Lewallen, even though they were British, would be able to find out whether simple insecticides were available in the camp. I'd take a breather until they returned.

"Very little," Harmon replied. He was reading a paperback, something by James Hilton. Or maybe he was rereading it. I don't know. "We've only had a trickle of new guys come in, one or two a day over the past week. It worries me a little."

"Why? It seems like fewer guys coming in here means the Krauts are shooting down fewer bombers. That's good!"

"Yeah, that's good if all of the sudden their flak gunners can't aim anymore or their fighter pilots suddenly chickened out. But think about this Bob: What if 8th Air Force has quit flying the deep missions into Germany? What if the losses on our Schweinfurt raid were so heavy that we're backing off?"

"You think that's why new arrivals are down?"

"I'm just thinking, that's all. I mean how many planes did the 91st lose? I can think of at least seven, eight counting us. Lose that many planes and men on one mission and it takes a while to recover."

I hadn't thought of it like that, but I could see Harmon's point. If the 8th Air Force was backing off, if we weren't intent on bombing the Germans back to the Stone Age every day, then we might be in for a long winter--or two.

A couple of more weeks passed. September in eastern Germany is a transition month, not like back home where it is simply another month of summer. In Germany, the weather was noticeably cooler. When we were roused out of bed in the mornings and made to stand in formation for Apel, or roll call, we could see our breath. My wool sweater was already coming in handy. Fortunately, we'd gotten Red Cross parcels again and I had handed over the last two packs I owed Freddie in exchange for a pair of brown shoes. They were GI shoes, which made me a little sad because I guessed that they had belonged to an airman who hadn't survived his last mission. I guess it didn't matter. He had no use for them anymore. It felt good to have real shoes again. I made a promise to myself to take good care of them.

Von Linden, the *Kommandant*, had finally sent word to Walling that no insecticide was available. Apparently the supply service in the German military works a lot like our own; when you don't need it you've got it coming out of your ears, but when you do need it, well, good luck.

Jeffers, Lewallen, Freddie and I were once again patrolling the back side of the bath house, watching our step and swatting at flies. There weren't as many as before; flies don't like cooler weather. Still, we needed to do something.

"Freddie," Jeffers asked, "can we get a work party in here to dig up the drain as Foster suggested?"

"Perhaps so. I will check with the adjutant."

Jeffers turned his next question to me. "Any other alternatives on insecticides?"

I scratched the back of my neck and breathed in the pleasant aroma from Freddie's cigarette, which used to be my cigarette. "Back home, some people used a homemade insecticide on their gardens. It might work here." I looked up. "Freddie, is there a flower shop in the town?"

"A flower shop?"

"Yes, a shop that sells flowers."

"I suppose so, why?"

"You can make a natural insecticide by crushing the petals of chrysanthemums and drying it into a powder. But you have to have the chrysanthemums to start with." We all stared at Freddie, who simply shrugged.

"I'll have to find out. It will give me a good excuse to go into town."

"Perhaps I could go with you," I volunteered. "In case there's a question about the flowers," I added.

"Perhaps," Freddie exhaled. "But you will have to give me your promise not to escape."

"Sure, sure. This is about fixing a problem, not about escape. No joking."

"Look, that's him," I nudged Harmon in the ribs. We were strolling around the perimeter. It was a pleasant afternoon, a warm sun beaming down from a bright blue sky. Perfect flying weather, I thought. And here we were stuck on the ground.

"Who?"

"Dalberg. Your twin." Dalberg, in addition to having facial features similar to Harmon's, was also about the same height and build. Where Harmon usually adopted a leisurely pace, especially now when he had no place to be and nothing much to do, Dalberg was a bundle of energy. He moved purposefully through the compound, varying his direction and ducking between the huts. At times, he'd dart behind a building, out of sight, and linger there, attempting to listen in on nearby conversations. Like Freddie and the other ferrets, Dalberg spoke English very well. Unlike Freddie, Dalberg wasn't friendly; he was all business and business was thwarting escapes.

"You think I look like that guy?" Harmon squinted into the sun.

"Yeah, I do. You wouldn't pass as twins, but maybe as half-brothers."

"A dubious compliment." Harmon smirked.

Two days later, I climbed into the back seat of a *Luftwaffe* staff car with Freddie. One of the camp guards acted as our chauffeur. The guards, or Goons as we called them, were different from the ferrets. We had little contact with guards, who were dressed in the usual blue-gray garb of the *Luftwaffe*. They manned the gates, stood watch in the guard towers lining the perimeter and rarely ventured inside our compound. The ferrets, on the other hand, were in our midst daily and we knew many of them, like Freddie, by name.

"Don't cause me any trouble today, *Leutnant* Foster," Freddie said as he slid into the back seat next to me. *"Fahren Sie bitte,"* he said to the driver and off we went. We turned south out of the headquarters area, then east on the road Harmon and I and the others had marched along on our arrival at Sagan. From there, we turned north, then east again and crossed the railroad tracks. I pretended to be enjoying the sunny weather, but I was working hard to remember every turn, every junction, every bridge. Who knew when knowledge of the local geography might come in handy?

The driver turned the car onto a street lined with shops and stores. There was a butcher shop and a bakery, both of which made my mouth water and my stomach growl. Farther down there was an apothecary and what looked like a tavern. We continued down the street, the river some hundred yards to the east. The car pulled up in front of a store front with a large glass window filled with colorful flowers. Pink, blue, red, white, yellow, copper, orange and purple blooms were jumbled together in different sizes and styles of arrangements. The sweet fragrance of the blossoms spilled out the door onto the sidewalk.

"This looks like the right place," I said to Freddie as he reached my side.

"Come," he said nodding to the door of the shop. We pushed open the door causing a bell to tinkle and walked in, removing our caps.

"Guten Tag," Freddie greeted a stout, middle-aged women who emerged from the back of the store. She had strong hands and graying hair around her temples and she was wearing a worn blue apron. Her smile faded as she

caught sight of me. *"Haben Sie Chrysanthemen?"* Freddie asked.

"Natürlich, mein Herr. Welche Farbe hätten Sie gerne?"

Freddie looked sideways at me and asked "What color?"

"Doesn't matter," I said, smiling at the shop keeper. *"Jede Farbe wird gut."*

The woman cocked her head, a puzzled expression on her face. *"Jede Farbe?"*

"Ja, bitte," Freddie replied.

The poor woman asked another question and Freddie again turned to me. "How many?"

I looked at the woman and then at Freddie. "How many does she have?"

"Wie viele haben Sie?" Freddie asked.

"Ein Moment," she replied and wiping her hands on her apron, bustled into the back of the store. We stood silently for a moment and I realized this was my first visit in a town since our dinner with Louie. That seemed months ago. *"Wir haben achtzehn Chrysanthemen, mein Herr,"* the returning shopkeeper said with a smile.

"Eighteen. She has eighteen."

"Buy them all," I advised. "I have no idea how much powder we can get from one flower. We might as well get all we can."

Freddie translated my instructions to the lady and her smile broadened. I suspected our purchase would be the biggest single transaction of her career. I couldn't imagine people walked in every day and purchased her entire stock of chrysanthemums. The shopkeeper and Freddie continued to converse, but at a pace I could not follow. After a moment, she turned and again disappeared into the back of the store. "Come," Freddie said pulling me along by my elbow.

We could each carry four plants at a time without damaging them. We took them back through the shop and set them at the trunk of the car. We left the loading to our driver and went back for more. I carried the last four out while Freddie arranged payment with the shop keeper.

The driver and I were taking a smoke break by the time Freddie emerged with a smile on his face and a bouquet in his hand. "She gave us these for the *Kommandant*," he laughed. "And she said to come back anytime."

"So now you have a lady friend in town," I teased.

He looked at me and grinned. "It's a good thing he doesn't speak English," he nodded at the driver and glanced at his watch. "Time for an early lunch!" Freddie bought me the best lunch I'd had since leaving Bassingbourn--and the best one I'd have for quite a long time to come.

"Freddie," I asked as I munched on a tasty sausage, "do you mind if I take one of these back to my friend Berly?"

He thought for a moment then nodded. "Yes, but you must be discreet." He spoke to the lunch counter cook who shifted his stare between Freddie and me, and then nodded. He turned back to his grill and a few moments later handed Freddie a fat sausage wrapped in brown paper. Freddie left some coins on the counter and we headed back to camp.

Freddie escorted me back through the gate and turned me loose into the compound. The chow line was snaking between the huts and I wandered along it until I found Harmon, mess tin in hand. "Hey, pal," I said from behind him, "you need to report to the *Kommandant*'s office. You've got a telephone call."

"Who from?" he said without turning to look at me.

"Hitler. He wants some advice on strategy."

"I'm pretty busy right now," Harmon said, stretching his arms out to his side. "What is it he wants to know?"

"Well, apparently things aren't going so well in Italy and he wants to know how to make the Italians fight harder."

"Turn them around so they're facing the Germans. That ought to do the trick!" Harmon answered, shaking his hand.

"No, but I really do need your opinion on something over here," I said jerking my head toward Hut 112. "It'll be worth giving up your place. Promise." Harmon reluctantly stepped out of line and followed me back to our barracks.

We sat on the barracks' wooden steps and I reached in my pocket and pulled out the paper-wrapped sausage. "This is better than anything you're going to get from that line!" I smiled. Harmon unwrapped the wiener and took a bite, a stream of juice trickling down his chin.

"Oh, oh," he moaned. "This is better than sex! Well, almost. Where'd you get this?"

I explained my little excursion into Sagan with Freddie and his resulting generosity. Harmon chomped down on the last bite of sausage, a satisfied look on his face, and proceeded to lick his fingers. The sight made me feel pretty good--until I looked up and saw Wilcox watching with a sly smile on his face.

I'd seen a lot during my months at war: violence, cruelty, destruction, death. But I'd never seen anything to compare with Freddie and four other ferrets strolling through the compound carrying our cache of chrysanthemums. The ferrets drew quite a crowd and were the objects of all manner of catcalls, some good-natured, others tinged with anger. I was tempted to join in, until I realized that Freddie and the others were heading toward me.

"Ah, *Leutnant* Foster!" Freddie called out as he closed the gap between us, "here are your flowers."

"My flowers?" Jeffers and Lewallen had poked their heads out the barracks door and were watching with amused grins on their faces.

"Ja! The *Kommandant* sends his compliments and requests you proceed with your insecticide program immediately!"

"Immediately?"

"Ja. As you Americans say, 'right away!'" Freddie and the others tramped into the barracks, down the hallway and entered our room. I followed them to the door.

"Just, uh, put them anywhere," I shrugged as Harmon peered over my shoulder.

The following morning found Harmon and me plucking petals in the ornamental garden our room had become. He dropped them into an empty powdered milk can. Once the petals were dried, it would be my job to grind them into powder, a task for which I was equipped with a simple mortar and pestle.

"You look like some mad scientist," Harmon muttered, glancing up at me.

"You look like a either a homicidal horticulturalist or a hopeless lovelorn who can't decide whether she loves you or not," I retorted. Our playful banter was interrupted by a knock on our door frame.

We looked up to see a medium height, medium build man outfitted in an RAF squadron leader's kit. "Good morning. Lieutenants Foster and Berly, I presume?"

"That's right," I said, setting the mortar and pestle aside.

He stepped past some denuded stems and into the room. "Miles Beauchamp," he said, holding out his hand. He had pale blue eyes and light brown hair and his face was marred by a scar alongside his right eye socket. "I thought I might stop by. David Hastings suggested I pop in for a visit."

"No trouble finding us?" I asked, taking his hand. It was hard, like a rock, but he didn't squeeze when he shook.

"Oh my, no! I could smell your quarters three huts away!" Beauchamp chuckled. "I've heard that each of you has some rather special talents. Lieutenant Berly, I must say you live up to your billing. You look remarkably similar to Dalberg, one of the more aggressive ferrets. And you, Lieutenant Foster, I understand you not only have managed to acquire a new pair of shoes," he looked down at my feet to confirm his reports, "but that you also arranged a tour of the local merchant district." He cocked his head to one side as if waiting for an answer.

"Forgive me, Miles, but why would this interest you?" I asked.

"Ah, yes, well we have established procedures here in the camp," he began cautiously," and Group Captain Walling has delegated certain duties to me." He paused.

"You're the X," Harmon stated.

Beauchamp pursed his lips and nodded. "It seems each of you chaps has some skills that would be useful to our extracurricular efforts. I wondered if you would be interested in joining our band of mischief makers. First, of course, I'm compelled to ask just what on earth you're doing with all these flowers?" A boyish grin tugged at the corner of his mouth.

We spent the next hour plucking chrysanthemum petals and talking. I offered to sketch a map of the town for Miles, but he preferred I describe it to him orally. The danger of being searched and found in possession of a map was too great a risk. After each sentence or two, he would repeat to me what I'd said to make sure he'd heard it correctly. Most of us were familiar with the railroad station since we'd arrived by train, but others, like Miles, had been delivered by truck and didn't know anything about the town or the nearby river. Knowing the topography and landmarks in the area--especially the station and the river--would be advantageous to any soul daring an escape.

"I hear you're something of an escape expert," Harmon ventured after I'd completed my description of downtown Sagan.

"I'm more of an expert at getting recaptured," Miles chuckled again. "I'm afraid I've yet to make good on an escape, to hit a 'home run' as you Yanks say and make it back to England."

"Think you can get out of here?" I asked.

"Oh, we'll get out all right. It's really a question of staying out."

"'We?' How many guys are planning to escape?"

"Oh, a few," Miles's face parted with a Cheshire Cat smile. "A few. Actually, I was hoping you both might help with the effort."

"What kind of help can we offer?" Harmon asked.

"Lieutenant Foster here has shown an ability to barter rather effectively with Sommer. He's one of the more capitalistic of the ferrets. He may be able to provide us some of the more difficult-to-come-*by* items we need." Miles glanced from the flower in his fingers to my eyes. "I'll get you a list if you're willing."

I thought for a moment and then replied, "Glad to help."

"And Lieutenant Berly, since the good Lord has blessed you with certain helpful physical features, here's what I have in mind. . ."

Freddie and I were standing in the warm afternoon sunshine smoking and watching a gang of Russian prisoners dig up the drain from the bath house. Four guards with rifles topped by bayonets continuously shouted at and prodded the prisoners. I felt uneasy watching. The Germans generally treated us civilly even though we were clearly prisoners of war. Their treatment of the Russians was far different. I watched as a Russian took too long between blows of his mattock. He was rewarded with a rifle butt to the shoulder which sent him sprawling in the muck he was helping clean up. The guard leaned over and shouted something that I couldn't understand, his face contorted with anger.

"What did he say, Freddie?"

"He said next time the bastard wanted to take a break it would be a permanent one."

"I'm glad I'm not digging. You and I get along a lot better than that."

"You and I are not barbarians," Freddie replied, spitting a stray piece of tobacco off his tongue.

"Good cigarette?" I asked, knowing the answer.

"American cigarettes are the best, much better than the English. And the French? Merde!"

That was one of the few French words I knew and I laughed, which was hard to do while watching the Russians. They were smelly, unshaved and filthy, but I figured they weren't getting weekly Red Cross packages. Once again I was reminded that luck is relative.

"How's your supply holding up?" I asked Freddie, nodding toward his smoke.

"Getting low," he replied keeping his eyes on the work detail.

"I wondered if you'd like some more."

"That would be very nice," he answered without looking my way.

"Well, you were good enough to get me these shoes and I wondered if you could acquire something else for me."

"Like what?"

"A magnet."

"A magnet?"

"Right."

"Why?"

"Freddie, do you ever gamble? Have you ever played craps?"

From the corner of my eye, I could see Freddie subdue a grin. "You must be very careful, my friend," he advised. "Very careful indeed."

"But can you get me a magnet and maybe some electrical wire?"

"Of course." Freddie and I watched the Russians dig.

A week later, on a cold October morning, Harmon and I waited in the shadows just inside the north end of Hut 109. Instead of his uniform, Harmon was dressed in the tell-tale blue coveralls and cap of a ferret. Don't ask me how Beauchamp had come up with the uniform; he wouldn't tell us. He said it didn't matter and that we didn't need to know.

Miles had sketched out a plan that was so simple it might actually work. It depended on timing and the attentiveness of the compound's guards. "We have a series of watchers all around the compound," Miles had explained to us in an evening session three days after our first meeting. We'd sneaked out of our hut after dark to meet with Miles and some other members of his X committee. The only other member I recognized was Jeffers, from our hut, who'd helped with the sanitation project. We were gathered around a low table, our faces lit by candlelight as the hour was already after "lights out."

"Lieutenant Berly will be positioned here," Miles pointed to a sketch of the compound stretched out on the table in front of him, "between Huts 104 and 109. Lieutenant Foster will assist. Watchers will be here, here and here," he tapped a pencil on the sketch at each "here." "We wait for Dalberg to enter. He's one of the less predictable ferrets, which makes this a bit dicey, but it's also what makes this work. Hugh will be our 'master of ceremonies' so to speak. Once Dalberg's in and past this point here," another tap on the diagram, "Operation Ferret goes into action! All clear so far?" he asked the assembled faces.

Everyone nodded and Miles continued. "Hugh monitors the watchers' signals until Dalberg has rounded the corner here, or until he goes into one of the five huts that can't be easily observed from the gate. The watchers and their relays will have to be on their toes and Hugh, you will have to make a quick decision."

"What do I do, Miles?" I asked.

"Your job is support and assistance. First, you help Don get ready and get into position. Whatever he needs during the first phase of the operation, you'll have to provide. Everyone else will be tied down specifically watching a sector, a particular ferret or the goons. Once Hugh gives the go-ahead, Don, you walk around the east side of Hut 104 and stride briskly toward the compound gate, just like you're Dalberg, head up, but don't make eye contact with anyone. Timing is critical. The guards on the gate have to believe that Dalberg has made his rounds and is on his way back out. That's where our delayers come into play. Paul, this is your assignment."

Paul was a dark-eyed man I hadn't met before, apparently a member of the X committee. He gave a short overview of his band of merry men and how they would distract Dalberg once our surrogate began his way toward the gate. "After all," Paul smiled, "it won't do for both of you to arrive at the gate at the same time, will it?"

"What do you want me to do once I'm outside the gate?" Harmon asked.

"Get out of the camp as quickly as you can. This ruse won't hold up long. Once Dalberg reaches the gate to exit, your lead will be over. The goons will figure something's amiss pretty quickly. If you can get into town, go to the train station and memorize as much of the morning departure schedule as you can: destination, track, time. Train schedules are very important for our future plans."

"Any particular destination?" I asked.

"Everywhere. The more of the schedule you can remember, the better--but don't write anything down."

"How many men are you planning to get out?" I asked, my curiosity piqued.

"Two hundred."

A deafening silence filled the room as I struggled to comprehend the figure. I glanced from Miles's scarred face to Harmon's. "You better work on your memorization skills, pal."

Now here we stood, me just inside peering through the slightly open door, a nervous Harmon looking over my shoulder. Jeffers was just across the way, perched in the window of Hut 105, smoking a pipe. I said a silent prayer for about the twentieth time, beseeching God to make this work and to keep Harmon safe.

Jeffers struck a match and touched it to the bowl of his pipe. "Dalberg's in the compound," I whispered to Harmon. "Get ready." I caught a glimpse of fast-pacing blue pass the opening between Huts 105 and 108. The seconds passed at the same rate as when were kids, waiting to fall asleep on Christmas Eve. Harmon shifted from one foot to the other. I felt the urge to pee, but I couldn't leave him now. I kept watching Jeffers, who was watching the team of watchers. Jeffers continued to puff away on his pipe.

In his window perch, Jeffers removed the pipe from his mouth. "Get ready," I said again, my intense gaze never leaving Jeffers.

"What the hell's going on in here?" I turned to find Wilcox staring open-mouthed at me and the blue-suited Harmon. Jeffers slapped the bowl of his pipe against his hand, knocking out a wad of burned tobacco.

"Go," I said quietly, giving Harmon a gentle nudge. "Good luck!" And he went out the door. I wheeled on Wilcox.

"I shoulda known you were up to no good," he sneered. "First you give away performance specs on our airplanes, then you smuggle a German into our midst! What are you doing, Foster?"

"Shut up, Wilcox," I said, keeping my voice as quiet as possible. "Don't say another word." I glanced back at Jeffers. He was repacking his pipe. I didn't have to start worrying about Harmon until Jeffers lit the pipe again--that was the signal that Dalberg was on the way back toward the gate. But I did have to worry about Wilcox, who was advancing on me.

"I want some answers, you traitor! I'm going to turn your ass in! You're going to get what's coming to you!"

That's when I had my brilliant idea. "Okay, you little prick," I snarled. "Let's take it outside right now!" I reached behind me and pushed the door open. I looked at Wilcox, bowed slightly and swept my arm toward the now open doorway.

Wilcox smiled nervously and said, "With pleasure." What an idiot! As soon as his foot hit the top step, I was on him, leaping on his shoulders and toppling him into the dirt! Jeffers mouth fell open as I laid into Wilcox's head with both fists. It was all he could do to resume his vigilance. Wilcox struggled to turn over, thrashing like a fish on a line. I kept slapping him about the face and ears, using my open hands now to keep from inflicting too much damage on either of us. My tactic was working, because within seconds, our little altercation had attracted a small crowd of prisoners. When you don't have anything to do, anywhere to be or much to eat, a little diversion can be a pleasant break from monotony.

My arms were getting pretty tired by the time I heard the first whistles, but I was still enjoying myself. I picked up a handful of dirt and threw it in Wilcox's face. He was now sputtering, mad as a thirsty drunk at a temperance rally. We were now encircled by a crowd of prisoners, many of them yelling at us, some urging us to fight harder, others urging us to stop. The circle parted and I heard an accented voice.

"No fighting! No fighting!" I looked up into the face of the ferret Dalberg and smiled to myself.

It took several minutes for Dalberg and two of the other ferrets to calm things down. Every time it seemed that things had finally come to a peaceful conclusion, I would throw some kerosene on the flickering embers of Wilcox's suspicions. I lunged at him a couple of times and made threats of further bodily harm. Wilcox, his face red from my repeated slaps, responded with a cold stare and clenched jaw. In front of the Germans, he really couldn't say much. I mean, if you suspect the home team has infiltrated a spy into your midst, who are you going to tell, right? I suspected Wilcox was biding his time until he could gain an audience with Group Captain Walling. I'd have to make sure I got there first.

Wilcox and I had occupied Dalberg for around ten minutes when I finally dusted myself off and took my leave of Wilcox. I figured that ought to gain some valuable head start time for Harmon. I learned later that sometimes fighters were thrown into the cooler, the solitary confinement building, but usually only if somebody got hurt pretty badly. After all, the Germans didn't really care if the Allies fought with each other. In a way, that was to their advantage. If we were fighting amongst ourselves, it would be harder to work together to create bigger problems for our hosts.

You never know what rumors to believe in wartime. We heard later that the poor sack working the compound gate on the day Harmon walked right through it was transferred to the eastern front so he could enjoy a proper winter.

Harmon's vacation lasted two hours. He was apprehended at the train station, doing exactly what Miles had charged him to do. As I think I've mentioned before, Harmon's a pretty bright guy. He was able not only to read and memorize a large portion of the train departure schedule, but was able to keep it memorized for the thirty days he was the *Kommandant*'s guest in the cooler.

"That was a shrewd move, starting that fight," Miles said, giving me an admiring grin. We were sharing tea in his hut. I had delivered the magnet and about twenty feet of electrical wire that Freddie had provided me.

"Thanks. It just came to me. Wilcox has been a pain in the ass ever since our train ride out here."

"I'll speak to the Old Man. We'll deal with Wilcox. At any rate," Miles resumed, "good work on both the diversion and on obtaining these little presents." He patted the cloth bag containing the magnet and the wire.

"What are you going to do with that?" I asked, curiosity finally getting the best of me.

"We're making compasses. One for every escapee."

"That's a lot of compasses," I whistled. "You got enough blue suits for two hundred men, with compasses of course, to simply stroll through the front gate?"

Miles chuckled. "I'm afraid that little trick isn't going to work again. Jeffers tells me that every ferret and goon who enters the compound now has to show his papers to get back out."

"Seriously, Miles, how are you going to get two hundred guys out of here?"

"Do you like history?"

"I'm not much of a scholar," I replied.

"There's an interesting chapter from your American Civil War known as the 'Underground Railroad.' It wasn't an actual railroad line below ground, but more of a network of safe points to which runaway slaves could be routed until they reached freedom."

"You're building an underground railroad?"

Miles smiled.

Rations were pretty slim in camp. The Germans provided a meager portion which we supplemented from the Red Cross parcels. In the cooler, you didn't get the supplement, at least not officially. One of the things I came to really appreciate about Miles was that, stern taskmaster though he was, he was also very careful to look out for those who undertook risks on behalf of his X organization. Rations for the guards and ferrets were only marginally better than our own, but without the added largesse from Red Cross parcels. That made some guards, like Freddie, willing to take on small jobs for under-the-table compensation. Miles's organization dealt with several such willing souls who could do things we couldn't, like smuggle extra food into the cooler. When Harmon finally got out of the cooler in late October, he had lost only a couple of pounds, but he still retained the outbound train schedule for Sagan.

Our camp was located in what, before the war, had been western Poland. The weather here was delightful--for about two weeks every summer. I'm exaggerating. By early December, the days had grown depressingly short. Worse, the temperatures had fallen and the wet season had arrived. At one stretch, I counted fifteen straight days without sunshine. Cold rain was typical and as Christmas neared, it began to snow often.

We began every morning with *Apel*, a formal roll call in which all prisoners were assembled in ranks at the front of the compound. Names were checked and the Germans would, of course, count us and then count us again. If anybody was too sick to stand in the ranks, one of the ferrets would have to go into the barracks and account for him.

Imagine standing in the twenty-degree darkness, wearing a wool sweater, watch cap and not much else. The cold made a tough situation more difficult and added to the boredom and misery. The best way to stay sane was to work, and there was no shortage of work that Christmas season! A third of the camp, many without knowing it, was working to support Miles's titanic escape machine. Forgers were forging, snoopers were snooping, scroungers were scrounging. You could have written a "Twelve Days of Christmas" song about all the activity going on. Then there were those whose efforts were more focused on individual survival than group rebellion. These guys were working hard to scrounge enough to eat or enough fuel to keep the stove in their hut going through the long, cold, boring winter nights.

Harmon and I were strolling the compound on a rare sunny December afternoon, attempting to stay out of the mud and the puddles. Because we prisoners had little to do, officially at least, we tended to stay outdoors when the weather allowed. As you can imagine, a few thousand pairs of feet continually treading across the same ground pretty much prevented any grass from surviving. As a result, the inhabitants of most huts spent a fair amount of time sweeping the floors clean of the mud and dirt accumulated the previous day. Of course, that same mud was always caking on our shoes, adding to their wear and tear.

We'd rounded the corner of Hut 101 at the northeast corner of the compound and turned west along the fence separating our barracks from the cooler, sick quarters and storage area. I nudged Harmon and said,

"There's your old home," nodding toward the cooler. "I'll bet you miss it."

He was trying to pull his head down to his shoulders, his hands jammed into the pockets of his trousers, in a futile effort to avoid a cold north wind whipping between the wooden buildings. "It wasn't all bad," he gave me a sideways glance. "I didn't have to put up with your idle chatter all day!" He attempted a smile, but his chattering teeth defeated him. It was mid-afternoon. The sun, making a rare appearance, was already hanging just above the fir trees to the southwest.

"How did you pass the time?" I asked, more serious this time.

Harmon looked down and sidestepped a mud puddle. "I reread the books I could remember. I'd go back over some Shakespeare. I couldn't really remember the verse, but I could walk back through the story. I'd think about what I'm going to do after the war."

"Yeah? Like what?"

"Law school, the General Assembly, Congress, Senate. . . who knows?"

"You really want to go into politics?"

"Family business," he smiled without looking at me. "Besides, I think I can do a hell of a lot better job on foreign affairs than my father and his cronies. Who would have believed we'd be back fighting the Germans just twenty years after the 'War to End all Wars'? We've got to do better after this one. We've gotten too good at slaughter. I doubt the world could survive another war like this."

"How would your father feel about that?"

"He'd welcome it. He'd be very supportive. He'd help me campaign, help me raise money." Harmon paused. "And he'd expect to call the shots."

"Yeah? How would that work out?"

"Not very well. Father and his clique made some bad decisions. If I do get into the family business, it will be on my own terms."

I wanted to ask him how he'd deal with the post-war world, assuming of course that the good guys prevailed, but we turned the corner and ran right into Miles Beauchamp. "Hello, chaps!" Miles grinned, his ears and nose red from the cold. He fell in with us and we walked between Huts 104 and 105, the wind now to our backs. When we got to the end of the building, we huddled against the leeward side of Hut 104, hidden from the main gate. Miles passed around cigarettes. They were a challenge to light in the wind, but we persevered and soon achieved success.

"Lieutenant Foster," Miles began, fixing me with a steady gaze, "I wonder if you could assist with another little acquisition?" I'd figured Miles's bumping into us was by design. He seemed like a good sort, but he was all business. We'd heard some rumors in the camp that he had been on the receiving end of some nasty treatment from the *SS* and that he intended to even the score.

"How can I help you, Squadron Leader?" I replied formally.

"Well, you did such a swell job on getting that magnet and wire that we thought perhaps you could help us with a very important item that is in short supply around here. Lieutenant Berly here," Miles tipped his head toward Harmon, "provided us with extraordinarily valuable information about the railway schedule. Remarkable, really, the level of detail he was able to retain during his stint in the cooler."

"You should get him to recite Shakespeare for you," I smiled as the wind swept away the smoke from our cigarettes. Harmon rolled his eyes. "What is it you need, Miles?" I asked.

"A camera."

"To take pictures with?"

"Well, yes, that would be the general idea."

"Pictures of what?"

"Ah, that's probably best left unsaid. Can you get one?"

"And film too, I suppose?"

"Well, naturally," Miles chuckled.

"Black and white or color?" Harmon rolled his eyes again.

Miles laughed, "Oh, black and white, yes, black and white. Color's too expensive. It'll never catch on." His laugh sailed away with the wind and his earnest expression reappeared. "Can you do it, Bob? It's of critical importance to our little project."

I took a long drag on my smoke. My brain had kicked into high gear, working out just how in the devil's name I was going to come up with a camera, much less film, in a place like this. I looked Miles in the eye and answered, "I'll see what I can do."

"Freddie," I asked the next day as we surveyed the outside corner of the bath house, "how would one obtain a camera and some film?" It was misting rain, the temperature slightly warmer than the previous day and the wind gone. The fly problem, which had posed a sanitation threat during the late summer when Harmon and I arrived, had been resolved. The drain had been replaced and after the careful application of our homemade chrysanthemum insecticide, the fly population had gradually diminished to zero. I had been hailed as something of a genius for solving the fly problem and had graciously accepted the credit. Of course the Russian prisoners had done the real work of replacing the collapsed drain line and the cold weather had done a lot more to rid us of flies than any crushed flower petals.

After our little deal for the magnets and wire, Freddie possessed an abundant supply of cigarettes, one of which now dangled from the corner of his mouth. "Why would you want a camera?" he asked without looking at me. He always seemed to respond to my questions without looking at me.

"To take pictures."

"Why do you want to take pictures?"

"Well, Freddie, my friend, someday after the Allies win this war and I go back to North Carolina and I meet the perfect woman and she marries me and we have a half dozen children, one day one of the boys is going to crawl up in my lap and ask me, 'Dad, what did you do during the war?'"

"What if you have all girls?"

"It doesn't matter! One of them is going to ask me, 'What did you do during the war?' and I'm going to say 'I bombed the hell out of Germany until I got shot down and met this really swell guy Freddie,' and then I'm going to get out a shoe box full of photographs and dig around in it until I find a picture of the ugliest guard at Sagan and then I'm going to say 'and here's his picture!'" Freddie started to laugh and finally looked at me, shaking his head.

"You'll want film, too, I suppose?"

"Of course, but only black and white; color will never catch on."

Freddie began walking around the south end of the bath house and I trailed along behind him holding my breath, hoping my request wouldn't arouse any suspicions as to the real purpose for a camera. He stopped, the building shielding us from view. "Such a request would be difficult and would be accompanied by some risk on my part. The price would be much higher than our last transaction." The last transaction had reduced me to begging for cigarettes for a month. I didn't care to go through that again, but I figured Miles wouldn't have come to me if he wasn't willing to pay a price. Besides, beggars can't be choosers.

"I understand," I said and I waited for his proposal.

Freddie studied the gray sky for a moment then looked around. No one was out and the windows of all the huts were shut against the cold rain. "Six cans of meat," he said.

"Six cans! It would take me until summer to come up with that much. Besides, I'd starve to death. Who'd show the pictures to my children? Four cans!" I countered.

Freddie watched my desperate face, looking for some sign of my resolution. He finally spoke, "Five," he said and turned away. "Three now, two on delivery."

"Two now, three on delivery," I responded and then waited silently, adrenaline coursing through my body. I kicked myself for continuing to push when I had reached an acceptable deal. Still, it was important for Freddie to believe he was doing this for me, one guy, not a whole committee of would-be escapees with the resources to come up with meat by the case if need be.

"Agreed," he said after about fifteen minutes. Okay, it was more like fifteen seconds, but it sure felt like a long time. "Let me know when you have the meat." Freddie flicked his cigarette butt into the mud and strode away. I exhaled deeply and smiled. Miles was going to be very pleased.

It was still dark when we fell in for *Apel* on Christmas morning. There was snow on the ground but it was still frozen, so we were spared standing in mud. The air was still, but frigid and we stamped our feet in a losing battle to stay warm.

Group Captain Walling took his place at the head of the formation and saluted the camp adjutant, Hauptman Handelmann, who I noted was bundled in a very warm-looking greatcoat. About that time, who should march through the gate but the *Kommandant* himself, *Oberst* von Linden. Walling called us all to attention and suddenly, there was no more stamping in the ranks. Walling popped up one of those open-handed British salutes and von Linden saluted back, a real military salute, not that 'Heil Hitler' straight-arm crap.

"At ease!" Walling commanded and then stepped to the left of the *Kommandant* and faced us.

"Good morning and Merry Christmas," von Linden began in a voice just loud enough for us to hear. "I am sure you would rather be with your families on this sacred day, as would your guards. Let us pray that this will be the last Christmas of war and that peace will prevail in the New

Year. We will be issuing extra Red Cross parcels in commemoration of the day. Let us please work together to make this a peaceful and quiet day." With that, he turned his head and nodded to Walling. The Group Captain resumed his position at the head of our formation and called, "Attention!" over his shoulder. He saluted von Linden who then extended his right hand. Walling shook it and the *Kommandant* marched back through the gate, followed by Handelmann and a couple of the ferrets. Must be nice, I thought, to come and go as you please.

Walling about-faced and put us back at ease. "Flight Lieutenant Dempsey will have the details on the Red Cross distribution. The lads in Hut 121 have been at work on a little holiday gift for all of us. They will be dispensing it from Hut 102 at 1200 hours. All are invited to partake. Merry Christmas!" With that, Walling dismissed us and we fled back inside, out of the extreme cold and back into the regular cold of our barracks.

Harmon and I were waiting in a long line that snaked through the camp, ending inside Hut 102, where Walling kept his headquarters. It was still cold, but at least now the sun was high in the deep-blue December sky. Each man had gotten his Christmas Red Cross parcel that morning, so there was a lot of bartering going on all over the compound. The guys who seemed to make out the best in these circumstances were the ones who didn't smoke. Cigarettes, as I'd learned with Freddie, were the preferred medium of exchange and a guy who didn't have to hold any back for personal use had more buying power. Of course we pooled most of the food we got, turning it over to the cooks who were then able to augment the meager rations provided by our hosts. One thing I wouldn't be contributing from this particular package was the one-pound can of Spam included in my parcel. It was earmarked for Miles's camera project, so I had shoved it in the side pocket of my jacket.

"Keep your eyes peeled for Miles," I instructed Harmon, "or for David. With all these parcels on the market, now's the logical time to collect enough to make Freddie's down payment. I'll need your can too." Harmon was the only guy in camp besides Miles who knew about Freddie and the camera.

"What's that in your pocket?" came a sniveling, small voice from behind me. "Looks like somebody's hoarding and not sharing for the good of all." It was Wilcox.

"Stuff it, pencil neck!" I said without looking at him. Maybe if I ignored him, he'd disappear. He didn't.

"You two only care about yourselves, don't you? We may be stuck in a German POW camp, boys," he lectured self-righteously, "but there will be consequences once the forces of good triumph over the forces of evil!" I kid you not; that's what he said: "forces of good."

Harmon turned to look at our accuser. "Back off, Wilcox. We're on a mission from President Roosevelt. It's 'hush-hush.' Can't talk about it and it's better for you if you don't either."

"Is that a threat, 'Lieutenant Berly'? I'll add that to my list of infractions. You may be able to pull the wool over the British officers, but not Ross Wilcox!"

Harmon stepped toward Wilcox, causing him to flinch, but I grabbed him and pulled him back in line. "Don't bother with him," I mumbled, "he isn't worth the trouble." It seemed like good advice at the time.

Word quickly filtered down the line that our Christmas gift was a holiday libation concocted from raisins. Now I hate wrinkled fruit; don't like raisins, prunes or anything else that looks all puckered-up and smells like Grandma. Harmon convinced me to brave the cold and wait it out, suggesting that we'd likely find one of Miles's guys in the headquarters hut. As usual, he proved to be right.

"Happy Christmas!" Miles Beauchamp smiled once we'd reached the distribution point for the raisin wine. We each held our cups as the wine was dispensed from a large clay pot.

"Merry Christmas," I replied, lifting my cup toward Miles. "Peace on earth and victory in '44!" I took a drink. It tasted awful, but was still the stiffest and best drink I'd had in more than four months. "Say, Miles," I said pulling him over into a corner of the small building. Harmon followed, shielding us from Wilcox's beady, prying eyes. "We've pulled our cans of Spam out for our little transaction. I need three more to get your camera."

"And three more you shall have, Bob," he smiled, "by the end of today. It will be delivered after dark, so be ready for it. I suggest that when you give Freddie the first two cans you let him know you already have the rest. That may motivate him to move more quickly." I nodded. "The sooner we get the camera and film, the sooner we get to work. We still have a lot to do and our time is dwindling."

"Have you set a date?" Harmon asked quietly as some of the boys in the wine line broke into a ragged rendition of "God Rest Ye Merry Gentlemen."

"There's a no moon period in late March. That's our target. Our railroad work is progressing with the help of some rather clever engineering and resourceful scroungers like Bob here," Miles nodded my way, his light blue eyes twinkling with mischief. "I expect we'll begin assigning numbers in a fortnight. That will get the lads excited and will help concentrate effort so we can reach our work targets."

Miles never told me, or Harmon either, more than he felt we needed to know. He didn't elaborate on what he meant by "work targets" and we knew better than to ask. There was no point in carrying a lot of extra information around in our heads, information that could prove dangerous to everyone if we were ever questioned. My mission right now was to secure that camera and film. I trusted that if I did my job and took care of Miles, he'd take care of me.

Our British allies observed Boxing Day on December 26. I had no idea what that was, but Jeffers explained it was the day when the English would give gifts to their servants. I asked if he was giving gifts to the ferrets. He thought that was a "jolly good" jest. I actually did give a "gift" of sorts to Freddie that day: two cans of meat, our down payment for something far more valuable. And, as Miles had suggested, I let him know that I could deliver the balance of our payment as soon as he delivered the goods.

The ferrets came a week later, but not for gifts. At about 1000 hours, watchers all over the compound sounded their alarms. Alarms were audible and visual, ranging from the way Jeffers held his pipe to the doffing of a cap or the rhythmic tapping of a stick of wood against the side of a hut. A blue-suited flood of ferrets flowed through the main gate and surged all over the camp, paying particular attention to Huts 104 and 105. The sun was out for a second straight day, so Harmon and I were walking in the yard enjoying a little exercise. We could hear rustling and rattling from inside both huts as their occupants came stumbling out, being herded by the ferrets. I looked around for Freddie, but didn't see him.

"Hope they haven't found Miles's railroad," Harmon muttered to me from the side of his mouth.

"Maybe they're just looking for their Christmas presents," I replied.

After a few minutes, the ferrets came tumbling out of the two huts. They stood around in a loose huddle for a couple of minutes and then, like a football team breaking for the line of scrimmage, ran at top speed to Hut 106. I guess they repeated whatever they had done earlier in 104 and 105.

"Sending signals, Foster?" It was Wilcox again.

"I swear, Wilcox," I said turning to face the little jerk, "if you don't buzz off, I'm going to box your ears again! That didn't turn out so well for you last time, remember?"

"Yeah, big man? You just try it! You'll get to spend some time in the cooler!"

"Yeah, well at least I wouldn't have to look at your weasel face and listen to you whine like a girl!" I spat back. This time it was Harmon who pulled *me* away.

"Remember your own advice," he counseled, tugging me by the elbow and turning back toward our hut.

We stepped up the two wooden steps and entered Hut 112. Jeffers was waiting at the door for us. Without saying a word, he raised his bushy eyebrows, nodded toward our room and held up one finger. It seems we had a visitor. I motioned for Harmon to wait with Jeffers and I walked down the corridor alone. I poked my head around the door post and sure enough, there sat Freddie on the bottom bunk, flipping through a ragged copy of *Life* magazine.

"I didn't know you could read," I said.

"I'm only looking at the pictures," he replied without looking up. "Speaking of pictures," he reached over and patted a leather knapsack sitting beside him on the bunk, "I brought you something."

I sat down beside Freddie and loosened the straps on the bag. I reached inside and carefully removed a small Franka camera and four foil-wrapped rolls of film. I was tempted to load the camera and take Freddie's picture right then and there. That would further the ruse and also provide some compelling coercive material should we ever need to blackmail our supplier. I decided instead that would waste time and film. "Very nice," I said, looking up from the camera.

"And now, you have something for me to put back in the pack?"

I stood back up and made quite a show of looking down the corridor in both directions. Even though Jeffers knew I was working for Miles and Harmon knew exactly what I was up to, I thought the charade would help put Freddie at ease. I pulled myself back in the room and dropped to my hands and knees. I ducked under the bunk and pulled out a low wooden crate we had fashioned into a lockable storage bin. I quickly snapped the box open and pulled out two cans of Spam and a tin of British meat roll. I stuffed all three cans into the knapsack and retied the straps.

No sooner had I done so than Freddie was on his feet, the bag slung up and over his left shoulder. "A pleasure doing business with you, *Leutnant* Foster," he said with a thin smile.

Although Group Captain Walling made his headquarters, such as it was, in Hut 102, you'd rarely find Miles there. He seemed to move like a phantom all over the compound. You never knew where he'd show up next--or what he'd ask you to do. But, as I mentioned before, once you did something for Miles, he was as loyal as a dog to his bone. I'd been out scavenging on a frigid, late January afternoon, attempting, without success, to find some additional electrical wire. Although Miles never said directly, I surmised that he needed it to help run lights through the tunnel.

I walked back into Hut 112 and immediately felt the heat from the stove. Even though its output was meager, it was a welcome relief from the cold outside. Jeffers and Lewallen were perched on crates, playing some kind of card game.

"Ah, he returns," Jeffers said, laying a queen face up on the table. "Miles wishes to see you."

"Where?" I asked, not too keen on going back outside.

"119. He said to go around back."

Around back was always the south side of any building as the north entrances were more visible from the main gate. I jammed my hands back down in my pockets and wheeled back around; do not pass GO, do not collect $200! A sharp wind bit at my nose and ears and caused my eyes to water as I covered the few yards to Hut 119. I didn't bother to knock; I just hopped up the steps and pushed through the door with my head bowed against the cold. I barged in and found myself right in the middle of five men who froze at the sight of me. It was as though I had caught them in the act, of what I don't know, but caught nonetheless.

"Oh, it's you, Bob!" Miles beamed once he recognized the intruder. He made quick introductions all around. I knew most of the guys by sight, though I'd never had a formal introduction to Hume, Willby or Dundalk. David Hastings and Miles rounded out the group. "I was just telling the lads here what a grand job you've been doing helping us acquire things."

"Happy to be of help," I replied. I figured I was about to be asked to acquire something else; maybe a Nazi staff car or a transport plane, you know, something simple like that.

"We're continuing to make good progress on our little project," Miles continued, "thanks in part to you and Lieutenant Berly. You've both proven most resourceful." I could feel another request coming on and I braced myself to keep an impassive face. "Come sit down," Miles indicated a spot on the low bunk next to the stove. Hastings slid over to make room for me. "Tea?" Miles asked. Now I know how the English like their tea. They offer it like we Americans offer coffee. I also knew how scarce it was in camp and I figured that none of these guys would be offended if I turned it down.

"No, thanks," I said.

Miles pulled a crate over in front of me and straddled it. "Bob, we're making final plans. We're going out during the no moon period in late March. We've still a few details to work out, one of which is assigning numbers in the queue."

"The queue?"

"That's the order in which men will leave," Hastings clarified. "Spots in the queue are allotted based on one's contributions to the overall effort and one's prospects for a successful escape. Detailed knowledge of Germany, say from business contacts before the war, or linguistic skills, that sort of thing enhances the likelihood of hitting a home run."

"A home run?"

"Yes, making it all the way back to England." I thought of Christy.

Miles looked me in the eye and said, "Your number is 95; about halfway along the queue. We wouldn't be nearly as far along without the electrical wire you supplied and without the camera, well," Miles shrugged, "we'd have no good identity papers or passports at all."

"What about Berly?" I asked. "What's his number?" Harmon had contributed invaluable information by memorizing the schedules for trains departing Sagan. He'd also become a member of Hastings' intelligence section, assisting with the monitoring of the guards and ferrets.

"He'll be number 52. We feel his language ability gives him a bit of a leg up."

I'd been wrong about the meeting. Miles didn't ask me to scrounge anything else.

"I'm not going without you," Harmon spoke quietly. It was past lights out and most of the guys in our hut were already asleep.

"I'll be right behind you," I argued.

"You'll be forty-something people behind me! No telling how much time will be between us."

"Well, you could just have a cup of coffee at the train station or something and wait on me to come along," I smiled in the dark.

"Sure. Why don't I just wait for you by the fence?"

We'd been arguing all afternoon. Harmon was adamant that we should go out as a pair, that his limited knowledge of German would offset my lack thereof and that together we'd have a better chance at a successful escape. He said he was going to ask Miles to assign us consecutive numbers. "After all the stuff you've turned up, he'll give us numbers together. I'm sure he will," Harmon said.

"I'm afraid it would mean backing you up a bit, Don," Miles replied. We were standing in the sun, trying with little success to soak up some warmth on another cold day. January had given way to February, but it was still bitter cold at Sagan. Harmon and I had come across Miles behind the camp theater. He'd been standing alone, staring off into the distant fir trees. I'd wanted to leave him to his meditations, but Harmon insisted this was the perfect time to make his request, and so he had.

"Presently you're number. . .what was it again?" Miles asked.

"Fifty-two and Bob's 95. As resourceful as he is," here I was gratified to see Miles nod his head in agreement, "he'll be lost on his own outside this wire. Together we both have a better chance of making it." I always found it interesting that in a camp where practically the entire population was engaged in ways great and small in planning the biggest escape ever attempted, no one ever uttered the word "escape." Or "tunnel" either.

Miles rubbed his chin for a moment, staring into Harmon's face. Harmon returned the stare without flinching. "Right," Miles said finally, "let me see what can be done." With that, he turned back toward the forest and was again lost in his thoughts.

A few days later, Harmon and I attended a performance of Shakespeare's *Two Gentlemen of Verona* at the theater. Understanding that men must have something to do or they will become disruptive, the *Kommandant*'s staff had worked with Group Captain Walling to provide some outlets for the prisoners' energy and creativity. They believed cultural outlets such as the theater would dampen the men's enthusiasm for escapes and other mischief. The prisoners, the majority of whom were British, seemed quite happy to stage plays, present lectures and perform concerts. All the while they were busy digging, stealing, forging, scrounging and planning mischief on a scale that would eventually impress even their captors.

Growing up, we'd never been to many plays. We lived far enough out of town that entertainments were a rare treat. I remember going one time with a group from my school to a play performed by some of the students at the university, but I couldn't tell you what it was about and I'd never been much of a Shakespeare fan. I found his verse hard to muddle through and that always caused me to lose interest in the plot.

Our British allies seemed to have a knack for theater. I was once again impressed by the ingenuity with which they set about fashioning costumes, sets and even musical instruments from the barest resources. They had obviously worked hard on the production. I'm no expert, but seeing our comrades performing Shakespeare on stage brought the story to life. I enjoyed seeing ugly guys like Jeffers dressed up as dames, speaking in high falsetto voices and really hamming it up. Stage hands hoisted and replaced the back drops with wires, ropes and pulleys just as I imagine they would in a real theater. Even though it was Shakespeare, it sure beat sitting around in the cold, dark barracks reading the same book for the umpteenth time!

After the show ended and the cast was rewarded with a boisterous ovation, David Hastings edged his way through the exiting crowd and fell into step with Harmon and me. "Miles asked me to give you a message," he said. "Numbers 81 and 82," he offered with a tight smile. Then he nodded his head, broke away from us and proceeded toward Hut 119.

"Thanks," I said to Harmon. He just smiled.

I don't know if the Germans have their own version of Ground Hog Day and if they do what the little bastard predicted for 1944, but by mid-March winter still clinched Sagan in an icy grasp. We'd have snow one day, sun the next and mud everywhere the day after that. Then we'd start the cycle again. The full moon on Friday the 10th was the brightest I ever remember seeing. The night sky was cold and clear and the moonshine reflected off of the snowy ground. The guards in their towers could have gone without their searchlights it was so bright. While anyone outside after curfew was subject to being shot, there were still usually some brave--or foolhardy--souls who would venture between huts at night. But not during this full moon! The moon's illumination drowned out many of the usual shadowy nooks and crannies. We all huddled beneath our blankets, trying vainly to stay warm as we waited for the dark of the moon.

Harmon and I were standing just inside a blacked-out Hut 105, watching the front gate from a crack in the door. Harmon had relieved a guy named Thorne who had scampered through the dark and into Hut 104. For the two hundred of us with escape numbers, Hut 104 was to be our last address inside *Stalag Luft* III. From there, we would descend into the tunnel, make our way along Miles's underground railroad, pass under the very fence we were now watching and then dodge tree roots as we surfaced in the shelter of the forest to the north of the compound. Some of us, if we were lucky, might make it all the way home. The rest of us, well, at least we'd keep the Germans busy for a while.

Harmon's job was to watch the front gate. If it opened, he'd flash a small penlight, a light for which a watcher in 104 was straining his eyes. If any ferrets came through that gate tonight, the escape would lock down; every man would freeze in place until the danger passed. If it passed. Harmon was also watching for any unusual patrols outside the wire. Typically, the German guards and their snarling shepherd dogs walked outside the perimeter fence. If they varied their routines, Harmon had a signal ready for that too.

Friday, March 24 had been the longest day of our captivity. I felt like a kid's balloon, never more than a moment from popping from excitement and anticipation. We'd tried to carry on as if it was just another boring, tedious, routine day. For the two hundred men with numbers and all those who had minor but critical roles to play in supporting the escape, it was anything but. This was one of the few early spring days in my life when I wasn't happy to note that the daylight hours were getting longer. When darkness finally descended on the camp, it set in motion a carefully planned choreography of movement. Each man involved had specific tasks to perform at specific places and at specific times. You couldn't just march two hundred men through the camp and have them all traipse up to Hut 104 and disappear inside. And you couldn't very well stage a dress rehearsal either. The ferrets had so far been unable to uncover evidence of the tunnel, but that didn't mean they weren't trying. And it didn't mean they were stupid.

I was lucky to be traveling tonight with Harmon Roberts III. He was resourceful, could speak passable though not conversational German, and he was brave. He was also smart, not likely to make a foolhardy decision. Since he'd prevailed on Miles to let us escape together, I'd gotten a much lower escape number than if I'd been leaving by myself.

It had been dark for quite a while. The bright white searchlights from the guard towers swept methodically across the compound, reflecting off the white-washed buildings and the snow that still lingered in shaded spots. I held my watch up when one of the searchlights momentarily splashed against Hut 105: 2155 hours. We were due to be relieved in five minutes. Once our relief took our positions, we'd time our dash across the few yards between us and Hut 104 and duck inside. Once in, Harmon's watcher duties were satisfied for the night. My pre-departure duty was chief scrounger. If anything was needed at the last minute, I would be responsible for finding it--and finding it fast enough to keep everybody moving on schedule.

Over the past three weeks as we'd prepared for this night, I'd developed a fuller appreciation for Miles Beauchamp and his incredible organization. Each escapee had a new identity with official papers sealed with official stamps. Thanks to Harmon's superb feat of intelligence gathering, those of us lucky enough to travel by rail held tickets on trains that would soon be chugging through the Sagan station. We had clothes that matched our new identities. Harmon and I, for example, were Czech workers on leave from one of the construction projects underway here at *Stalag Luft* III. Miles and his mischief-makers had provided us a cover that would explain why our German language skills were less than fluent.

"Cheerio, chaps." It was Abbott, Harmon's relief. Harmon pulled the door closed as the searchlight passed over us again. Then, without hesitation, he pushed the door open and pulling me along, hopped down the steps. We pressed our backs against the east side of the building, waiting for the right moment to make our last dash to 104. A bright shaft of light passed over our heads, lighting up our destination and then passing on.

"Now," Harmon said softly. We ran to 104's south end and jumped up the two wooden steps, the door swinging open from the inside as we reached it. Just as quickly, it closed behind us. We knew immediately that something was wrong; the hut was packed with men in various mufti, standing or sitting in every available space.

"What's wrong?" I whispered to no one in particular. The lights were out, of course, to facilitate the arrivals such as Harmon and I had just completed. My eyes hadn't yet adjusted to the darkness after the glare of the searchlights.

"Is that you, Foster?" I recognized Jeffers's voice.

"Yes," I answered, "it's Foster."

"Thank heavens! We need wire cutters, heavy gauge--very quickly!"

"Wire cutters?" I said. "Why?"

"It seems we've come up right underneath an old fence," Jeffers growled.

"An old fence?" My voice rose with disbelief, drawing shushes from all within earshot. "You mean there's another fence beyond the fence? Another fence in the woods?" I was in the dark both literally and figuratively. I had no idea what Jeffers was trying to tell me. I only knew the clock was ticking on our escape attempt and that we couldn't afford delays. Many of us held tickets for trains that would pull out of Sagan overnight. We'd have a helluva time trying to ride trains that had already departed.

"The tunnel's come up underneath an old farm fence or something. Apparently it ran through the trees and so none of our chaps ever saw it during our reconnaissance of the area. We need to cut it out of the way. We need to cut it fast!" Jeffers had made his way over to me in the dark.

I was the scrounger. It was my job to find whatever was needed and to find it fast enough to keep the whole escape from collapsing. I rubbed the back of my neck. Where could I find wire cutters and find them in time to make a difference?

"All right," I muttered. "I need Berly here and the biggest, sharpest knife you can find within the next ten seconds."

I knew the meter was already running on the escape attempt. Men were already in the tunnel, waiting at the far end for the wire cutters. More importantly, they were waiting for me to deliver it. My only hope for finding a pair of cutters was in the theater, at the southernmost corner of the compound. I remembered being impressed with the scenery used on stage during the play we'd attended and I figured it was, at least in some measure, held in place by wire--that meant cutters might also be found there. We were now in Hut 104, at the northernmost area of the camp, just inside the gate. To reach the theater, we would have to dodge the stabbing beams of searchlights and any patrols that might have entered the compound. Well, if it was easy, anybody could do it.

Jeffers was back at my side in about half a minute. "Here," he grumbled, carefully handing over a knife, handle first. "Don't lose it. Collingwood wants it back." Collingwood's knife featured a round, corded grip and a six-inch blade. If it was as sharp as it looked, it would do the trick.

"Let's go," I said to Harmon and he stepped in close behind me.

Jeffers took command of the doorman. "Ready, lad? When I say 'go', quick's the action. Steady. Ready. Go!" The door opened quickly, just wide enough for us to plunge through. We hurtled across the narrow opening between Huts 104 and 109 and dove under the latter. From there, we crawled across the frozen ground, staying under

Hut 109's raised floor and out of the glare of the lights. We moved along the north-south axis of the hut, reaching its southern end fairly quickly. I pulled myself to my knees, ready to assume a sprinter's stance to get a good start on the short dash to the next hut, Number 121. Suddenly, I felt Harmon's strong grip on my right ankle. With the constant swinging back and forth of the searchlights, there was plenty of light bouncing all over the compound. Fortunately, Harmon had been scanning our surroundings while I had focused on reaching the end of the hut. I looked back at him and he pointed to our right, toward the west. Two guards had rounded the corner of Hut 122 and were headed right toward us. I quickly inched backwards into the shadows and held my breath. If they saw us, they'd shoot. That would put an end to me and Harmon and would also pretty much finish off the whole escape. They got closer and I could hear their boots crunching through the patches of crusty, frozen snow. We could see only their legs as they passed by. We watched until they reached the main gate and exited through it. We'd lost valuable minutes.

We crossed quickly to Hut 121, the last building in its row, and again crawled its length. This time, the coast was clear of guards and all we had to do was time our next move to avoid the illumination of the searchlights. We'd been going south and now turned east and covered the fifteen or so yards to the next hut, Number 120. From there, we'd have to move in the open for about twenty yards to reach the theater. We sprinted to Hut 120 and rolled beneath it. We scrambled to its southeast corner and gauged the sweep of the guard towers' searchlights. The towers were positioned on each corner of the compound. Their lights typically moved from the sides of the compound to its middle in ninety degree arcs. We got a lucky break on this night; the guards were synchronizing their sweeps so that the lights from both of the east towers were reaching the center of the compound at the same time. That meant that when they swung them back to the north and south, we'd have a dark corridor to traverse.

I was on my knees waiting for the lights to move away, Harmon right behind me. As the lights began their arcs away from us, we dashed across the last open space and slid beneath the theater. I prayed that the door at the top of the two steps beneath which we hid was not locked. I didn't want to have to stand out in the open trying to pry the lock with Collingwood's knife and ducking searchlights every twenty seconds. "Get ready," I whispered to Harmon. He nodded in reply. Once again the bright white lights swept away from us, waves of illumination leaving a shore of darkness. I scrambled up the steps and pushed the door handle down. It opened! Within two seconds, Harmon and I were inside, running down the outer aisle toward the stage.

I ran into the side of a row of seats and stumbled in the darkness, my night vision compromised by the searchlights. Harmon leaped up on the stage and motioned for me to follow. I caught up with him as he pointed toward a work bench beside a pile of sandbags. The bags were used as counterweights for the backdrops. On top of the bench were several items, including the desperately needed wire cutters. Harmon picked up the bulky cutters and whispered, "Let's go!"

"How can you see in here?" I murmured as he shoved me back toward the door.

"Old Boy Scout trick," he answered softly. "Keep one eye closed in the light and it won't completely mess up your night vision." We were back to the door, ready to reverse our trek from Hut 104.

By the time we pushed our way back through the door of Hut 104, the air and the tension in the barracks were thick. Two hundred men were crammed into every square inch of space, many lying on bunks, others jammed together like cigarettes in a pack. "Here," I said slapping the cutters into Jeffers' outstretched hand. "And here's Collingwood's knife." I hadn't had to use it at all.

"Well done, Foster!" Jeffers said, and I could hear him smiling in the dark. It was 2230 hours and we were already running late.

I followed Jeffers to the middle of the hut and got my first look at the entrance to the tunnel. It had been carefully and cleverly concealed beneath the hut's stove, but now stood open, surrounded by eager men clad in an amazing variety of clothing, from business suits to working class garb, and even a German soldier's uniform.

Jeffers handed the cutters to the traffic controller at the top of the shaft. He gave me a broad smile and quickly dropped them to waiting hands below. From this close, I could feel the cold air flowing from the open end of the tunnel, the free end. I smiled, satisfied that I'd made an important contribution at a critical moment.

I made my way back as I had come, squeezing between men in overcoats and hats, some carrying briefcases, others bedrolls. In the darkness, I found Harmon. "Nice work," he said. That's high praise coming from a comrade under difficult conditions. I was elated. .

.and only eighty or so men away from my chance at freedom.

The men in the corridor and in the rooms began shifting and a murmur reached us. It had begun! Men were now not just moving into the tunnel, but also moving through it and out into the cold, moonless night!

Harmon and I had settled into a corner, near a pair of bunk beds that were occupied by brief case-toting men in business attire. Exhausted by our covert foray to the theater and the expense of nervous energy, I'd fallen into a shallow doze, vaguely aware of rustling, quiet movement around me, but resting all the while. A little before midnight, I was tugged from my snooze by the ominous wail of air raid sirens. Jeffers, whose job was traffic control up to the tunnel entrance, began quietly cursing his RAF comrades for picking this night to conduct a raid. I guessed they liked moonless nights for the same reasons we did.

While Jeffers fumed, fearful that the raid would slow our escapes, we quickly saw the RAF was having the opposite effect, for suddenly the Germans cut all the power, dousing all the lights in the camp--including the searchlights! Within moments, the pace of the escape accelerated noticeably. In near total darkness now, the men ahead of us were much less likely to be spotted by the guards. Every couple of minutes, another man, costume, kit, papers and all disappeared down the tunnel shaft. This efficient pace held for more than an hour, until the "all clear" sounded and the lights came back on. The pace through the tunnel now resumed a more measured rate.

We'd been briefed about our trip through the tunnel. We'd lie face down on a small trolley car that would run along wooden rails. Our belongings, at least the ones we would take with us, were to be held out in front of us. There was a transfer station called Piccadilly where we'd move from one trolley to the next. When we finally reached the tunnel's mouth, we'd climb up a ladder and exit into the trees, maneuvering around the phantom fence.

Jeffers continued to work his way among the men, quietly calling numbers and checking them off a list with the help of a tiny, red-shielded penlight. "What number are you, Jeffers?" I asked the next time he passed close by.

"Seventy-five," he whispered.

"What are we up to now?" Harmon asked.

"Sixty."

"Jeffers!" came a low but urgent summons from the direction of the stove. I stood up, my leg half asleep, and limped after him. If there was a problem, I might have to resume my scrounger duties.

"We've had sand fall!" explained Flight Lieutenant Penley, the traffic controller at the shaft. I peered down into the hole and saw men hugging the ladder and huddled against the sides of the tunnel head. I was surprised at how bright the lights underground were. No worries about blackout down there, I thought.

One of the many problems with tunnels is that they are subject to caving in, especially in Sagan's sandy soil. Throughout the tunneling effort, one of Miles's concerns was always acquiring enough wood to shore up the weak walls and ceiling of the tunnel to prevent potentially catastrophic moments like this.

"What caused it?" Jeffers snarled, leaning over with his hands on his knees and looking down the shaft and wishing he could see the problem. He was agitated, nervous and already tired. It was 0130 in the morning and none of us had slept that day, too excited to rest.

"One of the lad's blankets hit the wall before Piccadilly and jarred loose some supports."

"How long to fix it?"

"Not very, I hope," Penley replied, "but we are at a standstill until it's cleared."

Jeffers began to pace. He scribbled some figures on the edge of his list and frowned.

By 0200 hours, the sand had been cleared and the trains were rolling again. Fifteen minutes later, disaster struck again. Another man, carrying another blanket, had caused a second section of the wall to cave inward. Frantic shoveling cleared the obstruction within twenty minutes, but the damage was done.

Jeffers threaded his way through the dark corridor. "No more blankets, chaps. Sorry, but we can't afford any more delays. If you've got a blanket, leave it at the top of the shaft." He worked his way through the rest of the hut, filled with far more men than had been planned for this point in the operation.

I could just make out Jeffers's silhouette as he stood near the south end of the corridor. He flicked on his penlight and I saw him make some more notations on his clipboard. He stared at his notes for a moment, then clicked off his light and headed back through the waiting men.

"Listen, chaps," he began. "I'm terribly sorry, but there's just no possibility that we're going to get more than a hundred men through the tunnel. We've lost too much time with the collapses. Numbers 101 to 200 might as well stand down. You can either make your way back to your own huts or stay here for the night. I'm awfully sorry, lads."

"It's all right, Jeff!" came a voice from the darkness.

A dozen others echoed the sentiment. "Too right. We'll give the bloody Germans a Saturday morning to remember!" The men tried valiantly to laugh away their disappointment.

"Off with you now, Jeff! Number 70's up to the shaft!"

The men patted Jeffers on the back as he made his way to the tunnel to claim his place in line. I'd never see him again. Collingwood, who now knew he wouldn't be among those escaping tonight, took over the clipboard and quietly called out, "71!"

"Eighty-one, Berly; eighty-two Foster!" Collingwood said, clicking on the penlight and shining it in our faces. "Move up to the tunnel shaft. Good luck!" We shook his hand and approached the shaft.

"Don't foul things up, Foster." It was my friend Wilcox.

"How'd you get in here?" I asked as Harmon started down the ladder. "I thought you had to have at least one redeeming social quality to be invited to this party. Last time I checked, you had, let's see, zero!"

"C'mon Bob!" Harmon hissed from below and I felt that iron grip on my ankle for the second time that night.

"Yeah, Bob," Wilcox taunted, "you better do what 'Lieutenant Berly' says. Don't want to get into trouble."

I decided I had better options than to beat the tar out of the little jerk again, so I yielded to Harmon's tug and climbed down the ladder.

"Quit paying attention to that little dipstick!" Harmon scolded me. "Focus on what we're doing!"

"How'd he get in on this deal?"

"He's one of the forgers. A talented one from what I hear."

"Geez!"

"What?"

"I hope he didn't work on our papers!"

Harmon laughed. It was just after four o'clock in the morning. By the time we reached the mouth of the tunnel, the dark night would be giving way to the early grayness of morning. Time was running out, not only for us, but for anybody still hoping to follow behind us.

Harmon and I had been forced to leave our blankets behind. As a result, we were traveling light, even lighter than we'd planned. We huddled at the bottom of the thirty-foot shaft and I again marveled at the ingenuity of Miles and his team. The tunnel was far deeper than I would have expected, but that depth was one of the key traits that had kept it protected for months.

To our left, a man I didn't know was pushing and pulling on an odd contraption designed to blow air through the tunnel. This was to make sure there was sufficient air circulation so we didn't suffocate as we made our way through. Directly in front of us, a man named Doyle was busy hauling on a rope. It soon produced a small, flat wooden trolley car. Doyle lay stomach down on the trolley and tapped on its wooden rail with a small trowel. That was the signal at the Piccadilly station to begin pulling the trolley back. Rather quickly, Doyle's feet disappeared into the tunnel. The next man in line moved into position as the trolley rope snaked away, following Doyle to his transfer point. When we heard the tapping from the other end, the process of reeling the trolley back started over again. It had been going on for nearly six hours.

When it was finally Harmon's turn, he gave me a wink, laid down on the trolley, tapped on the rail and away he rolled. I watched the rope play out and waited. Despite my fatigue, I was getting excited again. Three more guys were lined up behind me, silently praying that it would remain dark long enough for them to make good their escape. The tap on the rails came and I yanked on the rope, pulling faster and faster. My arms were starting to tire when the empty trolley finally reappeared.

I tugged my workman's cap down on my head--I didn't want to lose it on the journey--and slid onto the trolley. "Good luck, mate!" the guy behind me muttered and I tapped the rail. The next thing I knew, I was rolling through the tunnel, electric lights illuminating my path. I watched the supports pass by and wondered where the sand falls had occurred. Within a few moments, a set of arms came into view. They were pulling on the rope, hauling me closer to Piccadilly, and they belonged to Harmon. Two other men were there with him in the transfer station, one ready to depart on the next leg to the tunnel's mouth, the other standing by on the rope.

We repeated the process here that we'd used at the tunnel head, waiting our turns. I guessed at this point there were probably four or five guys still in the tunnel ahead of us, waiting for their turns to exit into the woods and four or five guys behind us waiting to head through the tunnel. The trolley took off. I tapped the rails on the first trolley and it scooted back toward the entry shaft.

"Chelmsford," the other guy said, offering his hand to Harmon and then to me.

"Berly," Harmon said, holding onto his false identity with the ease borne of months of practice.

"Foster," I said.

"The scrounger?" Chelmsford asked.

"Yes," I nodded.

He grabbed my hand again and pumped it vigorously. "Swell to meet you! I'm the photographer, remember? I took all the portraits for the 'official' papers. Couldn't have done it without you, that's a fact!" The tap-tap came down the rail and Chelmsford turned back around and hauled on the rope. When the trolley emerged from the tunnel, Harmon helped him get in place and gave him a good luck pat on the back as he took off toward freedom. A moment later, a burly Australian in a German soldier's uniform appeared behind us.

"Tight squeeze, that," he said jerking his head back down the tunnel.

We waited with eager anticipation for the trolley to return. When it did, Harmon climbed aboard, turned his head and winked at me. "See you at the ladder," he grinned. He tapped on the rail and disappeared, the return rope snaking out behind him. I was next!

"You speak German?" I asked the Aussie.

"Ja! Ich spreche Deutsch!" he said convincingly. I heard the tap on the rails and began to haul on the rope, pulling the trolley--and freedom--closer by the second.

When the little cart reappeared, I shook hands with the Aussie and said "Good luck, mate," then tapped the rail and off I sped. The air grew colder as I rolled toward the open end of the tunnel. Harmon's feet, then hands, then face came into view as he hauled on the rope. Upon reaching him, I smiled and started to speak. He quickly held his finger over his lips. "No talking," he whispered just loudly enough for me to make out. As this point, we were too close to being outside. In the cold, dry winter air, sound would travel clearly. We couldn't take even the smallest risk that the German guards might hear us.

Behind Harmon, a square piece of black tarpaulin had been hung across the tunnel. It separated the trolley terminus from the final section of the tunnel, providing a measure of noise and light control. Harmon patted me on the shoulder and pointed back toward the tunnel from which I'd just emerged. He was telling me to send the trolley back for the Australian. I positioned in on the rails and tapped. Off it went. Harmon smiled at me and ducked through the tarp curtain.

Time dragged as I awaited the signal to pull my successor through the tunnel. My mind was racing ahead to the ladder, up to the surface, linking up with Harmon and then hot-footing it to the station to catch our early morning train. The Australian's head and shoulders appeared. I signaled him to remain silent and he nodded. I patted him on the shoulder and shook his hand, then slid past the tarp.

Harmon was waiting for me, one foot on the bottom rung of the ladder. Here, it was dark and my eyes had to adjust. Harmon leaned close to my ear. "See you at the top. Watch out for the fence."

I patted him on the leg and he began to climb. We were still several feet underground, but we wouldn't be for long. As soon as Harmon got above me, I took hold of the ladder. I followed as close behind him as I could without impeding his climb. When he reached the top rung he stopped. All I could see was his butt. He was still for several seconds, and then he scrambled out of the hole like a wary rabbit. Above me, I could see stars.

I carefully placed my hands on the next rungs and pulled myself up, vaguely aware of the gray-clad Australian below me. I stuck my head up through the hole and breathed free air! I climbed out, putting my knee down on the frozen ground. Then I heard a dog bark. I flattened myself out, trying to blend into the frost-covered pine needles. I turned my head to the left. Silhouetted between us and the compound was a rifle-toting guard and his dog, one of those mean-as-a-hungry-bear German shepherds that constantly patrolled the camps perimeter. Usually they roamed just outside the fence, but this pair had wandered over to the trees. It soon became apparent why. The guard had to pee!

I don't know if the dog heard something or if he smelled something, but he started a low, rumbling growl. *"Ruhig Schatz,"* the guard grunted, buttoning his trousers. I was barely breathing, lying still and invisible in the darkness. Unfortunately, the Australian picked that moment to stick his head up through the hole. The movement or a new odor caught the dog's attention and he began to bark ferociously, straining on his leash, eager to pull his handler in our direction. Before I realized what was happening, I heard a click and a beam of white light blazed toward me, splitting the night between the anonymity of the darkness and the certain exposure of the light. The big Australian figured things out first. As the beam swept inexorably toward us, as the dog and the guard came closer, the Aussie stood, kicked me on the foot and shouted *"Dort! Da drüben!"* I didn't know what the hell he was saying, but I had the distinct impression he was creating a diversion for my benefit. I pushed myself up, my feet sliding in the frosty pine needles, searching for purchase. The fake German was just behind me, the real one, the one with the real dog, the real mean dog, was to my left. I dashed to the right, my head and shoulder colliding with the old, forgotten fence.

By now, the commotion at the edge of the woods had invited the attention of the big, round searchlights from the compound. Great swaths of artificial daylight illuminated our predicament. Our Australian German had confused the guard, but not his dog. Unfortunately, my ungraceful collision had also attracted the dog, who could not decide which of us would make the tastiest snack. I had sat back up, my face stinging from its sudden introduction to the fence, and was attempting to stand when I felt Harmon's strong grip on my shoulders. He had reached over a section of the waist-high fence and was trying to help me stand and escape. The guard now turned his flashlight's beam on us, and dropping the leash, released the shepherd. As the dog charged the Australian, the guard swung the rifle from his shoulder and fired a single shot. It was the death knell of our escape.

We stood outside in the cold, morning darkness until the sun finally decided to appear. Then we stood some more. Harmon was to my left, in the third rank of the formation. The *Kommandant*, von Linden, was livid with rage! He paced, shouted orders, stalked away to inspect something and then marched angrily back. Group Captain Walling kept his place at the head of our formation, staring stoically ahead.

We didn't know for certain how many guys had gotten out, only that it was less than eighty-one, but our ranks were noticeably thinner on this cold morning. We finally heard an excited cry go up from inside Hut 104 and von Linden broke into a trot and bounded up the steps. Apparently, some hours after it was too late, the Germans had finally found the tunnel entrance.

"How's your eye?" Harmon muttered from the side of his mouth, a light breeze ruffling his dirty, blond hair.

My eye was swollen now and no doubt turning black and blue from the fence's sucker punch. And it hurt. "I can still see the future clearly enough to know I won't be home for Easter!" I couldn't actually see Harmon, but I think that made him grin.

It was close to noon and we were all dead tired by the time the Germans dismissed us. We watched silently as Walling, escorted by three of the ferrets, accompanied the *Kommandant* back to the headquarters building. One of the reasons he had wisely kept his distance from Miles and the escape committee was just for this eventuality. Once the escape was discovered, as it inevitably would be, the less the SBO knew, the better for him and all of us left behind.

"Hope they aren't too hard on the Old Man," I said.

"They won't be," Jones-Hatton said from behind me. He was one of Walling's staff members whom we'd met on our first day in camp. "Von Linden's *Luftwaffe*, a professional soldier. He'll understand that we're duty bound to escape. We might lose our Red Cross rations for a few weeks, but the *Luftwaffe* will act properly. It's the buggers in the *SS* that you have to watch out for." Even so, Jones-Hatton continued to stand and stare at the headquarters hut until Walling was returned to the compound late that afternoon. By that time, I was, sore eye and all, lost in sleep.

Eighty men made it all the way through the tunnel and out to freedom. Three of us were captured between the tunnel's exit and the bloody fence that no one had ever detected until it was too late. A few were captured before they could board their trains and promptly returned to camp. Others were the subject of a national manhunt.

Morale in camp improved rapidly in the days after the escape as we learned of its relative success. Eighty escapees was an amazing feat in a field where a three-to-four-man breakout was more the rule. We smiled as we relived our escape night experiences. We laughed with the few men who'd made it into town, living vicariously through their successful escapes and commiserating with them over their all-too-sudden recaptures.

Our pride in the accomplishment, in the trouble our escaped brethren were causing the Germans and in the replacement of von Linden, who had been relieved from his command, continued to grow for two weeks; continued to grow until Group Captain Walling was called to the office of the new *Kommandant*.

"Those dirty bastards!" Denys Jones-Hatton spat into the dirt, tears rolling down his cheeks. Few of us were strangers to death. We'd seen it, smelt it and dealt it, but that was war. This was murder. We were standing outside the headquarters hut on our side of the fence. Group Captain Walling had just returned from an interview with the new *Kommandant*, *Oberst* Baumann. Walling had been pale and shaking with rage.

"They murdered them!" he'd exclaimed, eyes wide with shock. He'd held out a yellow paper containing a list of our comrades who had, allegedly, been shot while trying to escape.

"But surely, sir, some of them were only wounded!" Jones-Hatton had protested.

"No, Denys," the SBO had replied, his voice breaking, "they are all dead, murdered in cold blood. Baumann would not, could not, look me in the eye as he reported the news." He held out the yellow paper. Jones-Hatton took it with shaking hands as I glanced over his shoulder. There were listed dozens of names, fifty in all, including Jeffers, Beauchamp and many of the others who had preceded us through the tunnel. Many, but not all. "Here," Walling coughed, "post this on the announcements board. Then find the bloody chaplain and have him report to me!"

Jones-Hatton and I were now standing a few yards away from the announcements board watching the reaction of the men as the word of the murders began to spread.

"We'll get 'em," I said, knowing I needed to say something. "We'll make 'em pay for this. We'll level their cities and burn the countryside. We'll win this war and turn Germany into a wasteland."

"You know what this means, don't you?" Harmon asked as we strolled around the perimeter later that day.

"It means the Germans are evil. They have to be destroyed."

"They have to be defeated, not destroyed. Their leaders are evil, but not the rank and file. They're just misguided."

"Mankind can't afford for the Germans to be 'misguided' every twenty years."

"Well," Harmon paused, "I've said it before: we have to do a better job of winning the peace this go round. Back to my question: You know what this means?"

"What?"

"It means you saved my life again!" he grinned.

"How so?"

"Well, if not for you, I would have kept my original escape number and I would have been through the rabbit hole and out! I would have been one of those who escaped and quite likely one of those who was caught and shot. Teaming up with you saved my life--again." He reached over and slapped me on the back. It felt pretty good.

The British had always been careful to compartmentalize information. If you didn't need to know something, it wouldn't be shared with you. For example, I hadn't known that Wilcox, pea-brain that he was, possessed sufficient skill as a forger to be included in the escape. He had been number 100, by the way. I hadn't known about the massive effort to cut and sew clothes until I was measured and outfitted with my escape kit.

Likewise, I didn't know there was a radio in the camp until Jones-Hatton approached me about ten days after the escape. "Lieutenant Foster," he called, as I walked the track around the perimeter, "might I have a moment of your time?"

"Sure," I said, seeing as though I had plenty of time to spare. "What can I do for you?"

"You've proven quite adept at acquiring certain items and we find ourselves in need again. I was hoping you could help us."

I looked Jones-Hatton squarely in his brown eyes and asked, "What do you need and why?"

"Ah, well, it's all quite confidential," he said lowering his voice, "as you might well imagine."

"Quite," I agreed.

"You see, Bob," he leaned in close to me and continued in a voice barely above a whisper, "the Jerrys confiscated something of ours after the escape when they went through every barracks with a clean sweep." This was a believable story. After the escape, the Germans had literally ripped apart every hut in the North Compound, confiscating anything which could be termed contraband using the broadest definition of the word.

"What did they take?"

"Our wireless antenna."

"You have a radio?" I asked, flabbergasted. Jones-Hatton offered a sheepish smile and a nod. I'm always the last to know these things. Maybe next to last, just ahead of the Germans. "How do you keep it hidden?" I pressed my interrogation.

"Are you sure you need to know that?" Jones-Hatton asked with a frown.

"No, but I'll tell you what I do need to know: I need to know what the news is that you're hearing and I need to know every damn day."

"That's a 'yes' then?" he asked hopefully.

"Sure," I said with more confidence than was warranted. "I'll find you an antenna."

I couldn't go to Freddie for anything. After the escape, the guards, ferrets and other workers in the camp had come under intense scrutiny from the Gestapo. Hitler's secret police pulled out all the stops to determine how an operation of such scale had been perpetrated under the watchful noses of a very capable *Kommandant* and staff. Von Linden had been replaced and shipped off somewhere, maybe to the Russian front. Fortunately for us, although the camp had been crawling with creepy looking guys in leather overcoats for a couple of weeks, von Linden's replacement was another *Luftwaffe* officer, *Oberst* Baumann. Our new *Kommandant* suspended the distribution of Red Cross parcels, confiscated all tools of any sort, imposed restrictions on contacts between guards and prisoners, installed a sophisticated system of microphones to detect the seismic vibrations caused by tunneling, and closed the camp theater. So, naturally I headed to the theater to search for something from which to fashion a radio antenna.

I figured the best bet for Jones-Hatton's antenna would be a thin wire about one hundred feet long. I thought it would be fairly easy to rig through the rafters of a hut. We could leave one end of the wire accessible through a hole in the wall and connect it to the radio. I had borrowed a small pocket knife from a former Boy Scout who'd been able to hide it from the Germans simply by moving it to an already searched place after every inspection. It wasn't much, but it was better than nothing.

I talked Harmon into helping me and we made another surreptitious evening trip to the theater, this time without the time pressure which had been imposed on us the previous visit. We snooped around in the dark building and found a fair amount of wiring. The trick was to steal wire that wouldn't be noticed or missed. We finally decided to strip some of the wire from beneath the footlights at the front of the stage. Once our plan was formed, a second trip was needed to complete the work.

Because the space beneath the stage was too constricted for two people to work, I convinced Harmon that I should go alone on the next trip. He helped me think through the sequence of actions I would need to take and we walked through the operation again and again. As we talked, I pictured every step in my mind. After a week or so, I was convinced I could get in, get the wire and get out with no problems whatsoever. Of course, things never work out like you plan.

I had been working for maybe fifteen minutes, pulling wire from under the footlights at the very front of the stage. I was holding a nasty-tasting flashlight in my mouth and working with a small pair of needle-nose pliers that doubled as my wire cutters. I was working fast and making what I thought was good progress. Then, the door slammed. I clicked off the light and froze, holding my breath. At this point, I belatedly realized the value of a second man on a one-man job: lookout. I was effectively blind underneath the stage and had no idea what was going on above me. Until I heard the floor creak.

Somebody was walking right above my head; two somebodies. I heard a muffled giggle and realized one of the somebodies was of the gentler sex. Now, my fertile mind could imagine only one reason a woman would be in this particular place at this particular hour. Here I was, middle of the night, all by myself in a place where I could be shot if discovered. I hadn't been close to a woman since Freddie and I had visited the florist the previous summer. I hadn't touched a woman since Candy Cane had kissed me nearly a year earlier. Yet, now I was forced to listen--listen, not watch--as some horny German bastard seduced a woman just inches above my head.

"Oooo! Heinrich!" a throaty voice sounded above me.

At one point I was fairly certain that I could have continued my work without being noticed as the amorous couple seemed quite focused on what they were doing, but I showed unusual judgment and patience and sat quietly in my cramped, darkened space. Now I don't speak German, but after they'd finished up, the giggling got more frequent. Before long, they were at it again. I was beginning to think the guy above me really was a representative of the Master Race when things finally began to quiet down. And I'd been worried about making too much noise!

I waited while the giggling subsided and expected them to tidy up and move out, but then I heard regular, heavy breathing. They'd fallen asleep! My legs were going to sleep too! There wasn't room to stretch out under the stage. I checked my watch and was starting to get anxious. I needed to finish my work, which I couldn't resume until the late-night lovers left. I couldn't afford to get stuck in the theater and miss morning roll call. If the Germans had to come looking for me and found me in the theater, chances are we'd never get the wire needed for the radio. That would be bad for the radio- -and even worse for me!

An idea lodged in my mind. I thought it over very carefully, considering it from every angle--for about five seconds. I quietly sat the flashlight on the floor next to my right knee, held my hands up and clapped them together one time, as loudly as I could.

"Was?" a sleepy female voice mumbled. *"Horsst du das?"*

I crossed my fingers as the guy stirred awake, prompted by his lover. They whispered for a second and I could hear rustling, then buckling. The boards above me squeaked and then I heard boot steps. A good sign, I thought. I listened as intently as I could, having to rely on my ears alone to let me know what was going on. I heard a door open and then close quietly. I was anxious to finish my work and get the hell out of there, but I forced myself to sit silently for ten more long minutes.

I completed my work and coiled the thin wire, placing it in a dark, green canvas bag Harmon had come up with. Now all I had to do was get out of the theater, evade the searchlights and the roving guards and get back to Hut 112.

This mission, unlike the night of the escape when we'd made our emergency run for the wire cutters, had begun from our home barracks, Hut 112. It was only two buildings removed from the theater, so the distance to cover wasn't great. The challenge was that the theater and Huts 119 and 112 were all along the eastern side of the compound and closest to the fence. Close to the fence meant close to the guard's watch towers and within view of the roving guards who patrolled outside the perimeter fence. It was sort of a triple threat.

I timed my dash across the few yards separating the buildings and rolled up under 119 as the searchlight swept past. I laid there and caught my breath, watching as two pairs of jackbooted feet strolled past me. You'd think after the calamity of the March escape, the Germans would have been on their toes, but like soldiers everywhere they had quickly become bored with the tedious routine of guard duty and had resorted to old, bad habits like smoking and talking as they walked along. These guys were never going to sneak up on anybody.

I crawled the length of Hut 119 and squatted, waiting for the patrol to move out of sight. I only had to cover about ten yards to reach the south end of 112 and secure my precious cargo. The beam of a searchlight flashed by and I scrambled out from my hiding place, across the open space, up the steps and pushed on the door. It didn't open. I was now standing fully exposed on the top step of the barracks. As soon as the searchlight swung back my way, I would be shot and my mission would fail. I was more concerned with the former than the latter. The beam of light reached the farthest point of its arc and began to swing back toward me. I couldn't very well pound on the door and demand entry. That would attract immediate attention of a most unwelcome kind.

I pushed on the door. The beam of light grew closer. I had only seconds. I hopped down off the step and rolled under Hut 112 as the white light rolled over the building. All right, I thought, I'll try something else since those bastards up there are asleep. I crawled a little ways under the hut and reached up with my fist. I knocked three times, very deliberately. I was sure the Germans wouldn't be able to hear the knocks since I was still well beneath the building. After a couple of seconds, a knock from above answered. We'd all been trained in Morse code as part of the communications section of our flight training, but my skills were rusty from disuse. I searched my mind and then rapped out dash-dot-dot, dash-dash-dash, dash-dash-dash, dot-dash-dot: DOOR. I hoped that would get the message across. I was encouraged when I heard the light tread of footsteps above. I moved back to the south end of the building and timed my second attempt at the door. When the light passed over the hut, I leapt up to the top step and pushed the door. It opened and I tumbled inside.

"Geez! What's the matter with you guys?" I fussed as loudly as I dared. "Didn't you remember I was out there?"

"Did you get the wire?" a voice asked from the darkness.

"Of course I got it!"

"We didn't think you were ever going to get out."

"I didn't think Heinrich was ever going to get out!"

"Who?"

The wire greatly aided reception of radio signals. In keeping with our agreement, Jones-Hatton or one of the other members of Walling's staff would casually bump into me each day. In the course of our spontaneous meetings, he would fill me in on the latest war news. The messengers never told me where the radio was, or how it was being concealed, only the news which had been received through the use of the new wireless antenna. That is until the first Tuesday in June.

"Ah, Lieutenant Foster!" I looked up to see Walling himself approaching me. He was leaning on a cane, his leg that was injured in the crash that had eventually brought him to Sagan bothering him on this cloudy, cool morning.

I saluted the SBO as he was technically my commanding officer even though we were of different nationalities. "Good morning, sir!"

"Good morning," he replied while returning my salute. "I wonder if you might pop over to Hut 110 for a cup of tea with Denys and me?"

"Why, I'd be delighted," I said, falling into step with Walling. "Is it a special occasion?"

Walling shot me a sideways look and smiled. "Quite!" he said.

I learned that morning that Hut 110 was where the wireless antenna had been run through the attic. The lead ends had been concealed in the wall; no one would ever know to look for them who didn't already know they were there. I followed Walling halfway down the building to a room right of the center corridor. A Canadian officer I didn't know was standing in the doorway, no doubt the lookout.

"Morning, sir!" he said.

"Good morning, Avery!"

I followed Walling into the small room where Denys Jones-Hatton and two other British officers were huddled around a small table. Sitting on the table, big as life, was a jerry-rigged radio receiver, attached to the wire I had snatched from beneath Heinrich and his unseen lover. Walling glanced at his watch.

"I thought you might like to hear this, Yank," he grinned. "We've been able to pick up the BBC quite nicely with the help of your antenna."

"Time, sir," Jones-Hatton reported. Walling nodded and pointed toward me. A surreptitious radio like this one, no doubt broken into pieces and hidden carefully away each day, doesn't include a big speaker like the one in your living room. Instead, one of the boys had hooked up a small earphone ingeniously cobbled together by somebody with more skill than me. Jones-Hatton handed the earpiece to me and smiling said, "Have a listen."

I held the earphone over my right ear and immediately heard the familiar static and pop of radio. Suddenly, I heard the gong of a large bell. It was Big Ben chiming the hour! I next heard a measured voice from London.

"This is the BBC and here is a special bulletin read by John Snagge. D-Day has come. Early this morning the Allies began the assault on the northwestern face of Hitler's European fortress. The first official news came just after half-past nine, when Supreme Headquarters of the Allied Expeditionary Force issued Communique Number One. This said: 'Under the command of General Eisenhower, Allied naval forces, supported by strong air forces, began landing Allied armies this morning on the northern coast of France'."

My British comrades were smiling broadly as I listened. They'd already heard the news on an earlier report. Jones-Hatton thrust a tin cup into my hand. "Up the Allies!" he said, lifting a cup of his own and tapping it against mine. It wasn't tea!

"It's wonderful!" Harmon exclaimed when I found him fifteen minutes later, "just wonderful!"

"We'll be home for Christmas, my friend! You mark my words!" I laughed, slapping him on the shoulder. I forgot to specify which Christmas.

The news was mostly good for the next few days. We kept waiting, along with the rest of the world, for the big announcement that Montgomery's forces had punched through the German front and were racing toward the Rhine. In the meantime, we learned that the news of our escape attempt--and the German reprisal--had made its way to London.

Anthony Eden was one of Churchill's protégés and served as His Majesty's Government's foreign secretary. About two weeks after the first news of the invasion, the BBC reported on a statement Mr. Eden had made in the House of Commons the previous day.

Denys Jones-Hatton shared it with me in the shade of the cook house as we waited for our evening meal on one of the early days of that long summer. "He called it an act of butchery and promised its perpetrators would be brought to justice after the war."

"Which can't get here any too soon as far as I'm concerned," I replied.

"It's good to know they know," he said.

The reports from the new western front continued to be encouraging, though not euphoric. We waited all through June for the big breakout, the beginning of the race to Berlin. All of us airmen figured that since we'd continued to pound the hell out of the Germans' industries and cities, the ground troops would have an easier time of it. Of course that was wishful thinking on our part and reflected the over-optimism of some of our Royal Air Force and 8th Air Force leaders. Still, we waited impatiently for our rescue, which we were certain was growing closer by the day.

The *Kommandant* must have thought so, too. The distribution of Red Cross parcels, which had been suspended following the escape, was resumed. We weren't sure if this was due to the invasion, the Allied blockade of Germany which was squeezing the Reich's ability to feed its own people, or the fact that our guards' rations were barely more than our own. At any rate, we were all grateful for the parcels' added calories, the chocolate and, most of all, the cigarettes.

Summer passed slowly as our D-Day euphoria gradually turned to impatience. Couldn't Monty hurry things up a bit and get us out of captivity? Even though we knew he had priorities higher than reaching *Stalag Luft* III, we still waited for each day's news with eager ears. The Allies finally broke through and began to race across France. Our long days turned warmer, both in temperature and in temperament. We began to ask questions about how we should prepare for our own liberation. Walling invited "Don Berly" to join his staff. He had finally replaced the several members who had escaped--and been murdered.

"The question now is who'll get to us first: the Americans or the Russians," Harmon explained one evening as we stood on the perimeter watching the sun sink in the west. We'd have to return to the barracks soon, but for now it was a pleasure to enjoy the close of a warm, sunny day.

"I hope it's our guys," I replied. "I'm ready for some real food."

"And a beer!" Harmon added.

"And a beer!" I concurred. "So we've still got the Germans on the run, right?"

"According to the BBC."

We kept listening, kept strolling the perimeter, kept combining our Red Cross packages with the meager supplies from the Germans. The Allies were kicking ass through July and August. Things were even going well out in the Pacific, though for obvious reasons the war out there wasn't as personal to us.

In late September, the BBC reported a major airborne offensive in Holland. The idea was to capture a crossing over the Rhine River. Though they never said so in their reports, after a week with no bridgehead, we figured out that the offensive had failed. My prediction of being home by Christmas had been set back.

By now, the sun was giving up time each day; the temperatures turning cooler. We'd passed one year at Sagan. Our German rations had been reduced. We were no longer getting regular portions of meat. What we got came only every week or so and was usually tough, stringy horsemeat. Our bread ration was down to a thumb-sized piece per man per day. We were all tightening our belts, our stomachs growling at us all the while.

The Allied offensive slowed down that fall. It seemed that not much was happening. That is, of course, until December.

"Walling said the *Kommandant* had a spring in his step this morning," Harmon told me a week before Christmas. "The Germans say their attack in the west is succeeding."

The weather had been frigid. Sagan was blanketed with snow and it was clear that the only home we were going to see this Christmas was Hut 112. A few days earlier, the BBC had reported a German attack through the Ardennes Forest, a heavily-wooded, ruggedly-hilly area of Belgium, just west of Luxembourg and Germany. The BBC, as one would expect, had chosen its words cautiously, but it was clear that the Germans were on the offensive for a change.

The atmosphere at Sagan had changed since the March escape. We'd gone through a period of heightened scrutiny by our captors immediately following the escape. After D-Day, the scrutiny had eased and our intercourse with the Germans had become a little friendlier. As the summer wore on and the Allies liberated Paris and landed in the south of France, our guards and the ferrets began to sense that their side was losing. Amazing the difference that realization made on camp relations. Now, with the Germans calling the shots again, we held our collective breath and waited for the next change. We didn't have to wait long.

The Battle of the Bulge, as it came to be known, failed to reach its objective and quickly collapsed. Everybody, except maybe Hitler, understood that the Germans had shot their bolt. From now on, they'd only be delaying the inevitable. We were cold, bored and always hungry, but we remained hopeful that we'd soon be freed by forces advancing either from the west or the east. Our captors, however, were not content to let fate determine from which direction our deliverance would appear.

"Wake up! Wake up!" Harmon was kneeling beside my bed, his hand on my shoulder shaking me awake. "Get up, Bob!" I blinked my eyes in the dim light of the hut.

"What is it?" I asked, trying to clear my head enough to understand the answer.

"They've panicked!" Harmon replied gleefully, wiping his nose on his sleeve. "The Germans are moving out!"

"Tell them to have a good trip," I said sleepily and rolled over.

Harmon slapped me lightly on the shoulder. "Get up, dammit! We're going with them!"

For a couple of days we'd been able to hear artillery fire from the east. Clearly, the Russians had been getting closer. Apparently, the *Kommandant*, or his superiors, had decided now was the time to leave. Who was I to argue?

I'm not sure when the *Kommandant* reached this momentous decision, but by midnight, we were marching westward, the sound of the guns at our backs. Of course, it hadn't taken any of us long to pack. Most of what we had we wore--every day. In fact, very few of the men had extra clothes. It had been so cold that most of us kept on every piece of clothing we owned except when we slept.

Even though it was dark, the six inches of snow on the ground reflected so much light that it was easy to follow the man in front of you. There must have been ten thousand guys walking right down the middle of that German road, right in the middle of that winter night. We were all sleepy and hungry and we didn't talk much, but every now and then I'd hear Harmon cough and I'd be reassured that he was nearby.

In time, the sky behind us turned gray, then pink as the sun began its daily climb over the horizon. By the time the sun painted the upper tips of the trees on either side of the road, no one was talking. Our focus was on putting one foot in front of the other, on taking that next step, on getting thirty inches closer to freedom.

With the brightening of the morning, I noticed a blue-suited ferret walking along beside me. I glanced over to see my old accomplice Freddie. He nodded at me and held out a cigarette. I gratefully accepted it as well as a light from his cigarette. "Where are we going, Freddie?" I asked.

"Spremberg," he answered, his eyes peering ahead of us.

"Where's that?"

"About eighty kilometers from Sagan."

"How far from here?" I asked. Freddie just shrugged. "When are we going to get some chow? We can't march eighty kilometers in weather like this without eating." Again, Freddie shrugged. I guessed that the *Luftwaffe* was a lot like the Air Corps. Decisions were made at echelons a lot higher up than the ones Freddie and I currently inhabited.

We marched on.

"How are you doing?" Harmon had come up behind me. It was now late morning and still we walked. An hour earlier, we'd passed by a makeshift water station the Germans had set up alongside our route. Buckets of water had been lined up on wooden tables. Those of us with cups had been allowed to dip them in, scoop up a drink and move along. I don't know what happened to the poor bastards who didn't have something to drink from.

"I could use a couple over easy and a side of country ham," I replied.

Harmon laughed, and then coughed. "Yeah, me too."

"Freddie said we're going to Spremberg, eighty kilometers from Sagan. How far is that in real distance?"

"About fifty miles, I guess. I'm not sure all of us will make it that far. Some of these guys are already pretty weak. Walling is having a hard time of it."

"His leg?"

"Yeah. It's hard enough to hobble around with a cane on dry ground. Add half a foot of snow and you can imagine how tough it is. But the old boy's giving it all he's got, I'll say that for him."

"Must be a lot tougher on an old guy like that. Hope I don't have to endure anything like this when I'm in my forties! Maybe the *Kommandant* would let him ride in the staff car."

Harmon coughed again. "Yeah, maybe."

Bad Muskau was a small town and when we finally trudged up its main street late that afternoon, we were a hungry, tired, ailing mass of men. Our guards herded us into every public building, church, barn, basement and any other structure that would hold us. They set up two field kitchens and cooked a thin liquid which they pretended was soup. It tasted more like flavored water. There was no meat, no bread.

We found places to lie down and slept huddled together, warming ourselves as best we could. Harmon and I stretched out on pews in a small church. We were told that trucks from the camp were following our route with blankets and Red Cross parcels and things would be better when we reached our destination.

We slept, rested and relaxed. We were fed again the next morning. Obviously, the truck with the Red Cross parcels hadn't arrived, for our breakfast was much the same as the previous night's dinner. There was a lot of scuttlebutt; everyone had heard a story of where we were going. I offered up what Freddie had told me about Spremberg, but nobody believed me.

Walling, in admirable British fashion, continued to hold a daily meeting with his staff. Harmon returned from the morning's conference with news. "We move out tonight. We've got a ways to go, but only half as far as we went the first day. Freddie gave you good information. The Germans are moving us to Spremberg, trying to keep us out of Russian hands."

"Us or themselves?" I inquired.

Harmon smiled, coughed and spat. "Both, I'm sure."

We gathered under a cold, full moon which cast bright shadows on the snowy ground. It seemed colder as we stepped off on our sixteen-mile journey to Spremberg.

"Keep your eyes open, Bob," Harmon instructed after we'd started walking. "A lot of the boys have gotten very weak. Let me know if you see anybody falling out. Too many of these guys don't have overcoats and hardly anybody has a blanket. If you see anybody sitting down, let me know. The Germans will just walk right by them. If we don't take care of them, they'll die from exposure." He sniffed his nose and dragged his sleeve across it.

"Will do," I said. "Where will you be?"

"Right behind you," he smiled.

He stayed right behind me the whole night. I could tell because he'd cough about every five minutes. The later it got, the more frequent came the reminders that Harmon was indeed with me. When we finally reached Spremberg about six o'clock the next morning, Harmon was shivering.

"You don't look so hot," I said as we entered a small barn. It was already crowded with other prisoners who were busy making beds from the farmer's small stack of hay.

"Don't feel so hot either," he replied through chattering teeth.

A day's rest helped us all. Harmon felt better after sleeping all day. When we started out after dusk, he seemed almost back to normal. He wasn't. As the night got colder, his breathing grew more labored. I resolved to stick by his side. By the time the sun came up, we'd drifted far back in the loose formation, Harmon being unable to maintain pace.

A harsh cough racked his body. In the dim light of the new day, I saw specks of red where he spat into the snow.

We were sleeping wherever we could. I'd found a place in a farm shed, peeled off my jacket and laid it over the top of Harmon. He was already asleep, but he was coughing frequently and he was running a fever. I had to find some food or medicine, so I went to the one guy who'd always come through in the past.

"Freddie!" I called out as I got closer. Freddie turned toward me, his ears and nose red with cold, rifle slung over his shoulder, hands buried in his pockets. "I need some help," I said.

He shrugged. I reached into my pocket and took out my last six cigarettes. I stood as close as I dared and quietly pleaded. "I need some medicine. Berly's sick." Using my body to shield them from view, I held the cigarettes out toward him.

"We don't have any medicine," he said, hands still in his pockets. "I can't take your cigarettes for what I can't deliver." Just my luck: an honest ferret!

"C'mon Freddie! What if you got sick? Or the *Kommandant*?"

"We die. And if the Russians catch us, we die. And when your side wins the war, we die. I'm sorry, Foster. We have no medicine and hardly any food. Keep your cigarettes. Maybe you trade with the Russians when they catch up." He looked away. Freddie and I had always been able to do business. He was a capitalist. If he wouldn't take my payment, then he couldn't get the goods. It was that simple. I'd have to think of something else.

Word passed that we'd move out again after dark. With Harmon sick, I was now relying on Denys Jones-Hatton for information. I found him inside a little church, sipping a cup of thin tea. "We're headed toward Dresden," he confided. "We should reach it sometime tomorrow. Beyond that is Chemnitz; beyond that, we're really not sure. We believe we're moving faster than the Russians simply due to the fact that the sound of their artillery has faded in the last couple of days."

"Any idea where they're taking us?"

"One of the ferrets mentioned Nuremberg, but that seems an awfully long way. I'm not sure all these chaps are up to it."

"Yeah, well that's part of why I'm asking. Berly's sick. He needs medicine."

"Most of the men are sick. They all need food or medicine," Denys replied gently, as though explaining to me a harsh reality which I'd overlooked.

"Yeah, I get it, but I've got to take care of Berly."

"And I've got to take care of the Old Man. He's growing weaker every day. I had a couple of the lads rig up a sled for him to ride on." Denys' red-rimmed eyes stared away into the distance. He was bone-tired. We all were. "We'd rather pull him than carry him. Listen," he continued, "if I find any medicine, or extra food for that matter, I'll hold some out for Berly."

"Any news from the outside world?"

He shook his head. "Afraid our wireless can't be put to much use out here."

I thanked him and asked what he needed me to do. With Walling incapacitated, I figured Denys was the next closest thing we had to a leader. He asked me for the same things I'd asked for: food and medicine, then added blankets. I told him I'd see what I could do and headed back to Harmon.

When I got back to the shed, Harmon was still asleep, but my coat was gone.

I guess they knew the war was lost. I guess they feared the oncoming Russians, because the people of Dresden did nothing more than stare silently as we trudged wearily through their city. Despite the theft of my coat, I had kept quite warm during the night. I'd spent the first half of the journey propping Harmon up, his arm across my shoulder and my arm around his waist. That had required a lot of extra effort on my part. Sometime after midnight, I realized I was dragging him, that his feet weren't moving at all. At that point, I shifted him onto my back as best I could and tried to keep up with our ragged formation. Harmon had lost a lot of weight, so he wasn't as heavy as he had been, but I wasn't as strong as I had been. Heck, it's not like any of us had eaten a real meal in a long time.

Throughout the night, I watched as men gave up and sat down or collapsed in the snow. Tom Hamilton dropped right beside me, but I was too tired to stop to help. I felt guilty about it, but I was afraid that if I set Harmon down, I'd never be able to pick him up again.

By mid-morning, we'd crossed over the Elbe River. Up ahead, I could hear the guards shouting orders. We were stopping again. We were on the western outskirts of the city and I began to look for a warm, dry place to sleep. I was exhausted, we all were. And I was afraid I might lose Harmon.

A guard in a gray greatcoat was escorting a small group of men toward what looked like a stable. I needed a place to rest and I needed it fast. I decided to follow. Before I got to the door, I felt a firm grip on my elbow. I glanced to my left and into the blue eyes of Freddie Sommer.

Freddie led me between two shops and up a set of stairs cut into the side of a small hill. With Harmon on my back, I could only take one step at a time. Freddie had to stop a couple of times to wait on me, I was moving so slowly. My legs felt like they were about to pop out of their sockets; my hips burned from exertion, and sweat, despite the freezing cold, dripped off the end of my nose. Every now and then, Harmon would groan. When his forehead rolled against my neck, I could tell his fever had worsened.

"Where're we going?" I panted. "I can't carry him much farther."

Freddie turned around and walked back to me. "Here," he said, pulling the rifle off his shoulder and handing it to me. "Don't do anything stupid." He pulled Harmon off my back and hefted his limp body across his back in a fireman's carry. He bounced once to shift Harmon's dead weight and then set off again. I was so tired that even freed of my burden I could barely keep up.

We walked for another ten minutes, through an alley that widened into a lane. I felt that we were heading away from the city, moving toward the northwest, but I couldn't be sure. We passed into a residential area, the snow-covered lane flanked by leafless trees behind which stood sturdy houses. Past the rows of houses, we reached a low stone wall, beyond which sat a low, brown brick building. Freddie pushed open the wooden gate and marched up the snow covered walkway with me trailing in his wake. We passed a carved, wooden sign that said "Franziskanerkloster." I couldn't decipher the word, but I was encouraged by the cross carved above it.

Freddie stepped up two stone steps and grabbed the iron knocker on the heavy-looking, wooden door. He banged it three times. "Take him," he said, easing Harmon off his back. I swapped the rifle for Harmon and tried without much success to keep him upright.

The bolt of the door was lifted and a man in a coarse, brown robe peered out. He frowned when he saw me and Harmon, then his eyes widened as he caught sight of Freddie. Freddie launched into a conversation with the man, who I guess was a monk or a friar or whatever the German version is. The man initially shook his head and repeated *"Nein, nein!"* but Freddie refused to be turned away. He kept moving closer to the monk, kept talking. Another monk appeared from behind the first, staring over his shoulder, his eyes darting from me to Harmon to Freddie and back. I was afraid I was going to drop Harmon and afraid they were going to turn us away, but Freddie finally prevailed. He turned to me and with a wink said, "They'll take him."

"Thanks, Freddie," I sighed. "You're a lifesaver!" I began to ease Harmon toward the door.

"Nein!" the first monk barked, holding up his hand in front of me. He and the other guy stepped out of the door and maneuvered Harmon between them. They turned and half dragged, half carried Harmon through the door. It closed behind them and that was the last time I ever saw Don Berly.

I turned back toward Freddie. We were both exhausted. He'd walked just as far as I had and on about the same rations. I pulled one of my remaining cigarettes out of my shirt pocket and handed it to him, my hand shaking from the effort. He stuck it in his lips and patted his pockets until he found a match. He struck it on the brick wall and lit up, then handed me the fag so I could light my own smoke.

"How did you know about this place?" I asked.

"The man who answered the door is my brother. We don't approach life the same way."

I'll say, I thought! "How did you convince him to take Berly?" I asked, exhaling deeply.

"Ich bin Gast gewesen, und ihr habt mich beherbergt. It's from the Bible," Freddie explained. "'I was a stranger and you took me in.' I shamed him." He blew a cloud of smoke into the cold air. "Come, we go back before we are missed." He stepped off the steps into the snow and stopped, turning toward me and wagging his finger in my face. "Not a word of this, Foster; not one word."

I nodded my head.

I stole a chicken. It was a scrawny bird, but it made a pretty good stew. Denys and I cooked it in an old beet can along with some water, a turnip, half a carrot and some green, leafy stuff that he found in a trash can behind a small restaurant. We'd shared the stew with Walling, who was holding his own and who declared it the best meal he'd eaten in Germany. He was exaggerating of course, but it was the best meal any of us had eaten since we'd left Sagan. The Germans had practically given up on feeding us. On the rare days when we got any food at all from the camp administration, it was quickly devoured by the thousands of hungry, ragged, sick men we had become. Daily, more men dropped by the wayside. Many fell out, fell down and died of exhaustion, starvation or illness. Some were taken in by farmers or villagers, but most of us who continued on did so only with the help of our fellow prisoners. I had always considered myself in good physical and mental condition--heck, you couldn't make it as a B-17 pilot if you weren't--but even I began to lose strength, began to lose heart.

Some of the men used the growing laxity of the guards to slip away, but by now I felt at least partly responsible for Walling. I wanted to make sure he got through this ordeal alive. Each night, I vowed to make it through one more day; one more day of little or no food, bitter cold, filthy conditions, ravenous lice, no shelter or heat, no sanitation.

Finally, after more than two weeks of walking, after endless hours of putting one foot in front of the other in darkness and in light; in rain and snow; in hunger and sickness; we finally rounded a bend in the road and looked up to see the high fence of *Stalag Luft* VII-A. We'd walked more than three hundred miles in the dead of winter, through the middle of a war and we'd finally made it "home."

We managed to survive in *Stalag Luft* VII-A for two months. The camp was packed tighter than Fibber McGee's closet. More than a hundred thousands of us from all over Germany had been stuffed into a compound built for a fraction of that number. We were crammed into barracks, guys sleeping on floors underneath bunks to keep from getting stepped on every night.

We had little food other than what we could scrounge or trade for with our guards. Red Cross packages were merely a happy memory. Apparently the German transportation system was wrecked to the point that only vital military supplies were moving--and not much of that. About the only good thing about *Stalag Luft* VII-A was that it was too big for me to run into Wilcox!

Walling remained very sick, but at least he didn't appear to be getting sicker. Denys and I tended to him daily, making sure he had a warm, dry place to sleep and feeding him as much as we could. It was a tough task. Fortunately, we were able to put the radio back into operation. From the daily BBC bulletins it was clear that the war wouldn't last much longer even after we heard the stunning news that the president had died. Knowing that the end was near lifted our morale and helped those of us at the margins of life to hang on a little longer.

On April 29th, our guards melted away like a late spring snow and a short time later a Sherman tank from the 14th Armored Division of the United States Army rolled right through the compound gate! We were finally free! It would take us a few weeks to get back to England--you know how the Army works. We'd have to be counted, fattened up, our health monitored, our records checked and all that paperwork for which the Army is so well known. I spent a large part of those weeks thinking: thinking what I could have done differently to save Harmon; thinking what I might do with the rest of my life. I found out pretty quickly that all the answers weren't up to me.

Part 3

May 1945

The war in Europe ended less than ten days after that tank smashed down the compound gate. General Patton paid us a visit and in his high, squeaky voice promised immediate food and blankets and evacuation as quickly as possible. In less than a week, groups of prisoners had begun shipping out to a repatriation center in France. From there, I expected a leisurely cruise home to the United States, some well-deserved home leave, some time to rest and relax and then, and only then, a reassignment to help finish off the Japanese out in the Pacific. I sort of hoped the Navy and the Marines would finish that assignment before I had to come bail them out.

We arrived at our repatriation facility neat St. Valery, France in early May. I think the same architect had been at work all over Europe throughout the war for once again we were confronted with low, rectangular, white-washed barracks and administrative buildings. We arrived in the late afternoon of our second day on the road, tired, dusty, but happy to be back among friendly comrades who treated us as guests rather than prisoners. Sort of.

The first thing we did after having our names checked off some master list was march into a delousing chamber, strip off our rags and get sprayed with some white, smelly insecticide powder. From there, we marched into the next building, which, mercifully, was a shower facility. I enjoyed the single best shower of my life for about twenty minutes, and then shaved with a shiny new razor that I got to keep. Next, we were medically screened and those with serious conditions were immediately transferred to the camp infirmary. It was almost dark by the time we got a new issue of uniforms and our first hot meal this side of Germany in many months. It felt wonderful to lie down on a clean cot with my own pillow and blanket in a warm, clean, free place. After the long journey, a thorough cleaning and a filling meal, sleep came swiftly.

I'd been to the state fair in Raleigh and to a couple of big college football games, but I'd never seen anything like the celebration that broke out on May 8th. The German surrender was announced early that morning and by the time all of us former prisoners of war gathered for our morning formation there was a festive air in the camp. **GERMANY QUITS!** read the headline in that morning's edition of *Stars & Stripes*. The thick black letters covered the entire top half of the front page. It was a great day to be alive. It made me think about Don, Joe, Al, Jeffers, Beauchamp and all the others who hadn't made it back. And it made me think of Harmon.

Every day, following morning formation and breakfast, a new group of men were summoned to a large barracks-like building which had been converted into a debriefing center. All interior walls had been removed and long rows of field tables had been arranged with a folding, wooden chair on each side. The same routine was repeated after the noon-day meal. It was here that each former prisoner was invited to share what he knew about the Germans and his fellow prisoners. The Army's personnel team was working long hours to account for every man possible--and to document German atrocities directed at the POWs.

My turn finally came about ten days after the German surrender. Ed Morgan and I had been pitching pennies against the side of the mess hall debating who had the most rotation points. The Army had devised a Machiavellian scheme under which soldiers would be returned home based on the number of points each had accumulated. You earned a point for each month in service, a point for each month overseas, five points for each combat decoration and--this is where it really hurt--twelve points for each kid back home under the age of eighteen. Ed had two daughters. That trumped my Silver Star, and on this particular lovely spring morning was a source of some contention between us.

"But getting your wife knocked up hasn't got anything to do with your contribution to the war effort!" I argued, flipping a penny toward the white-washed side of the building.

"Maybe not," Ed laughed, "but it has everything to do with the future. Why, Bob, that's why we fought this God-awful war in the first place--for the children!"

"I think heroism in the face of the enemy, daring death to come back later for a second try ought to count for more! That's all I'm saying."

Ed laughed again, picking up the pennies his toss had won. "If you think parenthood doesn't require heroism, you're crazy!"

The public address system popped to life with an ear-piercing whistle. "Attention all personnel, this afternoon's debriefing roster has been posted on the bulletin boards adjacent to the headquarters building. If your name is listed, please report to Building A202 at 1330 hours."

I shoved my remaining penny back in my pocket and tapped Ed on his shoulder. "C'mon. Let's go look and see if today's the day." It was, for me at least.

"Foster, Robert, First Lieutenant, United States Army!" I saluted as I stood in front of the debriefer's table. My uniform was sort of baggy owing to all the weight I'd lost; still, I thought I looked pretty presentable. The Captain on the other side of the desk was the picture of health: pink, chubby cheeks and a belly that strained against the confines of his shirt buttons. "When do I sail?" I smiled.

Captain Applegate, who looked about five years younger than me, glanced up from my personnel file with a frown glued to his face. "Not so fast, Lieutenant. First we've got to know what you know. Unit and home base?" I guess that even now, even here, they had to establish that I was who I claimed to be. Applegate asked a few more questions about my training and the missions I'd flown. Then, satisfied that I was in fact Robert Foster, he switched to more important matters.

"When you were shot down, the Red Cross reported that two members of your crew were killed and seven were captured." He looked down at the file in front of him and then fixed me with a steady, slightly bored gaze. "That leaves one guy unaccounted for. Do you know what happened to," he looked down again and then back at me, "Harmon Roberts III?"

"Yes sir, I do." I then told him the whole convoluted story of how Harmon, on my instructions, had switched identities with Don Berly's corpse and how, against the odds, the masquerade had escaped the Germans' attention.

"So Berly's been dead the whole time?"

"Afraid so, sir."

Applegate leaned back and shook his head. "Tough break for his family, to go all this time thinking he was a POW and get to the end of the war only to find out he's dead."

I nodded. It was a bad deal, but it didn't change anything, not really. It had just delayed their pain and grief. "Yes sir," I mumbled.

"I'm not saying you didn't do the right thing. Actually, that was pretty fast thinking. Roberts isn't on our camp roster here. Neither is Berly. What happened to him?"

I recounted the story of our long march, how we were forced to continue through horrible weather without adequate food and often without shelter. I told the Captain about dragging Harmon through the streets of Dresden and leaving him with the monks.

"Dresden!" Applegate exclaimed. "When was this?"

His response unsettled me, but I answered, "Well, it was probably early February. Yes sir, I'd say sometime before the middle of the month."

"Holy God!" Applegate stared at me. "You have no idea, do you?"

"No idea about what?" I was starting to get annoyed.

"We bombed the shit out of Dresden for three days and nights in mid-February. Left it a smoking hole in the ground."

I leaned against the back of my chair. The open windows let in a sweet-smelling breeze. A low rumble rose from the dozens of other conversations going on at the dozens of other tables in the large room, but all I could think of was Harmon. Had I struggled for months to keep him safe, stolen the identity of our crewmate, successfully hidden him from the Krauts, and dragged him half way across Germany, only to lose him to our own 8th Air Force comrades?

"Here." I willed my mind back into focus to find Applegate holding out a pack of Luckys.

I sulked around for the next couple of days, avoiding people I knew. I hadn't much appetite and so I wasn't gaining weight like most of the rest of the boys. I tried to read books from the camp library, but instead found myself staring at the same page for long stretches of time while my mind wandered.

It took eighty-five points to go home. I figured my tally was around sixty-seven. The *Stars & Stripes* had reported on some Sergeant whose wife had just given birth to twins. That gave the lucky bastard twenty-four new points, which gave him enough to get on the boat. If he'd only loan me one of the kids, I could have gone with him. . .in six more months.

General Eisenhower visited our camp on May 24th. According to the newspaper, Ike already had between a hundred-forty and a hundred-eight-five points! I was planning to ask him if he'd be willing to share some of his extras with me, but I couldn't get within thirty yards of the stage from which he spoke. It was a sunny day, and a portable loud speaker system had been set up for the Supreme Commander. An Army band had been assembled from somewhere. It played while some dignitaries gathered on the stage. There were two or three Generals, several Colonels and a group of gray-haired men in suits that someone said were members of a Congressional delegation. After some preliminaries, the Supreme Commander himself stood before us.

"I know you men are anxious to get home and we're going to get you there as fast as we can. Our transportation corps is working to unload every supply ship as fast as we can. Then we're going to get that ship ready to put back out to sea and ask you boys to 'hot cot' on board so we can make full use of our shipping capacity!" This brought cheers from most of the men and even made me feel a little better. Ike went on for a while about the challenges of transitioning European society back to peace. Then he continued, "I just want to say thanks! You men carried the ball for us in defeating Germany. We won't forget that. God bless you and God bless the United States of America!" The band struck up a marching tune and Ike and his entourage hustled into a waiting motorcade. Some of the men in suits departed with Ike and some started walking toward the headquarters building with the Colonel in charge of our camp. We all appreciated Ike taking the time to come talk to us. We understood that his pressing duties forced him to leave quickly. But I had hoped to ask him about points.

"Well, well, well! If it isn't my old pal, Lieutenant Foster!"

You know, I can get along with just about anybody. In the whole time I was overseas, there were only a few guys that I truly disliked. Jolly Tucker had been one. But Ross Wilcox was in a class all by himself. I hadn't seen the little bastard since we'd arrived at Saint Valery--and I hadn't missed him. Now here he was, all decked out in his Class A uniform, a duffle bag in one hand and a folder in the other.

"Excuse me for not saluting," he sneered. "I save that for superior officers."

Asshole. "Heading up to Paris, Wilcox? I heard they needed a eunuch to inspect the bordellos up there, you know, decide which ones were sanitary for the real men who won the war."

"Aren't you the witty one," he replied with thick sarcasm. "But no, Foster, I'm heading in the opposite direction. I'm shipping out to the States."

"How the hell do you rate the points to go home? You were still wet behind the ears when you got shot down! I'd already been flying combat missions for six months before you ever crossed the Channel!"

"Well, it's like this, pal" he said, stepping closer and smiling meanly. "I've got three bambinos back home who can't wait to see their Daddy. Three kids, Foster. Thirty-six points! How many you got, Bobby boy? What's that you were saying about a eunuch? " He was so close I could smell beer on his breath; so close I could have punched his lights out.

"Get out of my sight, Wilcox." I wanted to deck the little jerk, but I guess war mellowed me a little.

"Enjoy your summer in France, Foster!" Wilcox giggled, hefting his bag over his shoulder and turning away toward an idling bus.

Sometimes there just isn't any justice.

We continued to get medical check-ups and regular meals. Over the next couple of days, my appetite slowly returned. You get to a point where you have to ask yourself if you could have done anything differently. My answer was no; I doubt I could have carried Harmon another step. In the end, Freddie had actually saved him. At least temporarily. I decided it was time for me to let it go and get on with my life.

We'd all fallen into pretty lousy physical condition. A diet nearly devoid of calories and constant exposure to the elements take a toll on a man. To help speed our recovery, we were being fed well and often and recreational opportunities were made available. We could go on hikes, visit the nearby Channel beaches, borrow bicycles and sports equipment.

Ed Morgan and some of the other former 8th Air Force POWs challenged some infantry and armor boys to a game of high-stakes softball. The winners earned a beer party with the losers serving as waiters. The camp chaplains, a Catholic and a Jew, got drafted to be the umpires. Ed convinced me to play, offering me right field, which he claimed should be the least strenuous position to cover. We had just taken the field to begin the third inning when the deafness-inducing loud-speaker system sputtered to life. "First Lieutenant Robert Foster, report to Building A202 immediately. First Lieutenant Robert Foster, report to Building A202 immediately."

"What's up, Bob?" Ed asked as he trotted out from first base to retrieve my mitt.

"I think Eisenhower decided to share some of his rotation points with me after all. I guess this is so long," I quipped. Ed laughed and waved one of the other boys in to take my place as I jogged off the field and headed toward the debriefing building. I didn't really expect to be shipped home and honestly I was a little disappointed to have been jerked out of the ballgame. The exercise and the distraction both would have been healthy for me.

My eyes took a moment to adjust to the interior of the building, but I could see Captain Applegate standing at his table and motioning me over. At this hour of the afternoon, few of the tables were occupied. I guessed most of the guys had already had their turn. I guessed now Applegate and his colleagues were recalling their most interesting interviewees in order to keep themselves entertained.

I caught my breath and straightened my still-loose-fitting uniform and strode over to Applegate. I planned to let him know I had been enjoying myself at the moment of his untimely summons. So focused was I on expressing my annoyance that I failed to pay any attention to an older gentleman sitting beside Applegate's table.

"Hello, Lieutenant Foster," Applegate said as I got closer. That's when the man in the suit stood up and turned toward me. He was a little shorter than me with tired-looking eyes and salt-and-pepper gray hair that was short on the sides and thin on top.

The man stuck out his hand and said, "I'm Harmon Roberts. You're going to help me find my son."

At 0800 the next day, I met Senator Harmon Roberts, Jr. in front of the camp headquarters building. I had stuffed my meager belongings in a canvas knapsack and was turned out in my dress uniform, my raincoat over my left arm. The Senator was standing next to a dark blue Buick Touring Sedan, looking at his wristwatch.

"Ah, there you are, Lieutenant Foster. Duffy's inside filing our route with the headquarters commandant, whatever that means," he laughed. Reaching inside the jacket of his suit, Senator Roberts pulled out a buff colored envelope. "And here are your travel orders. I've kept a copy just in case. You've been assigned as my military liaison for the duration of my mission."

"What exactly is your mission, sir?"

"I'm on what we call a 'fact-finding' mission. I'm gathering information on the situation over here to share with my colleagues on the Foreign Affairs Committee. It's important that the Congress have first-hand information on matters of national importance. And right now, the only thing more important than the situation in Europe is beating the Japanese."

"How long do you think that's going to take?" I asked, opening the passenger side door and tossing my bag on the seat.

"Another year and a half maybe. Your Air Corps colleagues out in the Pacific are burning their cities down. The Navy has pretty much destroyed the Imperial Fleet. We're tightening the noose and choking off their shipping. It just depends on how suicidal the Japanese want to be. Ah," Roberts looked toward the headquarters building as a heavy-set civilian emerged through the front door, "here comes Duffy."

I introduced myself to Frank Duffy, the Senator's aide. He was an Irishman from Dublin. . .Ohio, and a member of the Senator's Washington office staff. He'd be our driver and also our photographer. I wasn't sure why we needed a photographer, but I'd find out soon enough.

I started to climb in the front passenger seat, but the Senator intervened. "Sit back here with me, Lieutenant Foster. We need to get better acquainted." The Senator slid into the spacious back seat and I walked around and climbed in behind Duffy. "What advice did the commandant give you?" Roberts asked as Duffy pressed on the starter and the engine roared to life.

"He said to stay on the main roads, no traveling after dark, and to always carry extra cans of gasoline."

"Do you have extra cans?"

"No sir, not yet, but we're stopping by the motor pool before we head out."

"Let's get a move on then. I want to get to Paris as soon as possible."

"Yes sir!" Duffy replied as he slipped the car into gear and the gravel crunched beneath its tires.

Roberts leaned forward and pulled a Michelin Guide of Western Europe out of his leather briefcase. "Show me where you left Harmon," he ordered, laying it on the seat between us.

I flipped the atlas open and began turning the pages. When I came to eastern Germany I stopped and traced with my finger until I found Dresden. "Right here, sir. Dresden."

"Dresden," he repeated flatly. I was pretty sure he already knew what I hadn't, that we'd clobbered the city not long after I left Harmon in the not-so-warm embrace of the monks. "How long will it take us to get there?"

"I'm used to flying to Germany, not driving," I joked. "It depends on traffic and the condition of the roads."

"Traffic shouldn't be a problem. There shouldn't be anything but our military traffic on the roads. The Germans don't have any gasoline and very few vehicles. Besides," he patted the pocket of his suit coat, "we've got priority travel authorization which should keep us moving along smartly. Right, Duffy?"

"Yes sir!"

I was beginning to get this Duffy guy. His job was to drive and to say "yes sir" whenever the Senator asked a question. Ross Wilcox would have been good at that job.

We left the motor pool fifteen minutes later with five jerry cans of gasoline tied down inside the trunk. As we loaded them in, I noticed that there were two nice suitcases plus a smaller bag already in the trunk.

We headed southeast along the Somme River toward Amiens. It was an overcast morning and cool. As Duffy drove, Senator Roberts began his first inquisition of me. "How did you end up on Harmon's crew?"

"To tell you the truth, he ended up on mine." I related the story of my meeting with Jolly and how my co-pilot had been promoted and I'd been relegated to the right-hand seat. I left out Jolly's supplemental instructions. The Senator sat sideways, leaning his back against the side of the car, his left leg crooked across the seat between us, his pale blue eyes searching my face.

"That must have made you pretty sore." I was beginning to notice a directness, even a bluntness to the Senator that surprised me in a professional politician. Well, I wasn't one of his constituents and I hadn't been old enough to vote when I went into the Army anyway. I guess he didn't feel he had to coddle me in exchange for a vote I couldn't cast.

Honesty's the best policy, right? "Yes sir. I was quite resentful. My crew and I had already flown several missions together. We were a good team and then we got busted up because the public affairs boys decided they needed a hero. You'd be right in saying that made me mad. But the longer we flew together the more I came to appreciate Harmon's skill and dedication to our crew and our mission. He turned out to be a legitimate hero." I was staring pretty hard back at the Senator, wondering if he knew what a fine man his boy had become, wondering how that fit into his plans.

At Amiens, we turned south. We pulled into Paris shortly after noon and the Senator directed Duffy to drive straight to the Arc de Triomphe. A giant blue, white and red French flag hung inside the Arc. The bright colors and its location at the center of the intersection of a dozen streets made it easy to find. Duffy pulled the car over to the side of the road and reached over to the floor in front of the empty passenger seat and whipped out a camera, just like the ones the boys in the press used.

Roberts climbed out of the car and buttoned his jacket. "Come along, Lieutenant." We dodged our way through the traffic which was composed mostly of bicycles, jeeps and delivery trucks and made our way toward the imposing monument to French martial success. There hadn't been much of that lately. Duffy snapped off several shots of the Senator with the Arc behind him, then took a couple of me with the Senator as well. Then we climbed back in the Buick.

"Let's get over to General Lee's headquarters," Robert's directed. "Do you have it marked on the map like I told you?"

"Yes sir!"

General Lee was J. C. H. Lee, Eisenhower's chief of supply. Lee had orchestrated the logistic miracle that had fed, fueled, armed and supplied the Allies in their build-up in England, during the invasion and on through the drive to the Rhine. He was also rumored to have taken advantage of his position on top of the supply chain. His headquarters was rumored to be more comfortably appointed and better supplied even than his boss's.

General Lee was absent when we reached his headquarters, but Senator Roberts was still treated as a visiting dignitary. He consulted with the General's chief of staff, requisitioned supplies he believed we would need for our journey and obtained overnight lodging for us. Duffy refilled the Buick's tank.

"I figured since we were passing through Paris, we might as well spend one night here. All right with you, Duffy?"

"Yes sir!"

"And you, Lieutenant?"

"Whatever you say, sir."

"Well, I say 'yes!'"

Our Buick was quite the oddity on the Champs-Elysees, drawing stares as we drove east. There were Army jeeps and trucks laden with supplies and everywhere bicycles. Hundreds of people strolled along the broad sidewalks. It seemed the Parisians were adjusting pretty quickly to peace. Of course, one could argue that Paris had always managed to avoid the worst aspects of the war. Senator Roberts certainly thought so.

"We can't trust the French," he said to no one in particular--which I guess meant me since I was sitting beside him.

"How's that, sir?"

"France is shot full of socialists and communists. Now that we've beaten the Germans for them a second time, they'll fall right back into trouble if we allow it."

"Harmon told me that you fought in World War I."

"That's right. I was an infantry company commander. Fortunately for me, I didn't come over until early 1918. I'd probably have been killed if I'd been here earlier. Most miserable experience of my life. Wonderful fellows mind you, just wonderful. But the conditions were just wretched. Mud, filth, death, decay, hunger, disease. And now here we are twenty-five years later and we've gone through it all over again. We've got to win the peace this time, Lieutenant Foster. I doubt mankind could survive going through this again."

I decided to have a little fun with the Senator, which maybe wasn't the smartest thing I could have done. "Harmon said you were an isolationist before Pearl Harbor, that you felt we should have stayed out of the war over here."

Roberts frowned. "Hindsight isn't wisdom, son. It pains me to admit it, but I was mistaken. If we'd backed the British sooner, this whole God-awful mess might have been avoided. But, back then, Hitler looked like a hooligan and, quite frankly we-- or I--didn't take him seriously. Why, my God, did you ever hear the man give a speech? Raving lunatic!"

Duffy turned north at the Place de la Concorde and then drove three of four blocks east, pulling up before the grand entrance to our overnight lodging--the Ritz Hotel. Apparently General Lee's reputation was founded at least partly in fact. The French tri-color, Union Jack, Stars and Stripes and red banner of the Soviet Union stood in colorful contrast to the facade of the luxury hotel.

"Glad to see this place back in proper hands," the Senator announced as Duffy stopped the car and a liveried attendant opened the back door. "Goering used it for *Luftwaffe* headquarters for the past five years." I wasn't sure whose hands he meant because the place was crawling with Americans in uniform. And I appeared to be the junior officer there.

We checked in at the massive reception desk and were quickly on our way to rooms. The Senator had his own while Duffy and I shared. We dined that evening in the main dining salon and based on this one experience I'd say the French deserve their reputation for culinary excellence. I couldn't pronounce anything on the menu, but ate what the Senator recommended and was never sorry for having done so. Along with dinner, we drank a bottle of white wine, which was a little lighter than what I was used to, but still quite refreshing.

After dinner was over, Duffy excused himself and I was left alone with Senator Roberts for the first time. I figured that either Duffy's Irishness had gotten to him and he needed stronger libations or the Senator had instructed him to leave us alone. Maybe both. Roberts pulled a pack of Chesterfields out of his coat pocket and offered me one. I accepted and a waiter magically appeared with a light.

"Tell me more about my son," the Senator directed.

"Well, as I told you back at St. Valery, I left him at a monastery on the outskirts of Dresden."

Roberts exhaled a small cloud of smoke and waved his cigarette impatiently. "Yes, yes. What I want to know is how he performed in combat. What was he like under fire. He worked very hard to get into the shooting war, despite my advice."

"He told me that. He told me you fought to keep him in the States instead of letting him do his duty like the rest of us." I put a little harder edge on this than I should have and the Senator responded in kind.

"Listen, son, the work being done in the States was vital to winning the war. Why, if we'd sent our boys over here without months of training they'd have been ground up like sausage. Now answer my question."

I stared into his tired eyes and saw a father desperate to know his son, desperate to know how the little boy, the teenager, the college student who should have been the focal point of his life had turned out. He didn't know because he hadn't known how to. He hadn't known how to relate to his namesake and rather than risk the vulnerability of holding his son close, he'd committed himself to what he did know: politics. I wondered if he was beginning to regret this choice just as he seemed to regret his isolationism.

"You know, Senator, that your son won the Distinguished Flying Cross, don't you? You can't buy those at Woolworth's. I sat beside your son on mission after mission. Time and time again he saved our crew through quick thinking, skillful flying and by just toughing it out. I wouldn't compare our experience in the Air Corps to what you went through in the trenches, but don't think what we did was easy. The fact that we got to come home from the war every night, got to come back to warm, clean beds and hot chow actually made it tougher to get up at four o'clock the next morning and go risk our lives again. A lot of guys couldn't handle it. The pressure built up flight after flight. After a few missions they'd cave in. Harmon wasn't like that. He bore the strain, not only for his own sake, but for the other nine souls that flew with him every day. Including me. I don't know how much of the credit you deserve,

Senator, but you've got a mighty fine man for a son." I wiped my mouth on my napkin and dropped it on the table, pushing back to stand up.

Roberts reached out quickly and grabbed my wrist. "Stay. Please." I had to get back in the car with him in a few hours. Plus, I could read sorrow in his eyes. I sat.

Roberts looked down at his empty wine glass and mashed out his cigarette. "I guess I should confess that I haven't always been the best father," he said, lifting his gaze and finding mine. "It's hard for me to admit mistakes sometimes. I guess that goes with my profession. Admit mistakes in politics and your opponents will crucify you. The press, too." He shook his head and looked away across the dining room. "Harmon wrote me after he'd gotten to England. He wrote me about getting his own crew. He couldn't tell me any details about the missions you flew, but he described each member of the crew. And he singled you out for special praise. He said one of the reasons he'd been so fortunate to that point was the high level of skill and teamwork you'd established for the crew before he took over."

"Yes sir, it's like--"

"Let me finish. He told me you'd saved his life on more than one occasion. The lives of the rest of the crew, too. In one of his last letters before you were shot down, he sent me this picture." Roberts reached inside the breast pocket of his coat and pulled out the picture Harmon had described to me. I leaned over and looked closely at it. He was wearing the DFC ribbon. I wondered if his father even knew what it was. "You know how I responded to these letters, son?" I did, but I thought it would be best if he told me.

"How?"

"I didn't. I was so pig-headed that I ignored my only son. My only son who was serving his country and fighting the enemy every day." He stopped for a moment and dabbed at the corners of his eyes with his napkin. When he started talking again, his voice was stronger, more assertive. "You're going to help me find that boy, Bob. We're going to find him. . . or his grave. One way or another. I may be too late, but I'll never forgive myself if I don't do everything I can to find my son."

In his plea, I knew that the Senator desired to find his son both physically and emotionally. I feared the odds that we'd find him alive were slim, but I nodded and looked Harmon's father directly in the eyes and said, "I'll do everything I can to help you."

"Good morning, Duffy," I said as I threw my knapsack in the trunk. "Did you see Hemingway last night at the bar?"

Duffy smiled, his red-rimmed eyes confirming my dim recollection that he'd tottered back to our room in the wee hours of the morning. "Nah, but there were some fine-looking French dames in there. That's for sure. How'd you and the Boss get along last night after I left?"

These were the most words I'd heard Duffy speak since I'd met him. It was like he was a real person as opposed to the cardboard cut-out he pretended to be while driving. "Well, I guess you could say we came to a meeting of the minds," I replied.

"That's great. Now listen, Lieutenant: the Boss doesn't need to know I kept late hours last night. He's an early-to-bed, early-to-rise kind of guy and he doesn't always understand that I'm not. Okay?"

"Sure, Duffy. Our little secret," I winked. I was anxious to gauge the Senator's mood as we started our second day on the road. He had spoken honestly the night before, laying open his festering emotional wounds and making himself vulnerable to me. I suspected that with Duffy in the car, the Senator would quickly move to reestablish his authority as our superior. I wasn't disappointed.

"Good morning, gentlemen," Senator Roberts greeted us as he strode from the door of the hotel to the door of the car, a bellman trailing behind him with a suitcase and what appeared to be a picnic basket. Turning to the attendant, Roberts pointed to the suitcase and said, "Put that in the trunk and the basket in the back seat." After the man had followed his instructions, the Senator dismissed him with a tip. He glanced at Duffy, then at me and said, "Let's go. Lots of ground to cover today."

We climbed in and Duffy started the car. "We're to go east, Duffy, toward Metz. Maintain a nice even speed and watch out for military traffic. It has the right of way over us as we are considered civilian traffic despite our official sanction. The hotel packed us a lunch for later. Plan to stop about one o'clock. Any questions?"

"No sir."

I wanted to ask him if he was going to tell Duffy which foot to use on the clutch and which on the brake, but for once my better judgment prevailed. Duffy handled the big car well, even down some narrow alleys as he navigated out of the city. Within half an hour, we were rolling through the French countryside. Farmers were cultivating their fields, traipsing along behind draft horses or oxen as they had for a thousand years. The gently rolling hills and open fields were littered here and there with the refuse of war. Destroyed houses, splintered trees, the occasional fallow field and burned out vehicles of all sorts served as vivid reminders of the hard battles that had taken place on this ground less than ten months ago.

From time to time we passed a makeshift camping ground with refugees huddled beneath a tarp, blanket or even a sheet, whatever they had which could offer them some shelter from the elements. Fortunately, on this morning at least, the sun was shining cheerfully, warming the land and its inhabitants.

"We're heading to Frankfurt," the Senator finally said after some time. It was the first time he'd spoken to me since we'd left Paris. He'd been staring out the window at the scenery, possibly wondering how to resume our conversation from the night before. Possibly not.

"That's not our most direct route, sir," I replied, happy to have something to say. "I think a route through Nuremberg might save us a little time."

"Eisenhower has just established his new headquarters there. I'm going to meet with him tomorrow morning to get his views on the situation over here and what Congress should be doing about it. As we discussed last night, there is a personal aspect to my trip but I am still here on official government business. You will accompany me to his headquarters. Duffy, open the side vents will you? It's getting a little stuffy back here." I cranked my window open about a third of the way.

So far, the Senator hadn't mentioned his son by name all morning. "I'm not a politician, but wouldn't you normally expect the President to set the agenda for Congress?"

"Harry Truman?" Roberts scoffed. "Harry's a nice fellow and he dresses well. His bowtie always matches his pocket handkerchief. But Harry's got no more foreign policy experience than you do. Congress, the Senate in particular, has to find out for itself what the issues and challenges are. As I mentioned last night, one of the lessons I've learned is that the United States can't leave Europe to its own devices. These people have been fighting every twenty or thirty years since the dawn of recorded history. The Normans and the Saxons, the Saxons and the Danes, the Danes and the Swedes, the Swedes and the Russians, the Russians and the French, the French and the British, and everybody and the Germans. No, this time we've got to be Europe's policemen. If we pull out hastily, the Russians are likely to fuel up their tanks and ride right through Germany. They'd probably stop on the Rhine, but who knows for how long. If we're not careful and smarter this time, you and your sons will be back to rescue the Europeans every generation for the next century."

"You seem to have come full circle on American intervention," I said, watching closely to see how he'd interpret my remark.

He smiled tightly. "A full three hundred sixty degrees. In 1917, I believed we should come to the aid of the democracies. Over the years, understanding the Europeans' proclivity to embroil themselves in senseless conflict, I decided we should get out and stay out. The folly of that position has been proven to me through the deaths of millions. Yes, I have come full circle. And being here now is the best thing I can do to make sure America helps keep the peace this time."

Up front, I noticed Duffy's chin slowly sagging toward his chest. "How you doing up there Duffy!" I called out, drawing a quizzical look from the Senator.

"Fine, Lieutenant, just fine!" he replied, sitting up a little straighter and putting both hands on the Buick's white steering wheel.

We were making pretty good time, except when we came to rivers and larger streams. As the Germans had retreated the previous summer, they'd destroyed bridges to delay their pursuers. At every crossing we found construction workers repairing ancient stone bridges or building new modern ones. In the meantime, traffic was forced to cross using mostly Army bridges. I was impressed by the ingenuity and skill of our engineers, knowing that many of these temporary structures had been completed while under enemy fire. I remembered what that was like.

At one o'clock, Duffy pulled the Buick off to the side of the road and parked beneath a stand of trees on the crest of a small hill. None too soon: my stomach had been growling for quite a while. To our right stretched a green pasture with a few cows lazily eating their fill. I wondered how many of their sisters had been caught in the crossfire as the Allies had battled the Germans. The cows eyed us suspiciously and slowly moved away from us as Duffy spread out a blanket in the shade of the trees. I fetched the picnic basket from the back seat. Senator Roberts wandered a few yards to the east and gazed out at the view. Stretching out before him, the road eased its way down a shallow ridge and wound its way to the wide Moselle River, beyond which lay the city of Metz.

Ours was the most elegant picnic I'd ever been part of. That's not really saying a lot, but we had tins of caviar, crackers, two bottles of wine, bottled water, smoked salmon, several cheeses, grapes, apples, pears, ham, mustard and, of course, bread. Plates, utensils and glasses were included along with cloth napkins. And when we were finished, we got to keep the basket.

My stomach was content and I was sipping a glass of wine when Roberts wiped his mouth and his hands and turned his attention to Duffy. Our driver had finished his sandwich and fallen asleep, snoring lightly, while the Senator and I ate at a more leisurely pace. Roberts leaned over and put his hand over the toe of Duffy's shoe and shook it gently. Duffy snorted and pushed himself up into a sitting position. "Yes sir?"

"Get the camera, will you, Duffy?" Duffy rolled on to his knees and pushed himself up, careful not to upset any of the containers spread open on the blanket. "Duffy's a talented fellow," Roberts said as our driver headed for the car. "He takes pictures of our travels to let the folks back home know how we're serving them."

"So will you make copies when you get back to the States and send them to key supporters?"

"Oh, my, no!" Roberts chuckled. "When we get into the city, Duffy will find the UPI or AP office and he'll arrange for them to put the best photographs on their wire. Why, with any luck half the papers in the country will print our pictures." I was starting to get the picture myself.

As Duffy headed back our way, Roberts stood and put his suit jacket back on. He cinched up his tie and wiped his face again on his napkin. Turning toward me he asked, "How do I look?"

"Senatorial," I smiled.

Roberts began walking toward the crest of our little ridge to where one had the best view of the city. With the sun now slightly behind us, the haze that had persisted throughout the morning was less of a factor. "How about right here?" he asked Duffy. "Can you get the city in the background?"

Duffy lifted up the Speed Graphic camera and peered through the sight. "Yes sir. If you'll move just to the left, I think readers would be able to pick out the spire of that big church."

"All the way down, as far as you can set the f-stop. I want everything in focus, got it?" I didn't understand why the Senator had to give such detailed instructions if Duffy was so "talented," but it occurred to me that he'd done pretty much the same thing with respect to Duffy's driving. Duffy fiddled for a moment or two with some kind of light gizmo to make sure he set the camera correctly, and then he took the picture.

"Got it, Boss!"

Within fifteen minutes, we were stopped dead still, sitting in a long line of vehicles, most of them olive green. After a couple of minutes, I opened my door and said, "I'll go see what's holding us up." I stepped out of the car and crossed back in front of it so I was walking on the narrow shoulder of the road. Up ahead I could hear gears grinding and the whole line of traffic moved forward the length of one vehicle. I must have walked half a mile before I came to the problem. Army engineers had constructed two long pontoon bridges over the Moselle River while French and American engineers worked to reconstruct and repair the city's permanent bridges. One direction served traffic leaving the city and traveling west toward Paris. The other served traffic heading east, like us. The military policemen controlling access to the bridges were letting only one vehicle at a time cross the span.

"Good afternoon, Sergeant," I said after I determined who was in charge. The startled NCO looked up and popped a quick salute. I guess it wasn't every day that he had an Air Corps officer walk up to his bridge.

"Good afternoon, sir! How can I help the Lieutenant?"

"I wouldn't bother you, Sergeant, but I've got a United States Senator in a Buick sedan about half a mile back," I said pointing over my shoulder down the long line of traffic. "He's a little impatient. He's on his way to Frankfurt to meet with General Eisenhower. I hate to ask you for favors, but can you help him out?"

"Is he willing to swim across, sir?" the MP asked with a twinkle in his eye.

"I don't think he wants to get his shoes muddy."

The Sergeant stepped out so he could see as far down the line of waiting traffic as possible. "I tell you what, Lieutenant. I don't think anybody else is in much of hurry. You head back to your car and when you reach it, stand out in the road and wave to me. Have your driver--"

"The Senator's driver--"

"Have the Senator's driver pull out into the oncoming lane. I'll hold westbound traffic and stick you in at the front of the line. How's that?"

"That's great, Sergeant. You've earned not only my thanks and the Senator's, but the thanks of the United States Congress and a grateful nation." We both laughed, exchanged salutes and then I headed back toward the car.

Once I reached the Buick, I stepped all the way over to the left side of the road, removed my cap and waved to the distant Sergeant, who waved back. I hopped in behind Duffy and told him what to do. As Duffy pulled into the oncoming lane, I turned to Senator Roberts. "Sir, when we reach the MP checkpoint I'd like you to stop and get out and thank the Sergeant in charge. He's going to quite a lot of trouble to keep us on schedule." I was only exaggerating a little.

Roberts looked at me with raised eyebrows, unused to taking orders from junior military officers. "All right, Lieutenant Foster," he nodded.

When we reached the head of the line to cross the bridge, the MP Sergeant waved us back over into the eastbound lane, sticking us in front of a deuce-and-a-half pulling a howitzer. Duffy slowed to a stop and Senator Harmon Roberts, Jr. stepped out of the back seat. "How do you do, Sergeant?" he said as he approached. Roberts was back in campaign mode now and he knew just how to handle this encounter. I watched from the open window as he shook hands with the friendly Sergeant. "I've got a meeting in Frankfurt tomorrow morning at General Eisenhower's new headquarters. I'll be sure and tell him how helpful you've been. Tell me your name, son, and where you're from." When the Sergeant said "Akron," I thought the Senator might dance for joy. Here he was four thousand miles from Ohio and he'd found a constituent!

"Well, Sergeant Obenour," the Senator said, "looks like we're going to be here a little longer than I thought. Why don't you send that truck there on ahead of us while my driver takes our picture? Why, with a little luck, you and I will wind up on the front page of the *Beacon Journal*!"

When we all climbed back in the car and started our slow traverse of the pontoon bridge, Roberts leaned over and patted me on the shoulder. "Well done, Bob. Very well done."

I was repeatedly impressed with Duffy's navigational skills. Within a few minutes of our arrival in the rubble-strewn center of Metz, he had pulled us up in front of the United Press International office. He and the Senator headed inside to see what political hay could be made of the Senator's picture with the MP Sergeant. With any luck, they'd find a local reporter in the office and the Senator would even get a wire story out of his side trip.

I took advantage of the opportunity to stroll around. I don't know much about France and even less about Metz, but it must have been the scene of heavy fighting because everywhere I looked buildings were damaged or destroyed. And it was not the kind of damage delivered by Air Corps bombs. For the most part, building walls and ceilings were intact, but windows and doors were destroyed or missing and the interiors, at least what I could see from the street, were often in shambles. Luck is relative.

Duffy preceded the Senator through the door about ten minutes later and they climbed into the car. I waved to them from down the street and Duffy drove over and picked me up. "Success?" I asked.

"Yes, Duffy has a way with the press even here, it seems," the Senator smiled. "Hopefully some of those pictures will turn out and the folks back home will gain an appreciation for what we're up to."

Less than an hour later, we rolled to a stop in front of another military policeman. This fellow must have stood over six feet tall and weighed more than two hundred pounds. He was physically imposing, the sort of man you wouldn't want to cross.

"I'll handle this," I said to the Senator, emboldened by my earlier success and eager to prove my value once more. "Let me see those travel orders." I stepped out of the back seat and approached the MP, who recognized the silver bars on my uniform and offered a snappy salute. I decided that the MPs are much better saluters than us fliers. "Good afternoon, Sergeant," I began in my most official voice. "I'm Lieutenant Foster, military liaison for Senator Harmon Roberts, Jr. He's on his way to a meeting at General Eisenhower's headquarters in Frankfurt."

"Good afternoon, sir," the MP replied without emotion. "May I see your travel orders? No vehicles are allowed to cross the border without specific authorization."

"Here you are, Sergeant," I said, handing over our authorization papers. "I'm sure you'll find everything in order." I don't know if he really read the orders or if he just looked at the bottom of the page to see Eisenhower's signature, but it didn't take long for him to hand them back.

"Sir, standing orders prohibit vehicle traffic between sundown and sun up. My guess is that you won't make it all the way to Frankfurt before it gets dark. There's an Army depot up ahead in Kaiserslautern. That's another forty miles or so east of here. You might want to make that your destination for tonight."

I glanced at my watch. It was nearly five p.m. "That sounds like good advice. Thank you, Sergeant." He saluted again and I climbed back into the car. Duffy slipped it back into gear and our journey east continued.

"What time is your appointment in the morning, sir?" I asked the Senator.

"Eleven a. m. or 1100 hours, as you fellows like to say."

"Good, because we can't be out on the roads after sunset and we're not going to make it all the way today." I expected Roberts to object to this. He did.

"It would be better for us to go all the way this evening, even if we arrive a little late. Don't you agree, Duffy?"

"Yes sir!" Another predictable response.

"Ordinarily I would agree, but your travel orders would be revoked at the first checkpoint we passed after dark and then you'd miss your appointment altogether. We just crossed the border, Senator. We're not in civil France anymore. Now we're in Army territory and the Army makes the rules. Welcome to Germany."

We located the Army depot in Kaiserslautern and were able to requisition some K-rations and fuel. The supply officer guided us into the town and helped us acquire rooms at one of the small German hotels that the Army had commandeered. Once again, the Senator rated private chambers while Duffy and I shared quarters. Our dinner wasn't quite as fine as it had been the previous night, but I think both the Senator and Duffy enjoyed sitting on the sides of our beds and eating the GI rations that had helped us win the war. It wasn't Jack Dempsey's, but at least we weren't cold, wet or hungry. It certainly broadened their experience.

We looked over Duffy's map and calculated that we were still about seventy-five miles southwest of Frankfurt. I searched around the hotel until I found a transportation officer. I asked him the best route to Frankfurt.

"Well, I'd go west and cross the river this side of Mannheim," he drawled. "It's easier terrain for one thing and the approach to the crossing is a little less congested. Plus, once you get east of the city you run into the autobahn, which is a whole lot better than the roads you fellas have been riding on. You got a jeep?"

"No, a Buick Touring Sedan."

"You're kiddin'! I haven't seen one of those since I signed up. I'll bet that beats riding in a jeep!"

"I guess so. It sure beats riding in a B-17!"

Unsure of what we'd find crossing the Rhine, and so we could minimize the risk of arriving late for the all-important appointment with the Supreme Commander, we pulled out of Kaiserslautern just after 0600. There was little traffic on the road at that hour and Duffy, unlike in Paris, had gotten a full night's sleep. By seven-thirty, Duffy had snapped a picture of the Senator standing thoughtfully on the banks of the Rhine and we had joined the light north-bound autobahn traffic heading toward Frankfurt.

Our destination was just north of the city's center, a park-like setting in the middle of which sat the largest office building in Europe, the I.G. Farben *Hochhaus*, or headquarters. "They say Eisenhower saw this place on some aerial reconnaissance photographs and decided it would be perfect for his post-war headquarters," the Senator explained as we continued north. "That's why it wasn't bombed. I love a man who plans ahead," he chuckled.

We stood in the cool morning sunshine staring up at a massive building clad in some kind of marble façade. The Farben building was seven stories high and longer than two football fields.

"You think he's got enough room in there?" I asked.

Roberts laughed. "Well, you know how it goes with government operations. I'm sure his staff will expand so that it can fill in any gaps."

It was only 0930. We--the Senator that is--still had an hour and a half before his scheduled appointment, so I suggested that we walk around the grounds. Frankfurt had been hit pretty hard during the war; not as bad as Berlin or some of the industrial areas, but hard nonetheless. Even so, the Farben building and its grounds were remarkably untouched.

"Farben was the company that made the nerve gas the Germans used in the camps," Roberts observed as we strolled around the green lawns of the structure.

"The camps?" I asked.

Roberts had his hands behind his back, his head down. "I don't know what you boys went through. I'm sure it was harsh, but it was nothing compared to what the Nazis did to the Jews. They industrialized murder. . .quite efficiently. They used nerve gas as part of their extermination program. I'd say there's some justice in turning this into supreme headquarters."

I agreed, but the heavy strands of barbed wire encircling the entire complex seemed out of place surrounding the victor's headquarters.

At precisely 1100 hours, the door to Eisenhower's inner office opened and the most famous man in Europe walked out. "Senator!" he said, his well-known grin splitting his face, "welcome to SHAEF!"

"General! Good of you to fit me into your schedule!" Roberts replied.

"You've had a smooth trip so far, I hope?" the Supreme Commander continued, playing the genial host.

"Very smooth. Your military policemen are doing an excellent job and traveling by automobile has given us a chance to see what conditions are really like. I must say that one cannot appreciate the devastation wrought by war unless one sees it with one's own eyes." Ike nodded at this keen observation and then the Senator turned to us. "I'd like you to meet Frank Duffy of my Washington staff and Lieutenant Robert Foster, my military liaison for this trip."

"How do you do?" Ike grinned, shaking hands with Duffy and then me. As any professional soldier would, he glanced at my uniform and then paused and looked me in the eye. "Where'd you pick that up, son?" he asked, pointing at the blue, white and red Silver Star ribbon on my chest.

"In a B-17 over the Ruhr Valley, sir."

"Well, let me shake your hand again, Lieutenant Foster. I am especially proud to meet you."

"General, might we take a quick picture before you and the Senator begin your talk?" Duffy asked, swinging the Speed Graphic up to his eye without waiting for an answer.

Eisenhower grinned and shook Senator Roberts's hand and Duffy's flash froze the scene for history. Another picture for the Columbus *Dispatch*, I thought.

With that, the General turned back toward Senator Roberts. "May I offer you some coffee?" he asked sweeping his hand toward the door. Roberts took his cue and went into the private office, Ike walking behind him and pulling the inner door closed. By previous arrangement, Duffy and I took chairs in the outer office and waited for our boss to reappear.

"Duffy," I began after the door closed, "there's a small PX downstairs. I saw it when we came in. I'm going to see if I can requisition some special supplies. I'll be back before they're done."

"Okay, Lieutenant."

Using my orders as liaison to Senator Roberts's mission, I stocked up on as many cigarette cartons and Hershey bars as I could. I also bought a few ink pens and two field watches. Even with my special assignment, there were limits to what I could purchase.

I was a junior member of the officer corps of the largest Army in American history. I'd had the good fortune to meet General Eisenhower who was that same Army's highest-ranking officer. That did not, however, give me any additional stature or authority. My job was to provide whatever military assistance I could to Senator Roberts in his official capacity as a Congressional fact-finder. I didn't have any right to ask him about his conversation with Eisenhower behind the closed door of the office. But I did it anyway.

"How was your meeting with the General?" I asked as Duffy guided the Buick north out of the city.

"Interesting, as I'm sure you would imagine. Ike said that sometimes he feels as overwhelmed with the challenges of peace as he did during the war. It makes a lot of sense if you think about it. He's gone from being responsible for the liberated territories to being accountable for the conquered areas as well." Roberts paused for a moment and then added, "And now he's got to contend with an ostensible ally whose cooperation is anything but a given."

"How so?"

"Well, the Russians aren't being cooperative on things like returning our liberated prisoners of war and they've acted lawlessly within the German territory they liberated. Ike's a little concerned that tensions may escalate as we and the Russians begin to establish the post-war governing apparatus. I've had some of the same concerns. You remember me telling you that the Europeans can't be left to their own devices?"

"Yes sir."

"Well Old Joe Stalin is already wiggling on the Yalta agreements. He's gone on record as opposing the Polish government-in-exile in England in favor of his surrogates already in Poland. We're afraid he's planning to abrogate the commitment to free, democratic elections in Russian-controlled countries. And then there's Tito in Yugoslavia whose guerillas occupy part of northern Italy and who is refusing to get out. The situation's not as bad as war, but it's not as good as it ought to be. Ike's proven he can manage coalition warfare. Hopefully he can manage coalition peace."

"He didn't offer to make us a picnic lunch, did he?"

The Senator chuckled. "No, but he did suggest that we travel only during daylight and spend the night with American military units. His G2 is still concerned about Nazi werewolves."

"Werewolves?"

"That's the label the intelligence boys have pinned on die-hard Nazis. G2's afraid some of Hitler's rabid followers still aren't ready to give up, that they might wage a guerilla war against the occupying powers."

"I don't know, Senator. You've seen this countryside and the cities we've come through. You've seen the refugees lining the roads. These people are war-weary and hungry. I'm a pilot, not an intel guy, but I don't see any fight left in these people."

Roberts looked over at me, a thin smile on his lips. "That's exactly what I told Ike."

We passed Oberursel and I wondered what ever happened to Felix, my interrogator. We'd been enemies, but I suspected in different circumstances we would have been friends. Our route gradually turned northeast. The farther we went in that direction, the more people we passed walking along the roadside in the opposite direction. Most of them were civilians dressed in dirty garments and carrying belongings on their backs, but we also saw a large number of men wearing the field gray uniforms of the German Wehrmacht. They'd been disarmed and I guessed they were walking home, however far away that was. I guessed they were eager to reunite with their families and I wondered how many still had families to reunite with.

We'd left Frankfurt after a late lunch and so none of us expected to reach Dresden before dark. We'd almost burned a whole tank of gasoline, so about 1800 Duffy pulled off on the side of the road and we emptied two of our five gallon cans into the car's tank. That left us a reserve of three cans if we didn't find another Army depot from which we could requisition more.

At 1930, we pulled into the town of Freiburg, about twenty-five miles southwest of Dresden. As Duffy slowed the Buick and coasted through the middle of the town, we saw Sherman tanks pulled off into side streets.

"This might be a good place to put up for the night," I said.

"Don't you think we could make it the rest of the way?" Roberts asked. "I'm. . . well, I'm starting to get a little anxious, that's all."

I could see it in his face. His lips were pressed together, his eyes restless. I was getting a little nervous myself. I wasn't sure we'd find any evidence of Harmon and if we did I wasn't sure it would be very encouraging.

"Yes sir. I understand. We'd be wise to settle in here tonight with this armor unit. We can get some food and fuel and a good night's sleep and then get a fresh start in the morning. That'll give us a full day to. . .to look around. Better than going in after dark, I think."

Roberts stared at me for a moment and then conceded. "You're right of course, Bob. We'll leave first thing in the morning. Tonight, it's food, gas and a good night's sleep."

He was right about the first two.

It was cool and still dark when I woke up. Duffy was snoring lightly. I rolled gently out of the bed we shared and pulled on my shirt and trousers. I'd slept in nicer places--like the Ritz--but also in much worse conditions and for far longer--like Sagan.

I tiptoed outside. The air was damp and the sky in the east was still gray. I pulled a cigarette and my lighter out of my pants pocket and lit up.

"Who's that?" came a voice from the shadows.

I took the smoke from my lips and answered, "Lieutenant Foster. I'm traveling with Senator Roberts."

A figure emerged from behind the corner of the Gasthaus where we'd been billeted. "He the VIP that came in last night?" As he drew closer I could make out the silhouette of a soldier, his rifle slung over his shoulder.

"That's right. You on guard duty?"

"Yes sir, for another two hours."

"How long you been here?"

"Ever since V-E Day. We just stopped where we were and took up defensive positions. Since then we've run some patrols out to the checkpoints, cleaned our weapons, repaired equipment and mostly waited. It's not quite as intense as fighting, that's for sure."

"And you get hot food and a warm bunk, right?" I laughed.

"Yes sir, but mostly we just want to go home." He didn't sound amused. I could just make out his face now. He looked pretty young.

"How long have you been over here?"

"We crossed Omaha Beach on D+18. So that's what, about eleven months? How about you, sir?"

"I came over in '43, 8th Air Force. I was a bomber pilot."

"I thought you guys got to go home after so many missions. How come you're still here?"

"Got shot down. Finished out the war in a German prison camp."

"Wow, that's rough."

"Not as rough as what you went through, I bet." I figured maybe this kid could tell me what was really going on around here. I'd learned early on that the official version of things and the actual version of things didn't always dovetail. "You ever have any contact with the Russians?"

"Not much, sir. You got to get almost to Dresden before you run into their checkpoints. The only time I really got to talk to them was kind of fun, though. They like to trade things, you know badges, hats, and they love watches. I traded my watch for two bottles of vodka. I would have gotten more stuff, but a Russian officer came along and everybody kind of clammed up. No offense, sir."

"None taken," I smiled. "Here," I said, pulling the pack out of my pocket again and offering the young tanker a smoke.

"Oh, I can't, sir. Not while I'm on sentry duty. It would give my position away. Not that anybody cares."

"You're right," I said. I didn't want to cause the kid any trouble. "Here, take the pack and smoke 'em later."

"Thank you, sir! Well, it was nice talking with you. I'd better get back to work."

"Yeah, you'd better do that. Thanks for the information."

I watched as the sentry trudged off across the road and disappeared behind a building. The last stars were fading from the morning sky. I checked my watch: 0500. We had a big day in front of us. I didn't realize how big it was going to be.

As planned, we pulled out of Freiberg at 0630. The sun was up by now and casting long morning shadows across the empty road ahead. I guessed it was too early for the refugees and military traffic that we'd seen on previous days.

Duffy had filled our two empty gas cans from the motor pool of the tank battalion the previous evening and I had stuffed my pack with some trinkets to trade if needed. I felt we were as well prepared as we could be. Senator Roberts was anxious. I could tell in the way he fidgeted, stared out the window and rode in silence. I was nervous, too. Who knew what, if anything, we'd find?

We traveled northeast along a forest of dark green fir trees, the road winding as it shadowed a clear brook. After twenty minutes, I felt the car slowing and peered out the windshield at an Army checkpoint just ahead. A red and white striped wooden pole stretched across the road, an olive drab Sherman tank and its crew keeping it company. A soldier, his face half hidden with shaving soap and a towel draped around his neck, hopped down off the back deck of the Sherman as we approached. Duffy stopped the car in response to the soldier's gestures.

"Good morning, sirs!" he said, bending over to look in the driver's window. "Where are you heading?" I figured this was why I was along on the trip--well, one reason anyway--so I stepped out of the back seat with our travel authorization orders in hand. Upon seeing my Lieutenant's bars, the young Sergeant saluted and smiled. "Sorry sir, you caught me shaving. We're due to be relieved in an hour and I wanted to be ready."

"Don't worry," I said, "we're just passing through on our way to Dresden. That's Senator Roberts of Ohio in the back seat."

"Wow!" the Sergeant exclaimed, bending over again for a quick peek. "What are you going to Dresden for?"

"Fact-finding mission," I said. I didn't want our trip to appear too self-serving for either the Senator or me. "Is this the last checkpoint between us and Dresden?"

"Yes sir. Well, between us and the Russians at least. The last time I went up this road we reached their first checkpoint at Freital. It's three or four miles ahead and then Dresden's three or four more miles beyond that."

"The Russians friendly?"

"Well, that depends," the Sergeant chuckled. "If it's just the soldiers, yes sir they're pretty friendly. If an officer's around, it's sort of fifty-fifty. But, if one of their political commissars is around, well, watch out; then everything's by the book. They won't even take a cigarette from you if those fellows are watching."

I held out our travel orders for his inspection. He hardly glanced at them before handing them back. "You're good to go, sir. If you didn't have valid orders you wouldn't have gotten this far."

"Thanks, Sergeant."

"Good luck with your fact-finding, sir." He saluted and shouted to one of his comrades to raise the barricade. I climbed back in the car and Duffy eased past the tank. We were leaving friendly territory.

A large red banner flapped in a light morning breeze above the Russian checkpoint at the southwest corner of Freital. Here two roads and the railroad tracks converged. The sun was in our faces as we approached the barricade, reminding me of the many times I'd squinted into its fierce rays to detect German fighters hurtling toward our bomber. I felt the same foreboding.

I stepped out of the car once Duffy rolled to a stop, familiar with the seemingly endless routine of checkpoints and soldiers. As I walked up to the soldier at the gate, I noticed that two of his comrades had leveled their machine guns at me. The guns had scarred wooden stocks and round, black magazines hanging beneath their firing mechanisms and were ugly to behold. The soldier who appeared to be in charge wore no discernable badge of rank. His face was covered by coarse whiskers and he smelled like a cowboy the night before his weekly bath.

I saluted and he nodded, but didn't return the courtesy. I held out our travel authorization and he took the papers without comment. He opened the orders and I watched as his eyes scanned the pages. My guess was that he couldn't read anything on the page, so I slowly pointed to Eisenhower's signature at the bottom of the page. "General Eisenhower," I said.

"Eisen-hour?" he asked, his eyes widening and a grin spreading across his face.

"Yes! *Da!*" Now we were getting somewhere! My new friend quickly shoved the orders back in my hand and shuffled over to the car, leaning over and looking inside. Uh oh! I thought.

When he stood back up an annoyed look had erased his grin. *"Nyet! Nyet* Eisen-hour!"

I held my palms up. "No, no, that's not Eisenhower. Here," I again pointed to the signature at the bottom of the page. I pulled one of my spare ink pens out of my pocket and mimed signing the orders, then repeated "Eisenhower."

"Ah," the light of comprehension dawned on the Russian's face. "Eisen-hour!" and he made a writing motion with his hand.

"Da!" I nodded smiling. Then I pointed to my chest and then to the car and then past the barricade down the road to the east. "Dresden." Casually, I glanced at the pen in my hand and then at the Russian. I held it out. "Here. Friend! *Tovarisch!"*

He smiled and accepted the gift, then turned and shouting, gestured for the barricade to be raised. *"Tovarisch!"* he said and shook my hand. I hopped back in the car and my new friend waved us through. That had been easier than I expected.

"Look for landmarks, Bob," Senator Roberts directed as we drove slowly through the narrow streets on the outskirts of Dresden. As if I needed instructions. Damaged buildings dotted every block, but most of them were still inhabited. Everywhere we looked, we saw Germans toiling to clean up their streets and neighborhoods. That is, except when we would encounter a group of Russian soldiers walking down the street. Then the Germans would melt into the closest building, disappearing until their conquerors had passed. As we rolled along, the Germans would glance at us and then resume working. The Russians would gawk until we were out of sight.

"See anything that looks familiar?"

"No sir, not yet." I had been here less than four months before. I felt that I should have been able to find my way back to where Freddie and I had left Harmon, but maybe we hadn't marched down this road. "Duffy, head north toward the river. Then we'll turn around and back track. Maybe if I see things from the same perspective I can figure out where we are."

"Right, Lieutenant."

We passed a long queue of people waiting for food in front of a partially repaired building. A banner hung above the door announcing "BROT," bread. As we approached the heart of the city, the mingled whole and damaged buildings began to give way to blackened stonework and masonry, then to bare, roofless walls open to the spring sunshine. The walls went from several stories high to knee-level as we finally reached the river and the center of the old city. I had never witnessed destruction on such a scale, but then I'd never paid a ground-level visit to one of our targets before.

"It's quite a testament to strategic bombing," Roberts said, a note of awe in his voice. Duffy stopped the car and we got out. A fine white dust covered the Buick. Here and there workers stacked stones and bricks. I wondered what else they were finding. I wondered how long they'd been working to clean up the rubble, and how much longer they'd have to go on. My thoughts were interrupted by the Senator, who had other matters on his mind.

"Well, here's the river," he announced, turning toward the Elbe flowing inexorably through the destroyed city. "Recognize anything, anything that's left?"

I slowly scanned the scorched and crumbled landscape until my eyes fixed on a bridge over the river. "There," I said pointing. "We walked across that bridge." The bridge, what was left of it, had partially collapsed into the water, but the arching superstructure remained visible. "We came across there and then continued down that street," I said pointing to our left. "I'm pretty sure that's the way."

"Let's go," Roberts said.

Duffy had to navigate his way around a couple of still-blocked streets. He stopped one time while a group of Russian soldiers marched in front of us shoving a couple of German teenagers ahead of them. We watched silently but did nothing to intervene.

It was a relief to be heading west again, even though I wasn't exactly sure where we were going. We had now left the worst of the devastation behind, but the area through which we now traveled would still rate as "heavily damaged."

"Turn right here, Duffy," I directed. "Now pull over. This looks right to me," I said to Roberts. "From here, we'll have to go on foot. Duffy, open the trunk for me, will you?"

Duffy did as requested and I stuffed my pockets full of cigarette packs, chocolate bars, pens and the extra watches I'd bought at the Frankfurt PX. "Here," I said to the Senator, "see how many of these you can cram in your pockets. You never know when they might come in handy. Duffy, you stay here and guard the car. If we're not back by dark, wait for us anyway." I winked at him and was answered with a nervous smile. "Follow me, Senator."

I led the Senator between two buildings, neither of which had glass in its windows, neither of which was adorned by a sign. Behind these, I found what I was searching for: a set of steps cut into the side of a small hill. We walked for another ten minutes, occasionally stepping around toppled masonry, through an alley that widened into a lane. We passed into a residential area, the damaged houses augmented with thatch-roofed lean-tos on their sides. Past the rows of houses, we reached a low stone wall, beyond which sat familiar low, brown brick walls, the roof they had once supported nowhere in evidence. Senator Roberts was breathing heavily from the exertion of our walk, both the physical and the emotional. He sensed without me saying it that I knew where we were. A splintered board lay on the ground. I looked down at it as we passed. It was blackened, but I could make out part of a word, "...erkloster."

The door through which I had once passed Harmon Roberts III was gone, but I knew we were finally in the right place. We passed through the open doorway, through a labyrinth of unroofed corridors. Roberts reached ahead and grabbed my elbow. "Listen," he said and I did, holding my breath. I could hear low voices and noises, an occasional clink and clack. We headed toward the sounds as well as the obstructing walls allowed. After a few minutes, we reached the rear of the topless structure. Before us spread a large garden-like area, an area being cultivated by a dozen men wearing ankle-length, brown woolen robes. Off to our right was an exterior entrance to a cellar. It reminded me of the one Dorothy couldn't get into in *The Wizard of Oz*, except that it was larger and nestled into the side of a naked brick wall.

I scanned the men in front of me, looking for a familiar face. So far, none of them had noticed us, standing still in the shadows. I took a deep breath and stepped into the sunshine. Immediately, work came to a halt. I sensed the Senator walking beside me. I couldn't imagine what was running through his mind.

"Hello," I smiled to the first monk we came to. I believe a friendly approach is always the best first option. The man stared at me and nodded slightly. "I wonder if you could help us? Do you speak English?" The monk shook his head. I turned toward Roberts. "You don't speak any German, do you Senator?"

From behind us a voice asked, "What are you fellows looking for?"

Harmon Roberts III was wearing a brown robe just like the monks. His blond hair was trimmed close to his skull, his blue eyes sunken into dark circles. He'd lost another fifteen pounds since I'd handed him over back in February. He was leaning on a thick wooden staff. He looked awful. I'd never seen a more welcome sight in my life.

"You should see the look on your faces," he laughed, dropping the staff and embracing me. Now I started laughing, wanting to ask a hundred questions but overcome with the joy of finding my friend, if not well, at least alive. He relaxed his embrace and held me by my shoulders. I felt it was as much to steady himself as to get a better look at me.

Harmon turned his head and maintaining his smile said, "Hello, Father."

The Senator stepped to him and hugged his son. Harmon wrapped his thin arms around the older man and I saw the Senator's shoulders begin to shake. By now, all the monks had stopped their work. I guess they'd figured out what was going on, because most of them were smiling.

Senator Roberts pulled out his handkerchief and wiped his eyes. "Hello, Son," he said and he too began to smile. "I'm very proud of you. I wasn't sure we'd find you and if we did, I wasn't sure you'd be. . .alive."

"What happened?" I asked. "Can we go somewhere and talk?" I thought there might be some parts of the story that might be better heard away from the monks. Since they didn't seem to speak much, I guessed that they liked to listen to other people's conversations.

"Let's go over there," Harmon replied. "There's a bench in the shade."

"We're not taking you away from chores or anything, are we? I don't want you to neglect your responsibilities."

Harmon laughed again and leaned over and picked up the staff and then led us over to the bench. It was cooler in the shade and we had some small measure of privacy. "So what happened?" I asked as we sat down, the Senator and I on either side of Harmon. "How come you're still here?" For once, the Senator seemed speechless, powerless. All he could do was stare at his namesake.

"Well, I don't remember much about how I got here. I was sort of hoping you could fill in some of those blanks, Bob. I must have been pretty sick. The first thing I remember is the brothers bundling me up in blankets and carrying me outside one cold night. The sky was glowing red and the wind was howling. They took me outside and then down into the cellar. We stayed down there for several nights and days, I really don't know how many.

When we came up, the monastery was largely destroyed. They told me the city center was obliterated."

"How are you feeling? You look like you've lost more weight."

"There's not much food here. I actually feel a whole lot better but it took me over a month before I could walk across these grounds without stopping. The brothers saved my life. Of that I'm sure."

"Why are you still here, Son?" Senator Roberts asked. "Was it because I. . ." His voiced choked up.

"No, Father," Harmon reached over and patted him on the knee. "No. I was safer here than if I'd tried to make my way across Germany. Besides, I wasn't strong enough. Once the Russians arrived, the brothers refused to let me go. They said the Russians were barbaric and couldn't be trusted to treat me as an ally. They'd heard that some Allied prisoners were being sent east instead of released to their own countries."

"These guys actually talk?" I asked.

Harmon smiled again and said, "Sure, when they've got something to say. Unlike some people." He elbowed me playfully. "Besides," he said looking me dead in the eyes, "I knew you'd be back. Of course I didn't think it would take you quite this long." He laughed again.

"Can you walk, Son?" his Father asked.

"Yes, but not too far. As I said, I'm much better, but there just hasn't been enough food available here."

"We've got a car waiting in town" I said. "It's probably a mile or so away. Can you make it that far?"

"I think so, as long as speed's not particularly important."

I looked at my watch. It was 1000 hours. We had lots of daylight left, but I didn't want to waste any more of it sitting in a garden surrounding by silent monks. "How long will it take you to say your goodbyes and gather up your things?"

"Not very," he replied and I saw the determination in his eyes that I'd seen on so many missions and on so many days in captivity. He leaned forward and with the help of the staff, stood. The Senator and I stood also.

"Listen, Harmon," I said, "we didn't bring much food with us and what we did bring we left with Duffy in the car. But our pockets are full of cigarettes. Maybe we could 'buy' you away from your friends here. I don't know if they smoke or not, but even if they don't, they can use the cigarettes to trade."

"I think they'd like that." Harmon smiled again and walked slowly over to one of the older monks. The man stopped hoeing and listened to Harmon for a moment, and then he called the other brothers around him. I could hear them talking, but it was all in German. After a couple of minutes, they all began to hug Harmon, shake his hand and pat him on the back. They seemed genuinely happy for him. Harmon waved his father and me over and introduced us. Hand-shakes all around. "Now would be a good time, Bob," he said. With that, Senator Roberts and I began to dig the cigarette packs out of our pockets and put them in the thankful hands of Harmon's benefactors. They couldn't eat them, but maybe they could trade them for something they could eat.

The farewells completed, Harmon stepped carefully down the steps into the dank cellar. He emerged a few moments later with a small cloth bag. "That's it? That's all you got?"

"Yeah. The porter who brought me here absconded with my luggage. I've got my dog tags, a tattered uniform and my shoes. And the brothers gave me a Bible. That's about it."

"Well, get dressed and let's get out of here."

"I think I'll just go like this for now. I can change later."

We turned to head back through the maze-like shell of the monastery. Suddenly, I felt a tug on my shoulder. Turning, I came face-to-face with one of the monks. *"Was mit meinem Bruder?"*

"Huh? Sorry?"

Harmon gave me a puzzled look and said, "He wants to know about his brother. Who's he talking about?"

I looked into the man's face and realized he was Freddie's brother; he was probably the real reason Harmon Roberts III was standing beside me. "You remember Freddie, the ferret?" I asked Harmon.

"Sure."

"This is his brother. He took you in the day we walked through Dresden. Freddie brought me to this place. Hell, he carried you part way here. He convinced this man to take you in. I'm surprised he didn't tell you."

"Surprised? This is the first time I've heard him speak!"

"Tell him that I'm sorry, but that I haven't seen Freddie since before the war ended. I don't know what happened to him. Tell him I'm sorry and tell him I am grateful to both him and Freddie."

Harmon conveyed my message. I could tell that his German had improved. I guess living with a bunch of German monks will do that for you. Freddie's brother's face registered his disappointment. He started to turn away, but I grabbed his hand and held it in mine.

"Thank you," I said. "Danke."

He nodded and sadly replied, *"Gott sei mit dir."* Then he turned and walked away.

"He said, 'God be with you.'"

"Yeah, I got it. Let's get out of here." I was reminded again that the Germans, our enemies, had also been our saviors.

"They've been ruthless. I haven't seen it myself, but the brothers relayed stories from the local people that made me wonder about our choice of allies. They say there's not a woman in the city who hasn't been raped at least once. They claim many were murdered, homes ransacked, property stolen. They call the Russians 'barbarians.'"

"Well," Senator Roberts answered, "the Germans have no room to cast stones. You haven't seen the atrocities they delivered on people all over Europe, including these very Russians." I remembered Freddie's attitude toward the Russian prisoners at Sagan. Maybe the Germans and the Russians deserved each other, I thought.

Harmon seemed to be holding up pretty well as we walked along. We took frequent rest breaks, but those were as much for his father as for Harmon. It was noon by the time we reached the stairway and descended toward the alley. We emerged from the shadows of the two buildings and turned the corner into the street. I looked to my left and then to my right. No Duffy. No Buick.

"Where the hell did he go?" the Senator asked, anger creeping into his voice. We were all eager, having accomplished our reunion, to get out of Dodge before sundown.

"He wouldn't have gone off on his own, Senator, not Duffy." I was pretty confident of that. What I was more worried about was that he'd had to go off with somebody else. Based on what little I knew about the Russians and on what others had told me, I was afraid that our driver and our automobile might have been confiscated.

I was considering splitting us into two and searching in different directions when I heard the big engine turn the corner and saw the blue Buick head toward us. Duffy pulled up beside us and jumped out, the engine still running. "I'm sorry, Senator!" he exclaimed. "Get in!"

"Duffy," I said calmly, "this is Harmon Roberts III."

"Hiya, kid! Now, get in!"

We scrambled into the car without asking for an explanation. Clearly Duffy was flustered and it seemed best to comply with his instructions and ask questions later. Once we were all aboard and moving again, I asked, "What happened? Where'd you go?"

"I'm sorry, Lieutenant! I was sitting in the car and I dozed off and when I woke up there were these two Russian guys staring at me. They started shouting and pointing at the car and then pointing down the street. I showed them our travel orders but they didn't know any more English than I knew Russian. They were getting more and more agitated and so I cranked up and drove off. I've been driving around in circles for two hours waiting for you to come back. I was getting really worried."

Harmon was in the front passenger seat, the Senator and I back in our customary positions in the back. I leaned forward and patted Duffy on the shoulder. "You did a smart thing, Duffy," I said. "Always obey men with guns, especially angry men with guns." I looked up at the dashboard and noticed that our gas tank was low. "Let's pull over in the next side street and fill up the tank. I want us to start the trip back with a full load of fuel."

As Duffy and I poured the gas from our jerry cans into the Buick's tank, Harmon struggled out of his robe and sandals and into his uniform. It was stained and ragged, the knees and elbows practically worn through and it hung loosely over his emaciated frame. Nonetheless, I felt easy passage through both the Russian and our own checkpoints would be more likely if our new passenger was in an American uniform. Sometimes I'm wrong.

The sun was once again in our faces as we retraced our route away from the city center. We were approaching a wide intersection when Duffy stepped on the brakes, bringing us to a rather quick stop. Ahead, crossing our route, was a convoy of Russian T-34 tanks. We sat watching as twelve of the armored behemoths rumbled past, rattling our teeth and stirring up clouds of swirling dust that sparkled like glitter in the sunlight. Behind the tanks rolled trucks, American-made trucks, emblazoned with the red star of the Soviet Army. The convoy passed and Duffy turned right onto the wider road. We left Dresden behind, but the stark vision of its blackened, shattered center remained seared into our memories.

By the time we reached the Russian checkpoint at Freital, the guard had been changed. My *tovarisch* from that morning was nowhere in sight. The soldiers on duty watched curiously as the Buick approached their wooden barricade. Two of them walked in front of us, standing between our car and the gate, their machine guns at the ready.

"Here we go again," I said, grabbing the door handle. "Duffy, if I need you to open the trunk, do so deliberately but slowly, got it?"

"Right, Lieutenant."

"The rest of you stay put." I climbed out of the back seat, travel documents in hand and saluted the nearest soldier. *"Tovarisch!"* I smiled. He just stared at me, standing as still as a mannequin. A heavily-armed mannequin. I decided to take the initiative, so I moved cautiously toward him. His comrade tracked my movement with this weapon, though he didn't actually raise it and point it at me. I wanted both of them to see I was unarmed, so I walked with my hands out to my side. When I got close enough, I held out our travel orders. "Eisenhower," I said. It had worked before. I pointed to the signature at the bottom of the page. "Eisenhower," I repeated. Maybe he was deaf, maybe he was stupid or maybe he was being watched.

I looked around just in time to see an officer stride purposefully around the corner of the small guard house. He wore dark trousers stuffed into high black boots, cloth epaulets on his tunic and red stars on each sleeve. He walked directly up to me and snatched the orders out of my hand without so much as a by-your-leave. He perused the documents and then looked me in the eye.

"What are you doing here, Lieutenant?"

"Just passing through, sir." I had no idea what this character's rank was so I figured respectful was the proper tone to adopt.

"I will ask again. What are you doing here? This is territory of the Union of Soviet Socialist Republics. You have no business here."

"Really? I thought this was Germany. I thought the United States and the great Soviet Union were allies, having defeated our common enemy the Germans."

"I ask you for the third and final time, Lieutenant: What are you doing here?"

"I am on a fact-finding mission for the United States Congress." I hoped that sounded more impressive to him than it did to me.

"What is the nature of this mission and why was it not coordinated with our Army headquarters?"

Thinking fast, I said, "It's an informal mission, but it's complete now and we're headed back to General Eisenhower's headquarters. You'll see he personally signed our travel documents granting us the authority to travel wherever necessary." He continued to stare at me with hard, black eyes.

"These documents are not valid in Soviet territory."

"I've got some more persuasive documents in the trunk of the car," I said, motioning to Duffy. He climbed slowly out of the driver's seat and walked around to the back. One of the machine gun toting mannequins followed him at a safe distance. "Come on, I'll show you," I said to the Russian officer. I walked to the rear of the car and whispered to Duffy, "Get back behind the wheel and keep the motor running." Duffy moved past me and the Russian who came and stood beside me. I leaned in and pulled a carton of Luckys out of the trunk. "Would you hold these, please?" I asked. I opened a paper sack and removed a field watch. I stuck two packs of cigarettes into my pants pockets. I turned back to my new friend and handed him the watch. "Perhaps now you would be kind enough to review our travel documents again."

He stared at me. I decided he wasn't my friend. "You expect me to throw in a couple of bottles of vodka and send you on your way now?" he sneered. Things weren't working out as well as I had hoped. "Do you think that everyone can be bought with a carton of cigarettes and a cheap watch? We are not capitalists, Lieutenant. Some things are more important than material goods. Or hadn't you heard?"

"Listen, friend," I said allowing the anger to creep into my voice, "just what is it you and your band of merry men want with us?" Respectful only goes so far.

"I want to know what you are doing snooping around in Soviet territory, friend. Perhaps you are spying. Ask your colleagues to step out of the car."

"That would be a mistake. Senator Harmon Roberts, Jr. is in the back seat and his son is in the front seat. As I've already told you, the Senator has been on a fact-finding mission on behalf of the United States Congress. He has been observing first-hand the conditions in conquered Germany so that he can make a full report to President Harry Truman upon his return to Washington, a return which you are now delaying." At the mention of

President Truman, I saw the slightest flinch. Maybe I'd finally blustered enough to bluff our way out of here.

My adversary thought for a moment. He folded our travel orders and tapped me on the chest with them. I reached up and took them out of his hand. "You will remain here until I return." He wheeled about and stalked off toward the guard house, my cigarettes and watch still clutched in his hand. I closed the trunk and slowly moved around toward Duffy's window. Without looking down, I rested my hand on Duffy's door handle and said quietly, "Don't look at me, just listen and then tell the Roberts boys what I tell you."

"Okay," Duffy replied continuing to look straight ahead.

I watched through the guard house window as the Russian picked up a telephone and cranked its handle. "Tell Senator Roberts to slowly, quietly slide over and unlatch my door. Don't open it, just unlatch it so all I have to do is jump in. Then tell him to slide back over. When I tell you to go, you hit the gas and ram through the weakest part of that barricade, closest to the unsupported end over there. Got it?"

"Check."

"Whatever happens, don't stop and don't slow down until you get to the American checkpoint. Understand?"

"Yes sir." Great, I thought. Now Duffy's calling me "sir." Through the window, I could see the Russian talking into the phone. He was gesturing with his hands, which struck me as funny because whoever was on the other end couldn't see them. I heard the latch on the rear door click. I saw the Russian nodding his head. He hung up the phone and stepped back outside, heading toward me with a look of satisfaction on his face. He came closer to me and opened his mouth to speak.

"Tovarisch!" I called to the guards. I reached into my pockets and pulled out the two packs of smokes. I tossed one pack to each. I'm not really a very good throw and the packs of cigarettes sailed on me a little. Both of the guards lunged to catch their prizes, laughing and lowering their weapons.

"You and your comrades will please accompany me back to 33rd Army headquarters," the Russian said. "We have some questions you will have to answer and some inquiries we will have to make." From the corner of my eye I could see the guards opening their packs and searching their pockets for a light. And why not? Their officer and I were having a friendly conversation. I mean I was smiling and everything. Right up to the point I punched the bastard in the nose and sent him sprawling!

Duffy had been paying attention, which I really appreciated. As soon as I dived into the back seat, he set the rear tires spinning, scratching for traction and shooting the Buick forward. The two guards didn't know what was happening and they stumbled out of the path of the car as it sped forward. Its back end was fishtailing, its screeching tires laying black streaks on the asphalt and throwing plumes of acrid, white smoke into the air. Duffy aimed for the far end of the barricade pole and hit it just as he shifted into second gear. The car shuddered, the pole snapped in two and Duffy swung us back to the center of the road, slamming the car into third and continuing to accelerate.

That's when I heard the popping and the glass behind my head turned into a spider web of fragments. I pushed Senator Roberts to the floor, but not before he punched me in the back. Two more bullets whined through the back window and out through the windshield. Duffy had already reached fifty miles per hour, the big eight-cylinder engine screaming like a banshee and winning my eternal gratitude. I told myself that the next car I bought would be a Buick!

"I don't know if they'll chase us or not," I shouted to Duffy over the whining of the engine, "so you go as fast as you can until we get back to our friendly checkpoint!"

"Yes sir!"

Harmon sat up and turned around. I was relieved to see that he was all right, although his face was very pale and his eyes wide with intensity. I helped Senator Roberts up off the floor. "You know, for an old guy, you pack a pretty good punch!"

The Senator gave me a puzzled look and I saw the same thing in his eyes that I'd seen in Harmon's. I was confused for a moment, until I realized that the blood on the back seat was mine.

6 June 1945

I woke up in a hospital ward lined with two rows of crisply-made white beds. Bright sunlight was streaming through the windows, which were open slightly at both the top and bottom to allow a cooling breeze to flow through the long room. I was thirsty, but feeling no pain, at least until I moved. I had a tube taped to my arm and my back felt like it had been moonlighting as Joe Louis' punching bag. I tried to sit up, but couldn't. I tried to speak, but my mouth was so dry I couldn't get the words out. Finally, I waved and got the attention of a pretty nurse who was making her rounds of the occupied beds.

"Good morning, Lieutenant Foster!" she said cheerfully. I'd have been cheerful too if I looked as swell as she did. "How are you feeling this morning?"

"Thirsty," I croaked. She stood next to my bed and I could smell her. It was quite a strange sensation for someone who'd been surrounded by foul-smelling men for the past three years. The nurse half-filled a glass with water and held it for me to drink. "Not too fast now," she ordered, smiling.

"Why is it so quiet around here? Am I your only patient?"

She giggled. "It's June 6th. General Eisenhower declared today a training holiday on account of the D-Day anniversary." She reached down and took my hand. I was beginning to like this place. She rotated my hand, placed her fingers on my wrist and checked her watch. "You seem to being doing a lot better. When they brought you in, we were worried about you. You lost a good bit of blood. If that field medic hadn't done a good job on you, well, let's just be glad he did!" She smiled and winked and gently set my hand back on my bed. I had fallen in love and I didn't even know her name. "I'll be back to check on you in a little while. If you need anything, my name is Nancy."

"Thanks, Nancy," I mumbled just before I fell back to sleep.

When I woke up again, it was dark. The windows had been closed. I looked toward the nurse's desk, but Nancy was gone. I turned my head a little farther to the right and was rewarded with the sight of Harmon Roberts III sitting next to my bed. He was reading *LOOK* magazine by the glow from a bedside lamp.

"Pour me some water, will you?" I managed through my dry mouth.

"Hey, buddy!" he smiled, laying the magazine on the floor and reaching for the pitcher of water. "How are you feeling?"

"Better, I guess." I wanted to sit up, but my back was still on strike. Harmon held the glass out for me and when I didn't take it right away, he brought it over to my lips.

"Easy does it," he said. Here I was a decorated veteran of the greatest war in history and nobody trusted me to drink water! I swallowed a couple of mouthfuls and felt better. "You really messed up the back of that Buick. Duffy got in all kinds of trouble for bringing it back in such shape. Not to mention the international incident you caused by slugging a Russian officer or the dangerous situation to which you exposed a United States Senator. My word, Bob, you're lucky they haven't already court martialed you and kicked you out of the Army!"

"Is that still an option?" I asked hopefully.

Harmon laughed. "No. If Father had his way, you'd receive another decoration and enough points to go home right away. He says you're a great American hero." I noticed that Harmon was wearing a new uniform, complete with his Distinguished Flying Cross ribbon. He was still painfully skinny, but his color was good and his old smile was firmly in place. "Father reported the whole adventure to General Eisenhower once we got back here to Frankfurt. I told him that I'd lost count of how many times you'd saved my life, but that you'd just done it again. By the way, you're no longer a first Lieutenant, Captain Foster. Congratulations!"

"Does that mean I can order you around?" Harmon laughed again and it made me feel better. "Your father and Duffy--they're all right? They weren't hurt?"

"No, they're both fine. Wilbur Shaw, the Indy 500 champ, asked Duffy for driving lessons based on his run from Dresden to Freiberg. He averaged seventy miles an hour over a winding road course. He and the medic with that tank battalion saved your life."

"And your father?"

"Oh, he's fine. He's back in fighting form you might say. Whatever you said to him, Bob, whatever you did to help put the two of us back together changed him for the better. Me, too. Father says you are a man of remarkably good judgment."

"Then how come I'm lying in this bed?"

"Father wanted to stay until you woke up, but duty called him back to Washington. In addition to his own report for his Senate colleagues, General Eisenhower asked him to personally deliver a message to President Truman and General Marshall. Father and the General seem to have hit it off pretty well. By the time we left the General's office, they were carrying on like old friends."

"What about you?"

"No, I'm not really that close to Eisenhower."

"Wise ass! What's next for you?"

"I'm under medical care, just like you. They've got to fatten me up and make sure I'm healthy before they release me back into the mainstream of the United States Army. Maybe some home leave and then off to the Pacific. Maybe get a chance to fly the B-29. Depends on how long the Japs hold out."

"What's the score out there?"

Harmon leaned in close and lowered his voice. "Ike says it looks like it could be another year and a half. He expects the invasion to come sometime this fall."

"What if they don't last that long?"

"Well, it's funny you should ask. One of the things I wanted to talk to you about is what happens after we beat Japan, whenever that is. I mentioned to you a couple of times that I was thinking about running for office. I've had a lot of time to ponder that idea over the last three months. The monks meditate and pray every day. I got in the habit too. It really helped me focus my thoughts and listen to God's plan for my life. The first election after the war's over, I'm standing for Congress."

"What's that got to do with me?" I was starting to get sleepy again.

"Well, we make a pretty good team, you and I. I was hoping you'd agree to become my campaign manager. It would mean long hours, lousy pay, little sleep, crummy food, and no thanks, but we might be able to prevent another conflagration like we've been through for the past four years. What do you say?"

"I say it sounds a lot like the Army."

"Will you do it?"

"After what we've been through, I think we can handle anything," I held out my hand and Harmon gripped it. Sleep tugged on my eyelids. "There's one thing you have to do for me, though."

"What's that?" Harmon's voice echoed.

"Find out when Nancy comes back on duty."

The Roberts Crew

Harmon Roberts III, pilot, Ohio
Bob Foster, copilot, North Carolina
Joe Johnson, navigator, Virginia
Don Berly, bombardier, Missouri
Eric "Sandy" Sanderson, flight engineer, Minnesota
Red Sutton, radio operator, Mississippi
Willie Trapp, right waist, Kentucky//Samuel Gold, New Jersey
Al Norris, left waist, New York
Rick Gonzalez, tail gunner, New Mexico
Artie Holmes, ball turret gunner, Florida

Author's Notes

Since I was a boy, watching "Twelve O'Clock High" on television, I have always been fascinated by the strategic bombing campaign in World War II. The losses sustained in the early days of the 8th Air Force's offensive were staggering. The destruction delivered by the B-17s and B-24s on occupied territories and later on Germany and its cities ushered in a new era of warfare. I have read many books on the US Army Air Force bomber campaigns of World War II and have worked to present an accurate if fictional look at the conditions in which the brave crews flew and fought.

I am grateful to my friend Bob Harmon and his wife Pat for taking the time to read an early draft of Part 1 of this book. Bob was a young navigator assigned to the 379th Bombardment Group (Heavy) at Kimbolton, England. Due to a bombing error not of his own making, Bob was awarded the dubious privilege of flying an extra mission and so ended the war with 36 trips over Nazi-occupied Europe. Any errors in this book are, likewise, not Bob's fault!

Kathryn Smith provided excellent editorial advice, helping improve clarity and consistency. I'm fortunate that Kathryn is not only an able editor, but also an historian. She made several suggestions from her own research which improved this story.

My gratitude extends to Dean Kay Wall and the staff at Clemson University's Cooper Library and to the staff in the Newspaper Archives section of the Library of Congress.

Even before we get to the editorial phase, brave souls must read and comment on the initial draft. Thanks to

Ina, Harry and Joe for sharing their constructive comments and helping recraft the telling of the tale.

My deepest appreciation and affection are reserved as always for my wife Yvonne who is supportive of my writing addiction and who always helps me find time to indulge it. I am wonderfully blessed.

About the Author

Kelly Durham lives in Clemson, SC with his wife Yvonne, their daughters Mary Kate, Addison and Callie and their dog, George Marshall. A graduate of Clemson University, Kelly served four years in the US Army with assignments in Arizona and Germany before returning to Clemson and entering private business. Kelly is the author of THE WAR WIDOW, BERLIN CALLING, WADE'S WAR and THE RELUCTANT COPILOT. Contact him at kelly@kellydurham.com.

Made in the USA
Charleston, SC
18 December 2014